THE
SONG
OF THE
NIGHTINGALE

THE
SONG
OF THE
NIGHTINGALE

FORWARD

To be fully transparent, I have been finding it difficult to make each forward in this series different from one another. So I am bound to repeat myself, but I will hope it isn't too redundant for those of you who take the time to read these words.

I was seventeen when I first became entangled in this Robin Hood world of my own creation. Seventeen when I first dove into the realm of self-publishing with no idea what I was doing.

To those of you who might have read the original series, I say the biggest and most heart-felt THANK YOU. I am always going to be humbled and amazed that anyone took interest in my little stories. To those of you who have no idea what I am talking about, let me explain…

When I started my self-publishing journey, I did so under the name Amanda Grace. The series I lovingly refer to as the OG Robin Hood series, five books in total, were all under that name. Dusty's book, the third of the series, I first published when I was twenty-one.

Her story is one that I was always fond of. In the first 3 books that I wrote (Lucy's story, Gisbourne's story, and Much's story) she was the mysterious woman. Seemingly emotionally stable and mature, full of wisdom and sage advice. And yet sometimes she would let her perfect facade slip and I would glimpse the pain that she hid beneath. I was insatiably curious about who she truly was.

In that first book, known simply as *Dusty*, I discovered pieces of her soul. In this new version that I have written for her, I found even more. She is infinitely complicated, feels emotions even more deeply than I do, and through it all has a stalwart faith in the Savior we share (except, you know, that she isn't real).

I adore Dusty. That much is true. I also happen to adore Will Scarlett.

Being able to dive into the idea of writing a love story— not just having the love story be there in the background or as a subplot, but being the main focus of the entire story—was strange for me. But I can't deny that I enjoyed it! In fact, I enjoyed it so much I'm tempted to switch genres altogether and start writing Romances for a living. I hope you enjoy the following story half as much as I enjoyed writing it.

to the girl learning to face her fears
to Dusty

Prologue

MARI-LU THREW BACK her head with laughter, amused by something young Edmund had said. Aunt Lucy smiled as she watched the interaction, a look of fondness softening her eyes. Edmund's eyes were sparkling as he spoke, and Mari-Lu looked as happy as Aunt Lucy had ever seen her.

Aunt Lucy sat perched on a fallen log near the edge of the meadow in the forest where she and the children had come for the day. It was a warm afternoon, the sun spilling through the tree branches above them and setting their hair aglow. Aunt Lucy had brought them deep into Sherwood Forest to a place she had once lived many years ago.

The huts she and her friends had called home were long gone. The fire-ring where so many memories had been made had long since disappeared, green grass and blooming flowers growing over the spot now. In the center of the open meadow was a tall four-sided pillar, with an inscription written on each of the four smooth sides.

"Though quiet now and full of sorrow, this small meadow was once the laughter-filled home of Robin Hood and his Merry Men. To them, we say, 'we will never forget your courage and your sacrifice. May you be remembered as long as England stands.'"

And below these words were etched the names of all those who had had the privilege of living and fighting alongside the great Robin Hood during the rebellion of Prince John Lackland of England.

Robin, Marian, Mark, Will, Little John, Allen, Dusty, Much, Lucy,

Ida, Faith

"Forever you will be remembered and loved."

Mari-Lu was sitting beside the stone, leaning over to watch as Edmund drew in the dirt. Whatever it was he was creating must have been amusing, because Mari-Lu started to laugh, and what a beautiful sound her laugh was. Mari-Lu's deep blue eyes sparkled as she threw her head back in merriment.

Aunt Lucy leaned forward, relishing the sight as her wrinkled face rested on her fragile hand, watching her great grand-children together. Edmund wasn't really hers by blood, but she claimed him all the same. He was descended from the gang, the same as Mari-Lu, which made him family. Edmund and Mari-Lu were nine years old, so young and so full of promise.

Aunt Lucy knew she was old. Far older than most people in her social circle. She was the last surviving member of Robin Hood's gang, and she knew eventually her time would come to join the rest in heaven. She'd spent most of her adult life collecting and cherishing the various life stories of the members of the gang, and sharing them with the people of Nottingham and beyond. But the stories about Robin Hood and his friends' exploits had bled from truth to legend in the sixty or so years since they had happened, and Aunt Lucy feared those legends would become myth if she left the world without leaving someone in charge of caring for the stories that she had collected.

She had made up her mind almost two years ago that little Mari-Lu was going to be that person. No one loved her stories more than Mari-Lu did; no one would care for them as diligently and faithfully.

Edmund looked towards Aunt Lucy, his curly chocolate-brown hair falling into his eyes. "Aunt Lucy, will you tell us a story?"

Mari-Lu clapped her hands. "Oh, do!" She leaped up from where she'd been sitting and darted across the open meadow to sit beside Aunt Lucy on the fallen log. "Tell us a story we haven't heard yet."

Edmund followed more slowly. "All your stories end the same; we know that." He sat on her other side, his dark curls falling across his eyes. "But can you tell us the story of one of Robin Hood's companions that we haven't been told?"

Aunt Lucy reached out to brush his hair out of his eyes. "A story you haven't heard yet…let me think."

Aunt Lucy reached down to the small satchel sitting by her feet which she'd brought with her to the old camp, pulling out a worn leather-bound book. "Why don't I tell you about Dusty?"

"Yes, yes, please!" Mari-Lu clapped her hands again.

"Well, to begin with, you should know that Dusty did not share her story with many people. She told me a little; she told Will more. Will kept a written record of the many things Dusty told him over the years. When Will died, Dusty gave that journal to me to preserve. This is Dusty's story…"

Aunt Lucy closed her eyes, beginning to recite the words of the journal Will had written precisely as he had written them….

My wife has always been a woman of unfathomable kindness and compassion which certainly helped her when she pursued her gift of healing. Yet despite her ability to relate to and understand people on a deep level, she always remained more guarded about herself—her history, her traumas, her life. Over the years, she slowly opened up to me and told me of her brightest and darkest memories, and I have collected them so that our children and grandchildren will know her as perfectly as I do myself.

This is the story of Andaleeb "Dusty" Scarlett. Dictated by my beloved wife, recorded by myself,

Will Scarlett

Aunt Lucy opened her eyes, flipping open the leather-bound journal in her hand. The first page contained precisely what she had recited. Both Mari-Lu and Edmund leaned forward eagerly as Aunt Lucy turned the page and began to read aloud.

"I've always been told that the stars were shining brighter than usual in the Palestinian sky the night that I was born. I do not know whether or not I believe this, but it is what I was told. I don't remember that night myself, having only just been born. My mother, Tahira, was worried because I was not a son. She worried my father would be disappointed. But my father, Habil, was overjoyed to meet me. From the day I was born, I was my father's daughter. He loved me more than the air and the light.

When I was only two months old there was a battle in the city where I lived—in Darum. Al-Nasir Sala al-Din Yusuf ibn Ayyb—better known as Saladin to those outside of Palestine-- attacked my city and tried to kill us all.

My city was founded by Crusaders from the First Crusade, and used as a strategic political and military headquarters during the Second Crusade as well. Most people who lived there were either descendants of European Crusaders, or were of mixed descent—such as myself—with both Crusader and Arab blood in their lineage.

My father fought in the battle against Saladin, as did our neighbor who died in the battle—his wife grew bitter as she only had a daughter and no son, and now her husband was dead. After her husband's death, she neglected her daughter Habibah, so Habibah spent much of her time with my parents and me and became as a sister to me. She was two years older than I was, and

I always felt she was the ideal elder sister. We became the best of friends as we grew up. Despite the tragedies that occurred that day during the battle with Saladin, I was given a blessing in the form of my sister.

Eighteen years later, Saladin returned…

Chapter 1

SCREAMS OF PAIN and roars of anger filled the air along with
the ringing of metal striking metal again and again and again. All
of the men—and many of the boys—in the city had taken up arms
to defend our city. They were trying to beat back the army that
had come to destroy us. The sound of the battle could be heard
from every corner of the city that was in uproar—women were
shrieking, children wailing, and panic reigned.

I was huddled in one corner of my dark house with my
mother's arms wrapped around me. She was weeping softly,
though her displays of fear were not nearly as violent as the
women I could hear through the window nearby. Daniyah—my
mother's friend—was rubbing her back while Habibah—the girl
who was my sister in all but blood—was sitting beside me, her
arms wrapped around her knees as she rocked back and forth.

I realized Daniayah was praying softly as she comforted
my mother. Listening to the screams from outside, I knew there
were others in our city who were in need of that comfort. There
were many in our city who did not know the Lord personally, who
would not know whom to turn to for comfort in this time of trial.

And there would be wounded. By the sounds of it, a great
many people were falling to the sword.

I removed myself from the group huddled in the corner,
standing up on shaking legs.

"Andaleeb, where are you going?" my mother asked in Arabic, the language we spoke.

"There are others who need help today, Ammi. I must go to them."

"Stay here, little one," my mother reached out a hand for me, her eyes filled with tears.

"I cannot hide here when people are in trouble—dying— and they do not know the Lord."

Daniyah reached up to grab my hand, her dark eyes boring into mine. "Go, Andaleeb. I will pray for you, and I will watch over your family."

"Thank you. God is with me."

I met Habibah's gaze, looking into her black eyes and seeing the peace written there. "Go, sister."

My mother was less peaceful, but she sank into Daniyah's comforting embrace and let me go.

I turned from my family and left the safety of my house. In the street there were women and their children running in all directions—presumably toward their homes—as others huddled against the sides of buildings. Everyone seemed to be crying.

I saw a woman stumble around the corner of a house nearby, her hand clutching her side as a crimson stain seeped across her tunic.

I darted forward, reaching out to catch her as her steps faltered.

"Easy, Ummi." I lowered her gently to the ground, reaching for the small bag of herbs I always kept attached to my belt as I peeled back her tunic to reveal the stab wound on her torso.

Saladin's army must have breached the fortress walls somewhere for wounded to be in the city already. I ignored the fear that rose at that thought, closing my eyes and praying for peace before I began to pray over the wound itself. I kneaded the correct dosage of herbs into the wound to stem the flow of blood.

Most of my knowledge of the medicinal properties of certain plants came from Daniyah, who had been my tutor in all things growing up. But the unnatural ability I could couple with the usual herbs was not something Daniyah shared. She said I had the gift of healing. All I knew was that if I used the correct herbs and spices along with prayer—relying on the Holy Spirit to do His work—most wounds I encountered could be healed.

Not all, though. I wasn't Peter healing the legs of the lame man at the temple or Ananias healing Saul's blind eyes. I was just…better than most healers I know, and I attributed it to Christ.

As the blood flow stopped I grabbed a needle and thread I kept with my herbs and carefully stitched the wound closed. It would hurt for a few days, but she was going to live and I told her as much.

"There won't be a few days to live," she said. "We're all going to die today."

I helped her to her feet and walked her down the street to her house. There were more wounded flooding into the street and the sounds of screaming and panic were coming closer.

After I got the woman into her house, I scanned the street looking for someone else who might need my help. That's when I saw three soldiers striding down the dusty street. One of them kicked a small girl who happened to be near him. She curled up on the ground, wailing.

The soldiers moved on, marching down the street—they didn't harm anyone who wasn't directly in their path, but they made it clear with the brandishing of their weapons that they could if they wanted to.

I ran past them to the little girl on the ground. I knelt beside her, putting my hand under her head and pulling it into my lap.

"It's alright, little one. Hush now." I brushed the tears from her small face. From the looks of her small form and chubby cheeks, I assumed she couldn't have been more than four years old. "Where is your mother?"

The little girl reached up, wrapping her tiny arms around my neck. She clung to me, burying her face under my chin. My neck was soon wet with her tears.

"Can you tell me where you live, little one?" I stroked her back in what I hoped was a soothing manner. Slowly, her tears abated. With a hiccup and a loud sniffle she pulled her head back long enough to point down the street. I followed her gaze. There were many houses on both sides of the street, yet in the distance I could see one with a door open with a woman lying in the doorway.

I stood up, scooping the little girl in my arms though I kept my hand on the back of her head to keep her face close to my chest. I wasn't sure what wounds I would find as I moved down the street toward the woman I saw. I didn't know if it was the girl's mother or if she lived in a different house, but if that woman was alive then she needed my help.

As I drew closer, I could see the growing pool of red spreading out from underneath the woman who was laying face down in the doorway of her home. My arms tightened around the child. If that was her mother, she was dead. The child's father was likely fighting in the battle. Everywhere around me were screaming, crying, panicking people as they rushed down the street seeking safety. What was I to do with this sweet child?

"Let me take her," a familiar voice spoke behind me and relief flooded my body. I turned to see Abraham—Daniyah's husband—with his clothes spattered with blood. He was sporting a cut on his face as blood dripped down his chin onto his tunic.

"Abraham!"

"The battle is not over, but we are being slaughtered," Abraham said. "We had to retreat. I will take this little one and look after her. Andaleeb, go and find your family."

As I transferred the small girl into his waiting arms she cried out in fear. Abraham immediately began to speak softly to her, stroking her back as I had been doing. When she was calm, Abraham spoke to me again. "Where is Daniyah?"

"She is with my mother and sister, at my home."

Abraham nodded, moving toward my home and I followed. "Where is my father?"

"Still fighting last I saw," Abraham said.

I breathed a prayer for his safety as tears stung my eyes. What was going to become of us all? I knew I should not worry; I knew who was in control of my life. Our Lord would see us through, one way or another.

I turned away from Abraham when I saw another bloodied man stumbling into the street. I hurried toward him to see what I could do for his wounds as Abraham carried the little girl to my home.

Once I had the man stitched back together, I moved down one street after another, offering help to anyone I could find. I healed some, I prayed with others. The sounds of fighting still echoed through the air, though I hadn't stumbled into any street with soldiers in combat yet.

I moved into another dusty street, scanning the terrified people scurrying along it for anyone who might be wounded. Then I heard the sounds of screaming from the far end of the street. A glance showed me Saladin's forces were marching down the street, cutting down anyone and everyone in their path. Unlike the three soldiers I'd seen before, these were killing everyone.

I ducked into a home nearby, pressing myself against the wall as I left the door open just a crack so I could see through. The house appeared empty—where the inhabitants were, I could only guess.

I peered into the street, watching the soldiers shove their swords through people as they marched past. More and more soldiers marched past, and it was all I could do not to sink to the floor as my legs wobbled beneath me. The screams were slowly quieting, as though there was no one left to cry out in fear or pain.

Slowly, the street emptied of the bulk of the soldiers. Soon all that was left seemed to be small groups of them pillaging homes.

I stayed where I was, forcing myself to keep breathing although my lungs were burning as my heart pounded wildly inside my chest. What was I going to do?

Two soldiers stopped just outside my door, chatting in the street.

"Any orders?" one asked, speaking Arabic as we all did.

"We're to let the rest live," the other said. "Saladin wants enough people to keep the orchards and farms going."

"There are few left."

"And there will be fewer still. All the remaining males are being killed unless they will join us."

When they moved past the house, I cautiously peered into the street, watching them walk away.

Once they were out of sight, I stepped into the street. It was empty, save for the bodies of the fallen. I stopped by a few to see if I could do anything, but they were all dead as far as I could tell.

I slipped down the streets of the city, trying to keep out of sight of any soldiers that moved about, heading toward my home.

When I reached my street, however, I realized I had no home.

Most houses on the street were piles of rubble and ash. There were still places where flames licked at anything flammable and others where mere embers smoldered as smoke drifted up from the wreckage. My home was one of the many destroyed.

I collapsed to my knees, staring at the disaster that had befallen this street as tears pushed against my resolve not to break down. Why? Why would they burn my home?

My family had been in there!

I struggled to my feet, rushing forward and clambering into the rubble. I was not strong enough to move the larger pieces, but I shoved aside smaller chunks of rock. I reached to push aside a plank of charred wood and then tore my hand away from it, wincing.

Inspecting my palm, I could see that I had burned my fingers.

I looked back at the wreckage of my house. I couldn't get inside. I wasn't strong enough to remove the heavier rubble, and I couldn't risk harming myself further by dealing with the still burning wood.

I couldn't tell if my family was in the pile of destruction, but something told me they were. I could hear no cries for help. If they were in there…

"Ammi!"

Silence greeted my call. I held my breath; I couldn't keep calling out for my family. The soldiers in the city might hear me.

My mother, Daniyah, and Habibah had been burned or buried alive in our house. If such was fact, there was nothing to be done about it now.

I stood for a moment, agony throbbing inside my chest with every heartbeat. The sound of voices drew me from my pain, and I glanced down the street. I saw soldiers in the distance. They hadn't noticed me yet.

I slipped behind one of the largest chunks of rubble, kneeling down. I could feel the heat of the fire that hadn't entirely gone out as the embers around me pulsed with warmth.

What was I going to do?

My father would be killed if he was not already dead, as would Daniyah's husband Abraham. But the soldiers I had heard chatting had said they were willing to let young men enlist in their army.

An idea was beginning to form in my mind.

I was the descendant of soldiers who fought in the Second Crusade–a third Crusade was rumored to be beginning even now.

Saladin had taken control of Jerusalem a year ago; that was why he was here, now, destroying my city and my family. Why should I not join in the Crusade against him?

But how could I?

I did not know how to fight, I did not know where the Crusading armies might be, but I did know where one army was —an army willing to train me and lead me directly to the Crusaders.

Of course, I was not a man. But that could be remedied. I had always been rather flat-chested and plain, so my hair would be the only real giveaway to my gender. If I cut it off, it was possible I would simply look like a young boy.

I peeked around the rubble to see where the soldiers were, and watched them until they moved down another street. Then I darted from my hiding place to the nearest house that wasn't a pile of rubble. I searched through the kitchen for a sharp knife and then knelt down and pulled a fistful of my hair away from my head. I reached the knife up, trying to gently saw it off. It wasn't particularly successful, although some hair began to give way beneath the edge of the blade.

I took a deep breath, setting down the knife long enough to brush aside my tears so that I could see more clearly. Pain was beating a rhythm inside my chest. My family—everyone that I loved—was dead and gone.

I grabbed the knife and a fistful of my hair again, and this time I hacked at my hair in more aggressive movements. Slowly the hair began to chop off as I hacked away. It was painful—my scalp reeled from the ache. Tears coursed down my cheeks as my shoulders shook from the sobs I tried to keep silent. I didn't need soldiers to find me like this, but I couldn't stop picturing what my family must have looked like. Crushed to the bone under the rubble, or burned to a blackened crisp.

Soon, however, most of my hair was shorn from my head and lying on the ground around me. I stood on shaky legs, looking at the detritus on the floor, and reaching up a hand to run my fingers through what was left of my hair. I could not remember my hair ever being so short. It wasn't a clean cut, and some places were longer than others, but for the most part it was cut above my ears.

My family was dead. Andaleeb was gone, and this new lad was taking her place.

I squared my shoulders, taking a deep breath and trying to channel my father's confidence. I'd idolized him all my youth—I knew how he talked, how he walked. I could do it. I could copy my father and become his son instead of his daughter. I had to. The alternative was death or rape—or both—and I did not relish the thought of either.

I searched the kitchen for certain herbs and spices so that I could clean and bandage my burned fingers and then replenish my little pouch.

Then I walked out of the door into the street, looking for soldiers. I was eighteen years old, and as of that day I was a man. I had to make this work—survival was my only option.

When I saw a group of soldiers, I paused. My hands shook at my sides and my breathing became hitched.

"Get it together, Andaleeb," I hissed. I had to approach them. I had to let them know I wanted to join them.

But what if I still looked like a girl after all? What if my face or the sound of my voice gave me away? What then?

The soldiers saw me and called out. My legs wobbled beneath me but I took a hesitant step forward, and then another.

The group of soldiers made my mission easier by coming toward me.

A sword was raised to my throat and the shaking in my hands increased.

"I…I heard you were looking for volunteers." A tear slipped down my cheek and one of the soldiers laughed.

"We've got a terrified whelp of a lad here. What should we do with him?"

"Bring him to the commander. He did say he's willing for recruits."

I tried not to shudder against the sword at my throat as the soldiers debated my fate.

"What do you think, lad? Should we kill you or take you to our commander?"

"T-take me to your commander?"

18

"That didn't sound too convincing, lad," one of the soldiers guffawed as he pushed my shoulder roughly. I stumbled a few feet—causing more laughter to burst forth from the group. At least now the soldier who'd had a sword to my throat had lowered his weapon.

"Come on, lad, let's see if you can stay or die."

They led me away and I told myself to just keep breathing.

My plan was going to work. The Saracen army would train me to fight, and I would go in search of the Crusaders the first chance that I got. I just had to survive long enough for the plan to work…

Chapter 2

THE COMMANDER SAT me down on the floor of one of the homes in the city that his men had looted—the inhabitants were most likely dead. He was tall, broad shouldered, with a thick beard and piercing eyes. His name was Asbat.

"Why do you want to join us?"

"I want to live," I answered honestly, curling my shaking fingers around each other and placing my clasped hands in my lap to hide them as I sat cross-legged across from him.

He nodded, stroking his chin and watching me for a time. I tried to hold his gaze without wavering, though my jaw was clenched to keep my mouth from trembling.

"We are accepting recruits, though you will be watched closely until you prove your loyalty so that we do not end up stabbed in our sleep. Are we clear?"

"Of course, sir."

"Can you use a weapon?"

"I…no, sir."

Asbat reached across the space between us, roughly taking my hands in his and turning them over. "Such soft palms. What do you do?"

I hesitated, but opted for honesty once more. "I am a healer."

I indicated the pouch on my belt and he nodded, so I pulled it out, unrolling the bag to show the contents inside—the herbs, the various utensils I used to sew up wounds or to collect more medicinal plants. I explained what the instruments were and he nodded slowly all the while.

"There is always room for healers in an army where there is often bound to be injured."

"Yes, sir."

"I have more use for soldiers, however, so I will see to it that you are trained."

"Yes, sir."

"Razon will see to your training and keep an eye on you until your loyalty has been proven." Asbat gestured over his shoulder to another tall, dark, muscular man standing in the doorway watching our conversion.

"Yes, sir."

"One final question, child…"

I clasped my hands in my lap once more to hide the shaking as I forced myself to meet his gaze. "Yes?"

"What is your name?"

"An…" I couldn't tell him my name was Andaleeb! That would break the whole charade. "Aban."

"Aban?"

"Yes, sir."

"Very well, Aban, go with Razon now. He will have charge of you until he sees fit to kill you or let you stay."

"Yes, sir." I stood on wobbling legs and willed myself over to Razon. He gave me a once over, shrugged, and then turned and walked away. I hurried out of the house after him. As I fell into step beside him, he began to speak.

"We will start training at dawn. You will learn to use a bow, a sword, and daggers. And when I say sword I mean both our scimitars and the longswords used by most of our enemies. You will be proficient, or you will end up dead in this war. Do we understand one another?"

"Yes, sir."

"Good. You will learn to ride as well, and fight from the back of a horse."

"Yes, sir."

Razon led me to a small tent in the camp Saladin's army had pitched outside the walls of the city they had nearly destroyed. There were a couple other boys who had joined the ranks of Saladin's army, and it appeared Razon had care of all three of us. We spent the night in that tent, with Razon keeping an eye on us and several other soldiers stationed around the tent to prevent escape—or to kill us if we tried harming Razon.

I did not sleep that night. I was still imagining what Habibah's face might look like charred black or what Daniyah's last words of comfort to my mother might have been as the house burned down around them.

Long before I or the other two boys were prepared, Razon dragged us out of bed and our training began.

The days that followed remain a blur in my memory. I was struggling to live each day, and not paying attention to much else.

About a week into our training, I came out of this stupor of what I can only assume was my grief and fear.

I awoke one morning to the groans of Sami—one of the boys I was training with. I had seen him once or twice in Darum, but we had not been friends or even acquaintances to any degree. The last week of training and sleeping together was the most time we'd ever been in the same company.

"Are you awake, Aban?" Razon kicked my side with his boot. It wasn't a hard kick—not enough to do damage. Just enough to nudge a sleeping soldier awake.

"Yes, sir." I rubbed my eyes and sat up. Sami was struggling out of his bedroll as Razon moved toward Karim to give him a good kick, too. Karim, however, was awakened by Sami's groans as I was, it seems, because he hurried to sit up as Razon's feet moved across the ground.

Razon grinned. "I will see you three outside in five minutes. We will begin with weapons today."

We'd been training for a week, most of which I no longer remember distinctly—as I stated before—but I do recall that the week was spent learning the simplest defensive and offensive stances for both hand-to-hand and sword fighting. We hadn't used any actual swords yet, however.

We'd occasionally been allowed to hold large sticks in place of an actual weapon, but there had been no sparring yet. I was okay with that; I am a healer, not a fighter, by nature. I knew in order to keep up my facade I would have to learn—and learn well—but I was not looking forward to it.

I hurried outside with Sami and Karim, every muscle in my body protesting from the brutal workouts I'd been giving it all week. We found Razon outside, arms crossed and scowling. As we emerged, he spun on his heel and marched away; we followed.

Razon led us through the tents of varying sizes to the edge of camp where he had been training us over the last week.

"Show me your stances," Razon said, the sharpness of his tone leaving no room for argument. Sami, Karim, and I dropped into one pose, and then another, moving between each carefully and precisely. I focused on placing my feet just so, and holding my hands exactly as Razon had taught us.

Once we'd moved through the stances he had taught us, he simply stood, arms crossed, watching us for some time. Then he gave me a sharp nod. "Aban, you dance as you should. Sami, Karim, you should take note. Now…"

Razon moved toward a large chest nearby, flipping it open and pulling out the curved swords known as scimitars. "You will show me your fighting and defensive stances when using this blade. Get used to the weight of it. Then we will use the longsword, and later the daggers."

Razon tossed a blade to Karim, who barely caught it, and then to Sami. It sailed right past Sami and he sheepishly moved to fetch it from the ground. Razon glared at him as he chucked a blade my way. My heart leaped to my throat as my hand darted out and my fingers curled around the hilt.

I'd caught it without hurting myself, which rather surprised me. Razon gave me another sharp nod. I was getting the impression I was his favorite pupil.

Razon took us through our paces for an hour before he let us eat breakfast. I sat apart from Sami and Karim as we ate our figs and carob pods.

"Were you trained before?" Karim asked, glancing my way.

I shook my head, not trusting my voice. I spoke as little as possible to avoid showing how terrified I was, and to avoid suspicion. Did my voice sound womanly? I didn't know. But I wasn't going to risk it if I could help it.

"You are a natural it seems," Sami said, resentment in his voice. He did not like me, which only served to make me that much more afraid of him recognizing me. Would he give me away if he realized I was Andaleeb?

"You do seem rather good," Karim agreed. "And *he* likes you." Karim gestured to Razon who was a distance away from us speaking with another commander in the army. "That's what matters right now, isn't it? We want to live so we have to fit in. You've already got someone on your side."

I glanced toward Razon. He was not a particularly friendly person in my estimation, and he'd never done anything to show he was 'on my side' as Karim seemed to think. Yet I did agree that

I seemed to have become his favorite pupil, so perhaps that would turn out to my favor.

Razon soon returned as we finished the last of our breakfast. "Come. We'll use our blades again."

"Yes, sir."

We trained with Razon everyday and I learned to use a bow, dagger, sword—both the curved and the straight. I was not brilliant with any weapon but that did not disturb me. I thought of myself as a healer and not a fighter.

Chapter 3

AS THE ARMY MOVED around the countryside engaging in various skirmishes with Crusaders—none of which I or Sami and Karim were allowed to participate in—my healing skills were put to use. Once the battles were over and the wounded were gathered, Razon would walk beside me as I helped first one and then another.

One day as I quietly worked over a man with a stab wound in his chest, Razon knelt on the ground across from me, arms crossed as he watched me. The sun was bright overhead and Razon's form cast a shadow over both me and the man I was trying to heal.

"Do you fear I will harm your men when you bring me to heal them?"

"Should I fear that?"

"No. Yet you watch me closely when I work."

"You can heal to far greater degrees than the others employed for that purpose. I find it fascinating."

I finished pressing my herbal tincture into the wound and wrapping a bandage around it to keep it in place.

"Who taught you such things?"

"A woman named Daniyah."

"Your mother?"

"No. A friend."

The thought of Daniyah's face crushed in by the rubble of my house, or charred black by the fire, flashed through my mind. My hands grew shaky as I finished binding the wound.

"I assume she is dead." Razon's voice was soft. I glanced up at him to find his dark eyes watching me gently. It was not what I expected; I could feel tears pushing to be let out and I looked down at my patient, hoping to gain my composure.

"I am sorry."

"You are not," I answered without thought as the first of the tears broke free. "You still fight with this army, and still kill other families. You are not sorry."

Razon sighed, stroking his chin as I collected my supplies and moved on to the next patient. This one was awake, writhing in pain as he held onto his leg where a deep gash was located.

I knelt beside him, laying out my pouch of supplies once more. A young boy came to me with a bowl of water. I had requested the ability to wash my hands after each patient when I'd first started being used as a healer for the army, and now I didn't even need to ask. They knew what I needed.

As I washed my hands and studied the wound, Razon came to sit beside me once more.

"Will I lose the leg?" the man groaned, his hands wrapped around his thigh as he grimaced in pain.

"I am not sure yet." I mixed together the herbs I used to dull pain, rubbing some into the wound and handing a small bunch of it the man. "Chew on this. It will help; you will feel less as I work."

He dutifully chewed on the mixture, grimacing from the taste now more than the pain. I gently pulled his hands free of the cut, gauging how deep it was.

"It cuts through every tendon," I said, mostly to myself. "And they nicked the bone…"

"It's bad," the man groaned.

I shook my head. The other healers in the camp would fail —give it up and cut the leg off, or try and heal it and then watch it catch infection and gangrene and slowly kill the man. But Razon was right; I was different. I could do more than they could.

I swiftly set about making another mixture of herbs—this one to promote the regeneration of the muscles and skin. As I kneaded it into the gaping wound, pressing down with enough pressure to slow the outpouring of blood, I closed my eyes. I lifted my heart to the true Healer, allowing His power to work through me. I knew in a moment that the leg would be fine.

I couldn't heal everything; I'd never brought back the dead. But for some reason, He had chosen long ago to use me in this fashion and I followed His lead.

It was strange to feel His warmth around me. I had been burying every part of Andaleeb—including her connection to Christ—so that I could survive as Aban. But this part of me, my relationship with Jesus, was the truest part of me and could not be buried. More than that, I could feel the comfort and warmth of

His love surrounding me and it was the balm my grieving soul needed.

As I finished my work and stood, looking for another patient, Razon put his hand on my shoulder.

"I am sorry, though you do not believe it."

I looked up into his dark eyes, studying the honesty written across his face.

"I do not fight to cause grief to other men. I fight to free my people from yours."

"How are my people different from yours?"

"You came from other countries, setting yourselves up as rulers here in a place you do not belong."

"I have as many ancestors who are native to these lands as I do those from Europe." I clasped his arm and pulled it toward my own, laying my tanned skin against his.

Razon nodded, pulling away and crossing his arms as he so often did. "The so-called Christians who invade our lands, subjugate our people to their laws and religion, these are what I fight against. They kill any and all who are different than they are, so we do the same."

"How is that better?" I asked. "If both sides cannot come together with open minds, this war will never end."

Razon shrugged. "We did not start it."

Life continued in much the same way for many months. The army fought—I healed. Razon trained—I learned. Sami bore his resentment toward my progress openly, while Karim tried to keep peace between us.

"We are all simply trying to survive," he'd say. It made no difference to Sami, who seemed determined to hate me as much as he hated our captors.

Eventually the army began marching toward Jerusalem and decided I could not stay much longer. Razon had declared me ready to join the fighting men and Asbat—the commander I'd first met—agreed. If we engaged the Crusaders once more, I would be on the opposing side; I would be fighting for the very people who had murdered my family.

Razon often spoke of the liberation that Saladin was bringing to *his* people, and that may well have been so. I am sure anyone not opposed to him was grateful for the protection he brought against the invading European armies. But I was not grateful for the work that he was attempting in uniting the Arab kingdoms against the Crusaders. I had grown up in Palestine; my parents both had a measure of Palestinian blood flowing through their veins, why were their lives so cheap to the man who claimed to want to save his people from Europeans?

One day the army was camped in a hilly valley, tents spread out in every direction as Razon led me, Sami, and Karim to his tent. Inside, he threw open a large chest and gestured to the weapons there.

"Choose."

"Are we training so late in the evening?" Sami asked.

"No. You are arming yourselves for the battles to come. You have all three proven yourselves over the last few months. I see no desire in you to kill me or your brothers in this camp. I will trust you with more responsibility. So, you will take weapons and tonight you will have your final test. You will be put on watch."

"We're guarding the camp?" Karim asked.

"You, along with many others. It is a large camp. But I will place the three of you along one section, yes. And if an enemy slips past tonight from your position—I will kill you each personally. Intimately. Painfully."

"Yes, sir," Karim said.

"If you fall asleep or escape, you will meet the same fate."

"Yes, sir."

"Good. Now, choose your weapons. I expect you to make me proud tonight and every day moving forward. You will fight beside me when next we encounter the Crusading army."

My heart raced as I stood listening to Razon tell us our duties for the night. We were going to fight with him? I couldn't do that.

If he was putting us on watch though, perhaps it was finally time for me to get away. I'd be alone, in the darkness.

"Aban!"

The sharpness in Razon's tone brought me back to the present. "Yes, sir?"

"Arm yourself, lad."

"Oh…yes, sir." I moved to the trunk, picking out a bow, a sword, and a dagger.

Razon looked between the three of us, all holding our weapons. We'd been using actual weapons in our training for several weeks—we knew how to use them. "If I find any of my men killed with those blades or arrows, you will all meet the most painful death. Are we clear?"

"Yes, sir."

"Good. Come along, I'll show you where you'll be on watch."

Could I run away tonight? Should I wait and try to plan it out further? But what if we ran into the Crusading army tomorrow and I had to fight them?

The main thing I knew about being on watch was not to fall asleep. There had been a man only yesterday who had the misfortune to fall asleep while on watch. He'd been beaten until the blood ran down his back, arms, and neck, creating a great pool of crimson at his feet. And then, he was beheaded.

Razon placed us a good many paces from one another. As the sun slowly set, I could see Sami and Karim less and less as the darkness stretched between us.

Razon came and stood beside me at the edge of camp. Did he know what I was planning? Was my eagerness to leave written all over my face?

I knew full well there were others dotted around the perimeter of the camp every few paces standing guard, not just Sami and Karim to my right and left. Could I truly sneak away?

I gripped my bow in my hand to stop the shaking of my hands.

"You are nervous."

I glanced at Razon as the sun continued to fall to the horizon.

"Yes." Honesty had always been the easiest way to lie to Razon, and tonight was no different.

"You will do well, Aban. You are the best of the three, you know."

I nodded.

"Just keep your eyes peeled for any suspicious movement, and don't fall asleep."

"Easy enough." I could hear how shaky my voice sounded, and I was sure Razon could too. He placed a hand on my shoulder.

"You will do well."

Darkness fell, and the camp quieted until only a few voices or sounds could be heard from within. Falling asleep while on watch was a capital offense. I assumed running away while on duty would be treated with no less anger. If I tried to flee and I failed, I would die.

But I didn't care. I hoped to be long gone before they discovered I had left my post. I couldn't stay and fight against the Crusaders.

Razon gave my shoulder a final pat and then moved away. I didn't know how far he was going. Would he stay close enough to keep an eye on Sami, Karim, and me? Would he notice if I tried to run?

I had my sword, bow, and daggers on hand as I was meant to be guarding the camp. I could potentially fight my way out if it came to that, but I had no desire to fight Razon. In some strange way, he was almost a friend.

I wrapped my cloak tightly about me to ward off the evening chill; I hoped it would also conceal me when I darted away from my post to the hill opposite me. I just needed to get up and over the hill without being seen, and then I might be free.

I took a deep breath, counting in my head. I wasn't sure how long I should wait and my toes began to tap in impatience and fear as I tried to distract myself.

And then I ran for it.

As I scrambled up the grassy hillside as quickly as I could, my heart racing, I listened for any shouts to cry out behind me, but I heard nothing. If Sami and Karim saw me, they said nothing. There was no angry or betrayed shout from Razon either.

I ran into the night with my weapons and my healing pouch but without provisions or money. I expected the trip ahead of me to be harrowing as winter was coming and I was alone in the world, but I had no choice.

Chapter 4

I RAN FOR MOST of the night, going the exact opposite direction I knew Razon's company would be heading. Eventually I found a narrow valley surrounded by large rocks of various shapes and I sheltered there for the rest of the night. I wondered what would become of Sami and Karim. If they'd seen me go, would they give me away? Or worse, would they be punished because I ran?

I couldn't dwell on the life I was leaving behind. I needed to survive. So when morning came, I left my hideout in the rocks and struck out toward the nearest town. I was armed, I looked like a man, it was likely I could use both to my advantage to obtain food and lodging.

When I entered the town, I made for a house at the edge. If things went south, I wanted an easy escape route. When I knocked on the door, a woman answered it. She was beautiful with her dark eyes, tan skin, and luscious dark curls that fall to her shoulders. My own hair had never been so lovely when it was long.

"Can I help you, sir?"

I started to nod when I heard coughing from behind her. "Is someone sick?"

The woman glanced behind her. "Both my children, and my husband, too. I'm not sure what it is, but our neighbor caught it first…and he's dead." The woman's eyes were wide with fear and uncertainty. I reached out to put a comforting hand on her shoulder.

"I am a healer. I can help."

She looked me over—probably taking in the many weapons I carried—and then hesitantly opened the door and let me through. She led me to the room where her husband and children were laying in bed, flushed with fevers as coughs wracked their lungs.

"Can you boil me some water?" I asked the woman.

She nodded, watching me with curious eyes as I pulled out my pouch, unrolling it to reveal the varied spices, herbs, and tools within.

"I'm going to make tea for them, if you will get the water."

"Of course, sir."

When she brought the boiling water, I made a simple tea to encourage their bodies toward recovery. Then I created a tincture to bring down the fever and another to purify the lungs.

The woman–Zara was her name–helped me as best she could, gently holding up her children's heads so I could tilt the tea into their mouths.

For several hours we watched over her family and I prayed. It wasn't long after that that the fevers broke and they became more lucid.

As I used a wet cloth to brush some sweat from the brow of the youngest girl, Zara's husband struggled to sit up.

"Who are you?"

"They call me Anab," I said with a sigh. I couldn't tell them the truth, but I did not wish to answer to Anab any longer. Anab was the boy training under Razon. Anab was gone.

"Thank you, Anab."

"You are not fully healed yet. You will need to continue with the tinctures I've created for several days yet."

"I'll be sure they do," Zara said, sitting beside her small son, brushing his hair from his face. "Is there anything we can give you as thanks?"

"Food. Money. Lodging for the night. Whatever you have, I will gladly accept it."

"You are a soldier?" Zara's husband asked.

"Yes, sir."

"You can have what you will, Anab. We owe you our lives."

I spent a few more days with Zara's family, nursing the husband and children back to health. When I left, Zara made sure I had provisions while her husband—Omar–pressed money into my palm.

"We will always be grateful you turned up at our door, Anab."

I nodded my thanks and strode away from the house. I would be forever grateful the Lord had taken me to their house. If He hadn't, they might have died from their sickness and I would likely not have been so fortunate in finding benefactors.

From there I set out for the port city of Acre. I had heard rumors from Omar and Zara that was where I would find the Crusading army so that is the direction I traveled. But winter was coming, so my travel was impeded and I spent several months in various town and cities along the way before I finally arrived.

Guy of Lusignan—King of Jerusalem until Saladin's rebellion ousted him—was laying siege to Acre, a city on the coast that was currently under Saladin's control. I hoped to join King Guy's army. It was rumored that more Crusaders were coming to aid him, and it seemed my best shot at life. I was alone, friendless. My family was dead; there was nothing left for me.

My options were limited; give up, which I had no intention of doing, or fight. Fighting meant with the Crusaders or with Saladin's army, and I had recently defected from the latter.

It was early in the morning when I arrived on the coast. Acre remained in the distance; there was no way to reach the city past the army that was laying siege around it, but that was just as well because I didn't want inside the city.

I approached as confidently as I could under the circumstances, knowing I'd be stopped by scouts eventually. I wasn't wrong. Men with drawn weapons approached me before I'd come within throwing distance of the camp itself.

"What is your business, stranger?" The soldier spoke French, which I only had limited knowledge of but I responded in kind.

"I would like to speak to someone in charge."

"To what end?"

"I would like to join your ranks, if possible."

They seemed rather unconvinced, but one of them agreed to fetch their commander while the others watched me closely.

"Don't even think about grabbing at those weapons, boy," one of them said. I raised my hands in mock surrender.

"I wouldn't dream of it."

I wondered briefly if my skills would be enough to match theirs. Razon was a master and a brilliant teacher, but I had no way of knowing what kind of training these men had undergone.

The soldier who'd gone to fetch a superior eventually returned with the man I assumed was his commander.

"You wanted to join us?" He asked, crossing his arms and eyeing me up and down much like Razon had once done. "Why should we trust you?"

"I realize you have little reason to…" I hesitated, my mind searching for words in the language I was not fluent in. Daniyah had taught me much, as had others in our community in Darum, but I did not believe I retained enough to be convincing. "My intentions are honest. I am from the city of Darum which Saladin attacked and ransacked a few months ago. In order to survive I joined their ranks."

"You fought with the Saracens?"

"I was trained by them. I did not, however, fight in any of their battles."

"Why did you join them then?"

"I had no other choice. It was to save my life. I left as soon as I was able."

"Are you a good fighter, boy?"

I would never grow used to people calling me boy, but after so many months I no longer flinched at it. "I do not know that I am good, sir, but I do my best."

"What is your name?"

"The Saracens called me Aban, but that is not my name."

"Shall we call you Aban?"

I hesitated. I couldn't tell them my true name, not without revealing I was a girl. But I did not want to be Aban. Aban was a boy training in the Saracen army under Razon. Aban was dead.

"No."

"Then what name would you go by, boy?"

"I do not know."

"You don't know your own name?"

"The name of my childhood is one I would like to forget, and the name given to me in Saladin's army is a thing of my past."

"Alright, fine. I'll just call you the Saracen for now." The man sounded angry and sarcastic, but I could not blame him. I knew I was being a pain.

"You say you were trained?"

"Yes, sir. I can use these weapons I carry with me quite well. The sword—both curved and straight variations—the bow, and daggers."

"Well, Saracen, my name is Emil. I'm going to test your training—let me see what you can do with those weapons." He drew his sword and immediately advanced on me. I dropped my bow to the ground, kicking it out of the way of my feet as I yanked my sword from its sheath to block his blade as it came bearing down on me without hesitation. Was he testing my skills or trying to kill me? Probably both.

For a few minutes we parried and blocked and attacked, dancing around each other. I had never fought anyone before— not truly. I'd sparred with Sami and Karim, and occasionally with Razon when he wanted to test my mettle. This felt like that, except I knew Razon was not attempting to kill me and I couldn't be sure with this Emil fellow.

After another of his blows was cast aside by a deft flick of my wrist, Emil stepped back and wiped the sweat from his brow.

"You were trained well. How do I know you are not a spy sent to kill me and my men in our sleep?"

"You don't know. You can either trust me or attempt to kill me, whatever is your preference."

Emil gave me a wry grin. "There is a truth about you, boy, that I cannot deny. But something in your eyes tells me you are not speaking honestly."

I nodded. "It is the name, I think. I will not tell you the full truth of who I am, and it bothers you."

Emil nodded. "I don't trust secretive people."

"My intentions are honest, sir, I can swear to that."

Emil studied me for a moment longer as he put his sword away. "Okay...I guess you're in for the moment. I will keep a close eye on you—if you try to kill us in our sleep, you're as good as dead."

He proposed a period of proving my loyalty much as Razon had done, and I agreed to it. With that, I was given a bedroll in one of the many tents alongside the men under his command. Here I was once more, in a tent with strange men pretending to be one of them.

The most surprising thing to me after joining the Crusaders was finding that very few of them truly knew the Lord at all. They claimed Him, and claimed to be doing what they were doing in His name or His church's name, but when I spoke to them it became oh so clear that they did not truly know Him at all.

I had been doing my best to ignore my past, to bury Andaleeb in the pile of rubble where the rest of her family had died. The one thing I did not try to bury was my Savior. I clung to the comfort that only He could provide, though in my denial of my pain I did not allow Him the opportunity to heal my wounds. But these men...most of them knew little of Christ at all.

Sometimes it made me question the battle they were fighting; if it wasn't zeal for the Lord that drove them—as in most cases of those I met, it clearly wasn't—then it was simply greed and avarice. A hatred for the people of this land, for people different than they were, and a desire to own their properties for their own. Power. Greed. Hatred. These were not things that I could stand by, and I found myself wondering if Razon's reasons for helping to kill the people of my city—my family—were not more reasonable than this.

The siege of Acre lasted for months. We did very little except sit in our camp and wait for the enemy inside to give in. I spent my days watching and listening. Learning about my fellow soldiers and learning the languages and customs of those I now lived with; there were few among them I could call a friend and none I trusted with the truth of who I was.

Emil kept a close eye on me, of course, but I did nothing to arouse suspicion. I was not there to harm anyone. I was there for protection. I hardly knew how to make my own way in the world. I didn't know where else to go, who to turn to, what to do. So I remained the soldier I had become since my family was murdered, albeit in a different army than when I began.

Chapter 5

I LAY MY HAND across the forehead of a young man named Jeremiah. His frame was frail—I could see more bones poking through his skin than was healthy—and his breathing ragged.

He'd fallen to fever and sickness as the last of the winter months faded away. The healers of the army had been able to do nothing for him and had put him aside as a lost cause. Their limited resources were not going to be wasted on someone who had no hope.

I had heard of Jeremiah from Maurin, one of the men who lived in the same tent I did. He and Jeremiah had formed a friendship since joining the Crusades and he had mentioned how distraught he was that the healers had given up. I'd asked him if he could take me to Jeremiah, reminding him that I knew how to heal. He'd agreed eagerly, ever hopeful.

As I knelt over Jeremiah, I tilted his head back to pour some of my tea into his mouth as I prayed. It would take weeks for him to recover his strength, but he could do it.

"So?" Maurin leaned over my shoulder, staring into Jeremiah's weak face.

"He'll live. You'll need to give him this tea twice a day. It should keep the fever and infection away. Once he regains some strength we can start him on solid foods once more."

"He's going to live?"

"He's going to live."

Maurin wrapped me in a bear hug from behind. I tensed for a moment, and then made myself relax. Maurin was not a threat. He was simply grateful.

"Thank you, Saracen."

"You're welcome."

The nickname Emil had given me had stuck. I refused to answer to Aban any longer, and equally refused to tell anyone my name was Andaleeb, so there was little for the men around me to do but pick up on Emil's nickname.

As the days passed, there was little for me to do. I helped those who were sick—after Jeremiah, word of my healing abilities spread and everyone would search out 'the Saracen' when they needed help beyond that of the army's hired healers. When not healing, my days were spent patrolling the camp and trying to keep my identity as a girl a secret.

Months passed in this way, with summer turning to autumn. I found laying siege to a city not nearly as interesting as it sounded. More to the point, I had no one to talk to, to confide in. I missed my sister Habibah, and I missed Daniyah. I missed having people who knew every part of me—the good and the bad —and loved me in spite of them all. I was surrounded by strangers.

And yet it was my own doing. Yes, I was keeping the fact that I was a girl a secret for my own safety, but I could have tried to be friends with Maurin and Jeremiah and others in the camp around me. Yet I did not.

I could not trust them. I could not let down the carefully created walls around my heart. The Lord I would let in; everyone else could stay as far away from me as possible. Did I fear the heartbreak of loving again? Perhaps I did. Whatever it was I feared, it was enough that I kept everyone at a careful distance.

With the coming of autumn came a change in our circumstances at Acre.

Something was finally happening. Saladin had sent thousands of troops to aid his garrison at Acre, and now the siege had turned into a drawn-out battle with fighting nearly every day as King Guy tried to maintain the siege of the city while fending off the forces that Saladin sent against us.

My skills were put to the test at last, and I found the use of them as distasteful as I thought I would. I was good, mind you; I was excellent. I rarely missed when I shot with my bow, Saladin's soldiers dropping one by one beneath my aim. And when the fighting became up close and personal, I could dance around my opponents with relative ease. Razon had taught me well.

And yet I couldn't help picturing Razon when I cut down the enemy. And Sami. And Karim. How many of these men were good men fighting for their own beliefs, fighting for their people? Or men like Sami, merely trying to survive?

We pushed back Saladin's forces every day, and yet he returned relentlessly. Thousands of our soldiers died. I could imagine what the enemy's losses must be.

Morale was failing.

"We are no longer laying siege to Acre," Emil sighed, staring out at the line of Saladin's forces that were marching in our direction once more. "We are merely trying to survive the siege of Saladin's army."

Emil kicked a rock that had the misfortune to be in his path and it skittered across the ground. "Food and water are growing so scarce, I will lose more men to starvation than from the battle."

"I know, sir."

Emil glanced at me. "Look, Saracen, I've seen you helping the sick around the camp. Don't stop. Sickness is spreading and killing more of my men than the starvation, thirst, and battle put together!"

"Yes, sir."

"I need you to help me, Saracen. My men need healing both on the battlefront and from the sickness that spreads…"

"I am doing what I can, sir."

"Just don't stop, lad. That's all I ask."

The winter months set in, and Saladin's troop set up camp around us, keeping us locked away from the hope of food or reinforcements. Given the dire state of our camp, I could only imagine how poorly the people within the city itself must be doing.

In December, Duke Leopold of Austria arrived with fresh troops, having taken control of the Crusading army as politics that were beyond my care left King Guy with little support. The

Duke's arrival raised everyone's spirits. He brought fresh troops and he gave those of us already stationed at Acre new vigor. He also brought news: King Richard of England and King Philip of France were on their way with an even larger army.

I had begun to believe this siege was all my life was going to amount to. I'd lost my family, I'd become this stranger I didn't know—first a boy fighting for the very people who had killed my family, and now a boy laying siege to Acre and on the verge of starvation because of the counter siege Saladin had set against us.

Now at least something was happening. I would still be this stranger, this soldier fighting a war I hardly believed in, but perhaps something would happen to bring some sort of meaning back into my life beyond simply survival.

"We just might be able to beat back the troops surrounding us," Maurin grinned at me as he pulled off his boots and prepared to settle in for the night.

"The Duke's reinforcements certainly help," I replied.

"And two kings are coming with more," Maurin said as he curled into his thin blanket. "Two kings…"

I was glad he could find some hope in the prospect of the kings coming to our aid. It was a bitterly cold night, and our blankets were hardly enough to keep off the frostbite. I was running low on my herbs and spices and had no way to get more, so it was difficult for me to help with the illnesses that were running rampant in the camp.

But the kings were coming…maybe that would change things.

It was nearly a month later before King Richard and King Philip landed at Acre, their fleets sailing toward the port city in all their grandeur. Cheers went up from the men on land, as Emil and the other commanders ordered various companies of soldiers to engage Saladin's troops so that the reinforcements could land and join us without being hassled by the enemy.

Maurin, Jeremiah, and I watched from the camp—our company wasn't set to engage unless the others fell too fast.

"Two kings," Maurin elbowed Jeremiah. "This'll change everything."

As we watched, thousands of soldiers were disembarking from the great ships and making it to the shore in smaller landing boats. Our soldiers fought along the shore, keeping Saladin's forces at bay while the reinforcements came to the camp.

"They just keep coming," Jeremiah said, hands on his hips and a smile on his face.

"I told you," Maurin said, grinning again. "I told you; two kings…" He shook his head as though he couldn't believe it either, despite his proclaimed faith.

In the days that followed, King Richard and King Philip's soldiers engaged Saladin's troops until they withdrew entirely and the city was conquered. Maurin was right; two kings seemed to change everything.

The camp remained outside the city walls with most of the combined armies staying there while a few of the higher ranking officials moved into town to take over the politics and truly seize control. I did not meet either of the kings—or the duke that had come earlier for that matter—but within a few days it seems there was a dispute among them. One night Maurin, Jeremiah, and I were on guard duty together and I listened quietly as they discussed the situation.

"Do you know what the King of England did today?" Maurin asked.

"I heard about it," Jeremiah replied.

"I saw it! I saw him pull down the Duke of Austria's flag and then shout in his face about not making himself equal to himself and the King of France."

"I wish I'd seen it…I just heard about it afterward. Severin told me about it. He says the Duke is leaving now; he won't remain in the Crusades to be humiliated further."

"I wouldn't stay," Maurin replied. "But the King of England might have a point. The Duke putting his flag up there with theirs was a bit pompous."

"I also heard the King of France is contemplating leaving," Jeremiah said.

"I hadn't heard that!" Maurin glanced at me. "Did you know that?"

"No," I said.

"Why the devil is he leaving?" Maurin asked Jeremiah.

"Because King Richard apparently got married to some princess from Navarre even though he was engaged to King Philip's sister…or some such."

"Royals," Maurin said with a sigh and a shake of his head. "Will King Philip take his forces with him? We need his men… will it only be King Richard's men left?"

"I do not know. Emil will probably tell us if it comes to that."

In a few days' time—after both Duke Leopold of Austria and King Philip of France had departed—King Richard marched the rest of the army, which he now had sole control of, down the coast toward Jaffa. Prior to departing, he lined up hundreds of prisoners of war from Acre and had them all beheaded. It was a horrifying and disheartening sight. My good opinion of the so-called Christian Crusaders had long since been lost, but this was the final straw.

When the king marched away from the port city of Acre, I volunteered to stay with the smaller garrison he left at Acre.

"Are you sure?" Emil asked. "We can use you; both on the battlefield and afterward. There are no healers quite like you."

"I know, but I do feel I would prefer to stay here, sir."

"I won't order you to follow, lad. We need men here, too, to keep the city under our control."

I took up my post on the city walls later that day, watching the army march away with little but disdain in my heart. Laid out across the ground below the city wall were the many dead bodies of the prisoners, their heads discarded nearby. It wasn't a pleasant sight.

I had no home and nowhere to go, so staying within the ranks of the army seemed my only viable option, but I longed to find a new path—this one did not suit.

Chapter 6

ONE DAY I walked down a street in Acre in search of a specific tavern. I had heard that King Richard had left his new wife and his sister in the city when he marched the rest of the Crusader army south, and I was looking for them. Living in the city was not proving to be any more purposeful or fulfilling than the siege had been, or training with Razon before that. I missed my family, though I buried my grief on a daily basis so that I would not weep. Once I started crying I imagined I would not stop.

I needed a change, however. I hadn't wanted to fight alongside King Richard's brutal army, but perhaps I could protect his family. That was more to my liking.

The chill wind had me wrapping my cloak more tightly about my shoulders as I glanced toward the sky—it would undoubtedly rain today.

I knew I was headed in the right direction not because I saw the tavern sign itself but because two women in elegant gowns were standing just outside, clearly in a heated discussion.

"I cannot believe he would leave us here alone!" the younger one threw her hands about in a wild manner as she talked.

"Now, Joan, he wanted to keep us safe."

"Alone. Unprotected."

"Away from the fighting."

"Your Highness? Your Majesty?" I stepped up to them, effectively interrupting their debate.

They both turned to look at me, studying me as most people did when they first met me.

"What do you need, lad?" the one I assumed was the Queen of England asked.

"I would simply like to offer you my services as a guard in the absence of the king."

The other girl, the one I assumed to be the princess, laughed. "See, even he can tell we were abandoned here."

"Joan!"

"I have a brilliant idea."

"And what idea is that?" Queen Berengaria questioned.

"We can follow my brother!"

"I don't know about that, Joan…"

I glanced between them, unsure if they had hired me on or not.

"You don't want to stay here, do you?" Joan asked, grabbing Queen Berengaria's arm.

"Okay, okay…we can follow my husband."

"I am not sure that would be wise," I said.

"We can get together some soldiers to protect us," Queen Berengaria said. "Starting with you, sir."

"Please, do agree." Joan turned to me, her big blue eyes pleading. She was rather sweet in a childish sort of way.

"I will agree to accompany you in search of King Richard." I could not believe I had agreed to it, but at least I was getting what I wanted: a change of scenery.

"Perfect!" Joan clapped her hands. "Berengaria, dear, make arrangements will you? How many soldiers do you suppose we need?"

Within a few hours I was lodged in the tavern in a room just beside the one where Joan and Berengaria were staying. Berengaria and I discussed payment for my services, and then she enlisted my help in gathering more men for protection. I suggested a few men from the garrison King Richard had left at Acre, and she made selections.

"You have been most helpful, Saracen," Berengaria said. "Have the men prepare for departure tomorrow. We will track down my husband from there, and I will have you all paid for your services."

"Of course, Your Highness."

Since I had been the first to approach the royals and offer my services, they had put me in charge of the few others soldiers they'd selected to guard them in their travels. We were more than a week behind the king and his army, but there would be fewer of us and therefore we would likely travel faster. The queen hoped to reach the king within a few weeks or less.

The following morning we set out from Acre. I led the group with a young man named Baldwin. The queen and princess walked behind us, and I'd placed Crispin and Florian on either side of them, with Ivar and Neville taking up the rear so that the royals had someone on every side to protect them from any foes we might encounter. Sebastian was at the very back, guiding the mule who pulled the cart filled with the royals' possessions and our provisions for the journey.

We trudged along the coast, following the clear swath of land trampled by many feet that had been left behind by the army following King Richard. On our second day out from Acre, we cut through a small valley between two steep hills.

"Keep your eyes sharp," I called to the men.

"Do you expect bandits, Saracen?" Joan asked, darting forward to my side, her eyes scanning the hilltops.

"You can never be too careful, my lady," I replied.

I glanced over my shoulder to be sure that Crispin, Florian, Ivar, and Neville were on the alert. They were all looking at the foliage along the edge of the roads and scanning the hilltops above. Satisfied, I continued forward. Joan stayed at my side, seemingly eager to watch for the bandits herself.

"Do you suppose we will be attacked?"

"Don't be frightened, my lady."

"Oh, I'm not scared, Saracen. I've been betrayed and thrown in prison, I've been lost at sea in a storm, and I've been abandoned by my brother in a strange city in a foreign land. Bandits are nothing."

"Were you harmed when you were thrown in prison?"

"No."

"I know you came to no harm at Acre, despite your protests against your brother. What of the storm at sea? Did you come to any bodily harm?"

"What are you getting at, Saracen?"

"Bandits attacking us on the road to rob or kill us seems a far more pressing matter than you are making it out to be, Your Highness. If we are attacked, you will not glibly suggest you have seen such things before. You will be terrified as swords come for your neck, or men deal with you in unseemly ways. This is not a game, Princess."

Joan studied me for a moment and then laughed. "You remind me of someone."

"Oh?"

"I have a darling friend named Robin—you would not approve of him, I think. He's too much like me. But his companion Much...he would be more like you. Taking everything far too seriously."

"There is merit in not making light of serious situations. You have to be prepared."

"Or perhaps there is merit in finding the lighter side of things, the joy and the laughter in spite of the darkness. Life would be dull and hardly worth living if we were all as serious as you."

I couldn't argue with that. Yet I had very little to laugh about anymore. My sister, my mother, my father, Daniyah...they were all dead. And so far, I had not risked making true friendships since then. I did not think my life was more fulfilling without fellowship and relationship, but though I could see what was lacking I could not change it. I had Jesus. He would be sufficient for me.

And yet I want so much more for you.

I closed my eyes briefly as His voice spoke through me.

I made you to be in community with others.

I opened my eyes, blinking rapidly to keep the tears from forming and falling as my heart squeezed inside my chest.

"And let us consider how we may spur one another on to good deeds, not giving up meeting together as some are in the habit of doing, but encouraging each other."

The verse from Hebrews flashed through my mind. I could almost hear Daniyah whispering encouragement as she spoke the verses to me when I was a child. Her dark eyes boring into mine as she brushed my hair from my face, tucking it behind my ear.

"Be devoted to one another in love," Daniyah's voice echoed in my mind. *"Honor one another above yourselves… rejoice with those who rejoice, mourn with those who mourn."*

"Look sharp!" Florian cried out, breaking my reverie. As I spun toward him, I saw him whip out his bow and take aim. I followed his arrow and watched it pierce a man running down the hill to the right.

A quick glance showed about fifteen bandits charging down both steep inclines on either side of the road. I grabbed my bow and took aim as the rest of the men did the same. Some of the bandits fell, their bodies tumbling the rest of the way down the hillside as they died. The rest reached the road with swords raised.

I shoved Joan behind me with one arm, reattaching my bow to the slot on my back as I whipped out my sword to block any incoming blows.

For a minute I was parrying and blocking with one hand as I kept hold of Joan behind me with my other arm, guiding her to stay squarely behind me as I turned this way and that to block the opponents who might wish her harm.

When I no longer had an immediate foe before me, I swung around, eyeing the rest of my men.

Crispin was shoving his sword into the last of the bandits, Sebastian was clutching his bloodied arm, and Neville was writhing on the ground. Florian was knelt beside Neville, trying to staunch the bleeding from his chest while Ivar tried to calm him down and Berengaria stood nearby, pale and wide-eyed.

Baldwin ran past me, chasing down the pack mule who'd apparently bolted further down the road once the fighting started.

I hurried over to Neville's side, pulling out my depleted pouch of herbs and quickly mixing together a few. Joan followed me.

"Is he going to die?"

"Not if I can help it. Keep pressure on that wound," I told Florian. "Ivar, Crispin! Check the hillsides for any other foes who might be in hiding. Sebastian, how bad is the arm?"

Sebastian came over, kneeling beside me as I mixed together my herbs. He held out his bloodied arm. "Not nearly as bad as Neville."

I studied the cut in his arm as I finished mixing my herbs. "You'll be alright. Give me a moment." I turned to Florian, instructing him to remove his hands from Neville's wound so I could press my tincture into it. As I pushed the herbs into the ragged skin and exposed muscles, I closed my eyes and began to pray.

Within moments I knew the herbs would take root and he would heal. I reached for my tools and began to stitch his wound closed and then I rubbed another mixture of herbs over the top and wrapped a bandage around it.

"What do you think, Saracen?" Neville gasped, his eyes gaining some lucidity as he looked at me.

"You'll be alright. It might take a few weeks for this one to heal, but you'll live. You'll have to ride in the cart with the packs; you can't walk or exert yourself too much until this heals up a bit."

Baldwin had brought back the mule and cart, so he and Florian helped Neville into the cart while I turned to clean and bandage Sebastian's arm. It wasn't a deep cut and didn't require the same concentrated energy that Neville's had.

"You are quite the skilled healer," Berengaria commented.

"I have had many years of practice," I replied.

Ivar and Crispin soon came back from scouting to say they saw no one ahead.

"We should continue on our way," I said as I finished packing away my medicinal pouch. "Crispin, stay ahead to scout for further bandits or unwanted guests. Baldwin, you take his place on the left, Florian stay to the right. I'll lead, and Ivar will bring up the rear. Sebastian, can you still guide the mule with that arm?"

"I believe so."

"Then do so. Keep an eye on Neville while you're at it."

"Of course."

"Princess, my Queen, are either of you hurt?"

"No, Saracen," Berengaria said. "A little rattled, but not hurt."

"You were brilliant!" Joan linked her arm through mine. "Absolutely brilliant. The only person I've seen fight like that before was my friend Robin—he's absolutely delightful to watch."

"Come on, everyone," I said, starting to walk forward down the road again, Joan still attached to my arm. "Let's get moving."

I glanced over my shoulder to be sure the men were falling into line around the queen.

"I'll come running back if I see anything," Crispin said before he darted forward to scout the road ahead of us.

The rest of our travel that day and in the days that followed were quiet. When we reached the city of Arsuf we discovered that the king's forces and Saladin's had battled there only two days before our arrival.

"Was anyone hurt?" Joan asked of one of the inhabitants of Arsuf whom we'd been questioning to ascertain the whereabouts of the army.

"There were losses on both sides, my lady," the man said.

"I know. That isn't what I meant," Joan snapped.

"Princess Joan," I said quietly, putting my hand on her arm. "You can hardly expect these people to know whether or not one certain man in an entire army was killed or wounded."

"If you are worried for the king, Your Highness," the man said, "he was uninjured."

"It isn't the king I'm concerned about," Joan sighed, turning away from the man.

Joan had been endlessly raving on our journey about a young man named Robin, and I assumed it was he that had her worried.

I arranged lodging for the night, and then our journey began anew with the dawn.

As we walked down the dusty road, I could see that Joan was still downcast. I sent Baldwin ahead to scout so that I could fall into step beside Joan without an audience.

"My lady, do you need anything?"

"No."

"You are unhappy."

"I am worried about my friends, that is all."

"Not your brother?"

"You heard the people of Arsuf; the king was fine."

"Who is this Robin to you exactly?"

"A friend. He came with my brother to rescue me in Sicily where I was imprisoned, and we traveled together until my brother left me alone at Acre."

"Do you love him?"

"That is a rather personal question, Saracen."

"I apologize. I am merely trying to ascertain your state of mind so I can best cheer you up."

"That is very kind of you. Once again, you remind me of Robin's little friend Much. I'm sure you'll be great friends if we ever catch up to my brother's army and find them again."

"I have no friends, my lady. Not anymore."

"I am sorry to hear it. Friends make life worth living, lad."

I glanced behind me to see the men still guarding Berengaria. None were paying too much attention to my conversation with Joan.

"None of these are your friends?" Joan asked, following my gaze.

"They are men that I happen to work with at the moment. If I never saw any of them again, it would not drastically alter my life in any way."

"Well that will never do. We must change this. We can start with me; I'll be your first friend."

"As you wish, my lady."

"Don't be like that, Saracen. Don't give me those sad, dark eyes. Here's how this will work. I'll tell you something about me, and you respond in kind, and we'll get to know one another on a deeper level. And voila! We are friends. Here: I was twelve years old when I was sold off in a political marriage, and yet that marriage has been the highlight of my life. My William was everything to me. Your turn."

I stared at her for a moment, wondering what I could possibly say without giving too much of myself away.

"Come on, Saracen, relationships must have two participants for them to work."

"I am glad to hear that your marriage was not a burden after all. I have never been in love, and I doubt I will be now."

"Oh don't be so dour! You'll meet a beautiful young woman someday soon and you'll fall at her feet and declare you'll do anything for her—die for her if needs must—because she is your everything!"

"That is rather dramatic."

"You'll do it; all men do eventually. Many have fallen at my feet, you know."

"Do you break their hearts?"

"Generally, yes. My husband I loved; but the rest I can do without."

"Even this Robin fellow?"

"He is an exception," Joan said, her lips forming a pout as her brow furrowed. "He refuses to fall at my feet like the rest. I can't get him to care for me however I try. There…I've shared another thing. Now you must. Tell me how the mind of a young man like yourself works so that I can understand Robin better."

"I am afraid I have no more insight into the mind of a young man than you do." My foot caught for a moment on a rock in the road and I stumbled forward, shocked by my own admission.

"Careful, lad. You don't need to be so defensive you hurt yourself." Joan seemed to think this comment of hers quite funny, for she threw back her head with a boisterous laugh.

I glanced at the men behind us, and Berengaria not far away. Then I looked at Joan, who looked back with her open and honest eyes. I knew, somehow, that I could trust her.

"Don't call me 'lad' please," I said, dropping my voice so as not to be overheard. "Or 'boy' or 'sir' or anything else that you have been since we met."

"Why not?" Joan asked, matching my quiet tone though her eyebrows raised and her expression was one of confusion and curiosity.

I glanced behind us once more and then took a deep breath, preparing myself to speak the truth for the first time since my family died. "I am none of those things, that is why."

"What do you mean?"

"I pretended to be a boy to survive," I hissed, glancing behind us again.

Joan stopped walking. "You're a girl!?"

"No," I said calmly, grabbing her arm and pulling her forward once more. I sent a hasty glance at our traveling companions, but none seemed interested in our conversation. "I am a woman."

My heart was pounding loudly in my ears. What was I thinking? I hardly knew Joan at all and here I was, spilling my truth to her.

"How on this good earth did you end up in the army?" Joan whispered, glancing back at the others as well.

"I had to pretend to be a man and fight in the army. I would have been killed or raped if I had not."

Joan's face paled and tears sprang into her eyes. My life since my family died had been so filled with hardship and secrecy that my simple statement had not disturbed me, but seeing her face I realized how deep I had pushed my own emotions. It was horrible, what I had been through, and I ought to feel it as Joan did.

"You poor darling," Joan said, wrapping her arm around my shoulders. "You will stay with us. My brother will find a safe place for you once we catch up to him. There now…see? Friends, after all. Do you have a name?"

"Not one I'm going to share. And please—"

"Your secret is safe with me, though I will tell Berengaria. We'll keep an eye on you until we reach my brother and he can figure out what we should do." Joan studied me for a moment. "Is that why everyone calls you Saracen? You chose to be a boy, but you couldn't answer to a man's name?"

"I did answer to a man's name for a while, but I grew tired of it," I said, remembering my life as Aban, training under Razon.

"And you won't tell me your real name?"

"No."

"Then I suppose you shall remain 'the Saracen' until you trust me enough to tell me your proper name."

As we continued down the road arm-in-arm, I couldn't help glancing behind at the others. None seemed to pay attention to us, but I was still concerned that someone might have overheard my conversation with Joan. What had I been thinking, telling her I was a woman? That it was the truth hardly mattered; I'd hidden my identity for safety and I was hardly safe yet.

Chapter 7

WHEN WE FINALLY caught up with the Crusading army, they were stationed at Jaffa. Our travels had been relatively uneventful after that first bandit attack. Neville was healing nicely, and Sebastian's arm was already good as new. When we arrived in Jaffa, we could see the encampment of the army spreading out for miles around the city. Berengaria led the way into the city, however, and not into the camp itself. After asking around, we found the king just outside the home where he was apparently living.

He was shocked to see his wife and sister, both of whom flung their arms around him for a hug.

"Berengaria! My love, what are you doing here?"

"Joan and I followed you, husband. We did not like being left alone."

Once the initial greetings had passed, King Richard paid the men Berengaria had hired and sent them to the camp under the direction of one of his commanders.

"Not this one," Joan said, grabbing my arm as I attached the pouch of coin the king had handed me to my belt. "You have to keep her, brother."

"Her?" King Richard turned to me, eyebrows rising.

"Berengaria will tell you all about it," Joan said. "I'm off to find Robin! I'll be back shortly."

Joan skipped off down the street in the direction the king

thought Robin and his companions had wandered. I was curious about her mysterious friend Robin, but I stayed rooted in place as the king eyed me from my toes to my forehead, as everyone else had done since the day my family died.

Berengaria linked arms with him, kissing his cheek. "Don't stare, dearest. It is rude."

King Richard turned to her, his eyes softening. "Berengaria, my love, you were far safer at Acre than here."

"But I was not happy,"

I started to step away to give them privacy, but the queen grabbed my arm. "Where do you think you are going? Richard, this is…well, the Saracen. We hired her to protect us on our journey. I want her to be a part of your personal guard."

"You want a woman to be a member of the Royal Guard?"

Berengaria crossed her arms. "She has served us well these last few weeks, and been a true friend to Joan."

"Do you know how to fight, young lady?" King Richard turned to me, eyebrows raised.

"I was trained by the Saracen army, and have fought with the Crusaders for a year now."

"Please, Richard," Berengaria linked arms with him once more. "Let her be one of your personal guard. She is remarkable as a warrior *and* a healer. She will serve you well! You will not be disappointed."

As the queen was speaking, Joan came hurrying toward us with two young men following her. Joan pulled one of them into the circle as we talked, but the second young man hung back from the group.

"Joan!" King Richard turned to her, shaking his head. "You should never have come; can you even begin to comprehend the dangers that could have befallen you and my wife? I'm sick with worry just thinking about it."

"You clearly don't need to worry, brother." Joan crossed her arms, arching an eyebrow. "We arrived safe and sound. We aren't in any more danger here than we were *left alone* at Acre."

"Regardless, my love," Berengaria drew his attention away from his sister. "It is done now. Robin, please do convince my dear husband to take on this young fighter. They are remarkable, I swear."

"She–her–he–uh…" the infamous Robin I'd heard so much about stumbled over his words. He was a young man around my own age. His blond hair was slightly unruly and fell into his blue eyes as he looked at me with something resembling panic. He took a deep breath and said, "I have heard good things about this fighter."

King Richard laughed. "As have I, but that doesn't change the fact that she is a woman. This will not end well."

"Richard!" Joan glared at her brother. "No one knows she's a woman, and no one will ever know if you'll shut up about it."

I was rather tired of always being treated as a man, but my secret was still too dangerous to share and the fact that Joan had been telling seemingly everyone since our arrival in Jaffa worried me somewhat.

"How can you be sure no one will discover the truth?" King Richard asked.

"They haven't figured it out yet," Berengaria said.

"I will leave if I am a problem to you," I offered. "I do not need your protection, King Richard; I simply wish to fight alongside your men."

"Why?" King Richard eyed me with obvious suspicion, which I was used to. No one let me join their endeavors easily since my family had died. "You are a Saracen, are you not? Perhaps you are here to spy for Saladin."

"I am not. I was trained by the Saracen army, yes, but I have never fought for them and I do not share their faith. I have, however, fought alongside the Crusaders."

"Why?"

"Because I am a disciple of Christ and I will not take up a sword against the Crusaders." *in spite of the fact I find them to be in the wrong more often than not* I might have added, but I held my tongue.

"So you joined them instead."

"We have a common belief in our Savior; I do not see why we cannot work together despite our different backgrounds."

"I am not sure we all–" the king began, but he cut himself off and simply stared at me for a moment. I am sure he was going to say that not everyone present did share the same belief in Christ, but of that I was already convinced. It saddened me.

I hadn't been sharing my faith since joining the Crusading army—I had limited my conversations with anyone as much as I could. But now that Joan had started me on this path to opening up, I suddenly felt the pull once more to share what I held so dear.

The king was still watching me with nothing but suspicion in his eyes, so I tried another tactic to placate him.

"I have no love of Saladin," I said, thinking of my murdered family.

The king was frowning but he said, "I will agree to take you on. You will remain a part of my guard alongside Robin and the others—not only to appease my wife, but to keep you safe as well. I will not have you mingling with just anyone in this army. You are safe with Robin and his companions; they are noble and honorable men."

"I appreciate the sentiment, Your Majesty," I said, though I knew I could handle myself and did not need their protection. I had been on my own in a sea of men for nearly two years.

The conversation wound down after the king agreed to let me stay; he soon went inside with his wife. Joan grinned, her eyes alight with mischief.

"That worked magnificently. I knew he would let her join you," she said to Robin.

"I am not sure this is wise," Robin said, eyeing me up and down as everyone did.

"You do not think I can fight?" I asked, giving him the same once over. He was not large or muscular—I could probably beat him in a fight. "That is alright, because it is true. I do not fight as well as some, but I can manage."

"This is Robin," Joan said, slipping her arm through his. "I've told you about him. The Earl of Locksley."

"So you have."

"This is his servant Much." The young man who'd held back from the group met my gaze and then glanced at his boots. "And the other member of the gang is Allen, though I haven't seen him today..." Joan glanced around the street for a moment.

"I'm not sure where he is at the moment," Robin said. "He wandered off when the king gave us the day to rest."

"It is a pleasure to meet you both," I said, bowing my head slightly in greeting.

"And your name is?" Robin asked.

I sighed, knowing this question had been coming. Was I ready to be Andaleeb again? Or perhaps the better question, *could* I ever be Andaleeb again? It was the name my parents had given me, and thinking of them only reminded me that they were dead, and had died horribly.

"I cannot say. I do not wish to be known by my childhood name, the memories are too painful to me. Yet I have yet to choose a name to answer to now."

"What do people call you in general?"

"Nothing."

"They must call you something!" Robin insisted as his friend Much watched me with quiet and thoughtful eyes. "What has Joan been calling you?"

"Some people refer to me as the Saracen."

"The Saracen, huh?"

"You may call me that if you wish."

"I suppose I'll have to if you'll give me no other name," Robin said. "But I'm sure we can do better than that."

Later, I was introduced to the fourth member of the King's Guard. His name was Allen and he seemed to find it hard to believe that I was a soldier. We were gathered in Robin's room in the house the king had taken over for his personal use while the army was staying in the city of Jaffa. Robin and Allen were lounging in chairs near the window, while Much sat on the floor at Robin's feet. I sat cross-legged on the floor across from them, underneath the window.

"You were a part of the guard that protected Joan and the Queen?" Allen leaned toward me, his eyebrows raised.

"Yes."

"Truly?"

"Yes."

"And now you are a part of the King's Royal Guard with us?"

"Yes."

"Is that the only word you know in English?"

"Allen!" Much scolded, shooting Allen a sharp glare. "That was rude."

"It is alright," I said. "He has not offended me."

"Why do you want to fight anyway?" Allen asked. "You're a girl."

"Do not say that so loud," Robin said, glancing toward the door and then to the open window. "We don't want that getting around to the men."

His concern was touching, but I could handle myself. I had up until this point just fine.

"But she *is* a girl!" Allen insisted.

"No," I said with a laugh, "I am not a girl. I am a *woman*. I am nearly twenty years old."

"That's certainly older than we are," Robin said. "All three of us are eighteen."

"Triplets?" I teased though I knew they were not related.

"We aren't actually related," Much said.

"But we are brothers-in-arms," Robin said.

"I know. I can see the attachment between you already; bound together by loyalty and love."

"Loyalty and love," Allen repeated, "That ought to be our mantra, Robin."

Robin laughed. "It does have a nice ring to it."

For the next week or so, guarding King Richard consisted of nothing more than following him around the camp or the city, or standing outside his room when he retired there. There was little to do but I was provided with ample opportunity to study my new companions. When boredom struck, Allen would be the first to complain, Much the first to encourage, and Robin the first to goof off.

Robin and Allen also pestered me with questions about my past and why I was in the army pretending to be a man, but I did not answer most of them. I told them I was doing so to survive and left it at that. My reticence did not stop their questions, though.

Within two weeks of my arrival at Jaffa, interesting things began to take place within the army. King Richard and Saladin were trying to negotiate terms of peace, sending messages between our two respective camps every day.

One day, King Richard told Much to fetch Princess Joan from her room as he was planning to use her as a bargaining chip in his negotiations, marrying her off to Saladin's brother. As Much trudged off to fetch Joan, and the king returned to his room, I crossed my arms.

"It is hardly a Christian thing to do, to force the princess into such a position."

"Nonsense," Allen shrugged. "They had arranged marriages in Scripture."

He wasn't wrong, but that was hardly the point.

"Have you ever read the Scriptures?" Robin asked.

"Nope." Allen grinned. "Have you?"

Robin shook his head and laughed.

"I still do not approve of this," I said.

"He's the king, he doesn't need your approval," Allen said.

"I do not approve of it either," Robin said. "Joan will not be happy."

"I imagine she will have a lot to say on the subject," I said.

My conjecture proved true, for Much soon returned with a princess in a passion. She marched into the king's room and jumped into her tirade immediately.

"We should move away," Robin said, "and give them some privacy."

"I do not think moving will help," Allen said, a wry grin spreading across his face. "Joan is already raising her voice; no doubt they will soon be in a shouting match."

"I agree with Robin," I said. "It would not be kind to eavesdrop."

The truth was that we had been privy to many private conversations of the king because it was necessary to ensure his protection. One could never tell when an ambassador would turn violent and we had to pay attention to everything around King Richard for his own safety. But this was different; the king's life was in not danger from his sister.

As we stepped away from the doorway, it became clear Allen was correct—the shouting from within was still easily heard. Much was watching the door with worried eyes.

"Joan will not kill the king," I said, placing a hand on his shoulder. "Don't look so afraid, Much."

"It is the king's anger that concerns me," Much said.

"He won't harm Joan," Robin said with a laugh. "Her will is as strong as his, and anyway, he adores her."

That much seemed to be true from all I had seen of King Richard and the princess, yet despite that affection and despite Joan's protests, he would not budge. Joan and the king argued for quite some time, but King Richard wouldn't change his mind.

Word was sent to Saladin later that day and soon the peace offering was accepted and plans were set in motion for a royal wedding.

Every night I and my companions took turns watching over the king and sleeping. I had the second watch and when I moved to relieve Robin who stood outside the king's bedchamber, I found Joan there as well.

Robin bade her goodnight and returned to his bed as I took up my post. Joan crossed her arms and leaned against the door beside me.

"Robin seems to have some influence over my brother." She spoke softly, her voice hardly above a whisper. "I had hoped he might be able to change Richard's mind about this wedding."

"I am sorry, Joan."

"As am I."

We stood in silence for a time, the hallway only dimly lit by a torch a few yards away. Even in the relative darkness, I could see the sadness written across Joan's face.

"You did say your previous arranged marriage turned out well; you said that your William was the best part of your life."

Joan's blue eyes darkened, her eyebrows pulling together. "Yes, I loved my husband. That does not always happen with marriages made for political gain…"

I waited, not wanting to push her farther. If she had deeply loved William, as her face and voice suggested, I could not bring her more pain. I still had yet to face my own grief. I swallowed past the lump forming in my throat at the brief thought of my own losses.

"What are the odds of such a happy arrangement happening twice?" Joan finally said. "And to be forced to stay here, so far from my home?"

"You moved to Sicily…"

"I have no desire to move here, or wherever it is that Saladin's brother keeps residence. I don't want to marry him."

"Do you think you will ever love again?"

"It's not that. I simply don't want to be used as a bargaining chip. I don't want to marry Saladin's brother; I'm not opposed to marriage in general."

Joan glanced the way Robin had gone, and I wondered if she had hope of marrying him. She certainly talked about him often enough.

The king's plans to marry off Joan came to a halt when church officials arrived from Rome. When Robin let them into the king's rooms, Allen, Much, and I stood outside keeping watch. Much looked as worried as ever, but Allen casually pressed his ear against the door.

A moment later Robin returned, shutting the door firmly behind him after giving Allen a knowing look.

It wasn't long before angry voices carried through the closed door.

"We should not be listening," I said. "This does not concern us."

"I am sorry, Saracen," Robin replied. "But I want to know what is going to happen to both Joan and the king."

The voices from within the room grew louder—both the king making his excuses and the church officials threatening excommunication if he married Joan off to a Muslim, peace treaty or no peace treaty.

Allen glanced toward me at the mention of how unseemly it was to marry Joan to a Muslim. "No offense to you, I'm sure."

"I am not a Muslim, Allen of the Dale. I am a disciple of Christ."

"Fair enough," Allen shrugged. "Makes no difference to me."

It makes all the difference in the world, in truth, but I did not have the heart or courage to say as much at that moment.

The church officials from Rome and the King of England had several more heated discussions in the days that followed, but in the end, Joan was free. King Richard rescinded his offer to marry her to Saladin's brother. Free or not, Joan was still angry with her brother and I don't believe she ever forgot that incident.

King Richard summoned Robin into his chamber after he'd made the decision and messengers had gone to and from Saladin as the change to the peace treaty was discussed. I waited outside with Much and Allen as always.

Robin had left the door open when the king had summoned him, so every word that passed between them was heard by those of us in the hall.

Allen leaned closer to the door, unafraid to show he was eavesdropping.

"Saladin is asking too much from me," King Richard told Robin. "I feel we need to teach him who is in charge here. We are only suing for peace for the good of the people, not because we couldn't demolish him in an all-out war."

"Whatever you think, Sire." Robin sounded tired and frustrated to my ears; I wondered if King Richard had noticed.

"That's Richard to you."

"Right."

"I have decided we are going to move out from Jaffa and march on Ascalon. That city was demolished by Saladin and his forces not too long ago, and I feel we could spend time rebuilding it, at least in part."

"As you wish, Sire."

"Why so formal, Robin?"

"It is a habit."

"A habit you fall into more often when you are upset with me, I think. What is your true opinion of marching to Ascalon?"

"You said you wanted to intimidate Saladin, yes? And rebuilding Ascalon will prove to Saladin, what exactly?"

"That he cannot destroy cities and lives without recourse."

"And yet," I whispered to Much, "we do the same here. Destroying cities and lives without recourse."

My disillusionment with the Crusading army was old; I had been growing accustomed over the last couple years to the idea that not everyone who claimed to be good was indeed good —or in this particular case, not everyone who claimed to know Christ truly did. Still, sometimes the frustration of that knowledge boiled over and I had to say something, if only to Much.

Chapter 8

THE ARMY SOON set off from Jaffa, heading toward the city of Ascalon. We'd set out early in the morning, staying beside the king. Allen and Robin chatted amiably together as we walked, and King Richard occasionally joined in their conversations. Joan and Queen Berengaria were further back in the procession, surrounded by the guards they'd hired in Acre, as well as others that King Richard had added to their retinue.

As the miles passed on we came to a place where the road cut through some hills, the steep slopes climbing down to the very edge of the road. It was similar enough to the last place I'd been ambushed that I kept my gaze on the hilltops and the trees sprouting along the hillside for any sign of danger.

It wasn't long before it came.

A flood of arrows came arcing down the hills toward the soldiers in the road. Men fell to the ground while others reached for their weapons. I whipped my bow from my shoulder and spun so that my back was to King Richard as I faced the hillside and searched for a target. A glance to either side showed Much, Robin, and Allen had done the same—drawing their weapons and closing in around King Richard.

The men who'd laid the ambush were running wildly down the hill toward our ranks, so I had plenty of targets. I shot down one, two, three as they came down the hill. Robin was doing the same, but there were more than either of us could cut down, and soon the enemy had reached the road, swords drawn. I tucked my bow away and unsheathed my sword, bracing for the oncoming wave of attackers.

A sword arced toward me and I ducked beneath it, darting forward to thrust my own blade in my foe's chest. I yanked it out again in time to block the incoming blade of another attacker. I danced around the enemy soldiers as they came forward, blocking, parrying, thrusting. The bodies began to pile up around my feet, which was in no way a satisfying ordeal.

The screams of the wounded and dying filled the air and my fingers ached to drop my weapon and pull out my pouch. I'd replenished my supplies during our stay at Jaffa, so it was likely I could help most of the wounded if only I was given the chance. My heart ached with every drop of blood that I spilled, knowing I could—and should—just as easily be healing and not harming. I hated this part, but such was life.

My three companions and I struggled to stay near the king, as was our duty. He was fighting as well, his sword cutting through his enemies with precision.

I could see the horror in Much's eyes every time I caught sight of him. I knew he felt similarly as I did to the violence we witnessed and incurred. He might have, in fact, felt it far deeper than I did. I do not think it would matter how many times Much fought in a battle, he would forever be shocked and disturbed by the horrendous things that he both saw and did. And so he should be; war is no pretty thing.

My sword was knocked from my hand a moment later and I scrambled a few steps backward—out of reach of any blade from an enemy—so I could pull out my daggers.

As my opponent approached, I blocked the sword thrust in my direction with one dagger and plunged my other dagger into his shoulder. He stumbled backwards, and suddenly Allen was beside me, shoving his own sword into my enemy's chest.

I grabbed my sword once more, and spun around in search of another foe. Despite our desire to stay near each other and near to King Richard, my three companions and I did get separated a bit in the heat of the battle, surrounded by the enemy. We were not too far from each other that I could not see all of them and perhaps reach them in a crises, but we were no longer standing side-by-side and back-to-back with the king.

I ducked under a spear thrust my way and then heard Robin cry out behind me. I spun around, using one leg to knock the spear-holder off of his feet, my eyes searching for Robin in the sea of bodies locked in combat around me.

Then I saw him—lying on the ground, blood gushing from his side, staining his shirt as a crimson pool began to form on the ground beneath him. Two enemy soldiers were descending up on him.

I ducked and dodged my way through the chaos around me until I reached Robin, shoving my sword over him just as the two blades of his opponents came bearing down on him.

The force of their swords crashing into mine caused me to grip my hilt in both hands. I took a deep breath, and then swung upward with all my might, throwing the two blades off of mine.

I fought back the two soldiers as well as I could, my sword dancing between both as I stood over Robin. Another soldier— one whose name I did not know—passed by the fight and cut down one of my enemies. He was then attacked by another soldier and their wary dance moved a few paces from mine. With only one soldier focused on me now, it was easier to catch him off guard and soon I'd ended his life.

I dropped to my knees beside Robin.

"Hold still, my friend," I told him as I set aside my weapons and pulled out my medicinal pouch. "Allen! Watch my back!"

I was not entirely sure where Allen was, but I hoped he was still near. I was relieved when I heard his answer just behind me.

"I'm on it."

I rifled through my herbs and spices as I eyed Robin's wound. He groaned, still clutching his side—it was staunching the bleeding for now, so I let him remain that way as I chose which herbs to mix together.

Once I was ready, I pulled his hands free and began to apply my mixture.

"Saracen…"

"Hush, Robin. Do not try to speak."

All around me I could hear the clanging of metal striking metal and the screaming of men dying terrible and painful deaths.

Every moment or two there would be the shadow of an approaching enemy, but Allen circled around Robin and I, keeping our opponents at bay so that I could work. What had become of the king, I wasn't sure. I hoped Much was still at his side.

With the blood flow lessened and the medicine doing its work, I closed my eyes and began to pray. It was, in my opinion, the most important ingredient in my healing art.

The battle continued to rage around us, but it seemed to fade into the background as I focused on my Healer. I was soon aware of nothing but Robin's wounds and the Lord's healing hand. I was wholly focused until I felt a hand on my shoulder and I jumped in surprise.

It was only Allen. "Saracen, the battle is over. How is Robin?"

"I believe he will be fine." I finished applying my herbs and then began to stitch his wound closed.

"Robin!" Much came running over as Robin opened his eyes and tried to sit up.

"I am fine, Much," Robin said, watching me work as I finished wrapping a bandage around his chest. "It isn't so bad."

Robin was right; it wasn't too bad. The blade that had cut him had sliced along his side and though the wound was deeper than I liked, it did not seem to have had any fatal damage. His organs were miraculously intact.

"You will be weak," I told Robin. "And in pain for some days, I imagine. This was not a small cut."

"But I will live, thanks to you."

"The wound is not so deep," I said as I began to clean up my supplies. "Perhaps you would not have died from it at all."

"But I was incapable of protecting myself either way, and would have died at the hands of those soldiers if you had not been there. You were magnificent! I've never seen anyone fight like that before; you are quite the warrior, Saracen."

"Thank you."

"I cannot continue to call you by no name," Robin suddenly grinned. Much helped him sit up as Allen knelt across from me. Along the road, soldiers were gathering the dead and the wounded. The road was soaked in blood and I grimaced.

"You have become a friend in the last month," Robin continued, "and now you have saved my life."

"What would you call me?"

"Warrior." Robin winked, seemingly back to his jovial self. I could not help but smile at his choice though I was unlikely to answer to it. It was hardly better than Saracen.

Allen snorted, shaking his head as he playfully whacked Robin's shoulder. "That is not a name."

"Dustin, then," Robin said. "It means the same."

"That does not seem very feminine," Allen said.

"You seem very opinionated about a name that isn't yours." Robin elbowed him.

"Dusty," Much said.

"Dusty…" I repeated softly. It was odd, that name. But something about it called to me.

It was not the name of my youth. Andaleeb had been a naive and sweet girl for eighteen years, until her family was murdered and she closed off her heart.

Aban had been a terrified girl pretending to be a boy and refusing to let anyone know her truest self.

The Saracen had been similar. Impersonal. Distant. It had worked because I did not intend to become close to anyone.

But Dusty? Maybe Dusty could finally let her walls down —if even a little—and let Robin call her friend. It was still true that I had no desire for friends beyond the Lord Himself, but He had other plans.

"I like it," I said at last.

"Dusty; the warrior, healer, and friend of mine," Robin said. "I like it, too."

"Dusty it is then," Allen agreed. "It will be nice to actually have a name for you now, instead of always calling you 'the Saracen' when we speak to and about you."

Silently, I agreed with him.

Dusty; a name given to me by Robin and Much—it was a token of friendship. It was a breath of fresh air to someone who'd felt stifled for longer than they could remember. I had not realized how painful it had been to shut myself in until that moment that I decided to open up again. All I had done was accept the name they offered, and yet for me it felt far more profound than that.

I hastily wiped aside my tears as Allen and Much helped Robin to his feet as King Richard approached.

"All in one piece?" King Richard asked.

"Thanks to Dusty," Robin said, grinning at me. Then he focused on the king once more. "Are you alright? Your Royal Guard failed a bit today."

"I survived," King Richard replied. He glanced at me. "Dusty, is it?"

"It is now," I said.

He gave a curt nod. "I assume you'll want to do your healing work with the rest of these men?"

"Yes, Sire."

I spent a few hours working alongside the other healers in the army, tending to the wounded. I attempted to heal the enemy wounded as well. As I knelt beside the first one, pressing my hand to a gaping gash in his chest, a sword appeared from nowhere and cut his head from his body. My stomach revolted and I nearly threw up in that moment.

With shaking hands and a shuddering breath, I looked up into the face of Emil, my commander from Acre.

"Saracen."

"Sir."

"The king only wants prisoners if they are high ranking in Saladin's army. This lot are not. We're killing them all."

"That seems harsh." I stood up with a sigh.

"Perhaps." Emil studied me, a bit of a smile forming on his face. "Strange to say it, but I missed your enigmatic presence while you remained in Acre. I hear you are now in the King's Royal Guard."

"I am."

"How did you manage that?"

"Mostly unintentionally." I took a deep breath, trying to steady the rapid beating of my heart. I felt ragged and raw from the day's events. "I was hired by Queen Berengaria to escort her and Princess Joan from Acre to Jaffa, and then before I knew it I was assigned a place at the king's side."

"You'll do well there—you are a brilliant fighter, and you can heal as well. Whatever befalls the king, you will be able to save him. It is a good fit."

"Thank you."

"Now, we still have wounded you can heal, just not these men," he gestured toward the enemy soldiers scattered across the road. I reluctantly returned to the gathered wounded of the Crusader army, trying to keep my eyes away from Emil and the other soldiers who were walking along the length of the road, putting their swords through any of the enemy who still breathed.

When my work was done and the army was on the move once more, I walked just behind the others. Robin was in one of the wagons carrying wounded, much to his chagrin, so Allen and Much walked beside King Richard alone. I followed close behind, of course, but I wanted a moment to myself.

The weight of allowing myself to accept the gift of the name Dusty had been an emotional strain I hadn't been prepared for, and then watching Emil and the others kill men I could have saved shook up my already tumultuous insides.

An arm slipped through mine and I glanced to my side to see Joan.

"I heard from little Much that you have a name now."

"Yes…"

"Dusty is such an odd name, but it suits you I think. And it will be such a relief not to have to call you Saracen any longer."

"Allen felt the same."

In truth, I was also relieved to have a name again. More than relieved, my emotions were a tangle of joy and pain, love and grief. I could hardly put them into words, but I was grateful to Robin, Much, and Allen for giving me such a precious gift.

Chapter 9

THE REST OF OUR journey to Ascalon was uneventful. Robin slowly healed—Much only left his side when forced to do so—while Allen and I kept watch over King Richard.

Upon our arrival in Ascalon, King Richard oversaw the construction of a citadel there. King Richard did not, in fact, do any of the work to build the citadel and therefore neither did we. Instead, we stayed near the king as he met with his advisors and made plans for the future of his war with Saladin. The ceasefire that had been in place while we were in Jaffa crafting a peace treaty was now over and what occupied the king's mind was what he might do next.

He soon decided taking Jerusalem directly rather than chasing down the bulk of Saladin's forces was the best course of action, and before too long we were marching in that direction.

The weather turned cold and our march to Jerusalem was slowed by days of heavy rainfall. When it wasn't raining, a heavy fog would descend so that I could hardly see my own hands when I held them up. Far worse, however, was the bitter cold that settled into our bones.

The ground beneath our feet became muddy and slick. We sloshed through it, getting mud up to our knees as we marched along the slippery road.

I remember one particular day as we walked along beside the king when I was suddenly splashed with mud from my left side. I looked over to see Allen jumping along rather than walking. He was keeping pace with us, but he looked ridiculous and every time his feet landed he sent mud flying toward myself, Robin, Much, and King Richard.

"Allen!" Robin scolded as he laughed at his antics. "The weather is bad enough, we don't need your assistance in our misery."

"Robin, my friend," Allen said, laughing himself, "can you not tell that I am trying to lessen said misery? If you cannot have fun, then what is life worth?"

I recalled hearing Joan say something similar not too many weeks before. Robin seemed won over by Allen's comment, for he was soon jumping alongside him, both of them splashing mud toward the rest of us.

Joan—when she chose to travel with us close to the front instead of toward the middle surrounded by soldiers where the king preferred she stay—was often seen jumping through the mud with them as well. I don't think King Richard much approved of her antics—or theirs, for that matter—but he let them be.

"Robin, can you see anything?" Much asked as we trudged along one day, surrounded by deep fog. King Richard was no more than a mere shadow in front of us.

"Not particularly, but at least it is better than the rain."

"Hardly," Allen interjected. "I can't feel anything—I've gone numb. Except for my nose, of course, which stings considerably."

"It is not as bad as all that," Dusty laughed. "A little water, a little cold. It will not kill us."

"It's more than *a little* water," Allen whined. "It rained for seven days straight!"

"Robin!" King Richard's voice carried through the fog in front of them and Robin strode forward, almost disappearing from view.

"Yes?"

"We will stop at the city of Beit Nuba tonight to take shelter. Pass the word through the ranks."

"At least we won't be camping again in this weather," Allen said as Robin walked past them toward the captain leading the company directly behind us in order to pass along the king's command.

"Being inside will be a blessing," Dusty agreed.

For some days the soldiers of the Crusaders' army shivered miserably in tents set up outside Beit Nuba while the king and his advisors—along with us, his personal guard—gathered inside a house on the edge of town. The rain continued, and soon it began to hail each day as well.

One day while we were staying in Beit Nuba, I sat in the corner of one of our rooms sorting through my herbs and other medicinal supplies. Sickness had begun to spread through the camp due to the damp weather, and I'd been using up my supplies once more. It was time to gather more and doing so while we remained inside the city seemed the best time to accomplish such a task. I wanted to be sure I knew what I needed before I went in search of a monk—they generally kept gardens perfect for my kind of work—or an apothecary in town.

The room was dark due to the weather, no sunlight could sneak past the clouds and filter into it. The fire in the hearth and a few candles scattered about on flat surfaces in the room were our only source of light and I held my herbs closer to my face than I might have otherwise as I sifted through them.

Much was shivering near the fire while Allen leaned against the hearth to watch King Richard and Robin as they stood over a table with maps and charts spread out before them.

"It's hailing again," Much commented as he moved to look out the window, pulling his cloak more tightly around his shoulders.

"So it is," I said.

"I am glad we are not forced to march in this weather."

"Yet we cannot stay in Beit Nuba forever," Allen said. "I wish a decision would be made. Either we move forward toward Jerusalem or we go somewhere else. Sitting here doing nothing is beginning to irk me."

"I wish we would move on as well," I said. "Less because I am irked and more because I fear what you and Robin might do once pushed past the brink of boredom." I recalled their antics jumping through the mud and shook my head, failing to hide the smile that came to my face at the thought.

Allen grinned and rolled his eyes. "We wouldn't do anything too drastic."

"You might," Much said, chuckling. "You two are not known for your patience."

Allen laughed heartily at this and then shook his head. "Much, you were meant to defend Robin and I. We've been friends long enough you should always take our side in an argument."

Much shrugged, his eyes twinkling. "I have known Robin his entire life; I know him well. He will start to be more than a little silly if he has nothing to keep him busy."

I felt a light in my chest at the easy banter in the room. This is precisely what I had been missing because I'd been too afraid to let my guard down and love again.

"A decision has been made," Robin called from the table where he and King Richard had been ignoring our conversation. "No one needs to fear any drastic measure."

I glanced toward the king.

"I have decided to leave off marching on Jerusalem for another time," King Richard said. "We should return to Ascalon and let the weather pass us by."

The return to Ascalon was just as cold and wet as our march to Beit Nuba had been, but we had not been in the city long before warm weather returned.

My birthday had come and gone during our short failed attempt to march toward Jerusalem. I was once more troubled with thoughts of my family.

This year, and for several years, no one but myself had noticed the passing of the day, but when I was a child the day had been celebrated with excess. My father always took care to make that one day in the year wholly about me. My mother would make special meals at my request, and would sew me a new dress—often the only one I received in a year. Habibah would go out of her way to find me a special gift. Daniyah would sit down with me to teach me something new from Scripture.

I missed my family.

I sat on a smooth stone wall warmed by the sun and looked out at the emerald Mediterranean sea, letting the tears fall silently down my cheeks as I remembered my family. It wasn't often I indulged in my grief, but sometimes it was too overwhelming to ignore. My heart ached inside my chest as I thought of all that might have been if they had lived.

"Dusty?"

I turned to see Robin seating himself beside me. "It is not often one has the opportunity to see Dusty vulnerable. It must be something truly awful to make you cry so."

I turned away from him, brushing aside my tears. "I was thinking of my family. They were killed by Saladin's forces two years ago."

"I am sorry."

I nodded, my throat closing over a lump and refusing to let me speak for a moment. I struggled to stop the tears from falling.

"I miss them…"

"I understand," Robin said, slinging his arm around me and pulling my head down to his shoulder. He exuded a comforting warmth that I longed for, so I melted into his embrace.

"I miss my father," Robin said. "He died not long after I came to join King Richard on this Crusade. I wasn't there with him…and we'd parted in some anger. I…well, truthfully, I ran away from home. He did not approve of me fighting in the Crusades."

"I am sorry. That must be worse than what I feel. My parents and I were on good terms. I have no regrets. I simply wish they had lived."

We sat in silence for a time before my crying came to a stop. I relished the comforting kindness of Robin's embrace—and I thanked the Lord for bringing me to my second family even when I was too stubborn to acknowledge I needed one.

"Will you be alright?" Robin asked.

"Yes. Thank you."

"If you need anything, I'm right here. You can talk to me."

"This was enough. Thank you."

I had forgotten what it could feel like to have someone care about me, to take an interest in my pain and feel it with me. I was grateful for Robin's friendship and thankful to the Lord for bringing me into his life. Robin, Much, Allen, even Joan…I had a growing group of friends I could lean on for support and it felt far more wonderful than I had expected.

As the weeks passed, we continued to watch over King Richard as he met with various advisors. Joan would be found with us as often as she dared—her brother would scold her for distracting his Royal Guard if he caught her—flirting with Robin every chance she could get. Robin, for his part, seemed to merely tolerate her advances. He seemed to care for her as he did for me, but his heart did not appear to be touched.

One night as I slept, I was rudely awakened by shouts from the hallway. I could hear Robin's muffled voice—he was on watch—and then the pounding of footsteps. I sat up just as Robin opened the door and came inside.

"Awake! An army approaches!"

Allen and Much began to stir as I rolled out of my bedding, pulling on my boots and strapping them in a hurry.

"What is going on?" the king's voice carried from his bed in the corner of the room.

"Saladin's troops have come looking for trouble," Robin said. "According to our scouts it is not a large number of men."

"I see. Well I am going back to bed then. Leave Much to guard me. The rest of you go join my army and deal with the rabble."

"Yes, Sire," Robin said.

I finished getting ready and strapped my weapons into place. A moment later, Allen was at my side. "Lead on, Robin."

Much took Robin's place outside the king's door as Robin led Allen and I downstairs and out of the house. In the street we could see more soldiers coming from their own houses and moving down the road toward the city walls.

"Come along," Robin said. "Emil is expecting us."

Up on the city wall we could see archers taking up position. Robin bounded up a set of stone steps that led to the battlements and we followed him.

Emil was shouting orders and directing soldiers from atop the wall and he waved us over when he saw us. "Who is with the king?"

"Much," Robin said.

Emil nodded. "Very well. Join the archers along the wall down there," Emil pointed down the line of archers.

The pathway on the city wall was lit every few paces by a brazier attached to one of the stone battlements and from the light they emitted we could see the archers kneeling beside the wall and taking aim at the soldiers storming the city gates below.

We followed Emil's direction and joined the line of archers, taking aim at the incoming soldiers and shooting them down before they could break open the city gates. It was not a long fight; within two hours we were returning to our beds. The incursion hadn't lasted long and had done no real damage to the city or the army.

When we approached the king's door after returning to our lodgings, Much seemed to sag with relief. "Are any of you hurt?"

"Not a scratch," Robin said cheerfully, clapping him on the shoulder. "You can wake Allen in a couple hours to stand watch." Robin turned to Allen and I. "For now, let's get some sleep."

After that skirmish, the weeks passed without incident. King Richard met with various advisors and military men making plans and hearing reports on what Saladin's troops were up to. I spent my days with Robin, Allen, and Much and was slowly coming to realize how much I enjoyed having friends once more.

Robin and Allen were quick to make us laugh, and Much kept a close eye on everyone's emotional state, offering comfort and support when needed. He rarely spoke his own opinion—particularly, I noticed, if the king was present—but he was quite wise when engaged in a one-on-one conversation. Joan was still in the habit of whiling away her hours with us, flirting with Robin and teasing Much. My curiosity as to the state of Robin's feelings on the matter was soon allayed.

One night as I was on watch, I could hear someone tossing and turning within the room and sighing every few minutes. After a time, I could take it no longer so I cracked the door open and poked my head inside.

"Would it help to talk about it, my friend?" I wasn't sure who was in such a state, but Robin's voice came out of the darkness toward me.

"Talk about what?"

"Whatever it is that is bothering you."

There was a slight pause, and then the sound of someone getting up and shuffling across the floor. Robin suddenly appeared in the dim light of the candle-lit hallway. I shut the door behind him so as not to disturb Much, Allen, or the king.

"I was just thinking…" Robin began and then trailed off. I waited patiently for him to continue. He leaned against the closed door and crossed his arms. "There is a girl—a woman—back home in England. Her name is Marian."

Something in the sound of his voice reminded me of my father when he'd talk to my mother.

"You love her."

"Very much. I am not sure she returns the feeling. Well…I think she does, but it is hard to tell with Marian." Robin sighed, shoving his hand through his hair.

"You miss her." It was not a question, I could see on his face and hear in his voice how much he missed this woman named Marian.

"Desperately. I just can't get her out of my head tonight."

"Tell me about her."

"I could not put her fiery nature into words."

"How did you meet?"

"We grew up together. Her father is the Sheriff of Nottingham, and my father is—was, rather—the Earl of Locksley. They did business together. More than that, though, our fathers were good friends. We both lost our mothers at a young age, and I think our fathers found kinship in raising families alone."

105

"I am sorry about your mother." My heart squeezed at the memory of my own mother and the questions I still had over how she died—the fire, or the collapsed house. Neither was a pleasant option. Or perhaps they'd been found by Saladin's soldiers before my house had been destroyed. I didn't know—I didn't want to.

"I do not even remember her," Robin whispered. "Or Marian's mother either."

I watched him in the dim light; his brows were knitted together and he pushed his hand through his blond hair as he frowned. Robin's face was usually full of laughter and amusement so it was rather unsettling to see him in distress.

"In any case, because our fathers were always together we were as well. Marian, her younger brother Mark, myself, and Much."

Robin's eyes began to twinkle as he lost himself in his memories and soon I could see his more natural jovial expression returning

"We went everywhere together in our youth. Marian is… bright and cheerful, and strong-willed and stubborn. She did not want me to come on the Crusades either. I sometimes wonder if she is waiting for me or if she has found someone else to love in my absence. Sometimes I fear I will return to England and find her already married, perhaps even have a child. Then there are other times when I believe with all my heart that she is waiting for me."

"I do not know your Marian, but she would be a fool not to wait for you."

"Thank you."

"She ought to be lacking in sleep herself, fretting over you in the same manner. Are you waiting for her, or falling in love on your wild adventures?"

"Nonsense, Dusty. You know I am not the kind of man to be unfaithful to the woman I love."

"I would not suggest you were unfaithful. Merely that Marian might have some cause for jealousy should she ever see you and Joan together."

Robin groaned. He crossed his arms, shaking his head with a deep frown. "That is unfair, Dusty. Joan and I are…"

"Yes? What are you, my friend?"

"Friends."

"Truthfully, Robin?"

"Yes. For my part, at least."

"You know she loves you."

"I'm afraid she does, but I cannot do anything about that. I will not give up my love for Marian, and I have said as much to Joan herself. I'm going to return to England eventually, and if she hasn't moved on, I'm going to marry her."

His voice held such conviction, I could only hope for his sake that the woman he loved truly was waiting for him.

"I knew even when I was a child that I would marry Marian; nothing will change my mind. With every passing year she grows more beautiful and confident and wise and…I love her."

Robin shrugged, grinning at me. Seeing his smile warmed my heart. I was glad he had someone to love. My parents' marriage had been one where they each delighted in the other. I had once held a dream of attaining that someday myself. Now, I wasn't so sure. Risking loving someone so much only to lose them as I had lost the rest of my family? The thought terrified me.

And yet I had begun to open up to friendship, and that had only been a blessing and not a curse. Still, friendship was one thing and loving someone so completely the way my parents had loved each other was another entirely.

Robin offered to take over keeping watch so that I could sleep, and soon I was left to my own thoughts as I lay beneath my blankets listening to the gentle snoring of both Allen and Much.

I wondered what she was like, this Marian of Robin's. I hoped for his sake that she did love him and was waiting for him as he was eagerly waiting to return to her.

Chapter 10

THE CITADEL OF Ascalon was nearly complete, the skirmishes between King Richard's army and that of Saladin's forces frequent but not monumental, and King Richard was itching to do *something* to turn the tide in his favor.

One day, he summoned Robin into his chambers along with his advisors. It was not the first time he had done so; it seemed King Richard had come to respect Robin's advice as well as the other nobles who claimed to be of his inner circle.

Allen leaned toward the closed door and I swatted his arm. "Stop eavesdropping."

"I'd like to know what's happening next."

"Robin will tell us when he comes out," I said. Allen ignored me and pressed up against the door. A moment later it swung open and Robin stood there grinning.

"The king says you can break for lunch, he's going to send for other soldiers to stand at your post while you eat."

Past Robin's shoulder in the room beyond King Richard was looking toward us with a look of exasperated affection.

"I think he knows you like to eavesdrop," Much said.

"Lunch it is, I guess." Allen shrugged.

Robin went back to his secret meeting with the king after assigning new soldiers to the post outside the door while Much, Allen, and I gathered a meager lunch and moved outside to find a place to sit and eat in the sunshine. We soon settled atop a stone wall overlooking the sea.

"It is hardly fair Robin is trusted and we are not," Allen said. "Besides, the king knows he's just going to come tell us what's happening anyway."

"It is possible they do discuss private matters that Robin does not disclose to you," I said.

It wasn't long, however, before Robin came striding down the street below us and cheerfully pulled himself atop the wall next to Much.

"I have news."

"Good news or bad news?" Allen asked.

"Just news. We're marching again. Apparently Saladin has captured another city that was under European rule and is now most definitely not, and he wants it back."

"What city?" Much asked. "And how long of a march will it be?"

"It's a city called Darum," Robin replied and I could not stop the gasp that escaped my lips as my heart leaped to my throat.

"We are marching to Darum?" Suddenly my mother's face flashed before my eyes, followed quickly by what I imagined her charred body might have looked like. I had a very vivid imagination.

"That is what the king has decided," Robin said.

"We're capturing Darum?" I could see Habibah smiling at me, and then pictured her screaming in pain as flames writhed around her body.

"Releasing it from Saladin's capture, but yes."

"I cannot go."

I pulled my legs closer to my chest, my shoulders curling inward as I tried to stave off the unwelcome images of my beautiful family in pain and dying. My hands began to shake despite my best efforts to remain in control of myself.

"Why can't you go to Darum?" Much asked, laying his hand gently on my arm.

"I cannot," I repeated, desperate to avoid returning to the birthplace of my nightmares.

"Dusty, what is wrong?" Robin asked as he leaned around Much to see my face.

I glanced between them, and then turned toward Allen who had stopped eating and was watching our exchange silently. I could feel tears beginning to fill my eyes and I bit my bottom lip to stop it from trembling. They were waiting for an answer, so I struggled to control myself long enough to speak.

"It is…Darum is where I come from. The city of my birth."

"You don't want to fight against your own city?" Allen asked. "It is only Saladin we are after, is it not? It is possible we won't destroy the town itself or its inhabitants."

"Like there wasn't a massacre at Acre?" I snapped, remembering all the Muslims King Richard had ordered beheaded before he left the city. "But no, it is not that I don't wish to fight my own city. The people of Darum are mostly descendants of the Crusaders from the First and Second Crusades, or like myself have both European and Arab blood in their line. The connections the people of Darum have to England, France, Germany—the Holy Roman Empire as a whole—are strong. That is likely why Saladin keeps attacking that city. Those who are left will not fight against the Crusaders."

"Those who are left?" Robin asked.

"Saladin captured my city when I was eighteen," Dusty said. "He destroyed the politically strong there, devastating the city and the people. So many families' lives were destroyed as he dismantled the power of the Crusaders there."

"That's when you lost your own family," Robin said.

"Yes." The single word seemed to hang in the air over the group, heavy and dark. Images of my mother, sister, father, Daniyah, and even Abraham drifted before me as I tried to keep myself from outright sobbing.

"I am so sorry," Robin said.

"So am I," I replied. "But I cannot go back to Darum. I couldn't…I haven't been back there since…"

"I understand, but we cannot leave you behind."

"I do not see why not," I said. "I only joined up with your army provisionally, given Joan's insistence. And I do appreciate the friendship the four of us have found together, but I can't go back. I won't. I don't have any allegiance to King Richard; I am not one of his subjects. I don't have to go. I won't."

Much shifted his hand off of my arm and wrapped his fingers around mine, giving them a gentle squeeze. "Perhaps going back will help you finally face your grief."

I closed my eyes, wrestling with the truth of Much's words. I had been burying my grief all this time; perhaps I should face it at last.

But I didn't want to do that.

Trust me.

I could feel the warmth of my Savior's love spreading through me and I reluctantly let go of the pain I was holding onto so tightly.

I opened my eyes and nodded, giving Much's hand a tight squeeze. "You are right. I will pray for the strength to return to Darum and face my past. Perhaps it will be good for me."

"I thought you were a Saracen," Allen commented. I turned to look at him, confused by his change in subject.

"What?"

"We all thought you were a Saracen, that's why we called you that before you had the name Dusty. But you said the inhabitants of your city were mostly descendants of the earlier Crusades."

"Yes, they were. I myself am a child of both descendants of the European Crusaders and also native Palestinians. I was

113

never a Muslim, as Saladin and most of his soldiers are, but when he attacked my city I hid my identity—dressed like a man, let them recruit me as a soldier and sympathizer. I lived with what you call Saracens—and then at the first opportunity I joined with the Crusading army."

"Why?"

"I do not often agree with the decisions of King Richard and those in charge—I do not feel the same fervor that they do in terms of who should live and rule in the Holy Land. Uprooting the people who live here or forcing them to abide by your customs and religions is not the way of life that I would wish to pursue. I wish there was peace. But Saladin himself? He destroyed my people, my city, my family. You are fighting him, and that is enough for me for now."

"Dusty, I am so sorry that this happened to you," Robin said. "I understand on some level the grief that you feel, and the anger. My own father was murdered by those seizing power in England during King Richard's current absence. I don't know the details, I haven't gone home yet, I don't know what all happened —but I understand."

"It is alright," I said, straightening my shoulders as I shoved my wayward emotions back into their place. Much was right; I needed to face them. But I could do that in Darum. "Do not fret over me."

"How long ago did you lose your family?" Allen asked. There was a bitterness to his voice, an understanding, that made me wonder what his own story was. Allen rarely spoke of serious topics or of his own past. He was nearly as reticent as I was. But in that moment, though I acknowledged my curiosity, I was too focused on my own pain to entertain his.

"Nearly two years ago," I said.

"Only two years," Robin said, shaking his head and shoving his hand through his hair. "I know you've told me about this before but…only two years. Dusty, I am so sorry."

"I have been looked after by my Lord," I said, gathering my composure once more. Facing Darum was a terrifying prospect, but I spoke the truth: God had taken care of me. "And now I have been given you, my second family."

"I would be proud to call you my sister," Robin said.

"Thank you." My eyes stung with tears once more as an ache filled my throat. How I had come to love Robin, Much, and Allen so deeply in so short a time I would never understand. Yet the truth remained that I did, indeed, love them. I hardly knew what I would do without them. The thought of something happening to them was enough to make my blood run cold.

Within a few weeks, the army had picked up camp and was marching toward the city of my youth. The closer we drew to Darum, the more familiar the landscape became. The glistening Mediterranean always to our right, the date palms standing tall and regal along the hillsides.

My father had worked in an orchard. I used to beg him to let me go along with him when I was a child. I can still hear my whining tone of voice, and my stern but loving father. He would always side with my mother's decisions, much to my chagrin, and I would run to Daniyah's house for comfort.

I always went to Daniyah whenever my parents' opinions differed from mine. Even still, I can hear her laughter and her gentle, sweet voice…

"Dusty?" I snapped back to the present as I heard Robin's voice beside me and felt his hand grip my elbow. "Are you okay?"

"Yes." I realized as I spoke that my cheeks were wet with tears. I hadn't noticed I was crying. I wiped my face clean and straightened my shoulders. "I was just remembering…"

Robin watched me closely as I took a shuddering breath.

"You are sure you are okay?"

"I am fine."

Robin let go of my arm and we continued to walk along the road together. He sent me curious glances now and again, ones filled with compassion and understanding, but he did not press me further.

I noticed Much and Allen giving me a few furtive glances as well, but no one spoke again as we continued on our way. I glanced to the side of the road and saw the tall palm trees once more, and once more my mind drifted to my father…

"You understand, Andaleeb, that everything I do is for your protection?"

I can still hear the deep rumble of his voice as he spoke to me, his gentle hand on my cheek. I can see his dark eyes and the warmth—the love—shining in them as he gazed at me. I remember the way he would put his large hands on either side of my face when he spoke to me, and the way he'd kiss my forehead and tell me he loved me.

The ache inside my chest was growing as my steps slowed. Much's arm slid around mine and I felt relief in the knowledge that I was not alone.

The city—my city—came into view on the horizon. I breathed deeply as I tried to remain calm.

We did not reach the city that day. Saladin's forces were occupying it still, so King Richard arranged the army in a siege around the city itself and began an assault that lasted five days. I spent those days at the king's side with my companions—my friends—trying not to remember the last time I'd been here when there had been a battle. Yet I could not help but remember.

When the sounds of screaming, dying men filled the air and the echoing of metal striking metal rang out my mind drifted.

Suddenly I was cowering in my house with my mother and adoptive sister, Daniyah speaking her words of comfort to all of us. I was standing in the road with a helpless child in my arms, speaking to Daniyah's husband Abraham for the last time.

If I had known my last words to Abraham were those I spoke that day, would I have said something different? And my mother and sister, would I have stayed in the house to spend my last moments with them? If I had, I would undoubtedly be dead alongside them. But who was to say that wasn't the better alternative?

When the battle was finally won, King Richard moved a good portion of his men into the city to occupy the space that had been recently held by Saladin's men.

One day King Richard strode through the dusty streets of Darum—streets that I knew oh so well—appraising my city. His personal guard, my companions and I, followed along beside him.

I kept my eyes on the ground, focused on the dirt puffing up around the toes of my boots and trying not to look at the buildings around me. I recognized so many; I knew who had lived in that house to our right and my eyes quickly found my toes again as my heart began to pound.

My palms were sweaty, so I wiped them along my pants, trying to breathe deeply. It was more than that I knew who had lived there—I knew which stall at the market had been theirs, and who their children had been. I had played with them as a child…

"There are few left here who were not of Saladin's army," the king commented. "I thought Saladin had kept the trade and commerce running…"

"Most were killed, Sire," I said quietly, my eyes darting from my toes to the king's face and then back again.

"Ah, that is unfortunate."

It was more than unfortunate, I felt. It was a travesty.

"Very little of the city itself appears destroyed," King Richard commented as we continued down the street. "Although that corner down there is a rubble heap," he gestured nonchalantly and I felt my heart plummet to my boots. That was the district where I had grown up.

"We will spend a few nights in the city, I think," the king continued. "Then we will plan another march on Jerusalem."

"We are going back to Jerusalem?" Robin asked.

"Yes. I feel rather invigorated from this fight; and now we have Saladin and his forces on the run."

That afternoon was spent in setting up a more functional camp outside the city walls—rather than the staging for the siege —and finding quarters for the king and others privileged enough to lodge inside the city walls. I would have preferred to be outside the city in the camp, but as the King's Guard, I did not have a choice.

One day, as we were standing watch over the king's chambers, Joan came to join us.

"Is Robin inside?" She waved at the closed door.

"He is," Allen said.

"Ah, that is a pity," Joan sighed.

"He might come out soon," Much offered politely.

Joan smiled at him, and seemed about to say more as her eyes drifted across myself and Allen and then snapped back to me. Her mouth closed, forming a firm line for a moment.

"I'm sure if you wait Robin will be glad to see you," Allen said.

"I'm sure he would," Joan agreed, flashing him a grin and a wink. "But I'm going to steal Dusty off your hands instead. We will be just down the hall, I'm sure, so don't let my brother get angry with her for abandoning her post."

Joan grabbed my arm before I was prepared for what she intended, and began dragging me down the hall. I didn't have the heart to put up a fight, so I followed along dutifully, rather as Much might have done if Robin had tried to drag him off somewhere.

"Dusty, what is the matter?" Joan asked, her voice lowering as she glanced behind at Much and Allen. She had taken us most of the way down the hallway away from them.

"Nothing is the matter."

"It took no more than a fraction of a moment to notice your discomfort. You are distressed, though I can tell you want to hide it as you always do." Her eyes bored into mine, keen and filled with compassion.

"I am not hiding my distress so much as trying to suppress it," I replied. "I do not like to…"

"I understand; you don't open up easily. We've had that discussion before. But what is it that is troubling you?"

"This is where I grew up," I said. "There are many memories associated with this place and not all of them are good ones."

120

"I can understand that," Joan said, wrapping her arm around my shoulders. "If you need to talk about it, let me know. I am all ears."

"Thank you."

I did appreciate Joan's offer; I knew she cared for me. And as it turned out, she knew me well enough that one glance had told her I was not my usual self. But I did not want to bare my soul to Joan, or to Allen or Robin for that matter. They would all care, they would extend compassion. But they would also *talk*.

I had only one friend I felt I could be truly vulnerable with and not have to face his opinions on my pain—Much.

Joan let me return to my post and then began to chat away with Allen while she waited for Robin to come out of the king's chambers. Her affection for the latter appeared to remain unchanged as the weeks and months passed, though he remained as faithful to the woman back home in England as he always had been.

As Joan and Allen chatted, I let myself sink into the roiling emotions inside my chest. The pressure was building and I needed to let it go before I erupted. I had a strong desire to visit my home despite knowing that it was a charred heap of rubble. I wondered if my family had ever been found or if they were still buried underneath the stones of what used to be my house. In any case, if I was going to crack under the weight of my grief, I wanted to do it there.

I knew I would need support.

121

That night when Robin and Allen took first watch at the king's door, I took the opportunity to speak to Much. I hoped he wouldn't be too tired to come with me; his quiet, gentle self would be more soothing than Robin's strong emotions.

When I asked him if he would come with me to my family's home, his eyes widened.

"Would you like me to get Robin for you?"

"No, Much. I want *you* to come with me. I need your support if you are willing to give it."

"Oh."

I began to walk down the hallway hoping he would follow, and he soon fell into step beside me. We walked in silence out of the house and began moving through the familiar streets of my city. Darkness had settled over the land, but the moon was shining down on us and there were fires lit along the street and shining from the windows and doorways of various homes where the Crusaders had taken residence or where the inhabitants of the city still lived.

When we passed from the smaller streets into the open area that had once been filled with a vibrant market, my heart squeezed inside my chest as my hands began to shake. I forced myself to speak, giving in to the promise I'd made to myself that I would not bury my emotions but rather face them here in Darum.

"This is where the marketplace was. I played here often as a child, especially at the milk stand. I loved to play with the goats." I felt a smile tug at the corner of my mouth as I thought about Abraham's goats.

"Did your father have goats?"

"No. My father…" I could feel the ache inside me welling up as tears began to fall from my eyes. Much took my hand and gave it a comforting squeeze. "He picked dates in the orchards outside the city."

As we passed through the empty and eerie marketplace, I could hear the sounds of my childhood; the shouts and calls, the loud bargaining, the laughter, the noise of the animals and the many feet crowded in the open square. I could heard Abraham's deep, warm laugh and see his bright smile…

I missed so much about Abraham and most of it was obvious, but as the memories danced in my mind it dawned on me that I also simply missed speaking in my native tongue. The Crusaders I now found myself living with limited themselves to English and French most days.

As Much and I continued our walk, I caught sight of the house where I had been hiding when I first heard that Saladin's army was willing to recruit young men. And when we turned down my street I could see the house where I had cut my hair and found boy's clothes to wear.

As we drew closer to my home, I saw a house that had once been as dear to me as my own.

"That was the home of Daniyah." I pointed and Much followed my gaze. "She was my mother's dearest friend. She, more than anyone else, taught me about God."

I knew Much had no context for my memories, but he did not pester me with questions. He merely slipped his hand in mine and listened as I talked.

I came to a standstill, my eyes clouding with tears. "There. At the end of the street. That is where I lived."

It was the same pile of rubble that it had been when I left. Burned, charred wood and the broken pieces of stone. Nothing more.

My hands trembled as I lost sight of my house and my vision blurred with my tears.

"I am sorry." Much gripped my hand warmly and I clung to the comfort I found in his friendship.

"So am I."

"Did you have brothers or sisters?"

"No." I hesitated a moment. Habibah was my sister, but not by blood. She'd been brought to live with us when her own family was gone. But I did not have the heart to speak of such things.

"Were you close to your parents?"

"Very." The one word came out in a sort of strangled way as my heart squeezed in my chest and my legs wobbled beneath me. More tears pushed their way down my cheeks and Much wrapped his arms around me. I melted into his embrace, letting my sobs wrack my frame as I thought of all that I had lost.

I do not remember what was said, but after I calmed down I do recall speaking to Much for a while as we stood there staring at what had once been my home. He was quiet and thoughtful and didn't try to say too much or try to understand my grief. He simply listened and offered sympathy.

In the end, I felt better. Emptied of my pain; there was a large hole left inside where I had once buried my memories and my grief, but it was quickly filling with the love and comfort of my Savior and of the friends He had provided me with.

"Thank you, Much."

"For what?"

"For being my friend. You care, and that touches my heart."

"We all care for you, Dusty."

"You were right, you know. Coming back here…it is facilitating healing in a way I didn't know was possible. I didn't grieve before, not like I should have. I ran. Partly for survival; I had to stay alive. But also because I couldn't face the truth." I shrugged, trying to regain my composure. "It was easier to fight to deceive Saladin's army, to pretend to be a man and lose my past and my identity altogether, than to face the pain. I turned to my Comforter to just keep breathing, keep putting one step in front of the other, but I didn't face all this grief, not truly."

"It's a lot to face."

I straightened my shoulders, taking a deep breath. "Thank you. I am grateful God led me to you, and to Robin and Allen. He has blessed me with a second family and I am glad of it."

Chapter 11

WE WERE NOT in the city of Darum for long; King Richard soon did as he had wished and used the momentum of his victory there to continue his push toward Jerusalem. As we left my city at the head of the army, following the king's lead as always, Robin laid a hand on my shoulder. On my other side, Much walked in silent sympathy, his eyes on my face.

"Are you okay?" Robin asked.

"I think I am. I am sad…and I do not think I will ever stop being sad that I lost my family in such a way. Yet even so, I am okay. I truly am."

"I am glad of that."

In the weeks that followed, I noticed my friends keeping careful watch over me—and I appreciated their concern—but what I had told them was the truth. Now that I'd stopped running from it and chosen to face it instead, it was so much easier to give it all to my greatest Comforter. My grief was not gone by any means, but it was less heavy.

Eventually, we came in sight of the city of Jerusalem. I had seen it before, having been stationed there at one point during my days with Saladin's army, but as soon as we could see the city shining in the distance Much's pace quickened beside me.

"Robin, do you see it?"

"Yes." Robin grinned at Much's infectious joy, though he did not quicken his speed as Much had done.

"I never dreamed I would see Jerusalem!" Much said.

"I never expected to see many of the things we have encountered on our journey," Allen said.

"It has been a strange and often exciting experience," Robin agreed.

We did not, however, reach Jerusalem. The leaders of our army began to bicker once more—which was not an entirely uncommon occurrence. He may have been a good king, may have been loyal and sometimes kind, but Richard the Lion-Heart had little respect for other royal houses and was often seen insulting one or another of the leaders he came into contact with. It was why the Duke of Austria and King Philip of France had abandoned the Crusade back at Acre.

The king's disagreements with the other leaders of the army had brought everything to a standstill. King Richard refused to change his opinion on what ought to be done next to further the war effort, and those opposed to him were equally stubborn.

When it became clear that we could march no further due to the ridiculous arguments between them all, King Richard brought the army back to Jaffa. It all felt rather futile and stupid to me.

In any case, negotiations for peace began once more. With what looked like the true end of the war at hand, King Richard decided to send his wife and sister home and made preparations to that end.

Before their departure, they came to say farewell to their friends. Joan could not resist hugging each of us. Berengaria refrained, but she was affectionate in her farewells to Robin.

"Oh how I am going to miss all of you!" Joan said, throwing her arms around my neck. "Who knows how long it may be before we meet again?"

She kissed my cheek and then turned to Robin and winked. "Will you miss me?"

"You will be missed, Princess," Robin said—rather gallantly, I thought— "and perhaps when things have settled down and I have returned home once more we can write to one another."

"I would love that!" Joan said, clapping her hands in excitement. "Dusty, you must promise me you'll keep in touch as well."

"Whatever you wish, Your Highness," I teased with mock seriousness. Joan's eyes sparkled with laughter and she pulled me into another hug. She knew as well as I did that my severe demeanor was melting away. My grief, and perhaps even bitterness, was slowly healing since my joining the King's Guard. The Lord knew what He was doing when He brought me to them.

After Joan's departure, our days were simple—we followed the king on his various errands making preparations for a departure for England, and we stood watch when he met with his advisors, which generally included Robin.

One particular day we were at the harbor as King Richard was overseeing the work being done on his fleet of ships so that they would be seaworthy when the time came to head home. The sea was sparkling in vibrant hues of green and blue, and Allen and Robin were amiably chatting and laughing together nearby as Much stood solemnly beside the king.

I wasn't sure what was going to happen when King Richard set sail for England. Robin, Much, and Allen would undoubtedly be going home as well. They had homes, friends, lovers to return to and were no doubt eager to do so. There was many a day when Robin could be heard eagerly anticipating his reunion with Marian and fretting over how much she may or may not have missed him.

But what of me? There was nothing left for me here; my family was gone, any friends that I had in my youth were lost to me. The people I loved most in the world were about to leave the country altogether. I was once more going to be fully and completely alone.

The thought terrified me.

Before I could get too lost in my own fear of losing the new family I had been given, I caught sight of several soldiers running down the docks toward us, shouting for the king.

"Your Majesty! Saladin is coming!"

"I did not know to expect him," King Richard said thoughtfully as he moved toward the out-of-breath soldiers.

"Though perhaps a meeting in person will move things along swifter than our missive have been able to."

"No, Your Majesty, you don't understand," one of the soldiers said, his eyes wide with fear. "They are mounting an attack on the city walls even now!"

"What?!" King Richard reached for his sword. "Show me."

The soldiers took off and the king followed them, not bothering to hide the anger on his face. I and my companions kept pace with him, as was our duty.

"What is Saladin thinking, with peace so near?" I asked no one in particular.

"He has been reluctant to relinquish his power," King Richard replied as we marched along the street. "This must be his last ditch effort to assert control so that he can demand a surrender—with terms to his liking, because we would have no negotiating leverage—rather than a peace treaty."

Before we reached the city walls we could hear the shouting of soldiers on both sides, and see the archers up along the city wall.

King Richard led us up a set of stone steps that led to the battlements atop the wall, striding along the top as we kept pace beside him. He sought out the commanders on the wall and began issuing orders.

Down below the wall, Saladin's army was advancing. The archers shot at those of us on the battlements that they could see, and others were attempting to climb the city walls. There were still more of them pressing toward the city gates in an attempt to break them open.

Robin and Allen were sent to join the archers along the wall while Much and I remained at the king's side.

As the archers and a few companies of soldiers kept Saladin's forces at bay along the walls, King Richard selected a few more companies of soldiers to follow him outside the city wall on the opposite side of Jaffa. This meant we were soon exiting the city opposite the battle and sneaking around the outside to flank Saladin's troops.

Within minutes, we were in the thick of battle. I was ducking under swords and darting around my opponents, jabbing my daggers into any available space where I could wound and maim. It was dirty work.

I kept beside King Richard as well as I could, fighting off any soldiers who came at his back while he ferociously moved forward through the throng, cutting down any foe in his path.

Much was nearby, slicing and cutting with his sword and keeping his eye on the king as well while the wake of bodies behind us continued to grow. The King showed no sign of slowing as he cut a bloody pathway through the thick of the fighting.

I tried not to focus on the displeasure of what we were doing, but I could hardly ignore the blood and the screams. The pouch on my belt seemed to grow heavier with every passing minute as I longed to lay aside my weapons and heal instead.

The battle was over almost before it had truly begun, or so it felt when we suddenly realized we had run out of enemies. The groans and cries of wounded filled the air, but the air was absent of any blades striking against each other.

With the battle over, King Richard's men began to gather their wounded to a central spot so that the army's healers could begin their work.

I checked my pouch on my belt and moved toward the nearest wounded man I saw. He was grasping his side and curling inward, coughing up blood. I knelt beside him and placed a hand on his arm.

"Let me see," I said softly, reaching for his hands so I could pry them away from his wound and get a good look at what I was dealing with.

He recoiled from me slightly, coughing again. His blood splattered my arm as he coughed and I reached for my pouch to begin mixing herbs.

"A…Aban…"

I froze, the spices in my hands sliding through my fingers into the blood-soaked dirt. My eyes moved from the crimson-stained hands covering the wound at his side all the way up to his eyes.

Razon.

He coughed again, more blood spewing from his mouth. I shook myself and set to work again, mixing a concoction to stem the flow of blood and then pulling his fingers away from his wound so that I could push the mixture into his wound and then pressed my hands on top. I closed my eyes, lifting him up in prayer as I worked.

"Aban…"

I opened my eyes, meeting his gaze. His eyes were dark with pain, but there was something more there. He could hardly talk because of his wounds and the coughing fits, but I could tell there was much he wanted to say.

Did he hate me for running away? For fighting against him?

He was a good man. I hated that it was true, but it was. He was a good man and I did not want him to die. The thought that one of us had cut him down made me sick to my stomach.

I focused on my work once more, desperately trying to encourage his wound to healing. I was afraid it was hopeless. The cut was deep—I could see past his skin and his muscle to his very bones.

The fact the Razon had been a part of the army that had killed my own family crossed my mind, but revenge was not my way. And more than that, I'd known Razon for months; I could not argue the fact that he was a decent human being.

I had to save him.

I bent over him, mixing more herbs and pressing them into his wound. I needed the blood flow to stop so I could start stitching him back together but more and more crimson flooded from his side. If it kept going at such a pace I couldn't help but wonder if he'd have any left at all.

"Dusty, what are you doing?"

It was Emil. He was standing over me with a frown on his face.

"What does it look like I am doing? This is my work. Let me be."

"He's not one of ours, Saracen."

"He deserves a chance at life as much as you do."

"I disagree."

Emil unsheathed his sword, but I thew my body forward to cover Razon. "Don't. You. Dare."

"Dusty—"

"I'm saving this one."

"We aren't taking prisoners."

"He didn't kill me when his army destroyed my home and my family; he recruited me, he kept me alive and trained me. The least I can do is save his life."

Emil glared at me, but he shoved his sword back into its sheath. I set to work once more, though the never-ending crimson floodgates kept on pouring forth.

135

"Aban…" Razon's eyes bored into mine and I wished I could speak to him. He wanted to say something and I couldn't understand whatever it was merely by his expression.

The light was fading in those eyes.

"No, no, no…"

I bent over his wound, my fingers working furiously to mix new concoctions of my herbs and spices. Everything I knew that might promote healing or congeal his blood. Nothing was working.

"Stay with me, Razon…stay with me…"

I hadn't realized I harbored any affection or respect for the man, but as my heart rate increased and tears filled my eyes it dawned on me that I did care about him.

"A…Aban…"

He just kept repeating the name that was not mine as I became more and more soaked with his blood until eventually he collapsed, lifeless, and I was left with nothing but regrets.

"There are more wounded being carried to our camp," Emil said grimly. "You are the best healer we have. Get moving."

I slowly stood, staring down at what had once been a vibrant man.

He was gone. I'd failed.

"Dusty!" Emil snapped, shaking my shoulder. "Our wounded!"

I nodded mutely, turning to follow the lines of men carrying wounded toward the tents set up for them. I spent the rest of the day busy there, healing many. I could not tell you what kinds of wounds I dealt with or if I knew any of the soldiers by name. I do not even recall if I lost other wounded to death that day. The only encounter I vividly remember from that battle was Razon.

With the battle lost and Saladin's forces destroyed, negotiations for a peace treaty resumed—this time with little grace on King Richard and the Crusaders side. There was tension on every side as messages were sent back and forth. Still, despite the tensions a treaty had been finalized within a week's time.

"What was the final outcome of the treaty?" Much asked as Robin joined us in the hall outside the king's chambers where he had just been speaking with King Richard.

"Jerusalem remains under Saracen control, but unarmed pilgrims and traders of other faiths and political views will be allowed to visit the city with no harm coming to them. Other than the city of Jerusalem and few surrounding areas, most of the 'Kingdom of Jerusalem' has been returned to King Guy's control."

"But we did not do what we set out to do," Allen said.

"Neither side is completely satisfied with this treaty, I think," Robin said. "But it is what it is, for now at least. Until someone decides there needs to be a fourth Crusade. But the monetary drain on the treasuries of the royals in Europe and the lives lost in this war that would potentially have no end—neither side being overwhelmingly larger in number, and every other battle being won by the opposite side—if we did not come to a compromise in this treaty, the Third Crusade might never end."

"So it's done," Much said.

"Yes, I believe it is."

"And we can finally return home," Much sighed.

"I don't have a home to return to," I said softly, closing my eyes briefly as I felt my heart begin to pound and the fear of losing this new family of mine washed over me once more. I hadn't faced that fear because Saladin's attack had distracted me, but it was still there just waiting to be acknowledged.

"You're coming with us," Robin said, throwing his arm around my shoulders. I could not hide the relief and joy that came over me as I looked into his grinning face. "You and Allen both are more than welcome in our home."

"Thank you," I said, trying to ignore the lump I could now feel in my throat as tears pricked my eyes. "I would be glad of that."

I felt a rush of love and gratitude for this new family of mine. Truthfully, I never wished to be parted from them, but I did not say as much aloud.

"So would I," Allen agreed. "You three are all the family that I have."

Chapter 12

NOT LONG AFTER the treaty had been signed, King Richard's army began to board his fleet of ships and prepare to set sail from Palestine. I, along with Robin, Much, and Allen, were aboard the same boat as the king. The war was over, perhaps, but we were still in his service as his Royal Guard.

Having never been on such a vessel before, my curiosity got the better of me. I wandered the deck, my eyes taking in everything from the rigging, the mast, the highest sails, the muscled sailors running about and the grizzled captain shouting orders from the stern of the ship.

I stood still for a moment, closing my eyes and letting the sounds wash over me: the creaking of taut ropes, the shouting and laughter of sailors, the pounding of footsteps as they scurried along the deck, the splash of the waves against the side of the boat. I could feel the accompanying quiver beneath my feet as each wave pushed the boat. Keeping my balance might prove to be a challenge.

When I opened my eyes, I caught sight of my friends leaning against the railing of the boat watching the shores of my homeland recede into the distance and I moved to join them. The only world I had ever known was disappearing into the horizon.

I peered over the rail at the swirling water below.

"What is England like?"

"Beautiful," Robin replied. "You will love it, Dusty. It's

lovely, it's green. We will live in peace and I promise you, you will not have so many hardships as you have had. You will have a good life."

"I am not afraid of hardships," I replied. "They do much to strengthen one's character."

"Have you ever left Palestine before?" Much asked.

"No." I glanced toward the horizon once more. I doubted I would see that shore again. Andaleeb was born and raised there. One might argue Andaleeb had died there.

I felt in some ways that I was sailing away from her and there would be no getting her back once I was gone.

Aban had been created and then discarded there, too.

There was a mingling of pain and hope in the tightness in my chest as tears pricked the back of my eyelids. But more than anything I felt excited for the future. That was a new sensation.

"I hadn't left England before coming on this adventure with Robin," Much said, watching me with his kind eyes. "It was surprisingly unsettling to wonder if I'd ever return."

"I know I will not return…but there is nothing to return to." I turned toward Much, noticing the concerned look on his face as I spoke. "But I have much to look forward to, a bright future ahead, so I will not regret leaving my past behind."

He seemed satisfied with that response and I returned to my view, watching the land of my youth disappear.

I stayed at the rail even after I could see nothing but the sea all the way to the horizon.

We had not sailed far when the sky grew dark and violent winds began to buffet the ship in various directions, the waves beneath us growing more choppy. If I'd thought it was difficult to hold my balance before, it was doubly so now. I had seen storms in my life, but never from a flimsy piece of wood at the mercy of the sea. I could feel my heart pounding with every wave that crashed across the deck, soaking anyone unfortunate enough to be in its path.

Robin, Much, and Allen dragged me below deck to a room filled with hammocks where many people were gathering to stay out of the storm and out of the way of the sailors at work.

Hours passed in the darkness of that room with nothing but the creaking boat and the shouting of the sailors to give any indication of the dire state of our situation. The boat itself pitched about in the rough waves, making us lose our balance and slide along the floor where we were sitting.

The constant erratic movement of the boat was causing my stomach to move in a similar fashion and I closed my eyes, trying to contain the mounting pressure. The boat shot forward and then rocked to the side and my head spun.

As dizziness overcame me I fell forward on my hands and knees, unable to stop the contents of my stomach from spewing forth. From the sounds around me, I knew I was not the only soldier vomiting in the room.

I felt a gentle hand on my back trying to soothe me, and then a handkerchief was held out to me. I wiped away the remnants of my ordeal from my mouth and turned to find Much's concerned eyes watching me in the relative darkness of the room.

The boat tilted violently and we both rolled into the wall behind us.

"Are you alright?" Much asked, struggling into a more natural seated position.

"I think so…"

I did not retch again during the storm, but I was miserable as the boat continued to pitch this way and that with no rhyme or reason and the hours passed in discomfort. Eventually, however, the storm began to clear.

Robin suggested we all go above deck and get some fresh air. I moved on shaky legs, but both Much and Allen reached out to steady me as we made our way toward the ladder that would lead us above deck.

When we emerged from the darkness below, I made my unsteady way over to the railing so I'd have support. The dark clouds still hung low overhead, and the waves were not calm yet though they weren't quite as large and violent.

Allen leaned against the rail beside me, looking up at the ominous clouds. "I hope it doesn't start up again."

"You and me both."

I noticed with some trepidation that the rest of the fleet was not in sight. Whether they had been blown further off course or had made it through the storm on the right path was unknown, but what was clear was that we were alone.

"Look, there's King Richard," Allen commented. I turned to look across the deck—the king was not far from us, speaking with the captain of the ship. Their conversation carried and Allen, as always, leaned forward to hear what was being said.

"You can't help yourself can you?" I asked, feeling amusement more than frustration at his antics. "You always have to eavesdrop."

"You'll find out all sorts of interesting things when you listen to people," Allen replied. "For instance, the captain is saying we're off course. He thinks the nearest port might be Corfu, Greece, but he's not absolutely sure."

"We're lost?"

"This tends to happen to the King of England. I think he's cursed." Allen winked at me. "Come on, let's tell Robin and Much what we've learned."

As I let go of the railing I became acutely aware of the wobbling of my legs. Allen must have noticed as well, for he wrapped an arm around my waist.

Allen hurried me across the deck, keeping me upright along the way, and then relayed his news to Robin and Much.

As the storm continued to settle, we made our way toward what did, indeed, turn out to be Corfu.

Once our limping ship docked, King Richard made arrangements to stay at an inn for the night with us, his four guards, while the captain of the ship and the sailors made their own arrangements for repairs to the hull, mast, sails, etc that had been harmed in the storm.

Once we went ashore and settled into our lodgings, the shaking in my legs and the unease in my stomach finally calmed down. We gathered around a table at the inn and my companions began to dig into a meal with gusto.

"I am rather tired of all my ships being sent off course," King Richard said around a full bite.

"Does this happen often?" I asked. "I have never sailed before this, but Allen commented that you might be cursed in this regard."

Allen choked on his drink of ale, sputtering for a moment and sending me a look that clearly meant he hadn't wanted that comment related to others.

King Richard, however, chuckled. "Allen may be right. We were sent off course on our way to the Holy Land as well. I believe Much was almost lost overboard on that adventure..."

I glanced toward Much and he shrugged, blushing deeply.

"We were above deck when the storm hit," Allen said, leaning across the table and grinning widely. "The huge waves crashing over the deck and sweeping all but the most hardened sailors off their feet! I'm sure you can picture it. The storm was wild. We'd all begun to run below deck, but Much here noticed Joan was in some trouble, caught up in a wave."

I glanced toward Much again and saw him inching downward in his seat as though trying to subtly disappear under the table.

"He ran to help her—very valiant of him—but what he actually succeeded in doing was being washed overboard!"

Much's face could hardly have turned more red as his eyes remained fixed on his lap.

Allen continued his tale, his eyes dancing with mischief. "Joan nearly went overboard, too, but Robin caught her. I'll never forget how he looked, one arm gripping the rail of the ship, his body dangling over the angry ocean, with Joan wrapped in his other arm, hanging on for dear life. And poor Much, practically drowning down below. It was a rather shining moment for our daring Robin of Locksley."

"It wasn't that exciting," Robin said. "I was soaked through, trembling with cold, and straining as I tried not to let go of the ship or Joan. It was actually rather painful, to be honest. I could feel that ache in my shoulder for weeks."

"Your troubles only make the act that much more heroic," Allen said.

"And clearly you managed to hang on and save Joan," I said. "And Much was rescued successfully..."

"Yes, it all turned out quite right," King Richard said. "I am glad, for Robin had been invaluable to me during this war."

When the meal came to an end, we retired to our rooms for some much needed rest. King Richard soon made it clear, however, that he had no intention of sailing the rest of the journey home. He had many reasons for his decision, but I always wondered if it didn't boil down to simply his belief that Allen might be right—sailing for him might be cursed.

Once we'd sailed from Corfu to a nearby port in Italy, King Richard intended to travel by foot. And in order to maintain his safety on such a venture, he insisted to go in secret. That meant he would not let us refer to him by anything other than his name—Richard—which I did not find a difficult task at all. He was, after all, only another human. And not even one that I particularly respected.

Chapter 13

WE STASHED ANY clothes that might draw attention, such as anything with the King's sigil emblazoned on it, and donned the most ordinary outfits we had in order to promote the idea that we were simple travelers. We kept our weapons on our person.

We spent a single night at the port in Italy where we had landed, and then the long march home began.

As we continued our journey we would walk for much of the day, stopping at various points to rest along the side of the road and eat occasionally. When Richard felt we had traveled enough for one day, we would take shelter at the first town we came to. Robin was sent to procure our rooms at a tavern, and we'd soon be sleeping soundly, exhausted from our exertion. Yet when the sun rose, we were immediately on their way again.

Travel continued in that manner for days.

Much occasionally slipped up and called Richard 'Sire' or 'Your Majesty' but as we were walking along the green countryside alone it did not signify.

One night as I slept on a small straw mattress and dreamed of my parents, sister, and Daniyah, I was awakened in the darkness by the sounds of footsteps in the hall outside my door. They passed by quickly, but I thought I recognized the gentle footfall.

I got up, exiting my room and moving downstairs and out of the tavern completely where I found Much sitting on the front step. The night was chilly and I pulled my cloak tightly around my shoulders as I seated myself beside him.

"Much?"

Much turned toward me, his face lit by the light of the moon.

"Why are you up so late?"

"Me?" I asked. "I could not sleep; I heard movements, like those of a mouse, and came to investigate."

"I am not a mouse."

"You could have fooled me. What is bothering you?"

"Nothing. I am merely thinking."

"So late at night? What are you thinking about?"

Much kept his gaze upward towards the moon. I studied my friend as he ignored me. He seemed to wrestle with something, but when he turned toward me again he appeared relaxed and at ease.

"I was thinking of home. I am eager to return to Locksley. I want to see the manor, to smell the garden, to see Sarah…yet it will all be strange without the Earl."

Robin and Much did not often speak of the Earl or their grief, but I could understand that—I had not spoken or even personally acknowledged my own loss for such a long time.

"Did you know Robin's father well?"

"Not exactly…I was merely a servant in his household." The tone of his voice and the downward curve of his lips as his eyes darkened with emotion belied his words.

"And yet I feel he was more than that to you."

Much nodded. "My earliest memories at Locksley…it felt like Robin and I were brothers. The earliest impressions I have of the Earl were that of a father. That soon changed, however."

"How long has it been since he died?"

"A year or so."

Robin had lost his father more recently than I had lost my family. I wondered why he was not more distraught or if he put up a facade of being fine when in fact he was in pain.

Much reached over and slipped his hand in mine. "Will it be hard for you?"

"Will what be hard?" I asked.

"Seeing all of us return to our homes and our families, when you don't have either to return to?"

I realized my silence and contemplation on Robin's grief must have made Much worried I was drowning in my own.

"No, Much. I have become content with where God has placed me in life. You helped me with that, actually. Besides, you *are* my family now. Where you and Robin go, there will be my home. I believe a person's home is where they find comfort, with those they love…where they keep their heart."

"Mine is at Locksley with Sarah and Robin."

"I know," I said, unable to stop smiling. Much was not afraid to show his affection for Robin at any given time and I loved that about him.

For a time we lapsed into silence, enjoying the stillness of the night and the brilliance of the stars above us.

"Dusty?"

"Yes?"

"How do you heal people?"

"With herbs and prayer."

"I know that; I have watched you do it. It's…amazing. I can't comprehend it. I watched a sword slice through Robin, and then the next time I saw him you had healed him up and he was talking and fine. Injured still, but…fine."

"It is God's gift."

"You healed so many while we were in the Holy Land."

"I merely helped where I could."

Much shot me a glance and then shook his head. For a moment he said nothing, and then he asked, "Could you teach me?"

"I can show you the herbs I use and how to mix them. But not tonight. We need rest. We have a long journey ahead of us."

"Assuming we make it to England at all."

"Why would you say that?"

"I don't know…I just have a bad feeling about our trip. We've already been thrown off course and forced to travel by foot across land—undercover no less—instead of sailing safely home."

"Things will play out how they are meant to be. You cannot stop them, and worrying about it will only make you anxious."

"I can't help it."

"Just pray for God's guidance as you travel through life."

"Does he answer your prayers?" Much's intense look surprised me. He was the most mellow person I knew, but at that moment there was something deeply unsettling in his soul and it showed on his face.

I took a deep breath, weighing my words. I didn't hide my faith from my friends, but somehow I didn't often speak of it either, not in depth. Still, I wanted to assuage whatever turmoil I could see in Much's eyes.

"Sometimes His answers are not what I would like to hear, but He always answers. He loves His children dearly."

"Does he?"

I was not surprised by Much's lack of faith. I had noticed early on that few of the Crusaders seemed to have a personal relationship with the Savior they claimed to be fighting for.

"Do you know the Lord at all then, as He so wants to be known by you?"

"Probably not," Much said. "I certainly don't share the kind of faith you do."

"Can I tell you about Him?"

"If you'd like to."

"I would like nothing better." I took a deep breath, trying to gather my thoughts. I wanted more than anything for Much— and Robin and Allen—to know the Lord as I did. Yet I knew that I could be too passionate at times and scare people off with my conviction. Or I had been, in my youth. I hadn't shared my faith fully since my family died.

Daniyah would be ashamed of me.

I wasn't sure where to begin or what to say, so I closed my eyes and began to pray for wisdom and guidance. When I felt ready, I began to tell Much my own story.

"When I was young, I was full of curiosity and questions. Annoyingly so. I grew up in a city filled with Christians and Muslims alike, and I hounded adults and childhood friends from both faiths with my questions as a child. I hungered for the truth."

My gaze shifted to the starry night sky above us and the moon shining so brilliantly overhead as Much listened.

"What I found from one faith was the expectation to be perfect, and if I did not live up to Allah's standards then I would perish."

Flashes of memories darted through my mind, too quick to latch onto. The crinkling of unrolling scrolls. Daniyah's laughter. A monk's keen gaze. The smell of fresh leather. The dark eyes of my Islamic mentors.

Pieces of the Quran they would quote to me so faithfully echoed in my mind and I concentrated on them and the way they had made me feel.

"'To those who disbelieve and do wrong, surely Allah will not forgive them or lead them to any path.' It left me feeling worthless; I wanted to do good, to be a good person, but I could never attain that kind of righteousness. And the books of religious text that my Muslim teachers would read with me told me that if I didn't attain that high standard, I would go to hell. I was left in fear and confusion, knowing I couldn't attain it but terrified of not trying because who wants to burn in hell?"

I turned to Much, hoping he could hear the truth in my words. As I shifted, his gaze moved from the stars to my face, his expression still open.

"My teachers tried to comfort me with things like 'They whose balances are heavy will be blessed, but they whose balances are light will lose their soul and abide in hell forever.' It was not remotely comforting to the little girl who wanted to do right but knew she could never live up to perfection. I was being told that if I didn't do the impossible, I would go to hell. That was it. That was the only reality. But what I found in the other faith was only grace."

As the truth washed over me, I closed my eyes. I could feel the love and forgiveness of my Savior wrapping around me and filling me up. I had clung to Him in my grief, but in a weird sort of way—holding on just enough, because I knew He was my only hope, and yet keeping him at the same distance that I kept everyone else.

Opening up to Much, Robin, and Allen had led me to open myself to my Savior further. More than just the Healer who worked through my hands, but my personal friend. And now that I was letting Much see the deepest part of me—my connection to my Savior—I could feel Him drawing ever closer.

I opened my eyes. Much was not shying away from me, so I took a deep breath and continued.

"My mother's dearest friend was the most patient person in my life, letting me bring all my doubts and questions to her without ever judging me for them. She showed me the difference between the salvation through works of one faith, versus the gracious gift of the other."

I could picture Daniyah's gentle smile, her carefully chosen words echoing in my mind. Her beautiful eyes bored into mine in all seriousness as she impressed upon the truth of the Scriptures that she held so dear.

"'But God demonstrates His own love toward us in that while we were still sinners, Christ died for us.' He didn't wait for us to be perfect—He knew we never would be. So He made a way for us to draw near to Him regardless of our imperfection. *While we were sinners*, He forgave us. Not after we'd worked hard to become perfect did He then deliberate over our deeds, both good and bad, and decide whether or not to be forgiving based on the weighing of our scales."

I took a deep breath, relishing the truth. Much appeared to still be listening to me, his expression still one of interest though he did not seem half as impressed by my words as I had always been by Daniyah's.

"To be fully transparent, there were quotes to be found in the texts of my Muslim teachers that spoke of God's forgiveness and mercy, too. But they also rely on works as much as Allah's grace for salvation: 'to those who believe *and do deeds of righteousness* has Allah promised forgiveness.'"

I closed my eyes for a moment, trying to remember all of the things that my mentors used to quote for me, all the things that made me shudder with dread that I could never do what was asked of me.

"'O you who believe! If you are careful of your duty to Allah he will grant you distinction.' They had a piece of the truth, but it was coupled with the ideas both that we are born good and perfect, not sinful—and I knew from my own experience, from my heart, that I was neither good nor perfect—and also the idea that salvation was about more than just God's grace; it also required something from me in the form of good deeds. Their teachings left me in fear because I knew that as I made mistakes I would constantly be in need of repentance, and if I didn't repent I would be punished eternally in hell-fire. What if I genuinely sought after God, and then made a mistake, and then died immediately after sinning? I hadn't had time to repent. What then? Trust a vague idea that maybe Allah would forgive me because the rest of my deeds outweighed this one big mistake I'd made?"

I remember taking my fear to Daniyah. I could hear her voice whispering the truth that assuaged the ache in my heart. I wanted Much to feel it, too.

"With Jesus, it is not vague. It is straight-forward and factual. He took the punishment of all sin, once for everyone. It's over and done with. All I have to do is accept His gift of salvation and freedom and my place at His side for all eternity is secured."

I met Much's gaze, praying that he could hear the truth of my words, that he would know Jesus himself.

"With one faith, there was no way to know for certain if my good deeds would outweigh my bad and therefore earn grace from a god they claim is so forgiving, but with the other I was told I was loved and forgiven because He chose to do so long before I ever thought to seek Him at all. I can rest in His grace knowing it is sure, rather than the arbitrary grace of an Allah who may or may not forgive me depending on how sincerely I may or may not repent or how many good deeds I may or may not do that may or may not outweigh my bad ones. You see my point?"

I took a deep breath, hoping I hadn't completely overwhelmed him. Once I'd started talking about my faith and my past, I couldn't seem to stop.

I smiled weakly. "So that is how I came to know the Lord. It is not always the same for everyone—don't get me wrong, Jesus and what He did for us is exactly the same, but sometimes we face different questions and doubts and He gently guides us to the truth in a way that suits our own needs. For you, for example,

I think you need to hear that you have inherent value because you are a Child of God. You are not less than."

Much shifted uncomfortably and I knew I had hit the bull's eye when it came to what he struggled most with.

"I haven't ever given a great deal of thought to any faith," Much said. "I certainly don't have the same questions as you did. I don't need to compare and contrast religions to find the truth."

I nodded, laughing and folding my hands in my lap as my cheeks blazed with heat. I had been rather inquisitive as a child and the embarrassment at having revealed so much of myself to my friend pressed down on me. After so many years of not telling anyone who I truly was, it was a bit overwhelming to realize I had opened up so much without fully realizing what I was doing.

Much was watching me still, so I shook off my embarrassment and continued,"I was searching for a different truth—that I didn't have to be perfect to be loved and forgiven. You, on the other hand, while you may need to hear that truth as well, your soul is longing for something else; namely, that you have value. Yes?"

Much shrugged. "I suppose."

"Robin's father is the one who convinced you that you are less than, isn't that right?"

"He made sure I knew the difference between the son of an earl and the son of nobody significant."

"And yet both the noble man and the servant are the same in the eyes of God. Both are made in His image, both are His creation. Both are seeking love, acceptance, significance—the things that make up our identities and where we measure our worth. God offers all of them—love, acceptance, significance—to His children in a way that no human could. Robin's love will inevitably fail you, his acceptance will fail you. The significance that he may lend you—if he lends you any—will not last. But God can give you all this and more securely than a human could, eternally, offering an undying love that will never change, accepting you exactly as you are and never wavering in His grace."

"You are so confident in what you believe."

"God has never been unfaithful to me; not once. His promises, both spoken to my heart and those found directly in Scripture, have always been fulfilled."

"I am envious of the assurance you have in your faith in God. And I do…I do wish I could be confident that I am… enough."

"You are, because He says you are. You are, because He made you to be. You are, because He is willing to forgive you and clothe you in His own righteousness and make you more than you could ever be on your own." I smiled, feeling the conviction in my own words swell in my chest. I'd nearly forgotten how wonderful it felt to live in the presence of my Savior. Not on the outskirts, but truly in His presence.

"That connection that you seek, the desire to be on equal footing with someone and not seen as 'just a servant', the ability to open up and be vulnerable with a friend without the fear of 'forgetting your place' is all found in God."

"But isn't it more terrifying to overstep the Creator of the everything versus offend a nobleman like the Earl? He's...I mean, He's God." Much's eyes were wide as he clasped his hands together in his lap.

"Yes, He is. And He is absolutely deserving of reverence and fear, of worship. But He gave up His glory willingly to meet you exactly where you are, Much."

Much gasped and shuddered suddenly and I wondered what he might be thinking.

"I'm sorry, was this all too much?" I asked. "I get passionate, I know. I am sorry if I have overwhelmed you."

"No. You didn't. It's interesting. The idea that I could be valuable simply because God says so is intriguing. I want that."

"God created all of us to desire community, connection... But the only place we can find true connection is with Him. Robin will not sustain you, Sarah will never be enough to assuage the longing for true acceptance and love that can only be found in Jesus."

We talked for several more hours—until the sun began to creep over the horizon. Much had many questions and my soul was on fire for the first time in so many years that I was grateful to have such a captivated listener to my ramblings.

By the time our heads hit our pillows, Richard was waking everyone up and demanding we eat and be on our way as usual. It had been an emotionally draining and yet fulfilling conversation for me, and I hoped Much felt the same.

His salvation was on my mind, as well as his inability to believe that he held any value on his own, and on top of my concern for my friend I was also feeling a bit raw at just how open and honest I had been all night.

Being so vulnerable was a new sensation considering how closed off I had become when my family died, but I did believe it was a good thing. A bit strange and painful at first—and certainly terrifying—but good.

Chapter 14

WE HAD NOT TRAVELED far the next morning before Much fell into step beside me at the back of the group. He usually chose to walk beside Robin—who was generally with Richard. In any case, I wasn't surprised that Much wanted to speak with me more. He'd had so many questions the night before, and I was certain all of my answers must have left his mind reeling.

My own heart skipped a beat as his strides matched mine. There was a pleasant ache in my chest from pouring my soul out to Much the night before—the sort I might feel in my muscles after training with Razon for a day. It might have been hard and might have left me exhausted, but in the end I could feel that it was making me stronger.

The sun was shining down on us as we made our way along the green countryside. In the distance, mountains cast their shadow across the land. There were a million different colored flowers scattered along the road beside us. It was a beautiful land, and unlike any I'd seen before.

"How are you not tired?" Much asked as we followed the others.

"I feel quite invigorated from our conversation yesterday, I must confess."

"The conversation was certainly interesting, but I am still incredibly tired."

I chuckled at the forlorn expression on Much's face. "It might also be that I am used to getting little sleep and my body learned to adjust long ago."

We walked in silence for a time; I did not want to rush Much. Whatever he was thinking and feeling, he needed the time and space to process it, and in many ways so did I.

Much suddenly yawned, and I felt a flash of guilt. I noticed then the dark circles beneath his eyes and the way that his eyelids drooped. He was exhausted. "I probably should not have kept you up so late. I know I can get passionate about the Lord. It can be hard to shut up about it…"

"I enjoyed our conversation. And honestly, I do have more questions."

"I would be happy to answer them."

Much glanced forward where Robin and Allen were flanking Richard, all three of them lost in a conversation of their own. I wondered if he was worried about how Robin might react to his questions about God.

"Take your time, Much. These questions—whatever they are—are likely the most important you'll ever ask. Finding the truth of who God is, is a powerful thing and so vitally important both for our lives here on earth and for the fate of our eternity in heaven or hell. But you should know that God does not shy away from our questions and doubts. He welcomes them, in fact, so that He can have the chance to prove Himself worthy. Because He is. Always worthy."

"I cannot get over how confident and assured you are when you speak of your faith, or about God."

"He has never failed me." I closed my eyes briefly, marveling that I could say such a thing with confidence. I may have wandered from Him a time or two, but He never wandered from my side. In all of the hardship and grief, He has always been with with me.

"Does He ever…speak to you?"

"All the time! When I read Scripture He has so much to show me."

"But does He ever talk to you…I wouldn't say verbally, but…"

I searched Much's face, my heart pounding as a jolt of excitement ran through me. "Yes. He does speak directly to me sometimes. It's not always a voice that I could hear with my ears, but my heart hears it. Did He speak to you?"

"I think…maybe."

"What did He say?"

"That I am his son, and he values me."

"Both statements are true." I couldn't help but grin at my friend.

Much nodded, though his expression was one of confusion.

"You said you had questions?"

"I can almost feel the fatherhood of God, and it is overwhelming and wonderful. But you touched on more than just

163

his affection yesterday…you spoke of Christ and what He'd done, but I'm not entirely sure I understand what that was exactly."

I took a deep breath, sending a quick prayer for wisdom as I considered how to answer Much. It had been so long since I had shared my faith, I almost wondered if I wouldn't do as well as I once did. But then I felt His gentle prodding, reminding me that it didn't matter how I expressed myself—He would use my words to His own purpose and glory. "Well, it starts with the fact that God is holy and perfect and good. Do you believe that?"

"I guess. I can't imagine Him being anything less if He's God."

"Exactly. And then He created this strange and beautiful world, and He created us. Humans. His children. At the beginning there was communion between God and man, until man sinned."

"Which means what, precisely?"

"Anything that we do or say that breaks His laws. It can be as extreme as murder or as simple as lying. It's our angry thoughts and our envious words. Anything that isn't good and perfect and true is apart from God. He cannot be near the ugliness and the horror of our sin and darkness. If we don't take the seriousness of sin—and our sinful nature as humans—into account, then we cannot truly appreciate what Christ did when He died to save us from those very sins."

"That makes sense."

"God is so serious about sin that His response is wrath. 'The wages of sin is death.' That's what Scripture tells us. We

164

cannot live with God if we are in open rebellion against Him, because He is a just and righteous God. He cannot let wrongdoing go without punishment."

I hesitated a moment, watching Much's face. He was as open and eager to hear my answers as he had been yesterday. The pounding in my heart eased and I smiled. As I continued, "This is where the Muslim faith I studied as a child begins to differ from the truth of Christ, both in the knowledge that we are, indeed, sinful people who deserve separation from God and eternal damnation, and also that we cannot do anything to assuage God's wrath. We do wrong, and He punishes. We can't 'be good enough' to ever change the fact that we are guilty. Our bad deeds will forever outweigh the good ones. Scripture even says that 'all of our righteous deeds are as filthy rags' because it's never going to be enough compared to the pure goodness of God."

I paused, hoping Much could hear the weight of my words. The way he always sought validation through serving Robin faithfully made me wonder if he would approach his salvation in the same manner and I didn't want that to happen.

"Our salvation is not through any acts that we might perform. God could have left us in our punishment—separation from Him eternally. But He chose something different because of His great love for us."

"Why didn't He simply accept us into His grace then, why the need for Christ to die?"

Much's mind was as keen and sharp as my own, though he rarely showed it. I wondered if that was because of Robin—or because of Robin's father. Perhaps both. They'd led him to believe that his opinion didn't matter, that he himself held less worth because he was of lower social standing. It broke my heart.

But I decided to hold off on accusing Much's best friend and his father-figure and instead answered his question. "Because He is a just and righteous God. There has to be punishment for sin. That doesn't change because of his love. Wrongdoing deserves correction. What He did was not remove consequences for wrongdoing, but rather taking those consequences upon Himself so that justice would still be upheld, but mercy and grace would be present. He didn't have to save us, but He chose to do so in the only way possible while still maintaining punishment for sin."

Much nodded, but I pressed on. "He carried the punishment so that we wouldn't have to. Only He could be that Savior for us—if anyone else had died, claiming to do so to free all men from sin, it wouldn't have done any good. But Jesus—being God—lived a perfect life here on earth, entirely free from sin, and therefore He alone was able to make that sacrifice. And it didn't end there—He rose from the dead victorious, powerful enough to bring us with Him to life eternal. *That* is why Christ is our only hope for salvation."

Much was quiet, his eyes flickering with emotion. I knew he was taking my comments seriously, considering them carefully and weighing their truth. He glanced toward the sky, as more emotion crossed his face and tears glimmered in his eyes. He was wrestling with something, I simply didn't know what.

After a few moments of silence, Much turned and smiled at me. "It is strange to say this…but I feel at peace in a way I never have before."

I could feel a grin stretching across my face. "Do you? I am so glad!"

"I do believe what you're saying—what God says. I don't understand it all…but I believe Him."

"That is the most wonderful thing I've ever heard you say."

"I feel…confident."

"You are valued and loved, and therefore hold inherent worth because your identity is found in your Creator who tells you precisely what you are worth. And He would know—He's the one who made you, after all."

"Thank you, Dusty."

"I only relayed His truth. These are not my ideas."

"I know. I appreciate you sharing it though. I know you don't usually talk so much—you don't usually share what's on your heart and mind."

"This is important."

"I'm sure it is. Even so, I do recognize the step you're taking into letting go of your secrecy and choosing to open up to someone."

I didn't respond. Much was right, of course. This was huge for me. It didn't surprise me that Much noticed; he seemed to always notice people's emotional states, though he rarely commented on them due to his unfortunate belief that his opinion wouldn't matter.

I could feel tears pricking my eyelids as Much's hand slipped into mine. It was comforting to know that someone cared for me in the same sort of way that Daniyah and Habibah and my parents had once cared.

I sent a grateful prayer to my Father who had so kindly provided a second family to assuage the loneliness that I had denied I felt at all for so long.

Not long after Much's decision to accept Jesus as His Savior and accept the love of His heavenly Father, our travels were slowed by the weather. It was late in the year and the rain and snow began to fall on an almost daily basis. We began to stay in cities for longer periods of time, though Richard refused to settle in for the entire winter. He felt we needed to keep moving to avoid garnering too much attention.

One night I stood by a window in the room at the inn where we were lodging, watching the falling snow with a measure of disgust.

"I do not like this weather."

Richard sighed from where he was sitting across the room in front of the fire in the hearth. "Neither do I. I would prefer to be traveling quickly. The sooner we get to Saxony—the seat of my brother-in-law Henry the Lion—the better I will feel. I wish to be out of foreign lands as soon as possible."

"Henry the Lion?" Much asked.

"Yes, Henry the Lion," Richard responded. "He is the Duke of Saxony."

I glanced toward Richard, brooding into the fire, and Much sitting off to one side of the room looking nervous.

"There is no need for the mouse to fear the lion," I said softly, causing Much to smile.

"The mouse?" Robin asked from his seat near Richard. Allen was sprawled across the ground near his feet.

I glanced at Robin with confusion for a moment, before it dawned on me that no one knew my pet name for Much. "Ah. That is what I call Much."

"It is a fitting name," Richard said.

Much lowered his head and I was convinced he wasn't comfortable with the sudden attention he was getting.

"I like my mouse," Robin grinned. "He is the most loyal person I know."

"And he loves so unconditionally," I added, smiling apologetically to Much. I hadn't meant to put him on the spot in such a way. I could see how uncomfortable he was.

Much shifted in his seat for a moment and then turned to Robin. "If I am a mouse, what are you?"

I grinned at Much's tactic for turning the attention on someone else.

Richard laughed loudly before saying, "Robin is a fierce lion like me."

"Are all royals lions?" Allen asked from his place on the floor. He had his arm draped over his eyes and seemed entirely unconcerned with the conversation he was now joining. "Henry the Lion, Richard the Lion-Heart..."

Richard shook his head. "Not at all."

"In any case, I think Robin is more of a playful puppy."

"And what are you?" Richard asked Allen.

"Allen is a horse," Robin responded. "Strong, powerful, independent, craving freedom."

I was almost surprised to hear such an astute observation from Robin. Much was the one I expected to understand people so well, but I thought Robin's description fit Allen rather well.

"And what does that make our resident lady?" Richard asked, turning to Robin.

"An aloof cat?" Robin teased, winking at me.

"A wise owl," Allen suggested, his hand still draped over his face as though he didn't care about the discussion despite participating in it.

As they bounced different animals around trying to find one to fit me, I could suddenly hear my father's voice in my head, whispering my name with the deepest affection I'd ever known outside of Christ Himself.

"I am a nightingale," I said softly.

Much's gaze turned on me as Allen and Robin both asked, "A nightingale?"

"Yes…it's…" I could feel my throat tightening as I thought of my father, of the way we used to sing together every night as he put me to bed. I shook my head to clear it before the tears could fall from my lashes. "It is my name."

"Nightingale?"

Andaleeb.

I shrugged without a word, turning back to the window as tears slipped past my defenses. For a moment there was silence.

"The snow is beginning to lessen," I said at last. "How long do you plan to stay here, Richard?"

"A few more days at least. We need to keep moving so people don't become too curious about us, but I do not wish to travel as long as this storm persists."

We stayed in that village for a few weeks in the end, and then moved on a few miles and stopped again. The weather remained cold and uninviting and our progress was incredibly slow. Richard hoped that once warm weather returned we'd be able to travel at a much better pace, but until then we moved across enemy lands at a snail's pace.

Much continued to come to me with questions about God and about Scripture, and I happily spoke with him for hours on end. We also discussed my healing practices, because Much still held an interest in how I used various plants to heal. He had little talent for it I thought, but even so we persevered with his studies.

171

In every village we entered there was plenty of gossip in the tavern common rooms about the politics of the world. The morals and justification of the recently ended Crusade, as well as lengthy discussions on how unsatisfactory an ending it had closed on.

There was also news about England. Rumors abounded that the country was in shambles because the king had abandoned England for his Crusade, and Prince John was ruining things. They were only rumors and wild speculation, of course, but coupled with the reports that Richard had been receiving while still in the Holy Land, it was disheartening to those who called England home.

It meant little to me, but because I cared for Robin, Much, and Allen it mattered to me that their homeland was in distress.

The winter months passed slowly, but eventually warmth returned to the air and our pace quickened.

Chapter 15

AFTER A DAY OF extensive traveling, Richard asked Much to hurry ahead to procure rooms for the night at a village we could see in the distance.

"Of course, Sire," Much answered dutifully. Before he could go anywhere, Robin and Allen clamped their hands over his mouth.

"How many times do we have to tell you?" Allen asked.

When they'd removed their hands Much looked rather sheepish. "I am sorry. I forgot."

Much set off, his shoulders downcast and his eyes on his feet.

"You shouldn't be so harsh," I told Allen.

"He's lucky there was no one nearby to hear him."

We kept walking down the road toward the city as the sun lowered itself into the horizon, hues of red, orange, and gold spread out around it.

Much disappeared ahead of us, hurrying along at a faster pace.

"How much farther do you suppose we have to travel?" Allen asked Richard.

"A good distance," Richard replied.

"Don't start up with your complaining again," Robin teased, playfully shoving Allen's shoulder.

As I watched their banter, I worried for Much. He was uncomfortable when he'd left us, and I hoped he wasn't internalizing his mistake and fixating on it. He had a bad habit of only noticing his faults. More than that, he had a worse habit of believing people when they belittled him.

I tried not to be frustrated with Robin for not noticing his friend's discomfort, but I couldn't help but shoot him a glare.

He didn't notice that either.

Much soon returned to us and we entered the village together, allowing Much to lead us to the inn he had chosen. Richard stopped outside, eyeing the building for a moment.

"I believe you've found us a good place, Much. I wasn't sure our mouse could manage the mission, but you did."

I winced at Richard's use of my nickname for Much, knowing it was far more condescending from him than I had ever intended it to be, but Much merely said, "Thank you, Sire."

"Much!" Robin cast a glance down the street at the villagers moving about their own business. "How many times do we have to tell you?"

"I am sorry, it was the slip of the tongue again."

"You have to stop doing that."

Richard placed a hand on Robin's arm. "Let us move inside. We don't need to draw more attention with this argument than his off-hand comment would have done on its own."

I didn't see anyone paying special attention to us as I glanced about the street, but we all hurried inside and to our rooms for more privacy all the same.

Tempers were flaring as we moved to our rooms, but after a brief argument over Much's slip up, we went down to the common room to eat some supper. Much remained downcast throughout the meal, and Allen whispered insults. He didn't discuss what had happened directly—presumably so he would not giveaway to the other people gathered in the common room who we were traveling with—but he still managed to quietly berate Much for his mistake.

Richard decided we would leave that village as soon as the sun was up in case anyone had heard Much, or Allen's whispered frustration.

Later that night when the others were preparing to sleep, I pulled Robin into the hallway to speak to him.

"You are too hard on Much."

"You mean with the Richard thing? He has to stop, Dusty, or he is going to give us away." Robin glanced down both sides of the hallway and crossed his arms.

"I still believe you are being too harsh with him. He isn't as presumptuous as you and Allen. He knows his place in society because *your* father drilled it into him. That is not his fault."

"But he knows the desperate need for secrecy here." Robin's voice was low and soft. "He should be able to overcome whatever excessive humility he has and just call Richard by his name."

"It is a lifelong habit and not easily broken," I replied. "He doesn't forget out of malice. And your constant reprimands and frustration are hurting him. You are his best friend. Try and act like it, for Much's sake. He hardly knows how to act when you don't approve of him."

"Much would tell me if I overstepped our friendship."

"No, he wouldn't." I crossed my arms, shaking my head. "I don't think you know your friend as well as you think you do if you believe for one second that Much would ever tell you when you offended him."

Robin frowned, his blue eyes darkening. "I've known Much his entire life; he's my brother. I do realize that he doesn't have as much self-esteem or confidence as he probably should and I do know the role my father played in shaping him into the humble man that he is. But I also *know* him—better than anyone —so don't presume otherwise, Dusty."

Robin returned to his room in a huff, and I felt I had most definitely taken a misstep. I didn't want to cause more fights. I had merely wanted Robin to be more gentle with Much. With a sigh of my own I retired to bed.

Early the next morning we set out; Richard so eager to leave that we did not bother to eat breakfast first. There were few people in the street so early in the morning and those who were up and about paid little attention to the group heading out of town.

As they passed the last house and left the village behind, I could see my companions relaxing. They had all been on edge, despite the fact that we had no proof anyone had heard Much's mistake.

The sound of hoofbeats approaching from behind caught our attention as we walked, and I turned to see what travelers might be in such a hurry. Richard turned as well and then stopped walking altogether.

"This does not look good."

What we saw as we turned was a company of soldiers on horseback charging down the road toward us. Robin and Allen drew their swords immediately, moving instinctively in front of Richard.

"There are twenty-seven of them," Allen said. "We're outnumbered by a large margin."

"Doesn't matter," Robin replied. "We defend the king regardless."

"Robin." Richard's voice was barely more than a whisper. "There is no need to die here. We will see what they want."

The men galloped up and soon surrounded us, every sharp sword and pointed spear pointed directly at our group.

"King Richard the Lion-Heart," the leader of the group called out. "You have been a hard man to find since your disappearance after the end of the Crusade. There is no need to hide your identity any longer. We have orders to arrest you and bring you to Durnstein castle."

"Who gave you such an order?" Robin demanded.

"We come by order of Duke Leopold of Austria, who is most displeased with the King of England."

"You cannot arrest a Crusader," I said. It was something I'd heard from Emil, and I hoped these men would abide by it. "It's an affront to the church of the Holy Roman Emperor, is it not?"

"We'll see about that," the man scoffed.

Robin and Allen clearly wanted to defend Richard, but he surrendered without a fight so there was little they could do but follow his example.

The soldiers soon took everyone's swords, bows, and daggers and then bound our hands behind our backs.

As a soldier roughly grabbed my shoulders and put me in line behind Much, I leaned forward to whisper, "This is not your fault."

The way his shoulders fell and his head hung low told me he did not believe me.

We were soon all bound and the soldiers began to lead us down the road once more.

During the long march to the Durnstein castle the soldiers took delight in mocking us, but I did my best to ignore them. I could tell that Much was taking it all to heart, however. The way Allen's eyes flashed and darkened by turn as he watched Much told me he took it all to heart as well, and undoubtedly blamed Much for the situation we were now in.

It was a week before we arrived at Durnstein castle, where we were promptly thrown into a cell in the dungeon. The long hallway on a lower level of the castle was lined with rooms that were used as cells, and it was into one of these that we were all escorted. The cell was roughly six feet across both ways, with stone walls on either side and along the back, with a dirt floor and an iron gate to shut us in.

The prospect of sharing the cramped space with these four men was not a pleasant one, but I'd been in dire situations before and survived.

As we were shoved into the prison, one guard caught sight of the pouch of herbs still on my belt.

"What's this?" He ripped it free before I could stop him.

"It's just medicinal herbs," I said.

"You don't need those," the guard grinned, pushing me toward the cell.

"Please!" I held out my hand, suddenly feeling the urge to beg. That pouch was so much more than herbs.

It was the hours I'd spent healing during the Crusades, it was my friendship with Robin, Much, and Allen blooming after I healed Robin. It was Daniyah teaching me as a child how to use the herbs properly, it was my life; my past, my present, my future. He couldn't take that from me!

Another soldier moved forward to push me away from the one with my herbs while a third slammed the cell door shut and began to lock it. I could feel a lump forming in my throat as tears pricked my eyes.

That pouch was my last link to home.

I was never going to see my homeland again, never going to see my parents, my sister, Daniyah...

I had nothing left.

Robin's hand on my arm suddenly jolted me from my painful thoughts.

I had not lost everything; I still had those that I had learned to love here by my side.

There was room for us to stand and sit in the cell but with only inches between us. We could not all lay down at the same time, which made sleeping an interesting endeavor. I dreaded the days to come. Being a woman surrounded by men was something I had grown used to since my family had died and I'd been on my own, but I had always been able to find privacy when I needed it. That would not be the case in this cell.

No one but my companions knew that I was a girl, and it seemed none of us were willing to disclose that fact now that we were prisoners of the Duke of Austria, so I was given the same treatment as the rest of them.

Much sank into one of the back corners of the cell, looking around at all of us in the dim lighting. "I am sorry."

"There's nothing to be done about it now," Robin said with a sigh. He stood by the bars of the cell, glaring at the guards at the far end of the dungeon.

Allen crossed his arms. "He could have listened to us in the first place and just called Richard by his name like everyone else."

"Leave him be." I glared at Allen, willing him to be more kind. "You've made mistakes, too."

"It's not my fault we're in this prison!"

"Maybe this is where God wants us to be for now, have you thought about that." I knew Allen wouldn't have considered any such a thing, but I was fed up with him bullying Much.

For a moment, silence greeted my question, and then Richard tilted his head to one side as he regarded me. "God? What does he have to do with us being thrown into prison?"

"I believe God is in control of everything that happens to us. So He has a lot to do with us being thrown into prison. Maybe there is something for us to learn here, maybe He wants us to witness to the prison guards and spread His love here, maybe something far worse would have befallen us if we'd continued on our journey and He is protecting us from whatever it might have been. There are endless possibilities."

Richard looked unconvinced and I shrugged. "Maybe whatever this experience turns out to be will strengthen our character in some fashion, or draw us closer in our relationship to the Father."

I glanced toward Much, knowing he was the only person present who could understand what I meant. "Who knows?"

"What are you going on about," Allen asked. "We're not Friars or monks or whatever."

"No, but we're Christians."

Robin shook his head. "Not like you are. You take everything far too seriously."

"Robin—"

"Not now, Dusty." Robin shook his head at me. "We're stuck in a prison and really ought to be working on how to get out, not arguing over theology that doesn't matter."

"It does matter," I said. "It matters more than anything else in this world. Your life depends upon it."

Allen rolled his eyes. "Now really, Dusty, don't be so melodramatic."

I sighed. I knew there was nothing more I could say. Allen wasn't ready to hear the truth. So I began to pray for him, and the rest of my companions as well. I prayed the Lord would soften their hearts to Him and open their ears to the truth that I was trying to speak to them. And I prayed that Much would have the courage to speak up about his newly found faith.

Robin loved and trusted Much; his faith might be precisely the influence Robin needed to open his own mind to the possibility of his need for Christ.

The days of our confinement passed in relative darkness— the dungeons being only partially lit for the convenience of the guards at the end of the hall. Food was brought at least once a day; an unpleasant assortment of moldy bread and rotting meat. In those first weeks, we ate very little of it. But hunger soon overcame our misgivings. I learned to be quite proficient at picking the maggots off of my bread in order to eat it.

The Duke of Austria himself made a habit of visiting our prison cell so he could gloat over King Richard. To Richard's credit, he rarely offered insults of his own, but Robin and Allen were quick to fire back at the Duke.

I spent most of these encounters praying for patience. I had plenty of things I wanted to say to the Duke and to my own companions as well, but I held my tongue and chose grace instead.

The only truly interesting piece of information gained from the Duke's visits was that he was holding King Richard for ransom. The prospect of someone paying that ransom and getting us out of prison was our only hope.

Allen ignored Much most days, but there were some days that he would turn the full brunt of his frustration on Much and yell and fume his insults across the cell. Much stayed quietly in the back corner of the cell, rarely leaving the darkness; his shoulders slumped, his face downcast. That he felt guilty was obvious, and Allen's attacks did nothing to assuage his feelings.

I wished there was a way to orchestrate privacy so that I could speak to Much without Allen overhearing, or speak to

Robin again about standing up for Much rather than belittling him.

Robin, however, soon proved a better friend than I hoped.

One night after we'd shifted around to try and find comfortable positions to sleep and settled in for the night, I heard Robin's voice softly break the silence.

"You cannot continue to blame yourself, Much. What's done is done."

I could hear both Allen and Richard snoring, and I imagined Robin had waited to speak to Much until he was sure the rest of us were sleeping so they could have some privacy. I wished I was asleep for that reason, but it was impossible not to eavesdrop in the limited space that we had.

"I truly am sorry. I never intended to get us thrown in this prison, and if there was some way that I could get us out, I would."

"I know. You don't have to apologize. Though I feel that I owe you an apology."

"For what?"

"For not being a good friend to you these last few weeks."

"How so?"

"I have taken out my frustration on you; being locked up is not sitting well with me. But you deserve more from me than to be insulted and belittled."

Much was silent for a moment, and then I heard his softly spoken, "I forgive you, Robin."

"I'm sure you do, because you're a saint, but I am sorry for it all the same.

I was glad Robin proved to be a better man than I gave him credit for, and proud of Much for extending grace—though Much would hardly have done anything else. I wished there could be reconciliation with everyone.

As the weeks passed, it seemed Allen was unlikely to ever forgive him. The hungrier and dirtier we all became, the angrier Allen appeared to be.

Robin and Richard had better attitudes toward Much with every passing day we suffered together, but Allen began to ignore Much's existence as far as he could. The few times he deigned to speak to him was only to scold and complain of Much's stupidity getting us caught.

Chapter 16

TO FILL OUR long empty hours I began to sit beside Much and teach him about my healing practices again. Without my pouch and the physical herbs on hand, it was difficult. But I described to him best as I could what I used and how I used it.

We also spoke of spiritual matters as well as we could; Much was eager to learn more about his Savior, but our conversations met with much ridicule from the others in the cell.

One day when our rations were brought, I began to methodically pick away maggots and pinch off the largest pieces of mold on my bread before I would deign to eat it. Suddenly Allen heaved his bread toward Much's head. The green chunk of bread hit Much across the face.

"You can have my portion of that rot," Allen hissed, crossing his arms. "It's your fault we're here."

"Allen!" I could not believe what he'd done. I stared at him, my heart racing as anger flashed through me.

Richard sighed heavily, looking about at the group. "This is no one's fault but my own. We are here, not because Much misspoke, but because I alienated Duke Leopold at Acre. If the Duke was not angry with me, he would not have seen fit to throw us in prison as we crossed his lands."

"It matters not," I said. "Nothing can be done about it now. Laying blame is not helping anyone."

Allen huffed loudly from the corner of the cell where he was sitting, but he said nothing.

"We have to stay together," I said. "We are all that we have left. If we turn on each other, we'll have nothing."

The fight did not progress, and for that I was grateful. There were times when Allen would go after Much and Robin would get fed up with him; usually Richard and I had to intervene before Robin and Allen tore each other apart, while Much shrank into his back corner of the cell. Today though things had settled down before anything got too far.

Life continued on in the same manner for some weeks, nothing of interest happening during the day except the changing of the guards at the end of the hall, the occasional scurrying of rats, and Allen's perpetual frustration with Much.

We all grew increasingly dirty as time went on as there was no chance of having a bath while locked in the prison cell. There was also little chance of relieving ourselves with any dignity. We'd designated one corner of the cell for that purpose, but still we all felt filthy and we all reeked.

The men began to grow out their beards the longer we were cooped up in there, and the guards took notice that I did not.

"We've got a little boy in here, too young to even shave!" they would mock. I let them say what they pleased; I had no intention of telling them I was not, in fact, a little boy too young to shave. Given our treatment thus far, I did not trust the men of that castle to treat me with any respect should they realize that I was a woman.

One night after everyone else had gone to sleep, Much nudged my shoulder with his foot. I pulled myself into a sitting position, listening to Allen and Richard snoring. Robin's even breathing told me he was still asleep as well, but I was careful as I adjusted my position so I didn't accidentally kick him.

"What is it, Much?"

"I wanted to tell you…I mean, have you noticed that Allen wasn't yelling at me today?"

"He ignores you fairly frequently."

"No, I mean…I apologized again last night. Allen hasn't been able to forgive me since we landed in this prison so I thought I should try and make amends."

"And he forgave you?"

"Yes. He even went so far as to apologize for the way he has been treating me."

"I am glad of that. He has been rather cruel. If we're going to get out of this then we need to work together. It pained me to see two of my friends so out of sorts with one another. And then, too, it is our duty as followers of Christ to live at peace with those around us as much as we are able. So I am glad that the two of you have worked through your differences."

"I am glad, too. The more Allen was angry with me, the more he and Robin would fight. We were tearing the whole group apart."

"You were not tearing anything apart, Much. You asked for pardon and forgiveness. It was Allen who was causing the rift. However, as the two of you have made up, I will not be one to hold this against Allen. We all have to be better or we won't survive this."

Our days continued to pass in relative boredom. We could not live in such close quarters without a few arguments arising between us, but for the most part peace was restored. Yet with the peace came the quiet—there was nothing to occupy our time, and conversation was limited as we soon grew tired of the same old topics.

I continued to teach Much about my healing skills, and about God as well. One day after we had talked I started writing out scriptures using my finger to carve letters into the dirt floor.

Writing them out in Arabic reminded me of home, and of learning with Daniyah, and the first time my fingers traced the familiar curves of the script of my mother tongue, a lump lodged in my throat and tears began to cleanse the dirt and grime from my face.

"What are you drawing?" Allen asked.

I took a deep breath to calm my emotions before I answered him. "I am writing."

"Writing what?" Much asked.

"Scripture."

"Do you think the next poor prisoner who gets thrown in this cell is going to read it and be blessed?" Allen asked, his voice dripping in sarcasm.

"No, Allen. I am writing these Scriptures to remind myself of what the Lord says, not someone else."

Robin scooted closer to see what I was writing. "Is that…?"

"Arabic," I answered his unfinished question.

"Can you teach me?"

"To read Arabic?"

"Read it, speak it, write it, anything! I picked up a few words in the Holy Land. It could be fun to learn more."

I studied him in the dim light, unsure what to make of his enthusiasm.

"Come on, Dusty, we have nothing else to entertain us!" Robin grinned at me, wiggling his eyebrows. "You know you want to."

I shrugged. "Alright."

And so I began to fill our endless hours with lessons. Robin had a keen mind and learned well, but not quickly. Much and Richard listened as well, asking questions now and again. Allen spent his days making fun of us, but I could tell he was also listening to my Arabic lessons and watching when I drew in the dirt.

Robin's carefree spirit willingly put up with Allen's abuse and returned it in kind, but Much seemed to shrink from their teasing. I found them amusing—at times, perhaps annoying—yet even when I felt a pull to join in their laughter, I could not.

Even then, after the Lord had used Much and Robin and the others to chip away at my bitterness and the walls I had put up to avoid vulnerability, I was still hesitant to commit myself too much. When speaking of Scripture and God Himself, I could open up to Much fully I had noticed, but on any other topic I was more reticent.

Much was an attentive student when we discussed our faith, though Allen and Richard still teased and mocked us. Robin would occasionally join them, but more often than not I saw him listening quietly, though he never joined our discussions unless I'd write out the Scriptures in Arabic.

The summer passed away while we were stuck in the relative darkness of that cramped cell, wiling away our hours with lessons on my favorite topics; my faith, my healing, and my homeland and native language.

After another visit from the Duke wherein he and the residents of our cell had an insult casting contest, Robin threw himself onto the floor of the cell in one of his melodramatic moods and groaned loudly.

"I give up!"

"On what?" Richard asked.

"Everything. We'll never get out."

"Nonsense," Richard replied. "The Duke has said he's holding us for ransom, has he not? I believe he is capable of doing something so treacherous as holding a king for ransom. And if he is, my people will pay."

"But your brother is running your kingdom, remember?" Robin put in. "Even if you have forgotten, I can still hear the voices of those who spoke of the terrible things that were happening in England by the hand of Prince John. I still recall the day you informed me your brother was most likely involved in the murder of my own father!"

"I have not forgotten all the reports," Richard said. "But I do believe the people will pay the ransom. Even if they will not, my mother Queen Eleanor will see to it that we are released. My sister Joan will be equally anxious to get you out of prison."

His mention of Joan brought a smile to my face. She was the first to push past my barriers and become a friend after I'd cut off that side of myself—even from me. I missed her exuberance.

Winter came, but there was little change to our situation except the temperature of the cell. The cool stone walls grew colder and we huddled together, shivering as our teeth chattered and we desperately tried to glean some warmth from one another.

Most days we could easily see our own breath form in the air as we exhaled. Allen's complaining became more consistent, but now that it was focused on the weather and our situation rather than on Much, I had more patience with him.

Both Robin and Allen were growing fed up enough with our situation that they began to dream of ways to get us out of our predicament.

"We know the guards' schedules at this point," Robin pointed out. "We ought to be able to use that to our advantage somehow…"

"But we're stuck in this cell," Richard said. "Knowing when the guards change out changes nothing for us."

Richard's melancholy did not dissuade Robin, and he and Allen would often discuss their ideas for escape. They never came up with any solid plans, however, so I had little faith in their endeavors.

Richard grew sick, likely due to the long exposure to the freezing weather coupled with the terrible diet and lack of exercise and sunlight. I was surprised more of us did not grow ill.

One day as Richard's wheezing rattled through the silence of our cell, I shifted to sit beside him.

"Would you mind if I prayed for you?"

Richard eyed me for a moment and then shrugged. "What do you suppose that will do?"

"There's no telling," I said, feeling a spark of excitement growing inside me. "My God is the master Healer. It is possible He will see fit to work a miracle here despite my lack of herbs and medicinal tools."

Richard shrugged again, so I took that as acquiescence. I reached over to lay a hand on his thin, frail shoulder and then began to pray.

In the days that followed, I prayed over him constantly and ever so slowly his illness began to fade. I was hopeful the small miracle might point my companions to the power of the God I served, which in turn might lead them to the truth. But only Much seemed awed by our Father's showing of healing.

The cold weather began to abate, and I assumed spring was upon us. I missed the outside world—the shining sun as I sat upon my father's shoulders when he picked dates, the feel of wind caressing my cheek as he raced me to the river, the starry night sky shining over us as we sang together.

The longer we stayed in the cold, dirty cell the more I longed for the days of my youth when I had no real care in the world.

I longed to be free of the cramped, fetid cell. But even if we did get out, I would never get my father back. He was lost to me...

One day during their planning sessions, Allen suggested to Robin that we dig through the back wall.

"It is out of the line of sight of the guards," Allen whispered, his eyes darting toward the iron gate and the hallway of cells beyond it. "We can see them, and they us, only when we're up at the front of the cell."

"But it would take so long," I said. "And when our meals are brought, and when the Duke visits, we'll be found out."

"Not to mention the difficulty in getting through the stone first," Robin pointed out. "And we don't know what's beyond the wall. You expect to, what? Tunnel to the surface? We're in the dungeons, likely underground…I don't see how that could work, Allen."

I continued to teach the group to speak and read Arabic. Much was slow to pick it up, though he was always attentive. Robin and Allen began to have more success. Richard seemed to have lost all interest in my lessons.

In truth, he seemed to have lost all interest in life at all. He was always apathetic towards Robin and Allen's wild schemes of escape, never smiled or laughed anymore, and now he didn't care to listen to my lessons. I didn't take it personally, but I was concerned for his state of mind.

One day as I sat beside Much at the back of the cell telling him about my favorite places around Darum that I'd go to in order to collect my herbs, I leaned against the back wall. Much watched me with rapt attention, as he always did.

After a moment, I felt a trickling of something cold by my ear. I turned around and squinted in the dim light toward the source. There was mud oozing from between the stones on the wall.

I reached up and pressed my hand against the stone. It sank into the wall, mud squeezing out of the wall all around it and covering my hand. I turned quickly, reaching out my foot and tapping Robin's leg.

I jerked my head toward the back wall, and he scooted closer to see what I was looking at.

"It's the moisture," I whispered. "It must have snowed through the winter, and given way to rain now that it's spring. It's softening the earth."

"So we *can* dig," Allen grinned, leaning around Robin to see what I was pointing at.

"But we're so far beneath the castle," Robin said thoughtfully, wiping his own hand slowly across the back wall and watching the stones shift and mud ooze beneath his fingers. "If we dig…we'll have miles, perhaps, to dig to the top. Where will all that dirt go? It won't fit in this cell. Once it spills out, the guards will notice."

"They'll notice before that, when they bring food and see us digging along the back wall," I said.

"But we can try," Allen said. "It's something; it's all we've got."

Robin shrugged. "We can certainly try."

Much shifted closer to the wall, running his own hand through the mud. "We cannot be too deep if the moisture on the surface is affecting this wall."

"It is odd," Robin agreed. "Allen's right; it's our only shot. I'm not so sure it will work, but we have to try something."

After that we began to work on the back wall, loosening the largest chunks of rock in order to use them as digging tools before carving into the wall. We had no idea what was on the other side of that wall, but it was our best shot. We picked a low section of the wall, one we could easily sit in front of and cover whenever food was brought to the cell. The idea was to shift the mud into the refuse corner of the cell where it would blend into the pile of brown already reeking there—in the dim light, the guards would not notice the difference, and as long as someone sat in front of the hole they would not see that either.

It wasn't a full-proof plan, but it was the best we had and it gave us hope.

Richard, however, showed no interest in our endeavors.

Every night we worked at our hole, grateful that it was blocked from view by the other stone walls of the cell. The guards could not see it from their watch at the end of the hall, and we always covered it when our rations were brought to the cell. The prospect of being able to eat real food if our plan succeeded made my mouth water.

One night, as I shoved my stone through the mud, dragging it inward and then pushing the mud toward the refuse corner of the cell, Robin gave a start. He and Allen had been working beside me and then suddenly Robin's hand disappeared completely through the wall.

He glanced at Allen, and then the two of them began digging with a vengeance, pushing the earth as much as digging it out until there was a hole large enough for Robin to shove his head through. I sat back and let them work, my heart pounding wildly in my chest. Was this going to work after all?

Robin's voice filtered back through the wall, muffled and distorted. I could not make out what he said.

Allen whacked his arm. "What?"

Robin pulled his muddied head back into the cell. "There's a hallway of sorts, a tunnel." He kept his voice low, presumably to avoid getting the attention of our guards.

"A tunnel? That is definitely our way out," Allen said.

"Why is there a tunnel by the dungeons?" Much asked.

"Castles have plenty of secrets," Robin said, winking at Much. "Ours certainly does, if you recall."

"We have to be quick," I said. "We have to carve a big enough hole to fit through, get everyone out, and then get far enough away that we won't be caught once the guards bring our food, realize what's happened, and come after us."

"It's risky, but we can do it," Robin said. "We'll be fast." He immediately started digging again.

Robin and Allen furiously worked at the wall and I moved to sit beside Richard. "We have a way out."

"So I see."

His eyes were almost vacant as he watched Allen and Robin. I wondered what he was thinking. I could only hope getting out in the fresh air and away from the Duke would lift his spirits.

I glanced toward Much and noticed he was asleep. As more and more mud fell into the cell as Robin and Allen worked, the hole began to take on a life of its own. As the integrity of the wall failed, the stones and mud began to sort of melt towards the floor, causing the hole to crack wide open.

198

"Time to go," Robin grinned, winking at me.

I worried briefly if we were about to bring the whole castle down on ourselves.

I shifted across the cell to where Much was fast asleep and began to shake his shoulder. "Much?" He stirred beneath my hand, his eyes blinking slowly. "We need to go."

"Go?"

"To England! Wake up."

Much slowly sat up. Before any of us could move through the hole, however, Richard spoke. "Robin?"

"Yes, Sire?"

"Your plan is risky."

"We know that, Richard."

"And you know that if you are caught—which is likely—you will undoubtedly be killed by the Duke."

"We are well aware, but we have to get out."

"I am no good to England dead, Robin. I cannot come with you."

"Richard!"

"No, do not try to argue with me. I cannot take the risk."

"It is dangerous," I said. He was being cautious, but he might have a point. "Perhaps if we wait, the ransom will be paid."

Allen crossed his arms. "I refuse to be too afraid to do this. I will not stay in this prison."

"Robin is no use to England—or Marian—dead either," I said. "If we stay, we have no risk of being killed by the Duke."

I didn't want to stay by any means, but I did want us to consider every option. Even so, my heart was trying to pound out of my chest as I thought about the blue sky above me and the wind on my face once more.

"Just of dying from the cold, the lack of real nourishing food, the fact we haven't seen the sun in who knows how long," Allen began to tick reasons off of the fingers of one hand.

"You have to go, Robin," Richard said. "We heard many terrible reports about what is happening in England. I believe my people are suffering. But I cannot leave here and risk it. I will wait for the ransom. Yet I cannot leave my people to their fate, whatever it is. You have to go."

"Richard—"

"No, Robin. Do not try to change my mind. Just go. I'm entrusting England to you. Keep my people safe."

Robin hesitated, but the loud guffaw from one of the guards stationed at the end of the hall set everyone's hearts racing, and Allen immediately pushed through the hole that had been created in the back of the cell. The guard seemed to be merely laughing at his companion, but it was best not to wait around and see.

Robin slowly reached out to clasp Richard's hand. "I will look after England. I promise, I will."

"I trust you."

"And I will see to it that your ransom is paid as swiftly as I can."

"Go, Robin! You are needed in England."

Robin squeezed through the small opening after Allen, and then Much followed suit. I pushed through last of all. I don't know what I expected to find, but the reality was merely darkness. I could see even less in the tunnel we'd found that I had in the dimly lit cell.

"We have to hurry," I said. "Who knows how soon the guards will notice what has transpired."

"Where are we?" Much asked.

"In a passageway in the castle?" Robin's voice carried through the tunnel. "The wall is clearly the back of our cell, the whole tunnel seems to be encased in dirt…there's no stone work on the walls or floor that I can see or touch."

"Where does it lead is a better question," I said.

"We will find out when we follow it," Robin replied. I reached out, my hand coming to rest on Much's shoulder as he walked. I didn't want to lose track of my friends. A moment later I felt Allen's hand grasp my own shoulder. We moved into the deeper darkness in that manner, the feel of Much's shoulder beneath my fingers, and Allen's hand weighing on my own shoulder my only anchors to reality in the world of darkness and silence.

I was worried for Richard. Leaving him behind did not seem like the wisest move, but he had chosen his path, and he had insisted Robin go. Much would always go wherever Robin did, and if my family was leaving then I was going with them. I owed nothing to Richard himself.

As we moved through the darkness, I became aware of the fact that it didn't matter if my eyes were open or closed, I could see nothing. I wondered how Robin was walking so confidently ahead of us. Much, too, seemed not to falter a single step, although that could have been due to Robin's lead.

After a time, however, the light began to grow dim rather than pitch black, and I could soon make out the vague shape of Much's head in front of mine.

A moment later the tunnel began to be more visible. I could see the walls beside us and the low dirt ceiling above, as well as the hard-packed earth we walked on. I kept my hand on Much's shoulder still, but his guide was no longer necessary.

Slowly, the light grew brighter until we reached the end of the tunnel where torches were lit and hanging in sconces along the wall. Passages branched off in several directions, most of them lit with torches, and the dirt floor gave way to a stone pavement.

"I think we've come to the portion of these tunnels people use," I commented, wincing at the brightness of the torchlight.

"For what purpose though?" Allen asked.

"Back home, where Much and I are from, there's a castle that is filled with secret passages," Robin said. "They were originally built for the nobility to have ways to escape if their fortress was overrun. I imagine these hold a similar purpose for the Duke."

"Which way do we go?" Much asked.

Robin shrugged and started walking, throwing his hands to either side. "I'm sure this leads somewhere."

The passage sloped gently upward, and before long it stopped at a door. Robin paused, glanced silently at us and raised a finger to his lips. Then he tried the handle.

It was unlocked.

Slowly Robin pushed the door inward. My heart was drumming an erratic beat inside my chest and my palms grew sweaty. We were nearly outside! And yet, we were unarmed, malnourished, and in need of proper sleep. What Robin expected us to do if we happened upon guards or nobles living in the castle, I wasn't sure. We clearly couldn't fight in our condition.

Robin glanced past the door as he slid it open, and then he visibly relaxed. He disappeared into the room a moment later and Much followed without hesitation. I was more cautious, but I crept forward as Allen finally let go of my shoulder and followed behind me.

Past the door was a small room with no furnishings, smaller than the cell we'd been cramped together in for so many months. Robin was already at the other side of the room pushing open another door to the hallways beyond. It was wide, well-lit, with a stone floor and many wooden doors on either side at various intervals.

"I think we're in the actual castle," I whispered. The secret passage, whatever it was used for, was behind us. Now we just had to avoid running into anyone as we tried to find a way out of the castle proper.

Robin nodded at me, putting a finger to his lips again. He began moving down the hallway, and we followed after him. I doubted he'd ever been here before or had any knowledge of the layout of the castle, but we all followed him regardless.

Judging by the grey light of dawn creeping through the windows we passed, it was quite early in the morning. It was likely most residents of the castle were still asleep. We saw few people as they traveled through the unfamiliar hallways. It was surprisingly easy for our group to keep out of sight until we found a door out to the courtyard of the castle.

From there we crept along the edge of the courtyard near the wall, keeping out of sight—hopefully—of any soldiers that might be on lookout or patrol. My heartbeat grew wilder with every step we took, but the moment we hit that courtyard I breathed in the deepest breath I had in a year.

When we reached the guard house near the gate on the opposite side of the courtyard as the castle we had just escaped, Robin ducked low to avoid the windows, and slowly crept along the ground.

I held my breath, glancing between Robin and the windows of the castle that we were now in view of.

He raised himself slightly, peeked in the nearest window of the guardhouse, and then grinned and glanced back toward the rest of us waiting at the wall. Robin mimed sleeping gestures, still grinning, and then stood up and sprinted past the guardhouse.

Much sprinted after him a moment later.

Allen glanced at me, grinned widely, and made a break for it. I took a deep breath, relishing the fresh, clean air that didn't smell of refuse and then sprinted after the others.

We didn't stop running once we were out of the gate, but simply kept going as far as our weak legs would carry us.

Eventually, Robin led us stumbling toward an outcropping of trees. Much collapsed onto the ground wheezing, his hand holding his side.

"What's...the...plan..." Allen panted as he sank to the ground beside Much.

"We have no money, no food." I glanced around at the group; Much and Allen on the ground, Robin leaning against the tree. All three covered in mud and refuse, with ratty clothes and overgrown hair, and bones sticking out in places they should not.

I was sure I looked no better. "We're weak and malnourished. What is the plan, Robin?"

"We go home."

"Yes, that much is obvious. But how do you plan to do that?"

"Very carefully," Robin said. His confidence and simplicity was rather annoying given our dire situation. He looked around at the trees and then shrugged. "We press forward. Maybe we can get work in a village in exchange for food and lodging, and then we keep traveling onward."

"And if we get arrested because the Duke sends people after us?" I asked, trying to be pragmatic. "Or if we get arrested because the village we beg for work in doesn't take kindly to vagabonds dressed in refuse-covered rags?"

"We'll deal with the situations as they arise," Robin said. "As it stands right now…we can sit in this bit of trees until we starve to death, we can go back to the castle and turn ourselves in, or we can press forward. I vote for the latter."

He was right, of course. We had no other option but than to keep going and pray for the best. I took a moment to do just that as I caught my breath from our run. Whatever the next step in our journey was, I knew Who was watching over us.

Chapter 17

AFTER OUR SHORT REST, we set off again. My feet dragged along the grassy hills we traversed, as it took every ounce of willpower I possessed just to keep moving. I longed for sustenance. And a bath. And what I wouldn't give for a bed...

Robin moved resolutely in front of us, determined to find us a better place than an outcropping of trees to truly stop and rest. The rest of us followed more slowly. I could hear my stomach growling. My tongue was thick and dry, but I was used to that sensation by now—we rarely had enough water while living in the prison cell at Durnstein Castle.

I glanced up at the sky, enjoying the vibrant blue shade and the puffy white clouds that drifted across its surface.

We were free.

My eyes still squinted at the brightness of the sunlight after so long in the dark prison. It made my eyes water, but I was glad of the sensation. If it meant I wasn't trapped in darkness, I wouldn't mind the slight pain to my eyes. They would surely adjust given enough time.

After a few hours, a town came into view in the distance, one large enough that it had a wall surrounding a portion of it and rows upon rows of buildings. It was by no means as large as some of the cities I had visited back home, but it was more than a simple village. A road came winding out of a gate in the city wall, snaking its way across the hillside—nowhere near where we had been walking across the countryside.

Robin came to a full stop and we all hesitated, watching him. He had his hands on his his hips as he surveyed the town in the distance.

"Do we go in?" Allen asked.

"We reek," Robin replied with a frown. "Dusty was right; we'll be no better than street scum to anyone of prestige. We'll get thrown out."

"It is always possible there will be people of compassion," I said, trying to counter my earlier pessimistic comments. "If there is an abbey or monastery we could start there."

For a moment we stood silently. I studied the buildings in the distance, wondering what we might find when we went in. I sent a quick prayer heavenward for guidance.

"Let's go in," Robin said at last. "We can't just stand here all day."

He set off toward the road to the left of us that led into the town, and I moved to keep pace with him, Allen at my side.

We reached the road within a few minutes, and made our way toward the city itself. When we entered, there were people moving about the streets going about their own business—most of whom stared at us.

Robin gave a wave and moved to speak to a man nearby, but he hurriedly turned aside and the other onlookers pointedly ignored us as well.

"We're disgusting and look ridiculous," Allen sighed, scratching his beard.

A tall man, muscular, with a sword at his hip, soon approached us.

He demanded something of us, but he spoke in a gruff language that I did not understand.

Robin replied in the same tongue, and I watched the man's face closely. He was studying us now, his eyebrows rising to his hairline as he took in what must be a rather disgusting sight.

Robin said something else, and the man responded, his face betraying nothing of what he might be thinking of the four vagabonds standing in front of him in tattered, reeking clothes, covered in grime and refuse and who knows what all.

Robin and the man continued their discourse, and I shifted my feet a bit, curious as to what Robin might be saying to persuade the man to help us. My legs wobbled beneath me and it was everything I could do to remain upright.

"If you are Crusaders," the man said, suddenly switching to speaking in French, which was a language that I could understand. Most Crusaders I'd dealt with over the years spoke French or English, so I'd learned both rather well. "That remains to be determined. In any event, I am Isenbern, the younger son of Count Jodok. I have charge over this town and surrounding lands, and I do respect the Crusaders, if that is indeed who you are."

"What can we do to assure you of our honesty?" Robin asked, also switching languages.

Isenbern studied him for a moment, his nose wrinkling. "I'm not taking you into my home just yet, so I'll ask questions here. What is your name?"

"I am Robin, Earl of Locksley," Robin replied. "This is my…" Robin glanced toward Much and his brows grew together for a moment. "My servant Much, my traveling companions, Allen and Dusty."

Isenbern nodded slowly, crossing his arms.

"Much and I met Allen in the city of Dover, just before we set out on the Crusades. We traveled to Sicily, Cyprus, and eventually to Acre where we joined the fight in the Holy Land."

Isenbern seemed reluctant still, but he uncrossed his arms and turned and began walking down the street. Robin walked beside him—though Isenbern kept a distance between them, likely due to Robin's stench. I glanced at Allen and Much, and then we all took off after them.

Robin and Allen began to speak to Lord Isenbern about our group's exploits during the Crusades, undoubtedly trying to prove we were, indeed, who Robin said we were.

When we reached a large manor on the end of a street, Isenbern paused. "I would like to continue this discussion once you are…less disgusting. I'll send my servant out who can take you through the servant quarters to get you washed up, and then you can join me in the house proper."

Isenbern disappeared inside the front door.

"This is going easier than I thought it might," Robin said with a satisfied grin.

"Assuming he does send his servant for us, and assuming he doesn't decide to kill us once we're inside," Allen said, "and assuming—"

"Okay, okay." Robin held up his hands. "Be alert, of course. Though without weapons I suppose there's only so much we can do if he is going to try and have us killed."

A young man exited the house a moment later, wrinkling his nose as he drew close to us. "You are far worse than he described," he said. Then he waved for us to follow him and began walking around the manor.

Robin followed without hesitation, and of course Much went wherever Robin did. I hesitated briefly, but Allen linked his arm through mine and pulled me forward.

"Come along, Dusty. Just think…we could be nearing a warm, delightful bath…" he titled his head to one side and shrugged slightly, "or we could be about to be murdered."

"So reassuring." I rolled my eyes.

The servant led us to the back of a house and through a simple door. From there he led us through a narrow hallway and then into a simple room with a small wooden tub.

"There. It's got fresh water. If it needs changing after each of you, fine. Knock on the door. I've got Bernhard boiling more water as we speak. Christoph will be waiting for the knock and get Bernhard and the water for you. There's clothes," the young man gestured toward a table near the wooden tub that had four sets of clothes laid out side by side. "Once you're relatively clean and dressed, I'll take you to the master."

"Thank you, uh…your name?" Robin asked.

"Friedrich. My father has run of the household, and I will once he's dead." And with that, Friedrich left the room and pulled the door shut behind him.

"Pleasant fellow," Allen commented.

"I'll wait outside," I said, glancing at the tub and then at Much and the others. I wanted a bath, but there was no way I was doing so in the presence of my friends.

"Oh, Dusty, we can wait," Robin replied, grabbing my arm before I could exit the room. "You go first. Come on," Robin grabbed Allen with one hand and Much with the other and dragged them toward the door. "Let us know when you're through."

Robin shut the door behind them and I stood alone in the room. The steam rising from the water in the tub drew me in closer. I shed my tattered rags and slipped beneath the warm water, closing my eyes as my body relaxed for the first time in over a year. The travel today had been exhausting on an already frail physical form.

I took a deep breath and sank deeper, letting my head slip beneath the surface. The water felt so smooth and warm, I wanted to stay there forever. But I knew the others were waiting for their turn, so I soon came up for air and reached for a bar of soap.

It took some time, but I managed to scrub the worst of the dirt and refuse from my skin and hair. The latter had grown long while we were in prison, reaching down to my shoulders now.

When I felt clean, I removed myself from the tub and slipped into one of the sets of fresh clothes Friedrich had pointed out. I felt like a princess to be out of the rags I'd been wearing and into the trousers and clean shirt.

I glanced at the tub and wrinkled my nose. The water was nearly black with all the disgusting things that had come off of me. I moved toward the door and swung it open to find my friends in the hallway with a different servant.

"Who's next?" I asked. "Also, I need my hair cut."

"We need a shave, too," Robin commented, rubbing his chin and the thick beard growing there. Robin turned to the servant. "Could you help with that?"

The boy glanced between us, his eyes widening. Given the number of people who hadn't questioned that I was a man for so many years, I was surprised this young servant could tell I was a girl, but it was clear from what he said next that he knew the truth by looking at me.

"Uh, yeah, I can get a shaving kit…and, uh…sorry, my lady," he awkwardly bowed to me. "I didn't…I mean…Friedrich said there were four men…"

I grinned. "Yes, that is rather the point."

He stared a moment longer before he shook himself and moved off down the hall, presumably in search of the shaving kit and some implement to cut my hair. The others took turns in the bath, the water needing to be changed out after each one. The servant who realized I was a girl returned with shears for my hair and a small knife for shaving the unwanted beards.

Once we were all clean, shaved, and my hair was cropped short once more, the servant fetched Friedrich who in turn led us through several corridors away from the servants' part of the house and into the nobility portion. Here the rooms were wider, ceilings higher, and furniture far more ornate.

Friedrich led us into a wide room with a large hearth, with several chairs pulled around it—wooden chairs whose legs were carved into elegant shapes, with pillows piled in the seats to make them more comfortable. There was a wooden desk, and several bookcases along the walls. Lord Isenbern was sitting by the low fire—far smaller than it could have been given the proportion of the hearth as a whole.

"Ah, I can almost see the Earl in you," he said to Robin as we entered the room. "Come, sit."

He waved to the chairs by the fire, and we all moved to sit down.

"I have been informed one of your number is, in fact, a girl. I apologize, my lady, for your treatment in this house thus far."

I shook my head. "I am used to far worse, Lord Isenbern. And I am not a lady—my parents were no more nobility than Much's, but I appreciate your concern. As it is, we have found it safer on our travels to let the world believe I am not a woman, so if you would be so kind as to keep our secret…"

Isenbern dipped his head. "As you wish, my lady." Then turning to Robin,"Now, tell me about your travel and battles during the Crusade."

Robin and Allen delighted Lord Isenbern with their tales for some time, and as they talked more of his servants appeared bringing platters of food along with a small wooden table upon which the food was placed.

The smell of the fresh bread, boiled beef and minced apples overtook my senses and I lost track of the conversation that Robin, Allen, and Lord Isenbern were having. I snatched a plate from one of the servants, shoveling food into my mouth.

I knew I should eat slowly and let my body get used to having more food to fill its stomach, but I couldn't help myself. I closed my eyes as the food melted into my mouth. It was possibly the most delicious thing I had ever eaten, though it was a far different meal than I might have found in Palestine.

"You have convinced me to let you show off your skill," Isenbern said suddenly, drawing my attention away from the food and back to the conversation. "I wish to see your archery."

He sent for Friedrich, and informed him to bring a bow and meet us outside. Once we'd finished eating, Lord Isenbern led us to the back of the manor where the sloping hillside provided a grassy enclosed area for them.

A bow was brought, and Lord Isenbern pointed out various targets for Robin—all of which he hit. I was surprised at how well Robin's muscles remembered their old skill, given his lack of practice over the last year. Though I could see in the shaking of his arms and the twitch in his wrist that it was a struggle for him.

"You are as good as you say," Lord Isenbern conceded. "And you speak and hold yourself with the authority of someone well-bred. I am inclined to believe your story, despite your lack of proof."

"I appreciate that," Robin said.

"You can stay here to rest and recuperate," Lord Isenbern said.

"We may need to work here," Robin replied, "as we will need to accrue funds for our further travels."

"I'm sure something can be arranged," Lord Isenbern agreed.

We did, indeed, stay with Lord Isenbern for several weeks—Robin, Allen, and Much joining the ranks of the town's guards who patrolled along the outer wall of the city to watch for intruders.

I asked Lord Isenbern for help in procuring certain herbs and spices, and when he realized I was a healer he was more than happy to help. I soon had a new pouch filled with the medicinal herbs I needed for my work, and I began to help the sick among the townspeople.

Once we had earned enough from Lord Isenbern's generosity, we set off on our travels again equipped this time with money, clean clothes, and freshly commissioned and purchased weapons of our choice from the town's blacksmith.

At the next village it was easier to convince the people that we were, indeed, soldiers returning from the Crusades because we were no longer covered in our own refuse and emaciated from lack of proper food.

Chapter 18

FOR TWO MONTHS we traveled across the countryside, using money earned in Lord Isenbern's employ and often staying with various contacts of his as well. When we weren't lodging with friends of Lord Isenbern, we would stop at abbeys and churches and use our influence as returning Crusaders to gain lodging. We made it to the coast without further incident, and were soon sailing across the channel to England.

As the white cliffs came into view, I leaned against the railing of the boat and studied this new land I was committed to living on for the rest of my days. Much was beside me, and a glance in his direction showed his misty eyes as he watched England draw closer.

"You are nearly home now," I said.

"Yes. I will be glad to return to Locksley for some well deserved peace and quiet."

"It will be pleasant to finally have some calm. And yet...it has been so long since my life has resembled anything close to calm, I am not sure I will know how to live."

"We were pretty calm in that prison, I suppose..." Much shrugged, grinning at me.

I laughed, feeling warmth spread through my entire being. I might be headed toward an unknown land, but I had family at my side; I was not alone.

Before I was quite ready, the ship came into harbor and we were soon disembarking. When my feet hit the solid wood of the dock, I could feel my throat constricting.

Robin moved away from the dock and knelt in the road for a moment, scooping up a small handful of dirt and letting it sift through his fingers.

"Planning on kneeling there all day?" Allen asked.

Robin grinned up at him, letting the rest of the dirt fall from his hand. "I can hardly believe we're in England again."

Robin led us to a tavern and booked us some rooms—he seemed to know the tavern keeper, and I gathered he and Much had stayed here before their departure for the Crusades.

There were only a few people in the common room when we sat at a table to order some food for our evening meal. When the tavern keep brought us a platter, it was merely a simple loaf of bread and a chunk of cheese. It seemed meager fare compared to how we'd been eating since meeting Lord Isenbern, but it was far better than having to take the time to flick maggots out of a slice of bread, so I was grateful for it.

"Sorry I don't have real meat as yet, but I can fry a few fish if you need it," he said.

"Why the meager fare?" Robin asked, taking a bite out of the bread.

The innkeeper filled our mugs of ale and spoke softly, "It is Prince John and his men. He has replaced almost every sheriff in England with ruthless men of his own. The taxes are unbearably high and we all suffer for it."

"Surely there is justice somewhere," Allen said.

The innkeeper glanced nervously over his shoulder at the other customers in the room. "If you can't pay the taxes, you'll be hung."

"Surely not!" Much gasped.

"If things continue as they are," the innkeeper said. "The Prince will have no more subjects left to tax."

"Is no one doing anything about it?" Robin asked.

"There are some who fight it," the innkeeper replied. "But they never live long. Here at the coast…you'll find more people leaving England as coming here. People are trying to get away from Prince John's ruthless reign."

It seemed the rumors we'd been hearing while on the Crusades had been accurate; England was in crisis. I knew Robin would take these people's troubles upon his own shoulders since he had promised Richard he'd look after them. I wasn't sure what he planned to do, but I was more than willing to help him in whatever endeavors he felt necessary to bring aid to the suffering.

"We are hoping for a speedy return to our home in Nottingham," Robin said. "Could you direct me to the nearest livery where I can procure horses?"

"Horses?" The innkeeper raised his eyebrows. "Where have you been that you think there are horses to be found?"

"Not in England, clearly," Robin replied. "Listen, it's been a long few years. I am sorry for your troubles, and I aim to do what I can about them for King Richard's sake. Don't worry about the horses, but if you can spare us some provisions for our travel that would be much appreciated."

"I don't have much," the man said. "But I can gather a bit for you, I suppose. Being Crusaders, and all…"

"Thank you."

We finished their meal quietly, and then Robin made arrangements for our provisions.

As we traveled across England by foot, we continued to hear reports of suffering, but also began to hear rumors of those who tried to stand up to Prince John and his sheriffs' injustice. The closer we came to Nottinghamshire—the home of Robin and Much—the more reports there were of people being saved from cruelty. There seemed to be a rebellion of sorts in Nottinghamshire that had yet to be squashed and the people we met were clinging to the hope that the rebellion would spread to the rest of England.

One night after we'd eaten in the common room of a tavern—with no better fare than any other we'd encountered—I laid a hand on Robin's arm as the others rose to retire to their rooms. Robin settled back into his chair and studied my face, undoubtedly curious as to why I had wanted to keep him here a moment longer.

"I've been thinking a lot lately," I said, keeping my voice low. There were few patrons in the room, and the innkeeper had returned to the kitchen, but I still felt privacy was the best course of action in this country where so many vile men seemed to live and enact their cruelty.

"About?" Robin asked.

"About the horrors we are encountering—the starving people, the corpses strung up in villages as warnings to those who would rebel against the sheriff, all of it. And about your promise to King Richard. The terrible things happening here weigh heavy on my heart and I do hope we can do something about it, but I know you feel it deeper; they're *your* people. What are you planning to do, Robin?"

"I'm not sure yet. I do have to do something to change what's happening here…but I'm not sure where to begin. I don't have contacts at court, I couldn't get Prince John's ear or change things politically with any ease. But what is the other option? Would joining these 'men of the night' we hear so much about bring any lasting change? They seem to rescue a few helpless souls, but they aren't overthrowing cruel sheriffs or the rest of Prince John's men who have authority over them…"

"Whatever you choose to do, I fully support you."

Robin grinned at me. "Taking on a fight against injustice does seem your style."

"We can't simply watch the horrors unfold."

222

"I know; I agree. Though Much is going to take convincing."

"His heart for people is stronger than most. I am sure he wants to help."

"His desire for peace is also strong." Robin sighed, shoving a hand through his hair. "I wish I could give him that... but if we make a plan to try and help people, he will be right beside me. He always is."

We heard more rumors and reports in every tavern we visited; the rebellion in Nottingham was spreading hope like wildfire. Executions were stopped and people set free; some said the 'men of the night' knew the Sheriff of Nottingham's very thoughts.

A few days later as we were gathered in another tavern eating an evening meal before retiring to bed, Robin leaned forward, catching the attention of Allen and Much. "You should know before we continue that I am hopeful of finding and joining these 'men of the night' in Nottingham, if we can."

"It does seem the most efficient way of making a difference for the people right now," I said. "At least until the King eventually comes home. The next question will be how we are to raise funds for the ransom to get him home."

"I am not sure about that yet," Robin said. "But I am beginning to have a plan. If the people in Nottingham really do know every scheme of the Sheriff before his plots are carried out, it is likely they are using the secrets of Nottingham castle to spy on him."

"Secrets of the castle?" Allen asked.

"There are many passageways," Much replied. "A bit like those we found under Durnstein castle."

"If the 'men of the night' are using those passages, that can only mean Marian is helping them!" Robin grinned.

"Marian?" Allen asked. "How do you figure?"

"It is just what she would do. She'd never stand by and watch all this suffering silently. I'm sure she would feel compelled to do *something*. I wonder if Mark is one of the 'men of the night' and that is how they remain undercover."

"It is possible," Much said.

"When we get home we'll have to go to Wetherby before we head to Locksley village."

Along with the rumors of the 'men of the night' that we heard so much about, the closer we drew to Nottingham the more stories of a mysterious person known as the Hooded Rescuer began to reach our ears. It also became clear that many of the taxes collected in that part of England passed through Nottingham before heading for Prince John. It seemed the new Sheriff there, whoever he was, had Prince John's trust. What Robin might do with such information remained to be seen, but I could see his mind at work as he listened to what people had to say of Nottingham.

As we drew ever closer to the place Robin and Much called home, they grew excited. Their pace quickened each day, and Allen and I were forced to try and keep up with them as they began racing homeward, pointing out familiar landmarks along the way.

When we reached Wetherby, I was delighted with the sweet little village. It was a collection of small houses dotted along a couple crooked streets with seemingly no attention paid to detail. There were twenty or thirty small homes, with chickens strutting around this front yard or that one, and a child or two playing in the streets here and there as their mothers watched through open doorways.

Robin paid little heed to his surroundings as he marched straight through the village to a home near the far edge of Wetherby. A young woman was outside, setting a bow against the side of her house. As she straightened, hands on her hips as she surveyed the horizon in the opposite direction where the city of Nottingham could be seen resting against a grassy knoll, Robin scooped her up from behind, spinning her in a circle before placing her back on her feet.

"Did you miss me, Marian darling?" Robin asked as Much walked toward them. Allen and I stayed a short distance away, Allen chuckling quietly to himself as he watched the proceedings.

So this was Robin's Marian. She was beautiful, that much I could tell. As to her character, that I could not make a judgment about yet.

Robin took Marian's hand just as a young man exited the house, leaning casually against the doorframe. He had a mess of brown hair and dark blue eyes that caught my attention immediately.

"Who's this?" the newcomer asked.

Robin dropped Marian's hand instantly.

"Will Scarlett, this is Robin of Locksley," Lady Marian said.

"The Earl?" the stranger asked.

Robin bowed stiffly to the young man named Will. "One and the same." Then he turned back to Marian. "I was sorry to hear of my father's death. I wish I could have been here."

"We were sorry for it, too. And you *should* have been here. Your father's death was one of the first things that spurred me into action."

"Ah," Robin said, "I wanted to speak to you about that. My comrades and I have heard tales of this Hooded Rescuer and the 'men of the night' in Nottinghamshire who seem to know the Sheriff's every move." Robin gestured toward the rest of us. "You remember Much, Marian? This is Allen, a brother in arms."

Allen stepped forward and gave a short bow. "It is a pleasure to meet you, Lady Marian. We've heard a great deal about you."

Allen winked at Robin, who shoved him aside, and then Robin placed a hand on my shoulder as I approached. "And this is Dusty, our master healer."

Marian ignored Allen and I and instead threw her arms around Much's neck. "It's good to see you."

"You, as well, Lady Marian," Much replied.

Robin turned back to Marian as she let go of Much. "Now, about these rumors."

"Rumors?" Marian asked.

"Even when he only tells his most trusted servant Sir Guy of Gisbourne in the darkest chambers of the castle, rumors say these mysterious heroes still know what the Sheriff and Gisbourne are planning and stop them. This has given rise to a belief among the superstitious that they can, in fact, read his mind." Robin winked at Marian but she seemed uninterested.

There was something glimmering in her eyes, a whirlpool of emotion, but I couldn't read her. Perhaps Much could; he'd always been better at understanding people than I was.

"Now I know perfectly well how one might obtain such secret information," Robin continued, "and I also know only a few people know of the castle's secrets. Now two of those people have been away from England, which to my knowledge leaves you, Mark, and your father. Have you been helping them?"

"Helping us?" Will laughed from the doorway. "She's one of us. You, sir, are addressing the leader of these 'men of the night'."

"Truly?" Robin asked, surprise evident in his voice.

"Truly," Marian replied to Robin. "You doubt I could do such a thing? It wasn't as though there was anyone else around to take care of the suffering people."

"Well it is a surprise," Robin said, "but not so shocking. You've always been a protector. Who is the Hooded Rescuer then, or do you and your companion," he gestured toward Will, "take turns under the mask?"

"No, that's Mark."

"Remarkable," Robin grinned. "Where is your father?"

"In custody, as he has been for a year. I've only been able to see him for the briefest moments when spying in the castle. Mark hasn't seen him at all. My father is ill, Robin."

"I am sorry," Robin frowned. "One of my friends has great knowledge of healing, as I said. Dusty's remarkable."

"I'm afraid the Sheriff isn't inclined to let my father have visitors of any nature, let alone physicians." Marian glanced down the street and then said, "You've all been introduced to Will Scarlett, my right hand, now meet my brother—the famed Hooded Rescuer, and the last member of our crew, Little John."

Marian gestured behind her and I saw two men coming along the dirt path that led into the village. One was small, with dark hair much like Marian's and I could see the resemblance in their faces. The other was a bear of a man, tall, muscular, and intimidating. Both carried parcels covered in cloth.

As they approached the group outside Marian's home, Robin's eyes widened. "Little John? Why didn't you name him Mountain John?"

"We thought about it," the younger man—the one I assumed was Mark—grinned as he drew near, setting aside his parcels, and then running forward to hug Much.

"Where have you been off to Mark?" Robin asked as he received his own hug.

"Nottingham. We went to Marcus to collect some weapons we commissioned."

"Marcus?"

"Don't you remember him?" Marian asked. "Of course you don't. You never notice anyone but yourself."

"Marian!" Robin laughed, but I could see there was some hurt in his eyes after her comment.

"What? Marcus is one of the blacksmith's in Nottingham. We used to play at his house as children if you recall."

"I do remember, I just couldn't place the name at first."

Marian shrugged. "It doesn't matter. Are you in a hurry to return to Locksley or can you stay for dinner?"

"We can definitely stay for dinner."

Robin re-introduced myself and Allen to Mark and Little John and then Marian graciously welcomed everyone into her home. We gathered in the small front room—there was a hearth along one wall, and a simple table in the room with chairs gathered around it.

I saw several doors leading to other rooms in the house, but we all gathered at the table as Marian brought out food from her kitchen for us to consume.

As we ate, Robin, Marian, and Mark fell into easy conversation—which Much occasionally joined in on. Soon Robin began to recount tales of our time in the Holy Land, with Allen cheerfully adding his own additions to Robin's stories. Their banter seem to bring even more ease to the table, and in no time at all Marian, Mark, and Will were telling their own tales of their escapades saving the people of Nottinghamshire from the Sheriff and Sir Guy of Gisbourne. We had a rather merry dinner that night as we caught up on the three years that Robin and Much had been apart from Marian and Mark.

Robin was most intrigued by Will's account of their camp in Sherwood.

"We couldn't stay with Marian and Mark here in Wetherby without drawing suspicion," Will said. "The same held true for Nottingham. We were both already outlawed in our home shires, and once we came here and began helping Marian's crew, it was too dangerous for the group for us to remain in the open. We risked exposing everyone. We do visit, as often as we can, for we have plenty of information to pass along between us as we plan our various exploits. But we live in Sherwood Forest."

"There ought to be a way," Robin sat thinking, "...if we learn the secrets of Sherwood Forest the way we did of the castle, and make camp deep in its heart..."

"What are you thinking, Robin?" Marian asked.

Robin seemed deep in thought, but I knew what he was contemplating so I said, "He's thinking he'll help you set up a more stable camp in Sherwood. Many caravans pass through the Sherwood road carrying the taxes supposedly collected for the king's ransom. The Sheriff here seems to have Prince John's ear and his favor, for most of the taxes seem to gather here and line his pockets before being shipped to London. If we knew the forest well enough, we might be able to way-lay the caravans, relieve them of their unjust shipments, and escape into the thick of the woods where no one could track us."

"We'd be a flash in the night," Robin said. "They wouldn't know what hit them."

"You must let me come with you," Mark said. "I can help! I'd love to be a part of the Sherwood gang."

"I do not know, Mark…"

"You cannot now say that I am too young," Mark laughed. "I have been fighting the Sheriff's men without you."

"You seem to already have a crew here," Allen said to Mark. "Would you abandon them?"

"Wouldn't it be better if we all worked together?" Mark replied. "We know Nottingham, we know the Sheriff. If you set up camp with Will and Little John and start raiding caravans, we can work in tandem to the benefit of the people of England."

"That's a decision for our leader, isn't it?" Will said, giving Mark a sharp glance.

"He's right," Marian said. "I appreciate the loyalty, Will, but we might as well join forces. It's not different than when you and Little John came to join Mark and I."

"I will return to Locksley," Robin said. "I might be able to assist as the Earl of Locksley as much as raiding the caravans."

"So you stay in Locksley, Marian in Wetherby, and the rest of us live in the forest?" Allen sighed. "I was so looking forward to an extended stay on an actual bed."

Much chuckled. "Allen is the biggest complainer you will find in the king's army."

"I like beds!" Allen protested. "There's nothing wrong with that."

It was late that night when Robin finally led us from the village of Wetherby across the open fields to his own village of Locksley. It was a dark night as the moon was relatively covered with passing clouds, but I trusted Robin to get us there safely. And if there were any highwayman, I knew we were more than capable of handling them.

Once we had passed through the quiet village of Locksley, Robin led us up the sweeping road that led toward a larger house —his manor. Light glimmered in a few windows, but for the most part the building was dark.

"Nice house," Allen commented, his voice breaking the silence of the night.

Robin chuckled as he moved forward to knock. Nothing seemed to happen at first, so he knocked harder.

Soon the door was swung open and an old servant stood there. "Who goes there?"

"Your master," Robin said, stepping forward and pushing past the frail man into the front room. It was lit by a fire in the hearth, and as Robin stepped into the light, the old man's face lit with recognition.

"Master Robin! You're home!"

"I am, indeed. I'll need my room ready for the night, as well as three guest bedrooms for my companions here. By the way, Much no longer works for me. He's a free man, so treat him as such."

The old servant glanced toward Much with a quizzical look.

"Let us know when the rooms are ready for us," Robin said. "We'll be in the kitchen, assuming that's where Sarah is."

"I imagine she is, sir," the man replied.

Robin hurried through the house and the rest of us followed. Much seemed to be crying, hastily wiping tears from his cheeks as we walked through the various corridors.

As soon as Robin entered the kitchen—a spacious room filled with a giant table and various workspaces—he ran forward toward a woman seated at a small table on one side of the room.

"Sarah!"

She turned at the sound of his voice, and her face brightened.

"Master Robin! You're home!" She rose from the table, wrapping her arms around Robin as he flung his own around her neck. "Oh, child…I will never let you go."

"You'll have to. Much will want a hug."

She pulled back from Robin and looked behind him and then with a smile wrapped Much in an embrace as well.

"My boys came home," Sarah kissed Much's cheek as she pulled back from the embrace. "I wasn't sure you would. But you're so thin!"

"There wasn't always a lot to eat on our travels," Robin said. "But we did come home. And we brought friends." Robin gestured toward the doorway where Allen and I were waiting.

"Oh, guests," Sarah straightened. "I'll have Matthew see to rooms—"

"Already done," Robin kissed her cheek. "This is Allen of the Dale, and Dusty."

"Pleasure to meet you," Allen gave a little bow, but I moved forward to give her a hug of mine own.

"I have heard a great deal about the woman who took it upon herself to love and raise two motherless boys as her own," I said. "I am glad to finally meet you."

"You can't believe the things Robin says," Sarah replied. "He's been known to exaggerate."

"Whereas our dear humble Much only speaks truth," I replied. "I have heard the report of your character from him."

Sarah ran her hand affectionately through Much's hair. "I was so worried...worried my boys would never come home...and then the Earl died..."

"I was wondering about that," Robin said with a sigh. "We have heard rumors that his death was not...natural."

Sarah crossed her arms. "It most certainly wasn't. It was that wretched Prince John and his servants."

"Have they done any more harm to our household, Sarah?" Robin asked.

"No. But I don't like them. The Sheriff is a terrible man. He hangs people for the fun of it. He almost hung Sir Godfrey! But the outlaws were able to stop that. I can't imagine how, but we're all grateful for it. You know Sir Godfrey has always been a beloved sheriff of our shire, until the Prince deposed him and put his own wretched man in his place."

"Sir Godfrey was almost hung?" Robin asked. "I'd heard he was in prison?"

"He is now, but he was nearly hung before that. How he was rescued, I don't know. It had to have been the guardian angels of Nottingham, no doubt, but having no idea who they might be I haven't gotten the detailed story from anyone."

"You don't know who the 'men of the night' are, or the Hooded Rescuer?"

"No, Master Robin. I do not. But enough of serious talk, you all must be famished after your journey! Let me get you something cooked up right quick, and then you can head to bed."

Sarah began to bustle about the kitchen with Much at her side as the rest of us found seats at the table. There were several small tables such as the one Sarah had been sitting at scattered along the walls, with shelves full of cooking utensils separating them. The middle of the room was taken up by a massive table where I imagined most of the preparation work was done, and one wall was filled with a large hearth and a clay oven where Sarah likely slaved away each day.

Much seemed perfectly at ease for the first time since I'd known him, moving around the kitchen in such a familiar way, he and Sarah performing almost a little dance as they skirted around each other, cutting bread, pulling cheese from the larder, and pouring drinks.

Eventually food was brought to our table and Sarah stood guard over us, making sure we all ate a decent amount. The older servant came to the kitchen to tell Robin rooms had been prepared, and soon enough I was sinking into the softest mattress I had ever slept on.

Chapter 19

THE NEXT DAY, after a hearty breakfast provided by Sarah, we went to Wetherby to meet up with the others so that Will and Little John could take us to their camp in Sherwood Forest. It was not far from the road that passed through the forest, and not too deep within the woods; the camp itself was simply two roughly put together tents made with what looked like any spare cloth that could be found. There was also a burnt patch of ground where they kept a fire during the colder evenings. It was all rather a sorry looking sight.

"This is hardly an ideal spot to create a well established camp," Robin commented. "It's too close to the Sherwood road. If we set up a large, functional camp here, we'll be noticed. We need to go deeper into the woods."

Will shrugged. "We basically just sleep here. If we need to go deeper to suit your purposes, Robin, then so be it. Lead the way."

Robin took the lead as our group trudged through the undergrowth. The sunlight grew somewhat dimmer the deeper we went under the canopy of trees, but it still found places to spill below the leaves so we weren't in true darkness. I walked beside Robin, not because I knew Sherwood or a forest terrain well but because I felt I knew what it was he was looking for.

"We have to become familiar with these woods," Robin said as we went further and further into the forest. "Intimately familiar. We need to know these trees as well as we know our own names, be as familiar with the paths here as we are with our own hands."

Will glanced at his hands with a mischievous grin. "I wouldn't say I'm that intimate with my hands, Robin."

"It may take us a while to become as acquainted with the forest as you want us to be," Allen commented, ignoring Will's humor.

"We'll spend as much time as we can in the forest," I said, "getting acquainted with it as we search out its secrets. If we know it better than those who might want to find or harm us, we will be able to hide effectively here in the trees."

Will moved slightly to the side, standing in front of a large tree and sticking out his hand. "Hello, there! I'm Will."

"What are you doing?" Much asked.

"He's getting acquainted with the trees," Robin said, unable to contain his laughter. It seemed Will was going to fit in well with Robin and Allen—I could already imagine the trouble the three of them would get up to together.

Will turned around, a grin on his face. He rejoined our group and threw a wink at me. "I suppose that is what you meant."

"Not remotely." I turned my attention back to Robin, but I could feel heat in my cheeks and feared I might be visibly blushing. I didn't know why, but Will and his piercing dark blue eyes had me flustered.

"Much and I will return to Locksley and bring supplies to the camp as soon as we start building one," Robin said.

"We will need to build shelters of some sort—tents, or huts, or something," I suggested.

"Yes, and we'll need food," Allen replied.

"We usually visit Marian and get supplies from her," Will said. "We visit every few days for that purpose, as well as to exchange information or plan rescues."

Robin shook his head. "We cannot continue to take supplies from Marian. The less we do through her, the better. I don't want her getting hurt."

"She's led us well this past year," Little John growled. He seemed offended at Robin taking charge of the group and seemingly leaving Marian out of it, but I knew Robin merely wanted to keep Marian safe due to his overwhelming affection for her.

Eventually we stumbled across a meadow that Robin felt sure would suit our purposes and so we decided to make camp there. As the days passed, the camp in Sherwood began to take shape. We spent more time in the forest than at Locksley manor, learning the various paths we could take to reach the camp—Robin wanted to be sure we didn't create an obvious trail to the camp we were meant to be hiding.

We gathered and cut wood from the forest to build huts to live in when we stayed in the clearing rather than at Locksley manor and slowly the meadow became more than simply a place to sleep.

Robin gave Allen and I a tour of the city of Nottingham, with Marian and Mark giving suggestions for the best places to turn if the Sheriff's men came after us. They had various contacts among the merchants and other people of Nottingham whom they'd been working alongside in the three years that Robin and Much were away from England.

During that visit, and many others afterward, I came across many sick and malnourished children playing in the streets.

One day as Robin and the rest of the group were busy hammering away at the huts they were building in our meadow, I suggested to Robin that I needed to visit an apothecary to replenish my medicinal tools. I had herbs and spices always, but after our stint in Durnstein I'd never properly restocked the rest of my supplies and tools.

Robin agreed it was a good reason to visit Nottingham. He took a step back from his work, wiping the sweat from his forehead.

"Could you wait an hour or so?"

I began to agree, when Will set aside his tools and came sauntering over. "I can go with her, Robin, if you're worried for her safety in Nottingham."

"There's no reason to think Dusty has run foul of the Sheriff yet," Robin said. "But I would feel better if none of us travel alone just in case."

"What do you say, Dusty?" Will grinned at me. "Will you allow me to be your escort? I do know where a couple apothecary shops are in town."

"Thank you. I will be glad of your assistance."

Before long we were tramping through the forest alone. Will kept up a cheerful chatter as we made our way through the forest and then across the hills to the city of Nottingham. I made a comment when the conversation required, but kept to myself as much as I was able.

Once we were within the city walls, Will grew more quiet, his eyes scanning our surroundings as we walked.

"You are an outlaw, are you not?"

The corner of Will's mouth quirked slightly in a bit of a smile as he glanced toward me and then back to the various people moving along the street. "I am. So is Little John."

"How did that happen?"

"How did I become an outlaw?" Will grabbed my elbow and steered me toward a cross street as several armored soldiers entered the street we had been walking along. "I saw soldiers like that beat a man to death because he couldn't pay taxes. I gave food to the dead man's wife and child, and I spoke out against our new Sheriff—appointed by Prince John, of course—to anyone who would listen. Tried to start a rebellion. Some people followed my example; they were killed and imprisoned. I was labeled a menace, an outlaw, a man to be feared and stopped at all costs."

"What did you do then?" I asked as we skirted around a group of merchants discussing their trade. The streets of Nottingham were a busy and often crowded place, especially if one was close to the streets connecting to Nottingham Square—a large open area where the market was held.

"I kept helping people as much as I could, but it grew harder and harder since the sheriff of that shire knew exactly who I was, knew who my friends were. He knew how to manipulate me. I began to do more harm than good simply by remaining there, so I left. I met Little John, who had a similar story, and we worked together as we traveled England until we landed here in Nottingham and joined Marian's crew. She led us well in the years that followed. And now the group's expanded, we may be able to do even more good."

"Will!" a small voice yelled out. Will spun around and I scanned the people in the street trying to identify the speaker.

Soon a little girl came running up to Will and he immediately knelt down to speak to her.

"What are you doing out in the street?"

"I saw you walk by! I came to talk to you."

"How is your mother?"

"She said to thank you for saving daddy."

"Have you heard from him recently?"

"Not since you helped him away from the mean old Sheriff." The small girl crossed her arms, her little lips forming a pout as her small brow furrowed. "But mama says he's safe thanks to you."

"He was when I last saw him."

"Can you tell me another story? I love your stories!"

"Not now, Leah. I have work to do."

"More people to save?"

"Yes, exactly." Will gave her a wink and little Leah giggled. Will reached out to tuck a strand of her hair behind her ear. "Get home before you are missed, Leah."

"Promise me you'll come tell me a story soon."

"Soon, Leah. Cross my heart."

Leah seemed satisfied with his response and went running off down the street again, presumably toward her home. Will stood slowly, watching her with an affectionate look on his face.

"Who is that?"

Will started and turned toward me, looking as though he'd forgotten I was there. "Leah. Her father was nearly executed by the Sheriff—couldn't pay taxes. Marian got wind of it and Little John and I were able to save him, get him out of Nottingham."

"She seems to like you."

"I brought news of his rescue to her mother, spent the night with them to make sure the Sheriff or his men didn't come bother them again. Leah couldn't sleep; she'd been crying since her father was arrested and nothing her mother tried would calm her down. So I started telling her a bedtime story, and one thing led to another, and I spent the whole night making up silly stories for her."

"And she stopped crying."

"She did." Will watched me for a moment and then shook his head. "Stop looking at me like that."

"Like what?"

"I don't know…your dark eyes got all big and emotional."

"Big and emotional?" I shook my head. "I was merely thinking."

"Thinking what?"

"That you are a kind and gentle man."

Will shrugged. "Just don't look at me like that, it makes me all soft and warm inside."

I laughed. I couldn't help it. He wriggled his eyebrows at me and grinned.

"Come on, let's get you to the apothecary so you can get your supplies."

I followed Will, wondering what he had meant by feeling soft and warm inside.

When we entered the shop I was accosted with the overpowering scents. My nose wrinkled and Will laughed.

"That was adorable."

"What?"

"Your nose all crinkly…"

I ignored him and moved deeper into the shop. There were rows of shelves covered in bowls, jars, and various bottles all full of powders and plants and potions. Above me on the ceiling hung various flowers, upside down and drying out.

A man came hurrying toward me through the shelves. He was dressed in simple clothes; whatever color his shirt and pants had once been they were now covered in stains of every color. He had an apron tied around his torso, also stained in a pastel rainbow of color. "Can I help you, lad?"

"I hope so."

The man caught sight of Will and grinned. "Scarlett."

"Abraham." Will took his forearm in a firm embrace. My heart skipped a beat and unbidden tears came to my eyes.

Abraham. The last time I had seen Daniyah's husband came flooding to my mind and I tried to shake it off as Will glanced back at me.

"This is my friend. We'll need healing supplies."

"Is someone hurt?" Abraham the apothecary asked.

"No, but our new friend here is a healer."

"Got one of your own, did you? I suppose you won't be needing me now."

"We'll always need you Abraham."

"What do you need?" Abraham stepped toward me.

I pulled my pouch from my belt and showed him what little I had. "I need healing herbs and spices. I'm not sure you'll have what I am accustomed to...I might need to learn the foliage of England before I can do much good here."

"Not from around here?"

"Not until recently."

"Come with me, lad. I'll show you what I use and you can decide what you want to take with you today."

"Thank you. I also need scissors, small knives, a pestle and mortar, and other supplies as well."

"Anything for a friend of Scarlett."

Abraham pulled me around the shop, stopping first at one shelf and then at another, showing me the different dried plants and powders that he used for different purposes. Some were familiar to me, others decidedly not. There were native plants that I did not know, and some imported ones I hadn't used before as well.

When my pouch was full of herbs and spices and utensils once more, Abraham pressed a small leatherbound book into my hands.

"This is my notes on certain plants and their healing properties. It isn't much, but a place to start for sure."

"I couldn't take this--"

"Please. And you're welcome back anytime. I'll talk your ear off about healing herbs. And I want to hear about what you used in Palestine, too. We can learn from each other—call it a trade if that makes you feel better about it, lad."

"Thank you."

Will and I returned to camp after that. A few days later Marian purchased a great deal of green and brown dyed cloth so that we could create clothing for everyone that would blend into the Sherwood environment while we lived there.

We gathered everyone at Locksley manor—gathering everyone at Marian's home in Wetherby might have been too obvious. When there were three or four of them using Marian's home as a base of operations they might go undetected, but a group of eight would be more suspicious in that small village.

Marian had asked Robin to gather everyone at Locksley so that we could take measurements in order to begin sewing the forest colored clothing for everyone.

Marian's basket full of supplies sat on the table filled with various pairs of scissors, piles of thimbles, needles, and the like though we were unlikely to need them at the time. We weren't diving into our sewing projects quite yet, but rather preparing for them. She had borrowed a few brown sticks known as ells from a tailor she knew in Nottingham to help with measuring our group, and we were both armed with long strips of cloth to wrap around our subjects and mark on them as we worked.

I wrapped my piece of cloth around Robin's arm, rolling my eyes as he flexed his muscles.

"Just want to be sure you don't make a shirt so small I break it," Robin said, throwing a wink toward Marian, who ignored him entirely as she measured Much.

Sarah was in the room, too, taking measurements for Little John while Allen, Will, and Mark watched the proceedings and waited for their turn.

I grabbed a quill from an ink pot on the table near Marian's basket of sewing supplies, using the quill to mark the measurement of Robin's arm on the piece of cloth.

"We should be good now," I told Robin as I set aside his strip of cloth filled with measurements and reached for another blank piece of cloth to measure the next person. I turned around to find Will standing before me and for a moment I was taken aback by his vibrant blue eyes.

Will winked, his face splitting into a grin and I ducked my head for a moment, trying to gain control of my heartbeat.

"Hold out your arms," I told him as I stepped forward.

Once his arms were held up and out of my way I reached around his waist, wrapping the strip of cloth around him. I could feel his breath on my ear as I bent my head down to see precisely how large his waist was so I could mark it on the cloth. A shiver ran up my spine and I quickly backed away from him, grabbing the quill and jotting down the measurement.

When I turned back around, Will's dark blue eyes were dancing with silent laughter.

"Hold still," I said. "And put your arms down."

Will's arms dropped dutifully to his side and I began to take in the measurement for his broad shoulders. As my fingers grazed his shirt, I could feel the muscles beneath. I glanced up at his face to find his eyes dancing with laughter again and I ducked my head.

What was wrong with me? I'd never reacted to a man this way before. I'd been living with them for years; this was ridiculous.

Will turned his head slightly to look at me as I worked, and I glanced up at him, suddenly realizing our faces were inches apart.

"Hi." Will winked again, and I immediately turned away.

"I'm trying to work here, do stop flirting."

"As you wish."

I hurried through the rest of his measurements as quickly as I could, all too aware of how close we stood together and how nice he smelled.

Once everyone's measurements had been taken, Marian, Sarah, and I set to work cutting the fabric for each person's outfits. We intended to make several pairs of trousers and shirts for everyone, along with hooded cloaks. In the days following, we spent many hours both in Locksley and in Wetherby sewing by firelight to finish the massive undertaking of clothing eight people.

One day as we sat around Marian's hearth at her home in Wetherby bent over our needles, I asked her about her father.

"You say you can't visit him, but you've seen him?"

Marian studied me silently, her eyes dark and distrusting.

"I do know about the secret passages, if that's what you are afraid of revealing."

"There's one that opens in the dungeons. I can see my father from there, but I can't speak to him or approach him."

"Can you tell what sort of symptoms he has?"

"He's ill." Marian bent over her work, focused on her sewing and ignoring me as best she could though I was sitting mere feet away from her. I was getting the distinct impression she did not trust or like me.

"Robin told you, I believe, that I am a healer."

"You can't get into the dungeons to help him."

"We might be able to think of *something*. Robin can be rather clever."

Marian's eyes shot upward, glaring into mine for a moment before she looked back down at her work.

Ah, there it was.

I knew why she didn't like me and I could feel the slightest twitch in my lip as I fought the urge to smile. "Did Robin ever tell you about Princess Joan?"

"What?" Marian glanced up at me again.

"Slightly off topic, I know…King Richard's sister traveled with us during the Crusades for a while. She had a strong affection for Robin, might have even loved him I think."

"And why do I need to know this?" Marian's eyes were flashing as she stared daggers in my direction.

"Because Robin never gave her what she wanted. He was staunchly adamant that the love of his life was waiting for him

250

back home in England and he would do absolutely nothing to jeopardize that."

Marian looked down at her hands again, meticulously sewing along the seam of the shirt she was working on, her hair falling over her face and obscuring it from view. Yet before her face had disappeared from my sight I saw the corners of her mouth turn upward.

Satisfied I had assuaged her fear of my claim on Robin, I returned to the first subject of conversation.

"If I know your father's symptoms I can perhaps figure out a treatment course. We'll still have to figure out a way to get the medicine to him, of course, but at least it would be a start."

Marian's fingers moved nimbly along the seam of her shirt and she said nothing. I focused on my own project—a pair of dark green pants for Will. The thought of Will brought a flutter to my chest and I bit my lip.

Why did this man I hardly knew create such strange responses in me? I blamed the brilliant dark blue eyes. I'd never seen anything quite like them. They gleamed like the twilight sky only just beginning to fill with stars.

I shook my head, putting Will and his insufferably perfect eyes from my mind as I focused on the task at hand.

Chapter 20

ONE DAY, after hours of manual labor finishing building our huts, we gathered around the new fire ring built outside of Much's hut—large enough to also serve as our kitchen—to enjoy one of his delicious meals. We had fallen logs pulled up around every side of the fire and it created a rustic but homey feel as we all sat together with plates in our laps.

Into this peaceful scene Marian burst, running into the clearing and straight toward us. She grabbed her side and gasped for air for a moment; her heavy breathing and windswept hair making me wonder if she'd run the entire way from Wetherby or Nottingham.

"What is it, Marian?" Robin asked, getting up to take her elbow and guide her to one of our log benches.

"I was in Nottingham, in the castle, and I just heard there's a caravan coming through Sherwood tomorrow. It is loaded with taxes taken from the people of England. The Sheriff will take his unfair share to line his own pockets before sending it on to Prince John."

Robin glanced at the rest of us with a clear twinkle in his eye. "Perfect!"

"We'll just relieve the Sheriff of that burden and responsibility," Allen said.

Marian discussed the details she had heard while spying on the Sheriff and Sir Guy of Gisbourne, and after a plan had been forged, I shifted from my seated position onto my knees to pray for the safety of our endeavors. If we were going to attack a guarded caravan we would need the Lord's protection. I also felt we would need His blessing to embark on a crusade to help the suffering people of England. No one could help them better than the Lord.

Robin insisted everyone pull out their weapons and inspect, clean, and sharpen them so we'd be ready for our ambush and we complied.

The next day, we were on the road that wound through Sherwood Forest, circled around Robin.

"Does everyone understand their roles?" Robin asked.

Allen rolled his eyes. "Seeing as you've only explained the plan four hundred times…yes, I think I can say with authority that we all understand our roles."

"In that case, get moving." Robin playfully pushed Allen toward the edge of the road, and then gestured for the rest of us to move off the road toward the hiding places we had chosen.

At his dismissal, the meeting in the middle of the road dispersed. As I positioned myself behind a tree not too far from the road, I glanced to either side; Robin was to my left, the closest to where the caravan was coming so that he could signal us once the last of the caravan passed his position. To my left was Will, only a few trees down from my position.

I gave a last quick prayer for our safety and then waited for Robin's signal. Taking a deep breath I pulled my bow from my back and nocked an arrow to the string, leaning lightly against the tree, waiting.

I shot a glance toward Will once more and when we made eye contact he winked at me. As the heat rushed to my cheeks I turned the other direction, intent on watching Robin instead.

In a few minutes, I could hear the caravan approaching as the wooden axles creaked as wheels rolled along the bumpy Sherwood road. Soldiers were laughing; someone was whistling a tune.

I stayed in position behind the tree, not daring to peek around it for fear of giving away our ambush. I had fought in battles alongside Robin before, but setting an ambush was a new experience and I wondered if we could pull this off.

Robin suddenly gave a long, high, piercing whistle and that was the signal I'd been waiting for. I spun around my tree and focused on the soldiers sitting atop various wagons and carts filled with wooden chests. I hurriedly selected a target and let my arrow loose. To my surprise, my arrow was trailed by another.

Out of all the soldiers guarding the caravan, Will had apparently chosen the same target that I had.

I ignored the flutter that raced through my chest and focused on another target as the soldiers began to draw their weapons and eye the trees in search of their assailants. Each member of the gang was letting their arrows fly in quick succession, and within minutes there was only one soldier left, still mounted on his horse.

Robin darted out of his hiding place and took the soldier's reins in his hand. "I thank you for your generous donation to King Richard and his subjects."

"You...you wouldn't dare," the soldier sputtered.

"Oh, but we would," Robin said.

As Robin spoke with the soldier, I ran forward to one of the largest wagons, jumping up to the seat in front and taking the reins of the frightened and confused mules who were pulling it. I directed them off the road; they were reluctant to obey, but Will, Much, and Little John began leading the rest away and my own mules soon acquiesced to follow the rest into the underbrush.

I glanced behind to see Allen grabbing a loose chest that had fallen from one of the carts and lugging it along behind us. Mark took up his place at the back of the group, doing his best to cover up the wagon tracks we were creating.

"Give my regards to the Sheriff!" I heard Robin shout. His plan had been to send one survivor back to Nottingham with news for the Sheriff that there were people willing to defy him.

Robin soon came running after us calling out, "Hurry! We must get all of this back to the camp. Little John, as soon as that soldier is out of sight, head back and bury those soldiers we killed."

"I'll help," I offered, pulling my mules to a stop and jumping from the wagon. Robin clambered up and took my spot.

Little John and I hurried back to the road. Once we were close to it, we crept forward cautiously, but the soldier was long gone. There was nothing in the road except the men we had killed.

Little John set to work digging graves and I moved from one body to the next, closing their vacant eyes and silently apologizing for the violent end we had brought them.

I was touched that Robin would expect us to do this. I didn't think of my friend as irreverent necessarily, but neither did I see him as overly respectful to his enemies. That he would care to give them the dignity of a burial surprised and pleased me.

Little John hefted the last of the soldiers into his grave and I knelt to push the dirt back into the shallow hole to cover him. Little John cracked his knuckles and grinned at me.

"For a first raid, I think that went well."

"We accomplished our purpose," I agreed, shoving the last of the dirt over the grave and wiping my dirty hands on my trousers. As I stood up, Little John tilted his head and considered me. "What?"

"Nothing."

"You were staring."

"I am trying to decide what my friend finds so intriguing in you."

"You mean Will?"

"Hmm." Little John shrugged and started walking off the road and back into the trees toward camp. I followed along behind him. I wanted to ask him what he meant, and see if I could get him to tell me about Will, what he was like as a person, a friend.

But asking those questions would give the impression that I was interested in finding out the answers—and though that was true, I didn't need Little John to know that. I'd barely managed to open up enough to let Robin, Much, and Allen be my friends. Now I had a handful of more people to be friends with, and I intended to try. But going so far as getting my heart involved? That was too much to ask.

It had ripped me apart to lose the people I loved. I was already risking so much caring for my new family—Robin, Much, and Allen—and I couldn't risk falling in love on top of all the rest.

Once we arrived back at camp—now filled with carts, wagons, mules, and horses—I suggested we pray to give thanks for the safety and success of our first raid.

"Is that really necessary?" Allen rolled his eyes.

"You may not think so, but I do."

Will shrugged. "I see no reason why we can't. Robin?"

"Whatever," Robin said. "I don't care."

I knelt in the grass and was grateful and proud of Much when he chose to kneel beside me. He didn't often speak of his faith with the members of the gang and I worried that he cared too much what Robin and the others would think of him. To my surprise, Will came and knelt beside me, too.

I ignored him, and instead focused my attention on my God, giving Him a quick thank you that none of my friends had been harmed, as well as a heartfelt apology for taking the lives of the soldiers.

When I was through, I raised my head and Allen perked up. "Now on to more important business," he said. "What are we to do with the horses and wagons we've acquired?"

"We can take the carts apart," Will suggested, "and use the wood to finish building our huts."

"And we can give the horses to a deserving farmer or two in the area," Robin said.

"Why not keep them here?" Allen asked. "They could prove useful."

"We'd have to feed them," Will said. "I'm not sure we could manage taking care of horses while none of us are here— we're going to be busy spying on the Sheriff, saving innocent people from unlawful executions, and so forth. At least if things follow the sort of pattern we've been living by these past years under Marian's direction."

"I agree," Robin said. "It might prove more nuisance than help to have the horses here."

Robin and Much set to work putting away the chests of gold as Will offered to find homes for the horses.

"We do know some of the farmers around here," Little John said. "I'll come with you."

"I'll come," Mark said. "People know me—my father used to be the sheriff of this shire and he was well-known and beloved. People will accept our help easier if I tag along, I think."

"There's enough horses it might do you good to have help," Allen said. "I might not know the farmers, but I can be an extra set of hands."

"I can help, too," I offered.

Soon enough Will, Little John, Allen, Mark, and myself had the animals lashed together and were leading the group of horses and mules away from the camp and through the forest.

When we broke free of the trees, Will turned to Little John. "We can do this faster if we separate."

Little John nodded.

"I agree with that," Mark said. "We can take half the animals to the farms south of Nottingham, and you can go north."

Soon Mark had the animals split into two separate groups, and he, Little John, and Allen began to lead them away. Suddenly it was just me and Will.

"There's a farm a few miles from here," Will gestured vaguely toward the horizon. He took hold of the reins of the horse at the front of the line of animals lashed together and began to walk. I fell into step beside him.

"Praying after the raid…" Will glanced at me and then looked forward again. "Do you do that often?"

"Pray? Probably not as often as I should. Scripture does say to 'pray without ceasing' after all."

"Does it?" Will's voice was soft and thoughtful; not the sarcasm that I was met with by Allen and sometimes Robin. Not as curious as Much. Just…thoughtful.

259

"How'd you end up with Robin and the others?"

"We fought together during the Crusades."

"Okay, but how'd they convince you to leave your homeland and come to this sorry mess? England is a disaster. Don't get me wrong, I love my homeland and the people here… but currently, it's a disaster."

I opened my mouth to say I had nowhere else to go; that Robin and Much and Allen were all the family I had left in the world. But I closed my mouth before I could say any of it. Why would I tell Will something so deeply personal? I didn't know him.

Marian knew and trusted him, and Robin knew and trusted Marian. So perhaps by proxy he was a trustworthy friend, but I didn't personally have any connection to Will yet so I bit my tongue.

"You are very quiet, you know that?"

"Oh?"

"Marian is fiery and will always say exactly what she is thinking—even if she probably shouldn't. Mark takes after his sister in that way, though amusingly enough Marian tries to keep him in check. Robin and Allen seem as outgoing and strong-willed as Marian can be."

"Is Marian your guide to measure a person's character by?"

"I don't know that I'd say that," Will said, chuckling as he glanced at me again. "I'm just trying to figure you out."

"Much is quiet and reserved."

"True. Though he was raised a servant, I believe, so that probably has a great deal to do with his upbringing more than anything else."

"Your friend Little John doesn't often have a lot to say."

"That's true," Will agreed. Behind us one of the horses nickered and I turned around trying to place the sound to the animal.

"Your eyes are expressive, you know. You might not say much about yourself, but your eyes…"

I turned away from the horses and back to Will, feeling heat rushing to my cheeks. This was becoming a bad habit since I'd met Will.

He grinned at me and I dropped my gaze to the ground in front of me as we walked.

"You don't have to tell me all about yourself just yet," Will said as we crested a hill and a cluster of buildings came into view. "I like that you present a challenge of sorts."

I shook my head. "I do not intend to issue any challenges."

"Finding out who you truly are will be rather fun, I think." Will winked at me and I could feel another blush blooming on my cheeks. "Come on, the farm's just there."

I followed Will down the hill to the cluster of buildings. He had a brief conversation with the farmer's wife—the farmer himself was out working in his fields. The woman seemed

261

incredibly grateful for the offer of an animal or two, and we left a couple horses there. Then we began walking toward the next farm.

Will didn't pry for more information as we walked, but rather chatted about nonsensical things—the shapes of the clouds in the blue sky overhead, the recent weather, the pining looks he saw pass between Marian and Robin when they both thought the other wasn't watching.

We made several stops at various farms that day until we had run out of animals to gift to the people and we turned our feet back to Sherwood Forest. I almost wished he would ask me more questions about myself—I certainly had plenty of questions I wanted to ask him. Will, however, kept the conversation light and impersonal for the rest of our time together that day.

After that first raid, news of a 'Robin of the Hood'—or the shortened version 'Robin Hood'—began to spread in Nottingham and the Sheriff issued a decree declaring him an outlaw, along with anyone in association with him. Up to that point we had visited Nottingham fairly frequently to gather supplies or keep an eye on things, but it became more important to travel within the city with as much secrecy as possible.

"Welcome to the guild," Will said one night, plopping onto one of the log benches around the fire ring. Everyone else was busy with various tasks—finishing their huts, cleaning their weapons—and I had been sitting alone for a few minutes watching the stars overhead. We had a good view of them in our meadow, though once we moved under the trees the canopy of branches blocked them from view.

"The guild?"

"Of outlaws," Will said, shooting me a characteristic grin and a wink. "Now, Little John and I have been here for a good many years and if you need pointers on how to effectively be a rule-breaker and make the local authorities despise you, just ask."

"You are not taking this seriously at all."

"Life is better when you can laugh."

"I believe Robin said something similar to me once."

"You have such wise friends."

"Are we friends?"

"Are we not?"

"We've known each other for less than a month."

"Time means nothing. I believe I was friends with Marian the very day we met."

"You bring up Marian quite a lot you know."

"We're good friends."

"Nothing more?"

"Jealous?" Will winked at me.

"Worried for Robin's sake, more like."

Will shook his head. "I don't love Marian—not like that, anyway. She is my friend, and over the last few years I think we have reached a point we consider each other family. But there is nothing more there. She might deny it and fight it, but she has always loved Robin and she always will. They belong together.

I've never yet been in love, but when I do fall someday, I can only hope I have the sort of epic romance those two are playing out as we speak."

"I hadn't given love much thought, to be honest."

"Oh?"

I bit my lip, turning away from Will's inquisitive gaze. He didn't need to know that I had started thinking about love quite recently.

"Well, anyway, I just wanted to tease you about officially being declared an outlaw…or at least an outlaw by proxy because of Robin."

We sat in an awkward silence for a time, listening to the sounds of chatter around the camp as the rest of the group went about their various activities. Eventually, Will spoke up again. "I have to warn you, Dusty, I fully intend to crack your shell open someday and see who you truly are."

"That sounds vaguely threatening."

"It isn't. Simply a promise that I will prove myself trustworthy enough for you to feel safe telling me all the secrets of your past, every circumstance that made you…you."

"Why do you care so much about knowing my secrets?"

"It's not the secrets. It's you. I want to know you. You won't talk about yourself though, which begs the question, why not? Hence the desire to know all the things. Plus, once I start to know about your history I might start to unlock the truths of this mysterious, beautiful enigma of a woman that has gracefully walked into my life recently."

I could feel the embarrassment rising in my cheeks again and I kept my face pointedly turned away from Will.

"I don't expect you to open up in a day. Just...beware that I'm a man on a mission."

"A mission to know me."

"Yep."

Will nudged me rather playfully with his shoulder and then stood up and sauntered away. I watched him go for a moment, until he spun around and winked at me and I quickly turned my gaze to my toes.

Our camp slowly became a home as the huts for each of us were completed, the fire ring with log benches around it became a usual gathering place, and Allen and Little John spent a few days building a small forge on one side of our clearing where they could create their own swords and other weapons. Robin teased that we were building a village in the middle of Sherwood, and it certainly felt that way at times.

We continued to raid caravans of unfairly collected taxes that passed through Sherwood. Sometimes Marian brought us news of when the shipments were coming through, and sometimes we heard the news ourselves. Robin had Much and Mark join him in teaching Allen and I the secrets of Nottingham castle—every secret passage and room, every entrance and hidden doorway—so that we could assist in spying on the Sheriff and his right hand Sir Guy of Gisbourne.

We kept a portion of the riches we stole from the caravans so that we could give it back to the people in order to buy food, pay taxes, and the like. We also sent a portion of the treasure to the coast and then passed it along through contacts we had made during our travels—such as Lord Isenbern—so that we could get the treasure to Duke Leopold of Austria to pay the ransom he had set in order to free King Richard.

Chapter 21

AS I PRESSED my back against the rough wooden wall behind me, I took a deep breath, fingering the pouch on my belt. Recently I had been visiting Abraham's apothecary shop. The plants and herbs in England were not all the same as those I had had access to in Palestine, and I had much to learn in order to properly use my healing skills here in this new land. Abraham was a patient teacher—and a student, too, as he truly did want to exchange information and learn from me the healing herbs and spices that were unfamiliar to him.

Right now, however, it was my other skills that were needed.

I let go of my pouch and grabbed my daggers off my belt instead. The Sheriff of Nottingham had sent his lackey Sir Guy of Gisbourne to hang a family who couldn't pay taxes. So Robin, Will, Allen, and I were in the village of Langlen to stop him.

Robin and Allen were across the street, pressed against the side of a house while Will and I were opposite them. In the middle of the street perpendicular to us there was a simple wooden gallows with two ropes dangling from it.

Sir Guy of Gisbourne was looking on as a handful of soldiers—ten, if I could count straight—were binding the hands of the man and his wife who had offended the Sheriff, to lead them up the steps of the gallows.

Little John was keeping an eye on Nottingham with Marian, while Mark and Much were distributing money to the south of the city, so the four of us here were the only hope for this couple. Robin was confident we could manage it. We'd been raiding caravans of treasure often enough that ambushes were starting to become routine. How different could this be?

The soldiers dragged the man up the steps toward one of the swinging ropes. He jerked around, calling out for them to let his wife alone. No one listened.

The main difference between our ambushes and today's events was exactly that; there were innocents this time that we had to protect. It wouldn't be a simple jump out and kill everyone within sight situation.

Will's breathing hitched behind me as the wife was shoved next to the husband.

"How long will Robin wait," he hissed.

As the soldiers reached for the ropes to wrap around both throats, Robin's high pitched whistle cut through the air.

I darted around the corner of the building and dove at my target—one of the soldiers on the ground below the gallows. I leaped through the air, daggers outstretched. He was not expecting the attack so as he spun around toward me my daggers sank into his neck.

I pulled back, repulsed by my own efficiency as his body slumped to the ground lifeless. I crouched, spinning to choose another target.

I heard arrows whistling through the air and knew Robin was cutting down soldiers from a distance. Will was in the midst of them beside me, his sword flashing this way and that as he fought the soldiers.

I ducked under a blade intended for my head and used both daggers to slice the arm carrying it. The soldier cried out, dropping his sword. As he reacted to the pain, I darted forward and stabbed his neck—perfect, precise. He fell, as lifeless as my first victim.

I glanced toward the gallows. The soldiers who'd been up there with the innocent couple were dead, arrows protruding from their bodies. Allen was there as well, untying them both. His job was to get them free while Robin, Will, and I dealt with the soldiers and distracted Gisbourne.

I heard the heavy footfall of someone behind me and swung around. Sir Guy of Gisbourne's sword was arcing through the air toward me and I dropped to the ground to avoid it, rolling to the side and springing back up on my feet. He turned toward me, fury in his eyes, and I took half a step back.

I wasn't afraid of this man. I had been trained well; I knew what I was doing. Yet even so, his reputation for being the best swordsman England had ever seen—unbeatable, people said— gave me pause. I needed to be smart.

Gisbourne's fingers and wrist twitched, swinging his sword in a dramatic circle at his side as he circled me, probably watching for weaknesses in much the same way I was doing.

I glanced toward the gallows and saw that Allen and the couple had disappeared.

Movement brought my eyes back to Gisbourne in time to see him lunging at me, sword outstretched. I dove to the side to keep out of reach just as another blade caught Gisbourne's and held it in check.

Will.

He and Gisbourne began to trade furious blows and I flipped one of the daggers in my hand, eyeing the fight. They moved around and around each other, swords flashing. The moment their fight twisted around enough that Gisbourne was close to me and Will was hidden behind him I threw my dagger. It sank deep into Gisbourne's calf and he stumbled.

Will tried to decapitate him but Gisbourne dropped lower to the ground, his own sword arcing upward and grazing Will's arm.

"Come on!" I heard Robin's shout and spun from the fight, running off the road.

Robin was just beyond one of the houses. He caught my shoulder as I came to a skidding stop beside him. "It's time to go. Allen has the couple and will get them out of the area. Get back to camp!"

I glanced over my shoulder, worried for Will, but he was running toward us.

"Go!" Robin ordered, pushing me. I took off running.

There was an outcropping of boulders not far from the

village and I made my way there to catch my breath. Will soon joined me, leaning against one of the large rocks and gasping for breath.

"Robin…is…leading…Gisbourne…" Will closed his eyes for a second and took a few gulping breaths. "He's leading him the opposite direction so we, and Allen with the victims, can get safely away."

"Let me see your arm."

I slipped my pouch from my belt and grabbed Will's arm, pushing back his ripped sleeve so I could see the crimson crack in his skin.

"It's not too bad," Will said.

I opened my pouch and found the herbs I would need to promote healing and stem the flow of blood, trying to remember all of Abraham's lessons as I mixed them and then applied them to his small cut.

Will was right; it wasn't terribly deep or long. Once I'd applied my herbs, I said a quick prayer to align myself with the True Healer, and felt the healing take root. Then I pulled out my needle and coarse thread and stitched his cut closed.

"Where did you learn to do this kind of thing?"

"Back home."

Will's hand caught my chin and lifted my face until he could see my eyes. "Always so cryptic. But your eyes tell a far deeper story."

271

I finished stitching and cut the thread, tying it off and then putting my supplies back in my pouch and back onto my belt before I stepped away from Will.

"I'm sorry." His voice was gentle and laced with concern.

I glanced back at him. "For what?"

"I push you too hard to open up to me. You're right; you don't know me. I can't deny my curiosity to understand you, Dusty, but I will try to respect your wish for privacy."

Will pushed himself off the rock he'd been leaning against and moved to look around it. "Doesn't seem like we have any followers. Every soldier but Gisbourne was dead when we finished as far as I could tell, and Robin took him on a different hunt. We should be safe to return to camp."

Our walk toward Sherwood Forest was quiet. Will did not pester me with questions, though I did notice him watching me intently on several occasions. I couldn't understand it; there was nothing interesting about me. I was just a woman doing my best to survive the harsh world we lived in, and hopefully make it a little better for others to live in it as well. I knew I wasn't particularly beautiful—hence how I'd managed to pretend I was a man for so many years—so what he found so intriguing I couldn't fathom.

In the weeks that followed, the gang grew busy; raiding caravans of treasure that came through Sherwood, rescuing innocent lives from hangings, beatings, and the like. I also visited the sick in Nottingham and spent more time at Abraham's apothecary to keep learning about English herbs. To my delight, Abraham's shop was well-stocked: he had imported herbs and spices from around the world, and I was able to gather some of my usual and familiar medicinal supplies along with the new plants from England.

Once I'd learned enough to feel sure I could manage on my own, I began to wander Sherwood Forest to collect my own herbs rather than buying them from Abraham himself. I enjoyed every aspect of my gift, and that included the finding and preparation of the plants I used in my work.

One day when I set off from camp to wander the forest in search of plants I could use, Will decided to join me. He had been true to his word and hadn't asked about my past since the day we'd rescued that first couple, and as we set off from camp he kept his conversation light and rather pointless.

I appreciated the effort he was making to curb his own curiosity; in some ways, that in itself gave me the desire to share something with him. He'd been patient and kind, and everything I'd seen of him since I met him led me to believe he was a good man. I did feel I could trust him as I did Robin, Much, and Allen.

As we walked along, I kept my eyes on the ground, searching for signs of plants that I could use. It was early autumn, and the trees around us were bursting with colors—oranges, yellows, reds, and golds glowing in the light of the sun that streamed down through the branches overhead.

Silence stretched between us, but it didn't feel awkward or stiff to me. I knelt down to inspect a plant that caught my eye, running my fingers along the leaves. It wasn't exactly like Abraham had described or the pictures he had drawn while teaching me, so I stood again and moved on, my eyes still scanning the greenery around us as we walked.

"What got you started with medicine and healing?"

I glanced toward Will, surprised by his question. He had been patiently holding his tongue, however, so I felt it was only fair that I answer his question.

"I think I was simply curious in the beginning. Anyone can learn the properties of healing, the plants and herbs to use... but some people have something more; a healing touch. And I turned out to be one of them."

"Robin said you healed a lot of nearly fatal wounds during the Crusades."

"Robin likes to exaggerate. I have healed some horrible wounds in the past, but I've never saved anyone that was beyond the point of saving. I have yet to perform miracles of that kind."

"That isn't what Robin says." Will shrugged and smiled at me, and I turned my gaze back to the ground and my search for the plants I could use.

"Robin, and the other soldiers on the Crusade, know nothing about healing," I said. "Would they have died if I had not been there? Possibly. Not because I performed a miracle but merely because I know the art of healing, and they do not."

"What is it like over there…your homeland?"

"Hot. I miss the warmth. England is always so…dreary. There is not so much rain there as here."

"But it does rain?"

"Of course it does. It snows, too. Just not as often as here."

"Do you miss your home?"

"So many questions."

"I am sorry. I know I was trying not to pester you…but you started answering my questions just now and that made me all the more curious." Will stopped walking, grabbing my elbow so I'd pause beside him. "I am sorry."

"You do not need to apologize. It's not that I don't want to tell you about my life, it's just…not easy for me to talk about. The honest answer to your question is no, I don't miss my home as it stands now. I do miss pieces of my childhood, but that is a foolish desire that cannot be granted because life has already moved on. I can't revisit the past."

"I still can't wrap my head around you coming all the way to England with Robin, or why you would do such a thing. My first thought was that maybe you loved him, but that has proved to be false."

"We thought the same about you and Marian."

"I know." Will shook his head, grinning. "Do you still have family over there?"

275

"No."

I turned away from Will, resuming my walk at a brisk pace, my eyes scanning the ground for plants though in truth I could see little through the sudden arrival of tears in my eyes.

My family was dead. I wasn't as bitter and cut off as I had once been, but it was still painful to consider that I would never see them again. Habibah's laughing eyes. My mother's crinkly smile. Daniyah's words of wisdom.

Will fell into step beside me again, though he said nothing.

Eventually I found a worthwhile plant and I knelt to pull it up by the roots, stuffing it into the bag I had brought along on this journey for that purpose. Will asked what the plant could be used for, and our conversation picked up again as I explained the various plants that I used and how they differed from plants I had used in Palestine.

The conversation remained focused on plants and herbs and spices and I steered clear of anything personal. Will, for his part, did not ask any more questions that did not pertain to the plants I was finding.

Chapter 22

ABOUT A WEEK after my conversation with Will, I sat on the dirt floor of our storage hut in the camp, my back against the wall. Robin was seated across from me atop one of the many chests in the hut, and there was an open chest on the floor between us that we were both pulling golden coins from and placing into smaller pouches. We were counting out money and separating it into portions to give to the people in Nottingham and the surrounding villages to pay for food and taxes and such.

"Marian said the Sheriff is talking about raising taxes again," Robin said as he dropped a handful of coins into the pouch in his hand.

We'd had a man in town—a contact of Marian's—create our horde of pouches that we used to give money to the people. We had an entire chest full of empty little bags for that purpose, but they still seemed to be used at a rapid rate and I was sure we'd need to commission more soon.

"Marian said he suggested raising taxes to Gisbourne half a dozen times this week."

"Do you want to raise the portions we're giving to the people then?" I asked.

"I'm considering it."

I picked up one of the bags I'd already filled and set aside.

"Does that mean we need to start over with all these portions?"

Robin looked like he was considering it and I considered throwing the bag of money at him. "You could have said something before we were halfway through with this, Robin."

"Sorry. We don't have to do it this week. We'll see if he chooses to raise taxes first."

Will stuck his head in the open door of the hut. "Hey, Robin? I have some news." His voice wavered and my attention snapped to his face. His eyes were intense as he stared down Robin.

"Did you hear form Marian?"

"No. Not from Marian. I saw an old friend of mine in Nottingham, a friend from my hometown of Middlesborough."

Will's eyes were almost wild and his voice betrayed the deeper emotions he was apparently trying to rein in. I sat up straighter, wondering what had him so distraught.

"I assume they are having the same issues our shire is," Robin said nonchalantly, apparently unaware of Will's distress.

"Yes. All of England is. But it's more pressing than that. My friend's son is going to be hung in three days' time."

Robin's head snapped up as he truly looked at Will for the first time during the conversation. "Let me guess, he didn't pay his taxes?"

Robin got to his feet, shoving a hand through his hair with a sigh. "I don't see why our rescuing escapades can't extend to Middlesborough as well as Nottingham. Take Mark and Little John and do what you have to to save your friend's child. Dusty, get together some of these money bags to take to the people of Middlesborough, too."

"Of course, Robin."

Within an hour Will and I were on our way to his hometown with Mark and Little John. I felt almost like an outsider in this group—these three men had been working together and building their friendship during all those years that I was doing the same with Robin, Much, and Allen. They shared a bond forged in fire, and it was obvious in the easy way they communicated together. I felt out of place without Robin or Much or Allen there.

Will kept us moving at a brisk pace, often sighing heavily and glancing toward the location of the sun in the sky.

"We'll get there in time," Mark said. "Don't panic yet."

"I don't know if we will. Cyrus didn't know precisely when the execution was going to be…"

"But it wasn't urgent," Mark insisted. "He said his son was imprisoned and threatened with execution, right? Not that he raced over here just as it was happening…"

Will nodded, but the tenseness in his shoulders did not ease.

It was more than a day's journey to Middlesborough, and Will spent the whole of that first day in a quiet and rigid mood. We stopped at a well-placed abbey along the road for the night— there was not a town, but rather a smattering of houses. The abbey had likely been built there so that travelers could have a place to sleep for the night on their way to and from Nottingham.

We were given a quick meal and then settled into the guest rooms we had been given. I still dressed as a man and kept my hair from growing too long and feminine, so the men at the abbey had us sharing their guest rooms. Mark and Little John in one room, Will and I in the other.

"Take the bed," Will said, gesturing toward the corner of the room where the small bed sat. "I won't be sleeping tonight."

I sat on the edge of the bed and watched him pace in front of the window for a few minutes. We had been faced with multiple executions and unjust beatings since coming to England and joining forces with Marian's crew, and at all of them Will had been concerned—empathetic even—but calm and entirely in control of his emotions and reactions to the situation. But now...

"Will."

"Sorry." Will turned toward me, his hands curling into fists at his side. "If my pacing will keep you from sleeping I can go to another room."

"No, that's not it. Just...sit down." I patted the bed beside me. Will hesitated, so I stood up and walked over to him, taking his hand. I carefully unrolled his tightly held fist and linked my fingers through his to guide him back over to the bed.

As we sat down, Will seemed to deflate as he removed his hand from mine. All of his tense muscles relaxed and he slumped forward, his head falling into his hands as dejection took the place of his anxiety.

"We are rather good at what we do," I said, placing my hand on his shoulder. "I have every confidence that we will reach Middlesborough in time to avoid disaster."

"And if we don't?" Will's voice was muffled as he spoke through his hands.

"Then we will grieve that tragedy."

"That is not remotely comforting, Dusty." Will sat up, turning to look at me and I could see the tears glimmering in his eyes.

"I'm sorry. I just…whatever happens in this life I have confidence that my God will be with me and get me through all of it. He has not failed me yet, even when disaster overcame my family; He was always there to be my comfort and I know He would be for you."

I shrugged, clasping my hands in my lap. I knew Will didn't believe as I did, so perhaps he would find my faith to be empty comfort. If only he knew the true depths of the love and grace of the Father whose own heart would be breaking at this situation. Jesus wept over his friend Lazarus whom He knew he was about to raise from the dead—He would surely be weeping over this child of Will's friend if we failed to save them.

Will didn't say anything. I glanced toward him and saw he'd returned to his dejected posture, curled forward with his head buried in his hands.

"In my experience, worry only makes things worse. If nothing terrible occurs, you've suffered for nothing. And if tragedy does strike, you've prolonged your suffering."

Will sat up, rubbing his forehead for a moment before he turned to look at me again. "It is difficult not to worry."

"I know." I bit my lip before continuing. "This is the first time I've seen you so distraught. You've saved many people over the last three years, haven't you?"

"Yes, but they were strangers. I was intent on saving them, and I feel guilty every time we fail, but I didn't know them. Aiken —Cyrus' son—I was there the day he was born. I haven't seen him in years due to being a fugitive outlaw, but…" Will glanced toward the ceiling and then stared at his hands for a moment. "I was there when Aiken took his first steps, said his first word. I love this kid."

I reached over and placed my hand on Will's.

"We have to save him, Dusty."

"We will."

He still appeared despondent, and I felt a sudden urge to do what my father would have done if I had been the one in such despair.

When I was a child and upset, my father would lay me down with my head in his lap and stroke my hair as he sang to me; the feel of his gentle fingers in my hair was always reassuring, and the sound of his voice brought comfort. I wanted to offer the same to Will.

But I hadn't sung since my father had died—not for anyone—and though I was holding Will's hand now, putting my fingers through his enticing brown hair seemed far too dangerous, like so much kindling about to burst into flame.

I could hold Much's or Robin's hands without feeling all fluttery inside, but even now when Will was distraught, holding his hand felt so right; I knew when I let go my hand would feel the emptiness the loss of him left behind.

And that scared me.

I was letting myself get so attached so quickly; it was as though everything I'd taught myself over the years after my family's death had been completely swept away by Will.

It was true that Robin, Much, and Allen had started the work of breaking down those walls and the Lord has used them for that purpose in my life—but with Will, it all seemed so much more real. Being open and vulnerable wasn't a choice, I simply existed in that space without conscious effort and whenever I became aware of it, it startled me.

Will curled his fingers through mine, looking up at me with those sad, intense, dark blue eyes. I could drown myself there and never feel sorry for it.

"We need rest," Will said, squeezing my hand. "I appreciate you trying to take care of me, but I don't think I'll stop worrying until I see Aiken truly safe. In any event, I am calm enough now that I am sure I won't pace and keep you awake."

"I was not worried about my lack of sleep."

"I know; you were just concerned for my well-being and believe me, that means the world to me." Will raised my hand to his lips for the briefest moment, and then let go and stood up. "Go to sleep, Dusty. I'm going to go sit and watch the stars for a bit. I don't anticipate sleeping at all."

"You do need rest, Will, if you're going to be any help to Aiken."

"I'll try and sleep, I promise. Just not right this minute; I've got far too much pent up emotion. I'll see you tomorrow."

Will left the room, and I felt the silence creeping into the space around me. I knew he hadn't gone far, but his absence was screaming from every corner of the room.

I curled into the bedding, pulling the thin blanket over my shoulders as I kicked off my boots and pushed them to the floor. I was tired from our day of travel, and exhausted emotionally both from comforting Will and from retraining my own emotions and wrestling with my vulnerabilities. It might have been easier to just give in and be open and honest with Will; but I wasn't brave enough for that.

When we arrived in Middlesborough late the next day, Will led us straight to his friends house. Cyrus eagerly let us inside and we gathered around his table.

"So far my boy's still under lock and key. Sheriff is threatening execution, like he was, but nothing's happened yet."

Will seemed to sag with relief—all of his muscles relaxing

as he brushed his shoulder against mine and smiled at me for a moment.

"I am glad to hear he's still alive."

"What's our plan?" Mark asked. "Rescue him from the Sheriff, or wait to stop the execution."

"Since we don't know how long we'd have to wait for an execution," Little John crossed his arms and shrugged. "I say we get the boy from his prison."

"I agree," Will said.

"You'll have to leave your home," Mark said to Cyrus. "Once we get your son out, you and your family will have to leave Middlesborough. You can live on the run in England if you can find a place to shelter, or we have been sending folks to live in Scotland for as long as it isn't safe here."

"We brought money for you," I said. "And for others in Middlesborough as well, if they'll let us help them. Robin Hood has been collecting the unfairly taken taxes and we are giving the money back to the people."

Cyrus nodded slowly, stroking his chin. "I have relatives from Scotland as a matter of fact; we can leave here as soon as you bring me Aiken. I'll have my wife help me get things packed and ready."

"Where is Aiken being held?" Will asked.

"In a pillory the Sheriff here had made especially for him —fitted for his tiny frame."

"That's appalling," I said. What kind of man would put a child in such a contraption?

"He's just outside the large manor house at the end of the village," Cyrus said. His voice shook as he spoke, and he put a trembling hand down on the table to steady himself.

Little John clapped a large hand on his shoulder. "We'll get your boy."

"Let's do this fast," Will said. "Dusty, get that money you brought distributed quickly. Little John, Mark, let's get Aiken out of the stocks and back here as fast as we can—Cyrus you have to be ready to go by the time we arrive so you can take flight immediately. If we are still pursued by any soldiers, we will take care of them while you run."

"Let's get to it then," Little John said.

I checked my satchel to be sure I still had all the pouches of money. I pulled one out and put on the table before Cyrus and he nodded gratefully.

"I'll have my family ready to leave, Will." He and Will clasped forearms for a moment and then our group left the house.

"Dusty, get moving. Hopefully we'll be back within an hour or less," Will said. "If we've left by the time you are done, or we're caught up in a fight but Aiken is free and with his family, then just head back to Sherwood. We'll catch up eventually."

"I am not going to abandon you all here," I said, crossing my arms. "I will do my job, and then I am coming to be your reinforcements should you need them."

286

Will, Little John, and Mark took off down the street, and I moved to the house next to Cyrus', pounding on the door. When a woman tentatively answered it, eyes wide with what might have been fear, I realized my eagerness might have sounded like aggression to the oppressed people of this village.

"Robin Hood sends his regards," I said softly, trying not to seem too frightening as I dropped a bag full of gold coins in her unsuspecting hands. I hurried away before she could say or do anything, running to the next house to do the same. All the while my heart pounded in my ears, telling me I needed to follow Will.

What if there were too many soldiers? What if he died? What if they all did, and that was the last I'd ever see of the three of them?

I took a deep breath as I reached the fourth house on the street. Closing my eyes and reaching toward the comfort of my heavenly Father. I felt it instantly; the calm, the reassurance, the love washed over me and I could feel my anxiety leave.

I continued handing out money as quickly as I could, wanting to be with the others so that I could assist them, but I was no longer panicking.

I heard Little John's roar of fury from across the village, and so did everyone else in the streets. People began to follow the sound, curiosity overcoming their fear, but I kept going door to door with my bags of money until I ran out.

As soon as the last bag was gone, I took off running. I hadn't gone far when I saw the gathering crowds. They were not clustered in the street, but rather lurking in groups of three or four in every doorway and window along the street. Those who had come from the other side of the village were joining the others in a rather slinking manner, and it seemed to me as though none of them wanted to admit they were witnessing anything so that if they got in trouble they could easily deny any involvement in the proceedings.

Because they weren't blocking my view in any way, I could see what was transpiring with perfect clarity. At the end of the street was a large manor, just as Cyrus had said. In front of it, Mark was engaged in a sword fight with two soldiers while Little John was wildly swinging his quarter staff at three more.

There was a tangled mess of wood in the street that must have been the remains of the pillory, and next to it stood Will, a child clinging to his waist from behind—he had one arm wrapped protectively behind himself, hand on the boy, as his other arm kept his sword dancing to the movement of his opponent.

I whipped my daggers from my belt as I pelted forward, skidding to a stop while using my momentum and trajectory to send the blades flying.

One pierced Will's opponent in the neck and he fell, the other grazed past the head of one of Mark's foes. It clattered to the ground, bouncing along the cobblestone street, but the spout of blood that came from the man's head as he dropped his sword and reached for his ear suggested I had hit him, albeit not where I'd intended.

Will came sprinting toward me, shoving the young boy into my arms. "Get him back to his house."

He spun back around just as more soldiers came pouring into the street from the manor; ten, twelve, fifteen of them. I didn't hesitate, didn't go back for my daggers. I simply grabbed Aiken's hand and took off running through the village toward his house.

I wanted to look over my shoulder, wanted to know that Will was okay, that Mark and Little John were still standing, but instead I kept running.

When we reached Aiken's house, he let go of my hand and bounded toward his door. Cyrus burst out of it and scooped his son up, practically crushing him to his chest, tears streaming down his face.

"It's time to go," I said, feeling tears spring to my own eyes at the sight of their reunion. It was the sort of hug my own father might have used if we met again—but we would never meet again in this life.

Cyrus nodded, carrying his son inside. His wife was there, bags packed. Cyrus grabbed a pack and slung it over his shoulder.

"Thank you, for all you have done. Tell Will I am eternally grateful. Should England ever return to peace…should we ever meet again…"

"I'll tell him."

I stood for a moment, watching Cyrus and his family leave their home and most of their possessions behind for what might be the last time. Once they were safely outside of the village, I sprinted back the way I had come, my hands shaking. I still had my sword, though I had left my bow at the camp in Sherwood.

As I dashed around a corner, I plowed straight into someone, both of us falling to the ground in a tangle of arms and legs. The impact knocked the air straight out of me.

I felt hands on my shoulders and heard Mark's voice above me. "Are you okay? Let's go!"

Slowly my brain seemed to come back into focus as my lungs took a great gulp of air and I reoriented myself. Shifting movement below me made me turn my head as I started to rock back onto my knees. Will was trying to push himself up; I had been draped across him when we fell.

Little John's shouting rang out and my gaze was drawn down the street. His quarter staff was still swinging wildly, knocking the legs out from under soldiers who were apparently in hot pursuit.

Mark grabbed me under my arms and pulled me to my feet while Will shakily helped himself up.

"We have to move!" Will said, glancing over his shoulder.

"Are you good?" Mark glanced between me and Little John's line of defense.

"I'm fine." I took off running down the street between Mark and Will. "What's the plan?"

"Let Little John deal with them for the time being," Will said as we sprinted through the village.

"What if he needs help?"

"We've used him like this before," Mark said. "He can handle it."

We broke free of the village and kept running. There was a spur of Sherwood Forest—a massive forest, by any standard—not too far from Middlesborough and I assumed that would be our destination. As we ran toward the dark shapes of trees on the horizon, I sent a prayer for Little John's safety.

The landscape was not remotely flat; there were rolling hills and outcroppings of trees, places where rock formations rose from the ground, and farmer's fields with tall stalks of grain. All of it swam before my eyes in a haze—I might have hit my head harder than I thought when I slammed into Will.

Once we'd gone far enough to be out of sight of the village, Will called for us to stop for a moment.

I bent over, my hands on my knees, as a fire burned through my lungs.

"We don't seem to have a pursuit," Mark said, glancing behind us. We couldn't see the village from here, just the gentle upward slope of the hill we'd just tumbled down.

"Did you get Aiken to Cyrus?" Will asked.

I nodded, trying not to gasp for air. "They…got…away…"

I stood up, closing my eyes and trying to breathe as deeply as possible to satisfy my hungry lungs.

I felt a hand brush my cheek and my eyes flashed open. Will stood in front of me, concern written across his face as his fingers grazed my cheek.

"I'm fine."

"It's a decent amount of blood, Dusty."

"Blood?" I reached up to my face and felt the sticky sensation there. As Will pulled his hand away, I could see the crimson stain on his fingers. Now that I was focused on it, I could feel the sting in my cheek. "I must have hit my face across a rock or something in the street when we fell."

"I am sorry."

"You didn't cause this, Will."

"What can I do to help?"

"Let's get to Sherwood where we know we're safe and then I can assess the damage and what needs to be done."

The three of us moved across the hills and fields quickly, but not at an all out sprint. Eventually, after several hours of travel, we made it to the forest. We moved under the cover of the trees, and then I plopped to the ground, my legs burning and my lungs protesting the exertion I had extended on this trip.

Will sat next to me, pulling his waterskin from his belt and pouring a bit into his hand. Before I realized what he was doing, he'd reached up and was wiping the blood from my face. He poured more water into his hand a few times as he gently scrubbed the drying flakes from my cheek and forehead. I sat as still as possible. My heart rate, already elevated by the run and the intensity of the fight and panic in the village, was now running faster than I had to escape the village.

I clasped my hands tightly in my lap to still their shaking.

Why did he make me so nervous?

"It's not a bad cut," he said once he was satisfied.

"Thank you." I pulled my pouch from my belt, wishing I had a mirror so I could see for myself. I chose a pinch of a mixture of herbs and held my hand out to Will. He raised his eyebrows, but let me drop the plant flakes into his hand. "Rub it into the cut, if you will."

Will did as I asked. I could feel the tingle in my cheek begin to fade. It appeared Will was correct in his assumption that it wasn't a bad cut. It had likely only bled a great deal because it was on my face—the head had a bad habit of being melodramatic when it got cut, I had noticed.

We waited in Sherwood for several hours, sprawled out on the ground resting our aching legs and our burning lungs.

Eventually, Mark moved away from the trees to keep an eye out for Little John. It was some hours before the latter arrived, but when he did we began our journey back to Nottingham and our own portion of Sherwood Forest.

Chapter 23

IN THE DAYS and weeks that followed it became more common place to hear harrowing reports from other villages and shires beyond Nottingham and it slowly became a regular occurrence for Robin or Will to lead one or two of us on a trip to rescue someone from a neighboring shire—or even farther away—or to take money and food to hand out to those in need far beyond the reaches of Nottingham itself.

On one such trip, I traveled with Will and Mark to a little village called Scarborough to distribute our small pouches of money to the people there.

After an hour or so of moving around the village, I approached the last house on the street. A man stood outside, having watched my procession down the street, stopping at every house along the way to give away a pouch of money. He appeared a few years older than myself, and was holding a baby in one arm, with a little girl hiding behind his legs and small boy holding onto his arm.

I reached into my satchel and pulled out my last pouch of money, holding it out to him. He took it with a slight bow and tears in his eyes.

"Thank you, laddie."

"You are most welcome."

He shepherded his children back into his house and I turned to walk back across the village in search of my companions. I did not have to go far, because almost as soon as I'd turned from the man's house, Mark fell into step beside me.

"You know if you grew your hair long again people might not always assume you're a man."

"What?"

"That fellow back there with the children," Mark gestured behind us. "He called you 'laddie' or didn't you notice?"

"I've been called 'lad', and 'son', and 'sir' so often in the last four or five years I hardly notice it anymore."

"But you aren't hiding your identity anymore, are you? I mean, you told all of us that you are a woman."

I thought about that, and then shrugged. "It's easier to maintain when there is less of it."

"Your hair?"

"Yes. And as for my clothes, which I'm sure is your next comment, how could I help with our raids and rescues if I were always in a skirt? It would impede my movement."

"Fair point. But you still could correct people when they think you're a man. I mean, you could…"

"I could what, Mark?"

"Look like a girl?" Mark shrugged, suddenly blushing and looking sheepish.

"Do I look like a man to you?"

"Eh…maybe not. A little. You did fool an entire army or two, right?"

"That was not a definitive answer," I said, feeling my mouth quirk up into a smile. Mark was clearly uncomfortable with the conversation that he had started.

"Is there a good answer to a woman asking if she looks like a man?" Mark glanced at me and then down at his boots. "What do you want me to say?"

"Don't look so uneasy. I do not care what I look like, so long as I am clean and healthy."

"But still…why didn't you correct him? The man back there?"

"I don't know…it didn't seem important." I glanced around at the houses we were passing. Some people were still in their doorways watching us, waving their thanks. The rumors of Robin Hood and his men bringing hope and salvation to England were spreading rapidly, and I had noticed people began to know who we were and expect our help when we arrived. It was less and less necessary to explain ourselves to them.

"I suppose it is still safer for the general populace to consider you a man," Mark shrugged.

"Why is this so important to you?"

"I guess it's not. I just…I have a sister. A fiery, unafraid of men, sister who is just as eager to fight back against the Sheriff and Gisbourne as you are. But she also doesn't hide her true self, you know?"

"What are we discussing?" Will asked, startling both Mark and I as he fell into step on my other side.

"Whether or not Dusty looks like a man," Mark said, grinning at me.

"Excuse me?" Will's eyebrows hit his hairline and I couldn't help but laugh.

"A man in the village called me 'laddie' and it bothered Mark," I said.

"Well the short hair and trousers are a bit misleading," Will said. "And you're not exactly...well-endowed, shall we put it? So that helps with the disguise, too. Though for the record, I have never once thought you looked like a man. You're far too beautiful."

I could feel heat rushing to my face and noticed Mark rolling his eyes.

"Have we gotten everyone?" Mark asked. "Hit every street with our money?"

"I'm entirely out of money bags," Will said.

"As am I."

Mark nodded. "Great. Shall we head back to Sherwood then?"

"Trying to change the subject?" Will asked, laughing and shoving Mark playfully to the side.

Mark didn't respond, turning away and striding down the street in order to exit the village. Will and I followed more slowly.

"I don't know how you fooled the army during the Crusade, or anyone else for that matter. They must all have been incredibly blind. I've never seen a more beautiful face."

297

"Don't be ridiculous," I said, biting my cheek as I blushed.

"I'm serious." Will leaned forward, trying to catch my eye as we walked, but I turned away from him. "Your eyes are so captivating, you know. And when you smile—it's a rare occurrence, but when it happens I can't even breathe sometimes. And I've never heard a laugh that makes me feel so happy myself, it's contagious."

It was hard to say whether my rapidly beating heart or my blushing cheeks held the most heat, but I was growing far too embarrassed for this conversation to continue. "Will…"

I felt his fingers curl around mine as he took my hand in his. We kept walking, following Mark out of the village. For a moment, there was a reprieve and I fought to regain composure.

"There's your keen and curious mind, too," Will said suddenly. My eyes darted his direction long enough to see his gorgeous blue eyes dancing. "Your healing skills, which are remarkable and evidence of your compassionate heart. Your accent that makes me smile simply because it is so you. Your staunch belief in your faith, the fact you show no fear or care for what the others say about it. Allen will tease you endlessly for it, but it doesn't phase you. You know exactly who you are."

"I'm not sure I do."

Will squeezed my hand. "You do. I think whatever happened before I knew you, the stuff you won't talk about…I think it is hard to look at and acknowledge. I think that's why you still don't correct people who think you are a man. Maybe it is safer to hide your identity, but I don't think that's why you do it. You're just not ready to face the truth yet—and that's okay, Dusty. Whatever it is, you don't have to heal from it to satisfy Mark's desire for you to be more womanly, or whatever it is he was thinking. It's your life, your pain—you are a healer, after all, you know these things take time and every wound is different."

I simultaneously loved and hated that Will knew me so well, that he could see straight through me. Much and Robin sometimes could, but they'd had years of practice. I'd only known Will a matter of months, but he *knew* me.

I felt seen and safe with him, and yet at the same time the very knowledge that he could see past my defenses so easily terrified me. I found myself pulling my hand out of his reach to create some distance between us, and yet as soon as my fingers were free of his I missed their comforting and warm presence.

I did not understand what was becoming of me, but I had an inkling. I didn't know how or why, but since the first moment I met Will I had been falling in love with him. He didn't help, either, with all his wonderful words and his kindness.

I *could* love him. I wasn't sure I wanted to; I wasn't sure I had a choice.

The fact that he didn't have Christ as his Lord was a problem, and one that I fully embraced. In some part because Scripture did suggest not being 'unequally yoked' by joining with someone who did not share the same faith. But also because I needed an excuse to pull away from Will's advances and my own heart's longings, and that was the best reason I could possibly find.

He didn't share my faith. That was the end of it.

Chapter 24

IN THE WEEKS that followed Nottingham began to swell as
merchants from around the world came to prepare for what Much
said was the biggest event of the year. The Nottingham Fair.
There were also travelers coming, not to sell wares but to enjoy
the Fair as party-goers.

"But what is it?" I asked. Much, Will, and I were
wandering the woods. I'd gone in search of more medicinal
plants, and Much had come along to continue his education. Will
followed because he always did, whether I liked it or not.

The air was warm—not too hot, not too cold. A perfect
temperature to match the way the light perfectly drifted through
the trees above us casting golden strands to grace the air and the
ground around us.

"It started as a harvest festival, I think," Much said. "But
since I could remember, it's always been a giant party. People
gather to sell fancy things you wouldn't always find in
Nottingham, and there are dances and contests—archery
tournaments and horse races and the like. It's a busy day."

"It sounds busy."

"There's also the tradition of accompanying a beautiful
lady to the Fair," Will said, throwing me a wink.

"It's one of my favorite times of year," Much said.

"You like courting the ladies?" Will said, chuckling.

"No, I like the different foods that are found in the various booths during Nottingham Fair. It always smells and tastes so perfect—a little slice of heaven."

That night as the gang was gathered around the fire ring enjoying the dinner Much had prepared for us, Robin came into camp in a foul mood. When Allen asked what was wrong, he was promptly barked at. No one else spoke as Robin disappeared inside his hut.

Once he was gone, the conversation picked up again.

"I wonder what's frustrating him now…" Mark said.

"He went to Wetherby to visit Marian, didn't he?" Will asked. "Maybe they had a fight."

"Or it could be Gisbourne," Little John suggested.

"What about Gisbourne?" I asked.

"The Sheriff's right hand has been spending a bit of time in Wetherby," Will said. "He's almost been courting Marian off and on over the years—when he isn't trying to execute her father, that is. It is possible Robin is jealous."

"But he can be in no doubt of Marian's affection for him," I said. "Why would he need to be jealous?"

No one could give me a solid answer, though they all seemed to agree that jealousy was a likely cause for Robin's mood—that, or a fight with Marian. That option seemed more likely to me. They were both rather hot-headed.

As the evening progressed, people began to retire to their various huts for the night, and Much went to speak with Robin, leaving Will and I alone at the fire. The logs crackled merrily before us as the air grew chill and the stars began to appear in the bit of sky we could see above our meadow.

"If we weren't outlaws, I'd ask you to accompany me to the Fair," Will said, shifting across the log bench to sit next to me.

"I suppose that means something," I said, studying his face.

"It's a whole thing," Will said, grinning. "Suitors asking their ladies to accompany them to the Fair. For the nobles, it can be the moment a man knows his chances with the woman he's pursuing. If she has multiple suitors, the one she chooses to spend time with will feel the weight of that choice."

"Seeing as you are the only person to suggest accompanying me to the Fair, it wouldn't hold that weight for you."

"Yes, but you agreeing at all would be a major victory."

I shook my head, trying not to smile at the way his eyes were alight with amusement and mischief.

"We can't go to the Fair; we're outlaws. It's dangerous to be in Nottingham at the best of times."

"And yet, with more people in the city for the Fair it would be easier to blend into the crowds. You've never seen the Fair, you might enjoy it."

"Perhaps."

Much came wandering over to the fire and sat beside us.

"I have gleaned the truth of Robin's mood."

"Which is?"

"Marian is going to the Fair with Gisbourne."

"So...Robin *is* jealous," Will said.

"Because she's spending time with another man?" I asked. "Robin is with me fairly frequently and Marian isn't jealous of that."

"You aren't courting Robin," Will said. "Gisbourne is definitely courting Marian. Plus...I think Marian has been jealous of you on occasion."

I sighed, thinking back to my arrival and Marian's icy attitude. Will wasn't wrong. She had instantly disliked me thinking I might be more to Robin than a friend.

"Still...Gisbourne is working for the Sheriff and often ruining innocent lives. Robin has to know Marian can't care for him."

"Have you ever been in love?" Will asked. His dark blue eyes were too intense and I turned away from him. "People will act foolishly when they are in love."

"Gisbourne did leave it rather late," Much commented. "Not asking her to go until the day before."

"Coward," Will said.

The next day Robin disappeared from camp, presumably going to the Fair to keep an eye on Marian. Much went with him, which was probably for the best. Robin sometimes needed a more steady hand to keep his impulsivity in check.

Instead of going to the Fair, I chose to take some of our store of money and travel to the surrounding villages, leaving donations at all the homes I could find. Most of the villages were entirely emptied out—everyone had gone to Nottingham for the day.

I was curious about the Fair, though I didn't know what to make of Will's comments about escorting me there. It didn't matter; I'd chosen not to accept his advances because he did not share my faith. Whatever other hesitancy I might have in regard to opening up and sharing the darkest parts of myself...it was a moot point.

The days and weeks continued to pass in quick succession. We were always busy; Marian—or anyone else spying in the secret passages of Nottingham castle—would hear of the Sheriff's schemes to hang someone and we'd set off to rescue them. The caravans of treasure continued to pass through Sherwood and we continued to ambush them. Robin made sure we weren't always setting up our ambushes at the same bend in the road so we never became predictable. Every week or two Robin would send us in small groups of two or three to travel beyond Nottinghamshire and check in on the rest of England, carrying money to the needy beyond our own city. There was no end to what we could do to help the people of England, and there were hardly enough of us to do it.

One night late in the fall, after the forest had burst into brilliantly bright colors all around our camp—reds, golds, fiery oranges—Robin came to camp in high spirits, waving about a bit of parchment. The rest of us were gathered around the fire ring enjoying Much's fine cooking when he came striding over, a mischievous grin lighting up his face.

"Your visit with Marian go well?" Will asked, elbowing Robin as he joined the rest of us around the fire.

"It did. But more to the point, I have a parchment!" Robin waved his stack of papers in Will's face for a moment, still grinning.

"Parchment?" Little John tilted his head to one side. "What for? Did someone write to you?"

"Oh no," Robin shook his head gravely. "It's blank parchment."

"And why is your blank parchment so important?" Will asked, trying to snatch it from Robin's hand.

"Because…now I can continue my studies with Dusty. I purchased this today for that very purpose. With all the excitement in England, I'd nearly forgotten about it."

"What studies?" Mark asked.

"While we were imprisoned, Dusty was teaching us Arabic," Robin said.

I'd nearly forgotten about that myself; it seemed a lifetime ago when I'd been writing in the dirt in Durnstein prison.

"We could have continued the studies without parchment," I said. "The ground worked just as well at Durnstein castle."

"Are these lessons private, or open to the public?" Will asked. "I'd be interested in learning Dusty's language as well."

"I am willing to teach anyone eager to learn," I said.

After that day, I began teaching the gang to read and write my mother tongue once more. As the autumn turned to winter, and the leaves fell from every tree as snow graced their branches instead, less caravans came through Sherwood and the Sheriff slowed his murder frenzy so we had more time on our hands and therefore more time for my lessons. Robin, Will, and Mark were my eager students. Allen only paid attention when he had nothing better to do. Much was attentive as always, but still not quite as quick at picking it up as Robin.

Along with rescuing innocents from the Sheriff's schemes, and confiscating the Sheriff's treasure to give to the needy and poor of England, we also spent time purchasing food in bulk from various bakers and butchers and then passing it out to the people of England. This became even more necessary during the winter months as the cold set in and food became more scarce for the less fortunate in England than it already had been.

Our job became more difficult during the winter months despite the need for it growing—traveling in snowstorms was not an easy feat. Even so, Robin still sent us off in groups as often as he could to distribute money and food across England.

One sharply cold day, Mark and I were sent to distribute food in Nottingham itself while Robin sent the rest of the gang traveling beyond our shire. The streets of Nottingham were covered in hard-packed snow and ice—here in the city the snow rarely stayed fresh and soft for long. Too many people tramping through the city for that; it quickly became a slush that would then harden into ice as the temperatures dropped every night.

"Aren't you glad we are assigned to Nottingham?" Mark asked, pulling his cloak tighter around himself with one hand while he carried a large basket overflowing with food in the other.

"I would have been willing to go anywhere Robin asked," I replied, carrying my own large basket of food that had been purchased earlier that day.

"But it is nicer to be in the city and not wandering the frozen countryside like the rest of the poor souls that make up our gang."

We walked side by side down the snow-covered street, stopping at each house to leave food on doorsteps. If the residents were outside or came to the door we would interact with them, otherwise we simply left the gifts where they could easily find them.

The colder the weather became, the less people would be seen moving around the streets. There were still a number of people on business here and there, and the market had a small gathering—though not quite a crowd—but it had been a far busier city when I'd first arrived in this part of England. It was more difficult to blend into the crowds and hide from the Sheriff's soldiers when they marched around the city now, but so far we hadn't been stopped or questioned.

Mark looked up toward the grey sky as fluffy white flakes started to float down towards our heads. "It's starting to snow. Again."

As he spoke, he slipped on the hard-packed ice beneath our feet, skidding several feet before regaining his balance.

"Careful."

"Are you actually worried about me, or just worried I'll drop and spoil the food?" Mark glanced toward me, his eyes dancing with laughter as he carefully placed his next step.

"The food, of course," I said with a laugh as I watched him dramatically and slowly place each foot before moving forward.

"That's what I thought."

After we'd left a few more gifts of food on several more doorsteps, Mark said, "When we finish here, we should stop at Marcus' home before returning to camp. That way we can warm up before our trek into the wild."

"Don't speak so loud," I chided, glancing around the mostly empty street. It was easy to be comfortable and confident the longer we were able to move freely in the city, but that did not change the simple fact that we were, indeed, outlaws and wanted by the Sheriff. Someday, if we kept on like this, someone was going to get caught. "Besides, the walk to Sherwood is not that wild."

"But you know you'd like to warm up, Dusty. You're not as invincible as you would like the world to believe."

The icy wind pricked my face and hands like so many small needles as the snow continued to fall heavily from above. "I cannot argue with that."

Once our baskets were empty of food, we turned out steps toward Marcus' home.

Marcus was a blacksmith that had worked closely with Marian, Mark, Will, and Little John long before the rest of us arrived in England. Though many residents of Nottingham would help us when asked, Marcus was an unofficial member of the gang. His house was a safe stopping point for all of us whenever we were in Nottingham. He would also provide us with weapons when we needed them.

"Here you are, Dusty." Marcus handed me a steaming mug as Mark and I made ourselves comfortable at the table in his front room. His wife Lillian was fixing us something to eat as well before we set off for the camp.

"Thank you, Marcus."

"If the weather gets truly bad, you can always stay the night."

"We should do that," Mark said. "It's way warmer here than at the camp."

"Mark." I shook my head at him. "You are coming back to the camp tonight. The weather isn't so bad that you need to be an inconvenience to Marcus and Lillian."

"It's no inconvenience," Lillian said, placing a platter of steaming meat pies on the table between us. "It's the least we can do after you have all done so much for the people of England."

"And it is cold, Dusty," Mark said, taking a large bite of one of the pies. "You have to admit that."

"I spent a whole winter frozen in a cell in Austria without any heat at all."

"Never one to be outdone, are you, Dusty?" Mark shook his head, chuckling as he continued to dig into Lillian's meal.

I slowly picked up a fork and started eating as well.

"You are always welcome here, Dusty," Marcus said.

"We appreciate that. But we do need to return to camp. Robin will be expecting a report. If there was a true emergency or the weather was too terrible to travel in, then I would say yes to your invitation. But as the only reason to stay now is because Mark is afraid of a little cold, I'm saying no."

"Yes, mum," Mark grumbled playfully, rolling his eyes at me. The smile on his face and dancing in his eyes proved to me he wasn't truly upset by my decision.

More than Robin needing a report, I was more concerned with whether or not Will had returned safely. Traveling in winter was dangerous and I often worried for those who traveled beyond Nottingham.

311

Chapter 25

SEVERAL WEEKS PASSED with snow and ice as our constant companions. We remained huddled around the fire as a group whenever we were in the camp, desperately trying to stay warm. Marian still visited often, bringing us news of Gisbourne and the Sheriff or simply coming to see Robin and her brother Mark.

One day in early February, Will and I were sent to Middlesborough to distribute food, money, blankets, and other supplies.

There was a dusting of snow on the ground, and the dark sky over our heads was cheerfully dumping more as we walked along the winding road in the open countryside. A harsh, cold wind pushed the snow in a spiraling dance through the air. I pulled my cloak tighter around my shoulders as Will whistled a happy tune beside me, leading a horse borrowed from Marcus that was weighed down with our supplies for the village.

"It's a beautiful day." Will paused his song long enough to shoot me a wink along with his comment.

It was a cold and harsh day, in my opinion, but the snow sparkled like so many diamonds whenever the sun would fight its way through the clouds, and I found that, at least, truly magical.

As we entered the village, Will shifted the basket filled with food that he carried, looking around the relatively empty street with a melancholy expression. He pulled his hood up, obscuring his face from view. I wasn't sure if that was to hide from my scrutiny, or from the sight of any soldiers we might come across who could recognize Will as an outlaw.

"Do you miss it here, Will?"

Will didn't reply as we moved to the first house on the street and laid out an offering of food and a bag of coins wrapped in a blanket on the front step.

We moved across the street toward the next house, and Will glanced at me. "I miss some of it; I miss the people, mostly. I have no family here, only friends I grew up with. Not being entirely sentimental, the town itself holds no more claim to me than Nottingham."

We moved to the next house and then the next before Will spoke again. "I think I miss the naivety and innocence I once had that this place represents…what about you, Dusty? Do you miss your homeland?"

"Not particularly. Everyone that I love is in Nottinghamshire, and I have no reason to pine for other places. Though I do miss the weather sometimes. Your country is far too cold."

"You don't miss more than the weather?"

"I don't have anyone to miss. Although it sounds like you do; when we have finished our task here, we could visit some of your friends if you'd like. You only saw Aiken's father the last time we were here, and we were rather distracted by Aiken's rescue."

"I'd like that."

We continued down the street, leaving offerings of food and money at every doorstep. Occasionally we met people in the streets we could hand our donations to directly. Eventually, our baskets were empty and Will led me through the streets of his village to the home of one of his friends, a man he called Adam.

As soon as Will knocked on the door, it swung open and a man of Little John's proportions stood before us—he was tall, muscular, and barely fit in the doorframe.

"What do you want?" His voice was not harsh, but there was a certain amount of suspicion to it as he looked us over.

"It's me, Adam."

"Will?" Adam reached forward and pulled Will's hood off of his head. He looked him over from head to toe before pulling him into an embrace. "Will! I have been so worried, and so has Agnes! Where have you been? You were helping people, and then the sheriff wanted to hang you, and then you were gone. When that Aiken kid was rescued a few months back, there were rumors you'd had something to do with it, but I hadn't seen you."

"I went to Nottingham when our sheriff came for my head."

"Robin Hood?" Adam asked, his eyebrows rising.

"Yes."

"Is it anything like people say?"

"Depends on what people are saying."

"Come inside, get out of that foul weather."

Adam stepped aside and waved us both forward. Before we went inside, Will tied the horse to a post outside Adam's house.

The moment we were out of the biting wind, I felt a sharp sense of relief. I set the last of our supplies on Adam's table.

"This is my friend Dusty," Will said as Adam ushered us to his table. "She's also a member of Robin Hood's gang."

"Nice to meet you, nice to meet you." Adam flashed a broad smile in my direction before turning back to Will. "Is it true? Is Robin Hood going to take down the Prince?"

"I don't know about that?" Will shrugged. "We help where we can though."

"But he is fighting—I mean you're all fighting—the Prince's men, gathering the ransom to free the King, all of that?"

"Yes."

I set the food and money on the table as Will and Adam continued their conversation.

"You're undermining the Prince's hand-appointed sheriffs, yes? Stopping the hangings, freeing the prisoners, feeding the poor?"

Will chuckled at Adam's enthusiasm. "Yes. We are doing all of that."

"What are you in Middlesborough for?"

"We brought food."

"Ah." Adam glanced toward the things I'd placed on the table. "How long are you here then?"

315

"Not long. We'll head back toward Nottingham today."

"Well I am glad you stopped by. Agnes is over at Maynild's house. You remember Maynild, Will? Can you wait till she gets back before you head off? She'll be disappointed to miss you."

"We can wait."

"Good! I'll get you something warm to drink, see if we have anything to spare to eat…"

Adam walked out of the room, but he soon returned with a plate of bread and mugs of ale. We'd barely taken a bite before a woman came bustling into the house. She'd only made it two steps inside before she froze, and then a smile broke out across her face.

"William Scarlett!" Her voice seemed to bounce off the walls around us. "Where the devil have you been? I've been so worried!" Agnes marched forward and grabbed Will's head where he still sat at the table, planting a firm kiss on his forehead.

"He's with Robin Hood, Agnes!" Adam grinned. "Can you believe that? Our Will is going to save England with the great Robin Hood himself."

Agnes continued to hug Will's head and kissed him a dozen times or so before she finally moved to sit down beside her husband.

"Oh, bless you, Will! I knew it. I knew you weren't just hiding or dead or scared of our sheriff and his threats to kill you. I knew it. I told everyone you were doing something good

316

somewhere. And Robin Hood? You're with Robin Hood? Oh, Will…I know for sure now, we're going to be alright."

It amused me to hear Adam and Agnes talking of Robin as some great hero. He was simply Robin to me. My friend, my brother. It was strange to think that the rest of England saw Robin —and likely the rest of us—as heroes sent to save them from their terrible fate.

In the weeks that followed our visit to Middlesborough, the gang continued to act on any information we gleaned from spying in the castle—setting up ambushes to steal back the kingdom's riches and give them to the people, and send some to pay Richard's ransom while we also distributed food and other necessities to any town and village that we could reach.

We were a small band of people, and our resources were limited, but we did what we could to help as many people as possible. This became easier as winter gave way to spring and travel became easier.

One day, as summer began to approach, Will and I found ourselves riding across the green countryside on Marcus' steeds, traveling south of Nottingham on a mission to spread some of our money beyond Nottingham.

As we rode through the countryside in search of any village or outlying farm that could use our assistance, Will glanced upwards toward the blue sky filled with puffy white clouds, and then glanced at me.

"Tell me about your childhood, Dusty."

"What?"

"I know you don't like to talk about it, and I know I promised to stop pestering you. But it's been months, and I could do with the tiniest bit of truth about this remarkable, secretive woman I wish I could know. It doesn't have to be a lot, just... something. I'm dying to know you: all of you."

I bit my lip, turning to watch the fields beside us instead of looking at Will. He'd been patient before, but I could hear the desperate eagerness in his voice now. I knew he cared about me— far more than he had any right to. And sometimes I wanted to return that affection.. I did desire to know more about him, too.

Some part of my heart whispered it was far too dangerous to grow fond of Will; what would I do if I lost him?

"What do you even want to know?"

"I don't know. I have loved every piece of information I've ever learned about you. I just wish there was more of it. I wish you would trust me."

"It's not that I don't trust you, Will. I do."

"Then what?"

I don't want to lose you.

"Here. I'll make it easy." Will's blue eyes softened as he looked at me. "Where did you grow up?"

"A city called Darum."

"There. I know something about you."

Will flashed me a smile and turned his gaze back on the road ahead of us. I knew he wasn't satisfied with that simple

318

statement about where I'd grown up, but he was once again trying not to push me too hard.

This man was far too generous and understanding; my heart couldn't take it. Was I really going to let fear deprive me of the beautiful friendship he was offering?

"Saladin attacked my city when I was just a baby," I said softly. It was easy to start there, with the history I did not recall in my own personal memories. "Many people died, including the father of a girl who lived next door. His wife grew bitter, hating the fact that she'd lost her husband and that her child was a girl and not a son who could provide for her."

I felt the ache in my chest building; I had tried to start vague but I'd immediately turned my conversation toward my sister Habibah and how she came to be part of my family. Could I tell Will all of that without weeping? I'd never truly spoken to anyone about my sister. Not even Robin and Much knew of her existence…

"Dusty?"

Will's voice broke through my reverie just as the first tears fell from my lashes. I shook myself, trying to bring myself back to a place of composure. "Sorry."

"What are you thinking about?" His voice was soft and gentle, like a tender caress, which only made me want to cry all the more.

"That woman—the widow—she was rude to everyone, at least in all the memories I have of her, but she was cruelest to her own daughter. My mother would bring the girl over to our house as often as she could to protect her from her mother's wrath. We grew up together…"

"That was good of your mother."

I couldn't respond as a lump lodged in my throat and more tears threatened to fall. Will said nothing else, letting us ride on in silence for a time.

"My mother was a compassionate woman," I said at last.

"So you must take after her," Will said, smiling gently. "Full of compassion and wisdom and gentleness."

"Hardly," I shook my head. "Compassion, yes. Wisdom, I wouldn't say so. If I have any, it comes from the Lord. And as for gentleness, that is a learned trait—not from my mother, in fact, but from Daniyah."

As soon as her name left my mouth I winced, but Will leaned toward me. "Who is Daniyah?"

"She…"

She was my second mother, and the one who'd told me everything I needed to know about who Christ was. It was she who had led me to the Lord and instructed me in the right way to live. She taught me righteousness as my mother taught me the beauty of kindness.

I took a shuddering breath around the tightening ache in my chest.

"She and her husband Abraham were good friends of my parents."

"Were?" Will's deep blue eyes seemed to darken a shade.

"She died, along with my parents and adopted sister; they were all killed the second time Saladin attacked my city five years ago."

"And then you met Robin and joined the Crusade."

"Well...I joined the Crusade first, and then met Robin."

"Oh?"

Tears were falling in quick succession and I resisted the urge to wipe them from my cheeks. I'd only talked about my life, my family, once before—with Much.

I took a deep breath. Will didn't say anything else, he simply waited.

"The only way to escape my city without being killed or mistreated was to pretend to be a man and join the Saracen army. I trained with them, and then when I was sure I could handle myself on my own, I left their army and went to find the Crusaders. I was with them for some time before I met Robin and joined the King's Guard. And you have heard from Robin, Allen, and Much what those years were like. I need not repeat them."

"I am sorry you saw so much suffering and loss."

"I appreciate that. I am sorry for it as well. And though I do still grieve—clearly, as I have already lost my composure more than once in this conversation—I have found myself content with my lot in life. Good did come from my hardship; I am here now, helping the innocent people of England. I have a new family with Robin and the rest of you. I am happy. Possibly the happiest I have ever been."

"Happier than when your own family was alive?" Will raised an eyebrow and I shrugged.

"I was young then, and hardly happy. Especially as a young child. I had a good life, but I could not see that. All I saw was that I wasn't allowed to do this, or that. My father could be stern, and I had a temper that often made things worse."

"You had a temper? I find that hard to believe."

"I did, though. I was a very angry child."

"I don't believe it."

"It is true! Daniyah taught me to be good, but it was a hard lesson. I had to bite my tongue so often to keep from complaining, I was often in physical pain just trying not to talk disrespectfully to my father when I was angry."

"I still find that hard to believe. You are the most emotionally stable person I have ever met."

"Years of practice and reliance on a higher power, Will."

Also I was good at hiding what I was truly feeling, but he didn't need to know that.

We fell into a comfortable silence and I breathed deeply. It hadn't killed me to talk about my past—in some respects it had even been nice to remember my childhood, and Daniyah's words of wisdom. It wasn't easy to talk about any of it, but I was finding relief in sharing with Will.

"Dusty." Will's voice suddenly held a sense of urgency and seriousness that I was not expecting. I looked to him, but he was gazing intently forward. Following the direction that had his attention, I saw what worried him.

"Is that smoke?"

"Come on!" Will kicked his horse into a gallop and I followed after him. We raced toward the rising shadow on the horizon. At first it was a vague shadowy shape, but it grew darker and began to billow about more as we galloped closer.

Cresting the final hill that blocked our view, a farm came into view below us. The house and barn were on fire, bright orange flames flashing amidst the black smoke that filled the air. Goats and cows were running in all directions and a scream rent the air.

I spurred my horse down the hill toward the sound. The closer I came to the wreckage, the more the air burned my throat and lungs. I held my breath, trying not to inhale the smoke.

Rounding the house, I found a woman clinging to what I assumed was her husband. She was on the ground, with the man in her arms, her head thrown back as she wailed. I leaped from my horse and sprinted toward her as the house began to crumble. We were some yards from it, but the heat of the fire rushed toward me and I stumbled.

Pushing forward, I dropped to my knees beside the screaming woman.

"Let me see him." I pried her arms free of the man so I could examine him as the flames of the house grew taller and the heat bore down on us. She began to rock back and forth, wrapping her arms around herself. Her screams abated, and she began to whimper.

Will dropped to the ground beside her, putting a hand on her shoulder. "Where is your source of water? Do you have a well? A stream nearby?"

The woman continued rocking, whimpering to herself and keeping her eyes firmly fixed on the man's face. I leaned close to his chest, listening for breathing or the sound of a heartbeat as Will questioned the woman.

I found nothing.

I sat up, a fist squeezing around my own heart. "He's gone."

"NO!" The woman began screaming again, her hands reaching up to grasp her hair on either side of her face. "No, no, no!"

A thunderous clap filled the air as the barn began to collapse, pieces of burning wood flying in all directions.

"We have to move!" Will scooped up the woman and began staggering back toward where we had left our horses at the far side of the valley.

I gently closed the man's eyes before I followed.

The woman was still screaming as I sprinted after Will.

Our horses were nowhere to be seen.

"Will?"

"The fire must have scared them," Will said, spinning around to watch the carnage we'd left behind. The woman was still screaming in his arms, but it was growing less frantic and morphing into a moaning sound. "If we don't put out that fire, it will spread to the crops."

"I think it's too late for that."

Will watched for a moment longer, and then set the woman down. "I'm going to look for a town or a village, see if I can get help here to put out the fire or to find this woman a place to live..."

The woman pulled her knees up to her chest, wrapping her arms around herself and beginning to rock once more, still moaning incessantly.

Will grabbed my elbow, staring at me intently. "Keep her safe and stay away from that fire. I'll be back as soon as I can."

"We'll be fine."

I said it with confidence, but as Will walked away I wondered if it were true. I sat down beside the woman as her grief consumed her and watched as the flames did the same to her home. The black smoke filled the air, blocking out any sight of the blue sky.

We waited for hours. Eventually the woman fell silent and we quietly watched the fire spread to the grass and rush toward the crops in the fields in the valley. Luckily, it didn't come up the hill toward us, as the wind pushed it in the opposite direction.

"My name is Dusty," I said at last, wrapping an arm around her shoulders.

She glanced at me, and then resumed her mournful vigil over the fire that was destroying everything she knew and loved.

"Do you know what happened?"

"Sheriff's men…" she glanced at me again, the expression in her eyes not unlike that of her dead husband. "Couldn't pay enough for the taxes, so they punished us…"

"I am sorry. We can find a safe place to live. Will—that's my friend who was here before—is looking for help."

"Doesn't matter," she said, her tone flat and lifeless.

I looked out toward the destruction below—we couldn't see the body from here, but I strained to see it all the same. The woman beside me was broken; she had been screaming, but now she was nearly devoid of life. I understood the feeling; grief had been far too overwhelming for me to acknowledge at all so I'd buried it for years when a fire had taken my family.

Is this what would happen to me if something ever happened to Will? I knew I was falling for him—is this how love ended? This broken shell of a woman?

I knew my God would be my comfort and refuge no matter what life threw at me, but even so…I had lost everything once before. Could I risk that again?

Maybe opening up to Will wasn't such a good idea.

Eventually, Will returned with a large number of men and women from a town he'd located a few miles from the burning farm. With all of them working together, they managed to put out the fire.

Nothing but the charred remains of the house and barn were left of the farm. The fire had even consumed the body of the woman's husband as we'd sat and watched the flames eat the countryside. I tried to keep the woman away from it, to shield her, but she seemed entirely unphased by the blackened corpse. The vacant expression in her eyes only intensified.

Once the fire was out, the village people offered to take the woman in. Will went in search of our horses, and once they were recovered we were able to offer the group money to both look after the woman and pay the Sheriff's taxes.

"I think we've had enough for this trip," Will said with a sigh as we watched the people walking away from the charred remains of the farm. "Let's head back to Sherwood."

I agreed. I needed to get back to camp and find some space from Will so I could reassess. When he was standing right beside me I couldn't think straight, but I knew my emotions needed to be put in check.

I'd opened up to him—truly opened up to him—for the first time, and then we met that woman…I couldn't risk becoming like her, so completely and utterly devastated at the loss of the love of her life.

Could I?

Chapter 26

MARIAN AND MARK'S father's health continued to decline as his imprisonment in the dungeon of Nottingham castle stretched on. Marian was worried, and Robin asked if I could do anything for him.

The secret passages in the castle did lead to the dungeons, but it was difficult to leave the passages and enter the castle itself without getting caught. Robin wasn't sure we should risk it, but the plight of Marian's father distressed him.

"I don't want you going into the castle, Dusty." Robin shoved a hand through his hair. "But…we have to do something…"

We were in Marian's home in Wetherby, my herbs and spices spread across the table in front of me as Marian and Robin stood opposite me.

"If I cannot see him, I will not know precisely what he needs. My healing work takes place when I am with someone, not from a distance."

"I understand that," Robin said. "But you are too valuable to risk getting captured…even so…we have to do *something*."

"I can get in there," Marian said. "I think I can manage to get to his cell."

"I don't necessarily want you to do that either," Robin sighed. "But I know I can't stop you; it is your father…"

Marian crossed her arms. "You most certainly can't stop me."

Robin turned to me. "Just do the best you can with what Marian can tell you of Sir Godfrey's illness."

"If I visit Gisbourne at the castle, I could slip away from him and get down to my father's cell for a visit."

Robin winced, a frown forming on his face, but he said nothing to Marian. Instead, he placed a hand on my shoulder and gave it a gentle squeeze. "I need to go to Nottingham. Little John and Allen are distributing money there and I want to check on them, see if they've noticed any suspicious behavior from Gisbourne. He's always up to no good. Do what you can, Dusty."

Robin soon left, and Marian began to describe the symptoms she noticed in her father when she spied in the castle and could watch him through the cracks in the stone wall that separated the dungeons from the secret passages. After we'd discussed his ailments—or what she suspected of them—and various remedies I might be able to offer, Marian thanked me.

"I only wish I could do more. If Robin were not so insistent that we don't enter the castle proper, I would tend to your father myself."

"This will have to do for now. We can't all defy Robin or he'll lose confidence in himself."

"You underestimate him."

"Perhaps." Marian crossed her arms as I began to gather my medicinal supplies back into my pouch. "You seem very close."

"You have no cause to be jealous," I said, failing to keep a smile off my face. "Robin and I are friends, as we've discussed before, but we share no deeper connection than that."

Marian flashed me a smile, one of the few she ever sent my way. "I am not jealous, merely commenting on the obvious. Robin trusts you a great deal—more than most people."

"I know. I am grateful for the confidence that he places in me. I would trust Robin with my life as well."

"I can't deny I was jealous of you when you first arrived, but Robin has been proving faithful ever since…"

"He never stopped loving you."

"So he says."

"You doubt him?"

"He did abandon me for three years, and then all hell broke loose here in England and I had to deal with it alone."

"I'm sure he regrets that."

"Perhaps."

"Does Gisbourne still court you?"

"He annoys me with his presence as often as he can." Marian rolled her eyes and smirked.

"Do you lead him on? I mean…let him think he's winning you over when you know you love Robin?"

Marian raised her eyebrows, a defiant look crossing her face. "Perhaps. He is the Sheriff's right hand; if I can get close to him, then I have a better chance of uncovering more plots of the Sheriff and saving more lives."

I nodded. I could understand the logic in her statement, though I could not agree with her methods. "Yet it does seem cruel to tease him in such a manner."

Marian shrugged. "He knows well enough that I am not fond of him, and he keeps coming back anyway. Maybe he likes the challenge. I don't know, but we need all the help we can get in this war against injustice, and Gisbourne is one method I can use to protect my people—and it works well. I am not going to stop, not so long as I can continue to use him to help the truly innocent."

In the weeks that followed, we continued to ambush the Sheriff's caravans of treasure and eventually he tried a new tactic —he arranged the path of the caravan to follow a different road than the one through Sherwood Forest.

Unfortunately for him, we were often within the very walls of his castle, and so we heard this plan quite clearly and Robin planned accordingly. We traveled as a group toward the village of Leicester, and stabled the horses we rode—those lent to us by Marcus—with the people there.

Most of the people of England were fond of our gang and eager to help whenever they could because they almost all had someone that Robin had saved from an execution or Will had rescued from prison or I had healed from illness.

Once we'd left the horses behind, we made our way along the road and Robin surveyed the area, searching for the best place to plan a proper ambush.

"There's less cover than in Sherwood, but we can manage with the ditch here at the curve in the road," Robin said. "There's enough bushes over there to make something work."

"Similar set-up as always?" Will asked.

"It hasn't failed us yet," Robin replied. "You and Allen go over there…" Robin began pointing to various spots and calling out our names until we each had a place to lay in wait for the caravan of stolen wealth.

I lay low in the ditch, my back on the incline leading up to the road, hoping my clothes—made to match the colors of Sherwood Forest—would serve me here as well. Robin was right; there was far less cover here than our usual raids.

I closed my eyes, whispering a prayer for our safety as I held my bow tightly in my hands, waiting. It wasn't too long before I could hear the sounds of wooden wheels creaking under the weight of their load.

I opened my eyes, tilting my head slightly to watch the caravan ease past me. I held my breath as I counted the soldiers and waited for one of them to notice me and ruin our ambush.

Another moment passed and then Robin's sharp whistle rent the air. I spun to my knees and raised my bow, whipping an arrow from my quiver and taking aim at the nearest soldier. He feel a second later with my arrow pierced through his neck.

Arrows flew from all directions as the rest of the gang shot down soldiers as well. I grabbed a second arrow and took aim, letting the arrow fly just as three soldiers came running toward me, swords drawn. I cast aside my bow immediately, pulling out my sword and snatching one of my daggers from my belt.

The dagger I flicked to the side, catching one soldier in the neck, while I brought my sword up to block the incoming swipe of the other two swords.

I shoved forward with all my weight, pushing them inches away from me for a reprieve, and then rolled backward down the embankment, and then jumped to my feet.

As the two soldiers came down the slight incline toward me, I grabbed my second dagger and flicked it with ease. The second soldier fell with my blade in his throat as the third swung his sword in my direction. I ducked beneath it and dove forward, plunging my own sword into his chest.

I yanked my sword out, collected my two daggers, and ran up onto the road, glancing around to assess the situation.

Some soldiers seemed to be trying to flee—or report to the Sheriff—but were shot down as they moved up the road, their horses hurrying along riderless. Some of the gang were in melee with other soldiers, while the rest continued to fire arrows into the chaos.

I chose a target and sprinted forward, leaping onto a soldier's back and plunging both of my daggers into his neck. He dropped to the ground and I sprang up, still holding my bloodied daggers.

It was rather sickening, this work that we did—I was painfully aware of how proficient I was at stopping a human's life. I wasn't proud of it; but I could justify it. These men were working for a cruel man who would beat innocent people and murder anyone with no good cause.

As I cut my way through the soldiers in the street, watching as others fell to the arrows of my comrades, a tiny scream rent the air.

I spun around, searching for the child who had let out such a cry of fear.

A soldier was marching up the embankment not far from me, dragging a child with him. He had a knife to the child's throat and a trickle of blood was staining the little one's neck.

Robin stepped into the road, arrow trained on the soldier. I flipped my dagger in my hand, wondering if I could kill the soldier before he killed the child.

"You let the boy go, and I might let you live." Robin's voice was as cold as ice and brimming with fury. I'd never heard him so angry.

"If you fire at me, this boy dies with me," the soldier spat, pushing the knife just a bit harder against the child's throat.

"My arrows fly faster than the muscles in your wrist could twitch."

"Try me."

Robin glared at the soldier. I hesitated a moment, but I wasn't convinced I could drop the soldier before he killed the child. I let my daggers fall harmless on the ground; I noticed Much drop his bow where he stood across the road, and others in the gang began to do the same.

"I and my surviving comrades are taking this treasure into town," the soldier said. "We're keeping this little play-actor with us. Wanted to be a part of Robin Hood's band of outlaws? He gets treated like one. If you don't let us go, I kill him. If you follow us or attack us on our route, I kill him. The Sheriff of Nottingham will likely kill him once we arrive safely, but who's to say? Maybe he'll be lenient, despite him being caught fraternizing with Robin Hood in the middle of an act of treason."

"He's just a kid," I pleaded. "Let him be, please."

"You can have one of us," Will offered from behind me. I turned and watched him inching forward, hands held out in a gesture of surrender. "Let the child go."

The soldier didn't even acknowledge Will. He started moving, keeping the boy in front of him and between himself and Robin—knife pressed firmly in place—as he slowly made his way down the road, past the carts full of chests of treasure.

Robin kept his arrow trained on the soldier, but apparently he had come to the same conclusion that I had; we couldn't kill the soldier without potentially getting the child killed, too.

The soldier called out orders for his remaining men to start leading the horses hitched to the carts down the road. They slowly moved to do as he commanded.

I saw Little John twitch, as though he wanted to stop them, but he held back and like the rest of us simply watched as the soldiers and the Sheriff's treasure slowly moved down the road.

Robin kept his bow aloft, but he didn't fire, and he didn't say anything else as he watched the boy being dragged down the road, knife to his throat.

Much moved to stand beside him as the carts wheeled by and Robin finally lowered his bow.

I hurried over to them as the soldiers lashed the reins of the horses who no longer had riders to the back of the last cart and the whole caravan moved down the road, leaving us behind.

"Robin?"

"I don't know." Robin flung his bow across the road and shoved a hand through his hair, his eyes turning to me with a look of pleading though I hadn't asked a specific question. "I don't know!"

The others gathered around us.

"We can take 'em," Little John growled. "Get the jump on him."

"He's not going to let that kid go," Will said. "If we try another ambush or attack, he'll slit the kid's throat."

"If we let him take that child back to the Sheriff…" I shook my head, imagining the horrors the Sheriff of Nottingham or Sir Guy of Gisbourne might inflict. "He'll never see his family again. We have to save him."

"We're going to save him." Robin sighed, kicking the road and causing a puff of dust to float above his boot for a moment. "I don't know how, but we're getting that kid back to his family, and we're getting the Sheriff's treasure. Just let me think…"

Robin marched off down the road and after collecting our weapons—Much grabbed Robin's discarded bow—the rest of us followed after him.

I wasn't sure what the best plan would be now; if we made the wrong choice, the child would die. But if we just let him go to the Sheriff, he'd probably die anyway.

The caravan disappeared from sight along the horizon as we hurried after Robin. My heart might as well have been in my boots for how heavy it weighed as I thought of the little boy with them. What had he been doing at the ambush at all? Perhaps he had followed us from the village after we had left our horses there…

Robin Hood and his band of outlaws were growing renowned in England; I'd seen children in Nottingham pretending to be us and 'fight' the Sheriff in their games. I could see this poor child thinking he could join in the fray with Robin Hood. If that had been the reason he was nearby, the reason he was now caught, I couldn't help but feel in some way responsible. It was our fault, and now I didn't know what we could do about it.

As we walked toward Leicester, a man came running toward us. My heart sank; what if this was the boy's father?

"Robin Hood!"

"We know," Robin sighed as the man ran up to him.

"You've heard? You have to return to Nottingham at once!" The man gasped, catching his breath from his run, his eyes wild. "The Sheriff is hanging six children!"

"Hanging children?" Much asked.

Robin shook his head as though to clear it. "Six? Now?"

My heart might have been in my boots moments before, but now it was in my throat.

"Lady Marian sent word; she's trying to reach you. It may be too late, already!"

"When is the Sheriff hanging children?" Will asked.

"*Why* is the Sheriff hanging children might be the better question," I said. I had been worried what the Sheriff might do to the boy we'd failed to rescue minutes before, but apparently we had a definite answer. He had no qualms killing children.

"At dawn," the villager answered Will's question. "Or so said the message from Lady Marian."

"We're too far from Nottingham to arrive before dawn," Little John commented.

Panic rising in my chest, I turned aside from the group. I knelt in the road, seeking the only solace I could.

My heart was still racing from the adrenaline of our fight, and there was an ache of worry in my chest for both the boy we'd lost and for the apparent six children in danger in Nottingham. If we couldn't save them, we'd need a miracle.

I began to pray for exactly that.

"We have to go," Allen said. "We can't let six kids hang."

"We can't get there in time to help," Little John said.

"And we have a kid here who needs help," Robin said. "If we run off to Nottingham, who knows what becomes of that little boy?"

The gang began to argue behind me, but I did my best to keep my focus on my Lord. I knew He cared about all seven children in question more than we ever could. If there was a way to save them, I prayed He would enlighten us.

"If we hurry we might make it by morning!" Allen said. "Not if we stand here arguing, of course, but if we leave and we don't stop all night...we might make it."

"But that still leaves the question of our own hostage kid," Robin said. "He's our priority. Marian and Marcus can figure out something for the Nottingham kids."

"What if they don't?" Allen asked.

"What if we leave to save them and our kid is killed instead?" Robin replied.

"Saving six over one...if it's down to math, Robin..."

"It's never down to math!" Will snapped. "All seven of the children in question matter. All seven lives are valuable."

I turned around, distracted from my prayers for a moment as Will voiced my own thoughts.

Robin sighed, his fingers curling into fists. His face settled into a hard expression, his set. It seemed he had decided what to do.

I rose from where I'd knelt in the dirt. I didn't feel confident in either choice—hurrying to Nottingham though we'd arrive too late, or trying to save the kid here with no good option for how to do so—but if Robin had a plan, I would follow him.

"We find a way to save our kid," Robin said. "We save the kid, get the treasure, and then make haste for Nottingham."

"We'll be too late," Allen said, crossing his arms.

"We'll likely be too late for the Nottingham kids either way," Robin replied. "We don't have to be late for the kid who's only a few miles down the road. Now let's move! We need to catch up to that caravan and make a plan."

Chapter 27

ROBIN'S PLAN TURNED out to be quite simple—race to catch the soldiers who'd taken the boy.

"I'll take Much and Mark and ride a good distance away from the road before we take up chase. The rest of you do the same on the opposite side. You'll want to stay far enough away from the road itself that you won't draw undue attention to yourselves before we catch up with them. When I see where the kid is, I'm shooting down the soldiers near him—if there are any—and the rest of you can take the rest of the caravan."

"That's assuming we can catch up to them, and assuming they don't see us coming…" Allen crossed his arms. "I don't see this working."

"We're doing it." Robin was firm, and as he swung into his saddle, Allen reluctantly moved to do the same.

Once we were all astride our mounts, Robin took off to the right with Much and Mark at his side while Allen kicked his horse into a gallop and led the rest of us to the far left of the road until we were some miles distant from the road itself and we straightened our course.

We'd wasted time arguing about what we should do, and I wondered what the chances were that we could catch up to the caravan. Though it was comprised of heavy, slow-moving carts which certainly worked to our advantage as we leaned low over our horses and galloped after the Sheriff's gold and the abducted child.

It wasn't too long before I could see dust ahead and to the right of us, which I assumed was evidence of the caravan. Since I couldn't see the caravan itself, I could only hope they couldn't see us either, and our horses wouldn't kick up as much dust running across the grassy field as their horses and carts did on the road.

Perhaps they wouldn't notice us following them.

Allen and Will's horses outpaced Little John and I; as we raced along, I kept sending desperate prayers heavenward for the safety of the little boy we were hoping to rescue.

"Trees!" Allen swiveled in his saddle to catch everyone's eyes as he pointed to the right; there was, indeed, an outcropping of trees ahead and to the right of us, presumably bordering the road itself. The dust from what we assumed was the caravan had been left behind; we'd outstripped them.

When we drew almost even with the line of trees Allen had pointed out, we turned our horses toward them, racing for the cover they would provide before the caravan drew close enough to see us.

As soon as we were under the trees, I pulled my horse to a stop and dismounted, running forward and yanking my bow from my back. I slammed into a tree near the side of the road, leaning heavily against it as I whipped out an arrow and took aim down the empty road, waiting for a target to come into sight.

Slowly the carts and soldiers came into view, inching along the road toward our second ambush of the day. I could only hope Robin and the others had followed the same line of reasoning that Allen had, and would be on the other side of the road. A one-sided ambush with fewer members of the gang might not end successfully.

There was also the chance that the soldiers had seen our desperate ride for the trees and would expect us.

As I counted the soldiers, my heart sank to my toes.

Somewhere between the original ambush and this outcropping of trees they had gained reinforcements. There were at least twenty soldiers guiding the carts and marching along beside them, all with weapons drawn. They were ready for anything.

I took a deep breath to steady myself, searching the caravan for the young boy. If Robin and the others weren't here, someone else would have to run for the boy. And if they weren't here...who would signal for the raid? Will knew how to whistle, I knew, but would he realize that might be his job without Robin?

As my eyes scanned the caravan, my fingers tightened around the arrow I had nocked to my bowstring, itching to release it. We had to save this boy quickly so we could race to Nottingham and attempt to avert the disaster of six murdered children there...

Robin's high note pierced the air and I felt relief wash over my shoulders. I picked a target and fired my arrow, immediately grabbing another one. If Robin had called for the ambush then he undoubtedly had the child in his sights; I trusted him to do his job while I and the others fought off the rest of the soldiers.

Little John let out a roar from somewhere behind me and ran into the road, his quarter staff swinging and soldiers flying off their feet in his wake.

I kept my arrows soaring toward various soldiers, dropping them to the earth one by one, as I saw Robin sprint toward a cart near the front of the wagon.

Mark and Will joined Little John in the street, their swords flashing as they fought the soldiers. I took careful aim amidst the chaos, dropping the soldiers with efficiency.

"We've got the kid!" Little John's voice echoed above the noise of the fighting, shouting soldiers. "Do we stay for the treasure?"

"We have six kids in Nottingham to deal with!" I shouted, letting another arrow fly into the eye of a soldier in the road.

"And we've got the treasure right here!" Little John shouted back at me, using his brute strength to knock aside several soldiers within his reach.

"I vote we leave the treasure and race for Nottingham!" Much's voice cried from across the road. "We could be too late as it is, why waste time?!"

"I agree!" I heard Will call out. Soldiers began to move off the road away from Little John and Mark, searching for me and Much no doubt.

"We have to go now!" I yelled.

"Get a move on!" Robin's voice suddenly joined the shouting match.

I snapped my bow in place on my back and spun around, racing back to where we'd left our horses. I jumped into the saddle, pausing a moment to ascertain that Will, Allen, and Little John were close behind before racing northward again.

As I broke through the trees I caught sight of Robin, Mark, and Much galloping along the road as well and made a beeline for them. There was a small boy riding in front of Robin, which was a great relief.

"The soldiers will be slow on foot," Robin said as we joined the group. I could see him counting heads as he looked around at everyone. We didn't slow our riding as he continued to speak. "Even if they unhitch the carts to use the horses to give chase, that will take time. We have a head start, let's get to Sherwood as fast as we can."

"Sherwood or Nottingham?" I asked.

"Wetherby," Robin called, spurring his horse into a faster gait. "If Marian isn't there, we'll go to Nottingham to see if we're too late, and then convene at the camp."

I leaned low over my horse, urging it to keep pace with Robin and the others as we raced for Wetherby—we had several hours of riding ahead of us. Little John was right; it was unlikely we would make it in time. But we had to try.

We rode through the night and into the early hours of the morning, and I didn't stop praying the entire way. Praying for a miracle; it was clear we were going to arrive after dawn. As the horizon grew grey instead of dark and the stars began to wane, I knew we wouldn't make it. Yet I continued to pray, begging God for mercy.

Eventually, as the sun rose over Sherwood Forest and lit the sky with bright golds and pinks, the village of Wetherby came into sight. Robin finally slowed our pace. My horse was panting for air and covered in sweat, and took to the slower pace with obvious relief.

When we arrived at Marian's home, Robin jumped from his horse. The child—James—remained in his saddle, watching with wide eyes as Robin ran to the house and knocked on the door. There was no answer. Robin turned to the rest of us, his shoulders sagging.

"We can't all ride into Nottingham in this state; we'll draw attention. I'll go and see if there's bodies swinging in Nottingham Square. Meet me back at the camp. Take James with you."

"We'll wait to hear the news," I suggested. "We'll meet you on the road between Nottingham and Sherwood."

Robin nodded. "Alright. I'll see you soon."

Robin handed the reins of his horse to Much. James still sat in Robin's saddle, and he looked more than a little overwhelmed by the ordeal he'd been through.

"Come on, everyone." I glanced around at the dejected group; it was clear from the darkness in Will's eyes and the droop in Much's shoulders that no one expected the six children to be alive. "Let's go."

I led the disheartened group away from the village of Wetherby and toward the main road that led out of Nottingham, keeping out of sight of the city. The sun was rising over Sherwood forest, dousing the land in shimmering light and painting the sky with hues of purple and pink now.

"We're too late." Much said, his voice filled with pain.

"Don't say that, Much," Allen snapped. "We don't know what happened."

"The children were to be hanged at dawn," Little John sighed. "It's past dawn, and we weren't here. Much is right. We're too late."

The child we'd rescued was crying where he sat in Robin's saddle atop the horse. Much edged closer to him. "It's alright, James. You're safe."

"And we'll get you home soon," I said, guiding my own horse over to him. I reached across the space between our horses to brush the tears from his cheeks."Just as soon as we get all this sorted, we'll get you back to your parents. Don't worry."

"Robin's coming!" Mark said suddenly. I spun in my saddle, following Mark's pointing finger. Robin was indeed approaching.

"The kids?" I asked as soon as he was close enough to hear me. I wasn't sure I wanted to hear his answer.

"No executions. Marcus doesn't know what went down specifically, but the kids aren't dead. The Sheriff hanged some of his soldiers this morning; they're still swinging in Nottingham Square."

"The soldiers are, but the kids aren't?" Will clarified.

Robin shrugged, pulling himself into his saddle behind James. "That's what I saw and what Marcus confirmed. I didn't see Marian. If she's not in Wetherby or Nottingham, she's probably at the camp. Let's go see what she has to say."

The ride to camp was quiet; I'm not sure any of us knew what to make of the night's events. We'd saved the child immediately in our care, and now it seemed the others weren't dead—but where were they? What had happened while we were gone? Marian had sent word of the execution, and it seemed more than a little strange that the Sheriff would hang his own men instead.

When we road into camp, Marian was sitting at the fire ring where we often gathered. She looked up as we entered camp, and then ran over to Robin and threw herself into his arms as he dismounted.

"Robin! So much has happened, I don't even know where to begin!"

"Start with the children," Robin said, helping James off of his horse as Much and the others also dismounted and gathered around Marian.

"The Sheriff was going to hang six kids because he was angry with their parents. You were all gone, and I didn't know what to do. I tried to talk to Gisbourne; I asked him to let them go, but he refused."

"Of course he did," Robin said. "What did you expect?"

"Wait, Robin, I wasn't finished." Marian crossed her arms.

"When I went to the Square, fully expecting to see the children hanging, the Sheriff was hanging his guards instead. From his angry ranting, I managed to make out that the children had escaped and he was hanging the guards who had been keeping watch over them."

"I did see the dead soldiers," Robin said.

"But what about the children," I asked. "What happened? Where are they?"

"Sir Guy–Gisbourne–came to see me late last night. He told me he'd taken the children from custody and brought them to the edge of Sherwood. He didn't know what to do with them so he asked me to bring them to you. He figured you could keep the children safe here, and Robin…" Marian bit her lip.

"The children are here?" I asked, spinning to look around the empty camp as Robin said, "What?"

349

"Gisbourne proposed after he rescued the children…"

"He what?!" Robin's eyebrows hit his hairline. Will dropped the bow he'd been holding and Little John started chuckling and then choked as he tried to cover his laughter.

I stopped searching for signs of the children and looked back at the dumbfounded group. How could they possibly be so shocked by the man proposing? He'd been courting Marian since before Robin came back from the Crusades and she had admitted on more than one occasion that she encouraged his affection in order to use him in her fight against the Sheriff.

The proposal did not shock me, but his rescuing the children did. It was possible there was more to Sir Guy of Gisbourne than we had first believed.

"Gisbourne proposed?" Robin asked.

"Yes," Marian said.

"And you said?"

"No! Obviously I said no. Really, Robin, why would you ask that? Sir Guy of Gisbourne is a wretched, cruel man. Why would I marry him?"

"I'm relieved you feel that way."

"I was worried after I refused him that he'd take the children back and go through with the Sheriff's plan to hang them…but he didn't."

"I'm rather surprised at that, but I'm glad. And of course we'll keep the children! They're here now?" Robin asked as the group moved toward the fireplace and seated themselves on the logs circled around it. James sat between Much and Robin, watching the conversation unfold with wide, confused eyes.

"Yes, they're sleeping in the huts; they had a long night."

"I'm sure they did," Robin agreed. "I'm surprised Gisbourne even rescued them, but to let them go even after your refusal? What a man wouldn't do for Marian." Robin bent and kissed Marian's cheek with a wink.

"Sir Guy might not be as vile as people say," I commented."Or at the very least, he does have a conscience and does struggle with the choices that he makes."

Allen shook his head. "Don't count on it. He did this for Marian, not for any other reason. His conscience is not getting to him."

"You don't know that," I replied.

Will placed a hand on my shoulder. "He's evil, Dusty. Don't try to make a saint out of him."

"I don't make saints," I replied. "I am only suggesting he is not fully evil, even as none of us are fully good. Only God can clothe us in any righteousness. We're all the worst of sinners before Him."

"I'd say we're better than Sir Guy of Gisbourne any day," Robin replied.

"Robin…" I sighed, unsure where to begin to express all that I was feeling. Sir Guy had done terrible things, but then so had everyone. None of us were guiltless, that was the very reason we needed Christ to begin with.

351

Robin held up his hands to silence me before I'd even begun. "Don't start. We all know how you feel. We don't need another lecture."

"Did Gisbourne not speak of anything else, Marian?" Little John suddenly asked. "He knows you are connected to our gang, that could mean trouble for you."

"I know," Marian replied, her gaze turning on Little John. "But he didn't say anything about it after we fought."

"He didn't mention Mark?" Little John pressed.

"Why would he ask about me?" Mark asked.

"I'm sure they've noticed you are never home," Little John replied.

"What Gisbourne will do with his information that Marian does indeed know who we are remains to be seen," Will said. "It might be too dangerous for her to continue living in Wetherby."

"We'll have to keep watch," Robin said, shifting closer to Marian and slipping an arm around her waist. "Gisbourne knows she knows us, if he came to her directly in order to get the children to us for safety…"

Marian pushed against his shoulder in a playful manner. "Don't look so grave. I will be fine."

"We'll keep an eye on Wetherby anyway," Robin replied.

"You do that," Marian said, kissing his cheek. "I need to get home anyway. Gisbourne might come back today."

"If he does, we'll be there," Robin said.

Marian gave him a last look and then slipped out of the camp.

"Little John, keep an eye on her today, will you?" Robin said.

Little John rose, grabbing his quarter staff from where he'd set it beside his hut. "Nothing will harm her today,"

Much set about cooking a meal for all of us as we slumped around the fire. The children were safe, which was good, but now that the danger was over the exhaustion was overtaking me—and I assumed the others as well.

Sudden movement caught my eye and I turned to look toward one of the huts. A small head was peeking out, and then another appeared just above it.

"The children are not, in fact, sleeping," I said.

Will turned to look and smiled broadly, gesturing them over. The two children tentatively stepped out of the hut, and as they slowly made their way across the clearing toward us, more small heads began to peer from other huts. Eventually Will was able to coax all six of them to come sit with us as Much set out some sausages and eggs for all of us to eat.

The oldest of the children—William, a ten year old boy—seemed in awe of us all as members of Robin Hood's gang, while the youngest of the group—four year old Peter and five year old Rachel—simply seemed starved for attention.

Will and Little John began asking questions and drawing the oldest children into conversation. It seemed their fathers had angered the Sheriff of Nottingham and that was why he'd attempted to hang the six of them before Gisbourne rescued them and got them to Marian.

"Being in the prison was scary," William said, his brow furrowing. He turned to Will. "Have you been to prison?"

"I haven't…I'm sorry it was scary."

"I didn't like it," William said simply.

"I'd imagine not."

Little Rachel, the five year old, crawled into Will's lap. I'd be lying if I said the sight of him being so gentle with the small child in his arms didn't make my heart flutter.

"Are you nice?" the little girl asked, staring up at Will.

"I don't know, little lady," Will winked, brushing a wayward curl out of her face. "Am I?"

Rachel tilted her small head to one side, her tiny brow furrowed as she studied his face. "I think so."

Allen shook his head with a laugh. "Don't be fooled, Rachel. You're only five, so maybe you can't see the truth, but Will is a—"

Before he could finish his sentence, I elbowed Allen in the ribs, causing him to nearly drop the plate of food Much had handed him.

Will raised his eyebrows. "I'm a what, Allen?"

Allen shrugged, glancing at me and shifting out of my reach. "I don't know. Nothing."

Robin laughed. "Don't worry, Rachel. Despite the silliness of our group, we're actually very nice, I promise."

Once everyone had eaten, Robin entrusted James to Much to return him to his family and they soon left the camp.

Robin divided up the new sleeping quarters—almost every member of the gang would share their hut with one of the children who would now be staying with us unless or until we could find a way to get them safely back to their families.

My little roommate was a girl named Beth. At seven-years-old, she was the oldest of her family, with six-year-old John and four-year-old Peter being her little brothers. They were sent to share huts with Mark and Much respectively.

As I tucked Beth into my bed and created a make-shift mattress for myself on a pile of blankets on the floor of my hut, she watched me with big dark eyes that reflected the candlelight by which I worked.

"When can we go home?"

"I don't know, little one. I hope soon, but I don't know. But you are safe here. I promise."

Little Rachel had insisted on remaining with Will, which I thought was rather adorable. As Beth drifted off to sleep on my bed, I couldn't help imagining Will tucking tiny Rachel into bed, brushing her hair out of her face. He was a good man, a gentle man; he would make a great father someday.

Which were definitely thoughts I did not want to entertain.

I curled into a ball under my blanket, pulling the rough wool up to my chin.

Rachel's older brother William seemed quite taken with Will as well, though he ended up sharing sleeping quarters with Allen. It didn't surprise me that Will was so good with the children...but I wasn't going to consider that any further.

The other child in the group was William's little sister Sarah, an eight-year-old girl who was bunking with Little John. They had all been through quite the ordeal, and were now stuck living with a group of strangers. I could only hope we would make them feel at home and safe until we could return them to their families.

Chapter 28

THE NEXT MORNING when Robin gave assignments for us, I was sent to keep an eye on Nottingham—spy in the castle, watch the market, and see if I could learn anything of use from the Sheriff, or catch Gisbourne up to some scheme. Allen was left in charge of the six children in the camp while the rest of us scattered on our various missions. Robin took Much and Mark to keep an eye on Marian for the day.

Slipping into Nottingham was a simple affair—the main gate into the city had guards posted, but they didn't stop or search the travelers and merchants who entered unless someone looked suspicious to them. All I, and the rest of the gang, had to do to get inside unnoticed was get in line with other travelers and groups and act like we belonged until we were within the city walls. We did this often enough that it was second nature by now.

Once inside, I made a stop by Nottingham Square where the market was located—the shops around the edge faced the large open courtyard from every side, and several booths and carts were set up in haphazard rows with more goods to be purchased.

I weaved through the crowds until I came to my favorite shop and slipped inside. Immediately I was bombarded with floral and spicy scents that made my nose wrinkle.

I breathed it all in deeply, and then slipped through the shelves stuffed to the brim with bottles and powders and plants until I found Abraham in the back of the apothecary, leaning over a table as he crushed a plant beneath his pestle.

"What can I get you now?" He didn't look up at me as I approached, but continued with his work.

"Has anything of interest happened today?"

"With the Sheriff or Gisbourne? Not that I am aware of. Haven't had to heal up any soldiers who survive your exploits today either...yet." He glanced up at me then, his eyes twinkling.

"If the world were as it should be, you'd never find anyone injured under my hand."

"I don't judge you for the harm you inflict. They deserve it." Abraham reached out a clasped my hand. "I know how much it wounds your tender, healing heart. But you have to know the work you do is good; you are helping, not harming."

"I don't feel that way when I'm covered in blood spilled by my own hand."

"I know." Abraham went back to his work for a moment and then paused. "Do you want to stay for tea and a chat? There's still more to learn from each other, I'm sure."

His eyes lit up at the prospect. Abraham was fond of my visits and eagerly listened to my explanations of my native herbs and spices whenever we traded information and studied together. But I had more pressing things to do today.

"Given the near-execution of the children recently, I think my time will be better spent watching the Sheriff."

"Next time then."

Since nothing seemed out of the ordinary at the market, I made my way to the street that bordered the castle wall. There were shops built along the castle wall, and one in particular that we in Robin Hood's gang often used to get into the castle.

There was a secret door at the back of a bakery that led into the narrow secret passages, and from there I could travel

357

around the castle wall into the castle proper without ever being seen.

I lingered in the darkness of the passages for several hours, stopping by the best places for spying—the passages that bordered the Great Hall where the Sheriff and Gisbourne did most of their planning, for instance. Nothing seemed to be brewing within the castle; Gisbourne wasn't home it seemed, and the Sheriff rarely planned anything without his right hand.

Learning nothing from the Sheriff, I began to traverse the streets of Nottingham, visiting the families that I knew to have been sick recently so I could spread my medicinal prowess to as many people as possible.

At one particular house I visited frequently, the mother eagerly let me inside her humble home with a wide smile. "Your friend came by yesterday; the children all seem to be on the mend."

"My friend? Abraham?"

"The apothecary?" Martha's brows knit together. "Oh, no. I meant the lady."

Martha gestured to the small table in the room and we both sat down. Across the room was a bed where three small children were sleeping. They had been taken with fever the last time I had visited. Almost every week they seemed to have a new illness to contend with, which is why I made it a habit of visiting their home frequently.

"What lady?" I asked quietly, trying not to wake the children. "Lady Marian?"

Martha rested her elbows on the table and frowned at me. "No, not Lady Marian. Someone I hadn't met before...I thought you must have sent her. Beautiful woman, but quiet. Won't talk about herself much. She made a tea for the kids, and the fever broke only an hour or so later. Here, I'll show you…"

Martha stood and hurried out of the room to the small kitchen beyond, and then came scurrying back with a pouch in her hand. She pressed it into my hand and then sat back down opposite me.

I opened the pouch, shaking a few flakes of tea leaves into my hand. I lifted them to my face so I could study their color, and then sniffed them.

"It's a good tea; the same as I would have made for them."

"You didn't send her though?"

"Whoever she is, no. I did not send anyone to visit you. I am glad that she did. It is good to know there are more healers in Nottingham. We need all the healing we can get during these broken times."

"Indeed."

I visited the apothecary to refill my stocks before I went home to the camp, since I had used much of them throughout my afternoon of healing. Despite Martha's family being miraculously helped by someone else, there were still too many people in the city who were malnourished, ill, and struggling.

Just as I stepped inside and the smell of dried plants and spices washed over me like a familiar friend, there seemed to be shouting and a commotion in the street.

"Dusty, always good to see you," Abraham said.

Before I could respond, the yells grew louder and then suddenly hushed to silence.

I glanced at Abraham and then toward his door. He was as curious as I was and a moment later, Abraham pushed open his door to lean outside and see what was going on. I leaned against the doorframe beside him.

The street was filling with spectators, but they were unnaturally silent—I assumed because they'd been threatened to do be so. Coming down the street as the crowd parted mutely was Gisbourne. He looked furious, with his eyes flashing and his chin set stubbornly; behind Gisbourne walked Marian, head held high and proud, surrounded by soldiers, with her hands bound behind her back.

"Lady Marian," Abraham whispered, his eyes widening. As soon as Gisbourne and his entourage were past, the people in the street began conversing again. I bounded forward, grabbing the arm of the first person I came to.

"What's happened?"

"Lady Marian was arrested…we don't know why, but rumor has it he burned her house in Wetherby!"

Wetherby…Robin and Much were there…

I spun away from the man who'd answered me, running down the street on my way out of the city. I didn't stop to say farewell to Abraham.

I sprinted past the city gate and across the open fields. Before I reached the village of Wetherby I could see smoke rising in the air and I was suddenly reminded of the burned corpse of the farmer Will and I had failed to rescue on one of our trips away from Nottinghamshire.

My heart pounding in my ears, I pushed myself to run faster. I skidded to a stop when I hit the village—Marian's home had been located near the edge of the group of houses. It was no longer there, all that remained was a burned out shell of a home.

I closed my eyes as my lungs froze, my fingers curling into fists, my nails digging into my palms.

I didn't want to think about it, but suddenly I was imagining Habibah's smiling face crushed by our own house as flames overtook it. I could see Daniyah's beautiful form morphing into the blackened husk my imagination suggested she might have looked like at the end.

"Dusty?"

My head snapped up and I realized I was kneeling on the ground. Widow Mary, a resident of Wetherby who lived near Marian, was standing over me.

"Marian's alive; Gisbourne took her to Nottingham."

"I know." I stood, brushing the dirt from my knees. "I saw them. I was worried for Robin and the others that I know were here today."

"They put out the fire, and then...I think went back to your secret camp in Sherwood."

"Thank you, Widow Mary. Was anyone else hurt?"

"No. We're all okay...just scared for Lady Marian. As soon as you hear something, you will let us know, won't you? Young Robin will come inform us?"

"I'm sure he will."

I turned away from Widow Mary and the charred remains of Marian's home and I set off for Sherwood. Slowly, my heart rate returned to normal and I gained control over my emotions.

I had been in such a state of terror at the thought of losing Robin and Much—my new family—and so overrun with memories and nightmares of losing my first family...I hadn't rested secure in the comfort of my Father and Savior.

I spent the rest of my walk to the camp praying, communing with my Strength and Comfort and feeling His love overtake me.

Even if I had lost everyone again; I would be okay. But even so, I had no desire to face such a tragedy again. That fear…that was precisely why I couldn't let Will all the way into my heart. I knew it—I felt guilty for it, for the lack of trust in my God—but I could not stop myself from feeling it.

When I arrived at the camp, Mark and Much were scowling at each other across the fire and Allen was sitting between them looking uncomfortable. He waved me over as soon as he saw me, flashing me a crooked smile.

"Oh good, a mediator…"

"Is everyone okay?" I asked, taking a seat on one of our log benches. The children were scattered about the clearing playing, and their laughter seemed a strange backdrop to the tension of our group.

"Gisbourne burned my home," Mark said, his eyes shooting sparks and his voice ice cold. "He took Marian captive."

"I know."

Mark shook his head, jumping up to start pacing around the fire. "Robin wouldn't let me follow. He went to Nottingham… now we're just waiting for news, and I hate it!"

"Do we know what happened?"

"I think it was her refusal to his proposal," Much said softly, his eyes tracking Mark as he paced around us. "He has a temper."

"He saved the kids and then he snapped," Allen shrugged. "He's not emotionally stable."

It was hours before Robin returned to the camp—in that time, the rest of the gang returned from their activities throughout the day and were filled in on the situation. Much made dinner, the children were eventually put to bed, and still we waited around the fire for Robin's return and news of Marian's fate.

"What if they have her executed?" Mark said, wringing his hands.

"Then we'll save her like we save everyone else," Little John said.

We heard Robin before he entered the camp, his cheerful whistling cutting through the tense silence.

Mark was on his feet instantly. "Where's Marian? Why are you so happy?"

Robin came to join the circle around the fire ring. "Sit down, Mark. She's alive, she's fine."

Mark sank back onto the log-bench with a sigh as Robin continued, "She's under house arrest and has a personal guard to tail her wherever she goes within the castle. It will be difficult to see her, but not impossible. Her room is, in fact, one of the many that has a door directly into the secret passages."

"That's a relief," Mark said. "But it doesn't explain your whistling! Why didn't you get her out as long as there's a passage that leads right to her room?"

"She wants to stay to be near your father, and also to pick up information from the Sheriff and Gisbourne that we might not be able to get simply from the secret passages. They don't connect to every room in the castle, it is possible there are plots and schemes that we miss, that she will now be able to hear about and help us foil."

"That's all well and good, but still not enough to be whistling for," Mark said.

"No, I suppose they aren't reasons for whistling. But Marian told me this evening she loved me, and that's enough to get me to whistle."

"We all saw that coming," Mark said with a roll of his eyes, still seeming unsatisfied by Robin's report.

Still, with the news that Marian was safe, albeit under house arrest, the tension in our group released. Soon enough they were all retiring to their respective huts to sleep.

Having Marian inside the castle would be a good way to finally get my medicinal things into the castle to her father. Gisbourne had sent for a physician on a few occasions at Marian's request, but now that he was angry with Marian it seemed wise for me to try and take over that duty as well as I could from a distance.

I awoke the next morning to the infectious laughter of children. When I exited my hut, I saw Will by the fire with little Rachel in his lap, tickling her to produce the delightful sounds that had disrupted my sleep. Other children were gathered around him as well, including Beth whom I had not noticed leaving our hut.

It warmed my heart to see the children leaning around Will, smiles on their faces as they were clearly enjoying themselves. Even after their ordeal, they could still find joy; their resilience was inspiring, of course, but I was more focused on Will. I was right; he was going to be a great father someday.

"What is all that racket?" Robin asked, stepping out of his hut. He was the only one of us who didn't have to bunk with a child.

"We have children," I said as Much, with Beth's help, began to serve breakfast. "What do you expect?"

More of the gang began to emerge, rubbing their eyes and yawning as they made comment on the noisy laughter of the children gathered around Will.

Allen sighed as he sank onto one of the log-benches. "Are you saying we aren't going to have any peace and quiet anymore?"

"I believe that is what she is saying," Mark said, playfully glowering at the children.

"I think I'd rather go to prison," Allen groaned.

"Allen!" I elbowed him in the ribs. "Don't be ridiculous. I think it was a true joy to wake up to the children's laughter."

Allen rolled his eyes, but Will shot me a smile that melted my heart. "I agree. This has been one of the sweetest mornings I've had since all our adventures began."

I maintained perfect focus on the food I was eating so as not to look at Will again; keeping my distance, not falling for him, was proving to be a difficult task. He certainly didn't help when he so gently brushed hair from little Rachel's eyes.

Chapter 29

AS WEEKS PASSED, Will took up teaching young William archery to pass the time. Marian would visit in the evenings as well to spend time with Robin and Mark. Though she was still under house arrest in the castle and she had a guard who was at her side whenever she exited her room, she'd begun sneaking out of the castle through the secret passages at night in order to visit the camp.

Mark had suggested she take over his old role as the Hooded Rescuer, the hero of Nottingham prior to Robin returning from the Crusades, and to that end I had helped craft a disguise of Marian's size to match what Mark used to wear. Marian would spend her evenings in the camp with Robin and Mark as often as she'd run around Nottingham as the Hooded Rescuer though.

The Sheriff began to send companies of soldiers into Sherwood Forest, wandering through the trees when no caravans were coming through at all. Robin believed the Sheriff was doing his best to find the camp and root us out. Robin declared that for the safety and secrecy of the camp to last, if we came across the soldiers and were not entirely outnumbered, we were to kill them quickly, or lead them to various traps that been set up around our camp in order to kill them there.

In spite of the Sheriff's roving bands of soldiers that never came back to him, the caravans of taxes still came through Sherwood. With every passing raid he sent more soldiers to guard each caravan, and every now and again he diverted his route to another road—like he had at Leicester when we'd had to rescue James. Sometimes the money the Sheriff and his lackeys unfairly collected slipped through our fingers and reached his castle, but such occasions were rare.

One day, Mark and I were in Nottingham at Marcus' home collecting supplies. As Marcus gathered our things into two packs for us to carry, he turned to Mark. "Have you heard from Lady Marian recently, Mark?"

"She was in camp a few days ago."

"Your father is very ill."

"I know." Mark crossed his arms, and I could see the worry written in his eyes. He turned to me as Marcus finished wrapping up our packs. "Is there nothing more that you can do, Dusty?"

"I'm not sure. What he needs is someone who can actually tend to him. It is tricky—if not impossible—to get me into the dungeons and to his cell without being caught or having enough time to do my work. And sending medicine and instruction through Marian now that she has access to him can only do so much…"

"Could he not see one of the physicians in town?" Marcus asked, holding out our packs. I swung mine over my shoulder as Mark grabbed his. "I suggested as much to Lady Marian, but she seemed to think Gisbourne would never allow it."

"I doubt he would," I agreed.

"I don't know…" Mark glanced between us and shrugged. "Gisbourne might. He did love Marian, or at least claimed to, before burning our house and putting her under house arrest. He's a wretched man, and I hate him, but I bet if Marian tried she could soften him up enough to get a physician to father."

"Don't encourage her to play with his heart again, Mark," I chided. "It is cruel."

"No crueler than Gisbourne burning our home to the ground, or helping to kill all the innocents who suffer under the Sheriff. Did you know he tried to execute my father once?"

I couldn't argue against the fact that Gisbourne was not a good man, but I was unwilling to have Marian lead him on. He was a bad person to be sure, I would not dispute it. But he was human, after all.

My Savior loved him, and had died for him, so I had to try to see him in that light as well. It was a difficult task, but starting with not causing him undue pain seemed a good beginning.

Mark appeared unconvinced.

It was several days later when I realized he had taken his idea to Marian. Mark came striding into camp one night after a visit to Nottingham in good spirits. There was a spring in his step as he came over to the rest of us gathered at the fire.

"What did you do?" Will chuckled, eyeing Mark's grinning face.

"Me? Nothing."

After a moment's silence, Mark shrugged. "Father should be on the mend soon."

"How do you know?" Robin asked, leaning forward and sharply studying Mark's face.

"Because the physician is seeing to him."

"Will the Sheriff allow that?" Much asked.

"Of course he will, because Sir Guy of Gisbourne is going to send for him."

"Gisbourne!" Little John and Allen responded, clearly incredulous.

"Yes." Mark shrugged, cool as a cucumber. "I made Marian go and…ask for his help."

"Marian and Gisbourne still aren't speaking to each other, are they?" Robin asked. "Last I heard they couldn't speak without arguing so they'd resorted to stony silence."

"Well…" Mark sigh dramatically, though his eyes were twinkling. "You won't like this, Robin, but I told Marian to charm him into helping!"

"Mark!" Much was aghast, but Robin only burst out laughing.

"Poor man! No one should be tortured in such a way."

I wholeheartedly agreed with Robin's statement, though my concern was much more serious than Robin's.

In the days that followed, it seemed the visit from the physician was not, in fact, changing Sir Godfrey's health, but both

Marian and Mark were in better spirits, believing it would eventually work.

A week or so later, we were preparing for another ambush. I leaned against a tree as I peered toward the bend in the road where we expected the caravan to pass through.

It was another ordinary raid; the sun was shining overhead, giving a golden glow to the tops of all the trees. We waited patiently, having grown accustomed to this work.

Robin would whistle—we would shoot down soldiers, and then jump out to kill the rest and steal the treasure which we wold then take to camp, split up between the people and the King's ransom, and life would go on as usual.

It was growing almost second nature now to raid the caravans, and as there were few occasions where we faltered they were no longer as nerve-wracking as they had once been. I was confident, and so were my companions, in our abilities.

Much had remained behind in the camp to watch over the children, as we always had to leave one person behind for that duty, but everyone else was in place and prepared.

As soon as Robin's whistle pierced the air, arrows flew and soldiers fell. Soon members of the gang were drawing swords and taking to the road to deal with the remaining soldiers while others of us—myself included—ran forward to jump up onto the carts and lead them off the road.

Just as I started to guide the horse tied to the cart I'd jumped on off the road, I caught sight of a figure in black racing into the chaos on his black stallion.

Gisbourne.

He snatched up Allen from behind and then spun his horse around, galloping away before we could respond. I stayed rooted to the spot for a moment, unsure what to do as the dust Gisbourne had kicked up settled back to the road.

Suddenly I felt arms grab me from behind, dragging me off the cart. I struggled against my captor and then heard Little John's roar of fury.

With a resounding crack, his quarter staff hit the back of the head of the soldier who'd grabbed me and Little John pulled me to my feet. He scooped a chest off the cart and started running. I followed him.

"We all got distracted by Allen," Little John huffed. "More than just you was overtaken…it's chaos back there. We just have to get what we can and escape for today."

As we stumbled into camp, I saw Will depositing a chest in our storage hut and felt some measure of relief, but the tension in my shoulders was growing.

Allen had been taken! And where was everyone else?

Mark came fuming into camp next, throwing his sword to one side.

"Mark!" I hissed, watching the sword bounce dangerously close to the group of children gathered around Much. "You could hit the children."

"What happened?" Much asked.

"All was going well," Mark said as Robin finally stormed into camp. "Until *he* showed up."

"Who?" Much asked.

"Gisbourne," Robin snapped, kicking a rock and watching it sail across the meadow. "We had nearly completed the raid and were just finishing off the last of the soldiers—"

"And then in rode Sir Guy of Gisbourne like a thief," Will said. "He bolted in on his black stallion, scooped up Allen, and rode off."

I closed my eyes, placing a hand over my heart to still the rising panic inside me. Allen would be fine…he *had to be* fine.

"Didn't Allen fight him?"

"Of course he did!" Mark said. "But Allen is no bigger than Marian is; he was no match for Gisbourne."

"Gisbourne was riding too fast," Robin sighed. "I was worried I'd hit Allen…my aim wasn't good. I pierced his saddle and did nothing worse."

"So Allen is…what? Taken in custody? Killed?"

"Probably in the castle dungeons by now," Robin replied.

"What are we going to do?" Much asked.

"We're going to rescue him," Robin said.

I opened my eyes to see him crossing his arms and glaring at the rest of us.

"We'll have to plan this carefully. I don't want anyone else being caught by the Sheriff! But Allen and I were already drawing up plans for an attempt to rescue Sir Godfrey, so we can just convert our plan to get Allen out as well."

The rest of the day I entertained the children and kept them away from the fire ring where everyone else was planning with Robin. I tried to remain positive to alleviate their fear— William, Beth, and Sarah could understand what was happening; the younger ones could only tell the adults around them were upset, which in turn upset them. So I tried to keep everyone calm. I volunteered to stay in the camp with the children during the rescue as well, for I wanted to spend my night focused on prayer.

Despite my attempt to remain outwardly calm for the children's sake, I was panicking. I knew the only place to turn was to my Savior. He would be my comfort should the worst befall Allen, and yet He could also be the powerful force that saved Allen from whatever fate the Sheriff was brewing up for him.

When the rest of the gang set off to find Allen, I knelt in the grass, the children gathered around me. Fear was beating an erratic rhythm in my heart and I bit my lip as my thoughts ran wild. Allen could be dead. Tortured.

I couldn't lose anyone else; it nearly killed me the last time.

I closed my eyes, focusing on my Savior and begging him to still my fears and quiet my mind. Slowly, peace began to steal over me.

Whatever happened to Allen, I knew my God would be faithful to me and carry me through it all.

Eventually the gang returned, and as soon as I caught sight of Allen among them I rushed forward to hug him.

"You have no idea how glad I am to see you."

"I am grateful to have limited this trip to prison to a single night and not a full year," Allen replied as he returned my embrace.

After we had put the children to bed, we gathered around the fire to discuss the day's chaotic events—though Mark stormed off to his hut and didn't speak to any of us.

It seemed that while freeing Allen the group had tried to convince Sir Godfrey to come to the camp as well, but he had refused and they had been forced to leave him behind. An extended argument might have gotten them caught—the whole scenario reminded me of leaving King Richard in Durnstein castle. According to Robin, Sir Godfrey was equally downcast as Richard had been.

Chapter 30

WILL WAS ENTERTAINING the children with fairytales and I couldn't keep my eyes from wondering to his animated face; the sparkle in his deep blue eyes, the way his lips quirked into a perfect smile…

I was sitting by the fire, trying not to watch Will and failing entirely.

Eventually his story came to a close, and among the cries for more and complaints about the relatively early hour, Will herded them all off to their beds.

Will returned to the fire where the rest of us were still gathered. He sat beside me, throwing me a wink. I ducked my head, trying not to blush too much.

Before I could get too lost in my thoughts of Will, however, Robin came bursting into camp. He marched into the clearing, kicking at a loose stone and then throwing himself onto the ground outside his hut.

"What is wrong with you?" Will asked.

"The passageways are being closed up! The Sheriff has discovered the secrets of Nottingham castle. I couldn't get in. He's blocking some off, and having others guarded…"

"So you didn't see Marian?" Mark asked.

"I went in through the stables."

The castle stables opened into the grassy hillside as a pasture on one side of the large barn and the opposite end opened into the courtyard.

"It was trickier than the secret passages because I could have been seen at any moment, but I got there."

"Does Marian have any idea about why the Sheriff found the passages?" Little John asked.

Robin picked himself up and came to join the group by the fire. "No…but I do."

There was something sinister brewing behind his eyes that I didn't like.

"How could he have learned of them?" Robin's voice was filled with ice as he asked the question.

"They have always been there for anyone to run across, Robin," I said. "It should not have taken the Sheriff as long as it did to discover them."

"Still…without the secret passages, it's going to be hard to spy on the Sheriff and Gisbourne," Little John said.

"And Marian won't be able to visit anymore," Mark added. "She's going to hate being cooped up in the castle…"

"Visiting her will be harder as well," Robin said, shoving a hand through his hair. He looked distraught at the news, but he'd said himself that he had been able to see her.

I wondered what was truly bothering him; he'd said he had an idea how the Sheriff had finally found out about the secret passages…what could that have meant?

Eventually the rest of the gang wandered off to bed one by one, reeling from the news that our way of spying on our enemies was no longer open to us. I stayed at the fire, and Will remained at my side.

"Marian can't be the Hooded Rescuer anymore," Will commented quietly. "Mark is right; she's not going to be happy being stuck inside the castle. She's the type of person who always has to be doing something."

"I believe you're right."

"I am not sure how we are going to get our information now either, with no way to sneak in or out of the castle. We'll be one step behind the Sheriff." Will sighed, staring into the smoldering fire.

"Robin will find a way; he always does."

"But it will be more dangerous: we'll have less information, which means we'll miss more of the hangings and beatings…more people will slip through our cracks—will die— than already were…"

"We can't think like that, Will."

He sighed again, keeping his gaze on what was left of the dying fire. Eventually he turned to look at me. "I wonder how the Sheriff found out about the passageways?"

"They were always there to be found—and were fairly obvious, if you ask me. It was only a matter of time."

"Maybe…"

"You think there's another explanation?"

"I'm not sure…I'd hate to think it. But Robin hinted at it, too, earlier…"

"What exactly was he hinting at?"

Will studied my face intently for a moment; the little I could see of his face from the firelight and moonlight was far more serious than I'd ever seen him look before.

Finally he shook his head. "It's probably nothing…we're just paranoid."

He didn't say anything else, and I no longer wanted to press the issue. I knew what he was thinking; someone had informed the Sheriff. But the idea that there could be a spy inside our camp was ludicrous.

Later that week we were preparing for another ambush. I chose a tree near the side of the road and jumped up to grab a branch, swinging myself up into the tree to give myself a better vantage point from which to shoot down the soldiers the Sheriff undoubtedly would send along with the caravan.

Will stopped at the base of the tree and smiled up at me. "Be careful, Dusty."

"I can handle myself as well as you can, Will Scarlett."

"I know."

Once everyone was in their designated place, we waited patiently for the caravan to arrive. Given the disaster of the last one—with Allen getting caught—I was on edge. My palms were sweaty and I could feel my heart pounding too fast inside my chest. I tightened my grip on my bow as the sounds of creaking wheels and chatting soldiers drifted down the road toward us.

The first of the carts came into view and I raised my bow, taking careful aim and waiting for Robin's signal.

As the caravan drew closer and more of it became visible to me, I began counting soldiers. There were more with this caravan, but it was not unusual for the Sheriff to add extra men each time as he tried to compensate for our ambushes.

As I counted heads, I felt a jolt of surprise run through me as one of the soldiers moved off the road, heading straight toward where I knew Robin was hiding.

I let an arrow fly toward the soldier immediately, and then as I whipped another arrow out of my quiver I realized more soldiers were running toward everyone's hiding places!

I loosed more arrows as I tried to rationalize what I was seeing. They would expect an ambush, of course.

I let loose another arrow and watched a soldier fall as more rushed toward the hiding places of my companions.

We always changed where along the forested road we set up our ambush. Maybe they checked the sides of the road at various points as they traveled...

Another soldier fell by my arrows.

But those soldiers weren't checking the general vicinity for potential highwaymen, they were going straight to our exact hiding spaces. Two were coming for my tree even as I tried to find an answer that didn't suggest someone had told them our exact plan—one we'd only created that night before when Robin had managed to get word from Marian about the caravan.

One of the soldiers raised a bow, but I shot both down before either could attack me. The rest of the gang were trying to fight off the soldiers attacking their positions as well.

A sharp whistle filled the air—not Robin's signal to attack, but one he'd created to indicate retreat, the sort of sound we almost never heard. We had often joked that it was used so little that we'd forget what it sounded like at all, but as the sound cut through the air I knew exactly what it was.

I swung down from the tree and started running. I heard footsteps behind me and glanced over my shoulder long enough to notice three soldiers following me.

I sprinted through the forest, ducking around trees, leaping streams, and leading the iron clad soldiers on a merry chase until I eventually lost them.

They could not move as swiftly as I could given their armor, and it had actually been easier to get away from them than I expected. Once I was sure I wouldn't be followed, I hurried to the camp, praying all the way there that the rest of my family would be safely there.

On the way, I caught sight of Little John.

"Are you okay?"

Little John paused to look me over, and then peered over my shoulder. I followed his gaze.

"I think I lost my tails."

"I killed mine," Little John said. Then he sighed. "Yes, I'm good. No injuries. You?"

"I'm winded, but not worse for wear. Have you seen anyone else?"

"Not yet."

"What happened?"

"I don't want to consider it," Little John said. He started walking and I fell into step beside him. I didn't want to consider it either.

More of the gang began to join us and I was soon satisfied that we had not lost anyone.

"How did they know where we were?" Allen asked the question we were all thinking about.

"They were obviously informed," Robin replied, his jaw clenched tight and his hand curled into fists.

The thought was a sobering one. Someone—possibly someone I was walking beside at this very moment—had betrayed us.

Much had been the one to stay in camp with the children, and he was surprised to see us return empty handed and brooding. I did not have the heart to tell him one of our friends was potentially feeding information to the Sheriff. I went to my hut and sat on the floor, staring at my hands.

No one in this family of mine would do such a thing; would they?

Had Marian been found out? She could have been discovered along with the secret passages, and possibly tortured or manipulated into giving up information on us. She would never betray Robin willingly, but the Sheriff might have threatened her father's life or her own in order to get her to talk.

It wasn't a pleasant thought, but it was better than believing that Little John, Mark, or Will had willingly betrayed us to the Sheriff and his men.

I trusted Robin, Much, and Allen too well to believe them capable of such a thing, and though I had been fighting it, I trusted Will, too.

Little John I wasn't close to, but he was a good friend, and Will trusted him implicitly, which in my mind spoke volumes of his character and trustworthiness. None of them would have done this.

That left Mark, but he loved the people of Nottingham, he would never do anything against his people. He'd been fighting this war against the Sheriff longer than I had.

Which brought me back around to Marian. She would not have done it willingly, that I knew, but it was possible the Sheriff had threatened or manipulated her in some way.

Much still cooked up a meal for everyone that night, but people were slow to exit their huts and it soon became clear that the perfect trust in our family was withering. No one wanted to eat beside the potential traitor.

As the days passed, relationships grew strained. I spent many hours a day on my knees in my hut praying for unity and peace to return to our camp, but it seemed unlikely to happen. I also prayed for the truth—whatever it turned out to be—to come out.

Chapter 31

THOUGH THE GANG had begun to eat separately and only speak to each other when necessary to plan our rescues and raids, I tried to maintain my friendships with everyone. It was nearly impossible to deny that someone had fed information to the Sheriff, but there could have been any number of reasons why that didn't include betraying us for the sake of betraying us. I couldn't believe that of any of them.

Robin still interacted with everyone because he had to—issuing orders and keeping us all in line—but he only confided in Much as far as I could tell, because he no longer trusted the rest of us.

Mark and Allen seemed quick to distrust everyone, and Little John was grumpier than usual, sparing no kind word to anyone but Will.

For Will's part, he seemed loathe to distrust his companions, but he was clearly sad and often seemed wary when speaking to the others.

One night I sat at the fire ring with Much, brooding over the possibility of a traitor in our camp. The crackling logs in the fire and the moonlight from above cast sharp shadows on Much's face.

"What are we going to do, Dusty?"

"Pray."

"The gang is fracturing…"

"I know, which is why I've been praying." I closed my eyes for a moment, reaching out to the peace I knew I would find in my Jesus. He was still there, as always, waiting with strength and power and love.

I turned back to Much, considering the pain in his eyes and confusion written across his face. What could I say to comfort him?

"Our God is the Way, the Truth, and the Life. I have to believe that He will lead us to the truth—whether or not there is a traitor in our camp—and He will give us wisdom on how to respond. He was betrayed too, you know, by one of his closest disciples."

"How did He take it?"

"With grace and forgiveness I'm sure, though Judas killed himself before Jesus was given the chance to show Him that mercy. And in the end, it was all a part of His grand plan to save us from our sins. He will use this, too, Much. I don't know how... but I believe He will."

As I said it aloud, I suddenly knew it was true. He promised to work all things for the good of those who loved Him, and He had always been faithful to keep that promise to me in spite of the horrible things that occurred in my life. He would use this, too, and I would be okay. We all would.

Later that week, when Robin got wind of another caravan of treasure coming through Sherwood, I offered to remain in the camp to pray while everyone else ambushed the caravan.

Robin sighed, shoving a hand through his hair. "I think we need all the help we can get. Go ahead and pray."

Once plans were made and the gang was ready to leave, I pulled Robin into a hug. "I am sorry, my friend, for all of this."

"Thanks…I just wish I knew who the traitor was so we could be rid of him."

Robin kept his voice low as the rest of our friends gathered their weapons and prepared to follow him out of the camp. It pained me to see Robin under so much strain; he was not his usual cheerful, playful self. He was frustrated and his appearance was becoming more haggard.

Once everyone had left, I had William gather the children to keep an eye on them, and then I knelt near the fire ring and began to pray. Not only for everyone's safety as I usually did, but I pleaded with my God to reveal the truth of what was happening and give us all the wisdom to know how to deal with that truth when it came to light.

Little Beth came and sat beside me, clasping her small hands in her lap. "Are you praying?"

"Yes, I am."

"Can I help?"

I smiled at her, reaching over to lay a hand over hers. "You can always talk to God."

"I want to ask Him to help all of you not be so worried anymore."

"I think that's a fine thing to ask."

"Okay."

Beth lowered her head to pray, and I felt a surge of affection for the small girl. I resumed my own prayers with a quick 'thank you' for the beautiful faith of a child.

We were interrupted far sooner than we should have been when we heard Robin shouting my name.

I looked up to see him crashing into camp, supporting Little John with Will's help. They both stumbled as they walked, practically dragging Little John between them, the latter's chest marred by a fast-growing dark path of crimson.

"Dusty! We need you!"

I ran forward, lifting Little John's shirt to get an idea of the severity of the wound as the rest of the gang arrived.

"Much, boil me some water. Allen, get my spare bandages from the storage hut. Robin, take him to my hut to lay him down —Will, get this shirt off so I can see what I'm doing."

The men sprang into action, doing precisely as I told them to.

As Will pulled off Little John's shirt and Robin eased him onto my mattress, I could feel my heart rate quickening. I knew Little John quite a bit less than any of the other members of our gang—we were not paired together for missions often, and Little John and I were both of such a quiet nature that we had few conversations—but I had known him long enough and been fighting a war alongside him for long enough that I counted him a friend. He was a part of our family.

"Dear Lord, help me," I breathed as I studied the wound in his chest. It was fairly deep, wider than an arrow wound. He'd likely been stabbed with a broad sword.

I began to wipe the blood away, revealing the jagged edges that surrounded the wound. A second later, they disappeared in a pool of crimson once more.

"Robin, help me. We need to staunch the blood flow before I can do anything else."

I feared Little John's lungs might have been pierced. My heart beat its drums in my ears as we worked, but I ignored it as best I could, instead focusing on praying unceasingly throughout the process as Robin helped me press down on the wound to stop the flow of blood.

Allen brought the bandages and we used them to put pressure on the wound and bind it until the blood slowed. Little John groaned, easing in and out of consciousness as I worked.

I knew my hands could heal; the Lord had given me a gift. But how much could I heal? I had never stopped a fatal wound before—this wound seemed beyond my skill.

Yet my God was capable of miracles beyond my imagination and I clung to that as I worked.

Much brought the boiling water and I grabbed fresh bandages and began to clean the wound, pulling out my well-worn pouch of medicinal supplies and quickly mixing together the things I would need to congeal the blood, promote healing, and lessen the pain.

Eventually, the blood flow stopped and I was able to ascertain that his lungs were not pierced.

With that relief, I applied more mixtures of herbs and then began to stitch his skin back together, earning a grunt from Little John. Glancing at his face, I could tell he was fully awake now. His eyes were clear—though filled with pain—as he watched me work.

"What's the verdict?" Little John asked softly, his voice lacking it's usual gruff strength.

"You'll live," I said with as much confidence as I could muster. It had been a near thing, and I wasn't satisfied yet.

Allen groaned, and I glanced outside the open door of my hut to where he was kneeling on the ground, clearly distraught.

Robin stood up. "Keep an eye on him, Dusty. I'm going to Nottingham to talk to Marian."

I continued to watch over the wound, applying more herbs and praying as Robin left the camp. Much had gathered the children on the other side of meadow, but every time I looked his direction I saw that he was nervously watching me work.

Will came and knelt beside me, watching me quietly. His eyes were filled with a darkness I hadn't seen in them before.

"I'm alive," Little John grunted. "Stop brooding."

"I'm allowed to brood," Will snapped. "My best friend nearly died, and it was the fault of someone in this very camp! I'm worried about you and I'm furious at whoever has betrayed us. Let me brood."

Little John grunted, shifting to a more comfortable position on the bed and closing his eyes.

I sat quietly watching over the wound and watching Will brood until Robin returned. When Robin did come back from his visit to Nottingham, he called a meeting of the gang, sending the children to the other side of the meadow so we could talk openly.

"I have asked Marian to keep an eye on things in Nottingham," Robin said, soundly disturbingly calm, though there was a veiled menace in his words that unsettled me. "Whoever is informing the Sheriff will be caught, and I will kill him."

"Him," Mark repeated, glancing toward me with obvious distrust.

"I do not believe that Dusty would do this to me," Robin said. Robin's firm trust in me sent a wave of affection for my brother washing through me. He didn't even hesitate.

"None of the rest of us would do this either," Will snapped, his voice ice cold.

"Obviously someone has!" Robin growled. "Little John nearly died today because of the coward who betrayed me! I expect to kill whoever has done this."

Robin was done with his lecture and stormed out of our circle to the edge of camp; I ran after him, grabbing his arm to stop him.

"Robin, wait! Surely you don't mean that. Killing the traitor wouldn't change anything—and it would mean killing one of your friends."

"I don't want to hear anything you have to say about right and wrong, Dusty," Robin snapped, jerking his arm out of my grasp. "They wouldn't be a friend of mine."

He marched out of camp, and I slowly returned to the circle of my friends where silence reined. No one seemed to have anything to say. Eventually, Much went to his kitchen to start preparing supper.

I went to my hut and checked Little John's wound. He was sleeping, the day's events and the trauma to his body having exhausted him, no doubt. The wound was looking better, and I could only hope and pray that he would, indeed, survive.

Will came and sat next to me, studying Little John silently as I re-bandaged the wound. When I was done, he said softly, "I agree with Robin."

"About what?"

"I don't believe you are the traitor, Dusty."

"Thank you. For what it's worth, I don't believe you are either, but I don't want to believe that anyone is so perhaps that is my own naivety. It is obvious someone has, I cannot deny that."

"Who do you think it could be?"

I moved away from Little John and settled against the wall beside Will. "I don't know. I would wish to believe in the innocence of all of you, but the evidence is against me. It is not Robin; I thought perhaps Marian had been coerced into it at first, but it seems that is not the case."

"I had a similar thought in the beginning."

"Much would never do anything to harm Robin, of that I am sure. I have a hard time believing Mark would act against Robin—whom he grew up with and whom his sister loves—and more than that, against his people that he's been fighting to protect for so many years."

"It is hard to think of any one of our gang being the traitor," Will said. "But someone is."

"Allen is a dear friend and brother and went through a war with us, I can't imagine him doing this. He was alone in the world much like I was, and finding Robin was like finding a second family for him as much as it was for me."

That only left one person...

Will's eyes flicked from my face to Little John's sleeping expression and back again, his expression darkening. "Little John could not have done this."

"I didn't say that he did."

"He's the only one you didn't defend."

"I don't know him."

"Well *I* do! And he didn't do this. He almost died because someone else did this to us."

"I believe you, Will. I do. I just…everyone has a reason not to be the traitor, and yet someone is."

"I hate this." Will dropped his face into his hands for a moment, sighing heavily. "Whoever the traitor turns out to be, I know it will break my heart to know the truth."

"Mine, too. My heart is already broken believing any of our friends could have done this."

The tensions in the camp did not lessen—they in fact grew worse after Little John almost died. Robin was angry, Mark was suspicious, Much was sad. Allen grew withdrawn, Little John was always in a state of frustration.

The children suffered, too. Some of them were too young to understand the betrayal, but they could feel the tension between all of us and it caused them a great deal of discomfort and grief as well.

Chapter 32

ROBIN RETURNED TO CAMP one night after a visit to Nottingham in a foul mood, but that had become rather standard for him in those days. Little John was on the mend—though his wound wasn't fully healed—so he joined us at the fire. It was the first time in a long time that we were all sitting around the fire eating one of Much's suppers together rather than separate and apart.

"I spoke to Marian," Robin said with his usual frustration. He said nothing else, and an uncomfortable silence fell over our group; had he found out who the traitor was?

I glanced around at my friends, knowing it would be horrible to find out that any one of them could have been feeding our information to the Sheriff and nearly gotten Little John killed.

The silence stretched on until it was finally broken when little Rachel began whimpering and Will pulled the girl into his lap.

"What did you find out?" Will asked.

"Nothing I didn't already know. Marian followed Gisbourne to a tavern where he apparently meets his informant, and she overheard Gisbourne speaking with the tavern keeper."

"What did they say?" Little John growled, leaning forward.

"Nothing of importance," Robin said.

"Then why are you telling us?" Allen asked, his voice strained. I felt that tense emotion I heard in his voice in my own heart—Robin had absolute proof now, if he hadn't already, that there was, indeed, a spy in our camp.

"Because Marian said they were speaking of a 'him' which means that I was correct in saying Dusty would never betray me. It's one of you men…and I will never forget this."

With that, Robin rose and stomped off to his hut. No one spoke after he left.

Eventually Allen got up and went to his hut, and Much went to his kitchen to busy himself with small tasks. Little John decided to take a walk through the forest to think.

"Be careful," I said as he stood up. "You are still weak."

"I know."

It wasn't long before Will and I were left alone at the fireside with the children. The atmosphere in the camp was clearly disturbing them, so Will began to tell them silly stories to keep them entertained until the hour was late enough to put them all to bed. Once they were all in their beds, we sat alone at the fireside once more.

"Robin said Marian followed Gisbourne," Will said. "What was she doing outside the castle walls?"

"Maybe she found a way out? I assume she's been as distressed by the suspicions of a traitor in the camp as the rest of us, and is likely as eager to find a solution to uncover the truth as anyone."

"She has a personal guard to follow her everywhere—I can't imagine how she could make it out of the castle unnoticed."

"Well however she did it, she's found where the traitor meets with Gisbourne."

"He likely won't do it again," Will said. "He'll find somewhere else to meet him now that Robin has let him know he's been discovered. He should have simply held onto that information and watched the tavern."

I glanced toward the dark treeline. "Where did Little John go, do you think?"

Will tensed beside me, glaring at me in a way he never had before. "Little John. Did. Not. Do. This."

"You don't know that—"

"I *do* know that! He's my friend, and I trust him."

"But you could say that about anyone in the camp, Will. Anyone. Yet it is clear that someone is the traitor. Where exactly is he going so late at night?"

"He almost died because someone leaked information to the Sheriff and Gisbourne! You don't think they'd protect their spy?"

"Maybe they wanted him wounded to throw off suspicion."

Will sprung to his feet. "I can't listen to this!"

He marched off to his hut, and I was left alone to watch the fire turn to glowing embers. Perhaps all that remained of the once vibrant friendships within the camp...

The strain on even my relationship with Will—whom I trusted, and who said he trusted me—made me feel the tragedy of a traitor in the camp even more that night. It wasn't only those I could not fully trust, such as Little John, whose relationships were spoiled now.

Days of tension and frustration continued to pass until the annual Nottingham Fair came around again. No one seemed inclined to go; Marian was under strict house arrest—although she had escaped at least once when she followed Gisbourne to the tavern to meet our traitor—Robin seemed too frustrated with the situation to care what anyone did, and the rest of the gang was equally broody.

I didn't want to remain in the miserable camp so I decided to go looking for plants to replenish my supply of medicinal herbs. Much decided to go with me.

We were both quiet as we wandered through the forest; I kept my eyes on the ground, searching for the plants I could use. Every once in a while I would see one and I'd bend down and collect a few flowers, stems, or roots—whichever parts of each particular plant I could use—and stuff them into the satchel I had brought along to carry all the things I collected.

Once I returned to camp I would dry them, crush them into powders, and restock my little pouch on my belt.

Much was rather moody as we searched for herbs. We worked in silence for a time, but eventually Much started to talk as I bent to pull a flower up by the roots.

"I can't believe we've been betrayed. I hate to think anyone would do this…and Robin is so angry! He scares me sometimes."

"You have no cause for fear," I said. "Robin would never harm you."

"But he is going to hurt someone, whoever the traitor turns out to be."

"I know." I stuffed the flower into my sachel and brushed the dirt from my fingers. Much was right; Robin did want to kill whoever had been feeding information to the Sheriff. I understood why he was angry, but I did wish he wouldn't threaten such violence.

I stood and finally met Much's gaze. "I do wish Robin wouldn't threaten to kill the traitor, yet he does have the right to be angry. This betrayal is no small affair. I'm angry, too."

"But still…aren't we supposed to forgive him, whoever he is? That's what you said before."

"Yes. As hard as that is going to be, we are called to forgiveness. But you have to keep in mind that Robin does not share our faith. He does not have the same conviction that we do, or feel the need to follow in the Lord's footsteps as we might."

"Who do you think did it, Dusty?"

"I don't know. I just don't know…"

I could walk through the members of our gang again, considering the reasons why none of them could be the traitor, but that was never productive. The truth of it was, I couldn't imagine any of them being the traitor—but the evidence showed that there was a traitor, so my hope was foolish.

That didn't change the fact that I could list reasons for each member of the gang to not be responsible. The way my brain went in circles trying to justify the innocence of all of my friends was beginning to hurt my head.

A week later, Robin went to visit Marian and then returned to the camp in a daze. He didn't bear the same angry look he usually did—he looked lost and confused. He went to his hut without saying a word.

I took a seat at the fire ring, wondering what could have caused him to look so wounded and confused. Much came and sat beside me.

"He's wasn't fuming this time."

"I know," I said. "He looked…"

"Like he wasn't completely here."

Other members of the gang began to join us at the fire. These days we only gathered as a group if Robin called a meeting. I suppose we all expected him to have news from Nottingham.

I tried to engage the group in conversation once or twice, but no one responded with any enthusiasm so eventually I stopped. We sat in silence, waiting for Robin to exit his hut.

The children had all been put to bed, and darkness was falling over the forest. But the moon was shining brightly and our fire was lit as usual so I could see the strained expressions on the faces of my friends as we sat in our tense silence together.

Suddenly the door to Robin's hut burst open and he stormed out, his face red with anger. "Allen!"

"Yes, Robin?" Allen tensed where he sat opposite me across the fire.

"You better start running now if you expect to live," Robin shouted as he marched toward the group at the fire.

"Robin?" Will glanced from Robin to Allen. "What do you mean?"

Robin drew his sword as he came toward the group and my heart dropped to my toes.

"I mean it, Allen."

Little John leaned forward, his face growing nearly as furious as Robin's. "He's the traitor?"

"Yes." Robin spat the word as he marched toward the fire ring with his sword raised.

Mark spun toward Allen. "I hate you."

"No," I whispered.

Not Allen.

Pain exploded in my head at the realization that Allen was the traitor.

It couldn't be Allen.

He was our brother.

Little John growled and then charged Allen, scooping him over his shoulder and running toward the edge of the meadow.

Allen was the traitor.

I could feel a darkness encroaching on my heart and mind, anger coursing through me and battling grief as the chief emotion swirling through my mind.

I stood to follow Little John, as did most of the gang.

When Little John reached the edge of the meadow he chucked Allen as far he could. Allen landed with a thud and then he scrambled to his feet and took off running as Little John and Robin chased after him.

Much sank to his knees in the grass at the edge of the meadow, putting his fists to his eyes as his shoulders began to shake—from his own grief or anger, I wasn't sure. Will leaned against a tree, staring into the darkness where Robin, Little John, and Allen had disappeared. Mark kicked at the ground and let out a string of curses.

I understood his feelings.

Allen was the traitor; the man who'd fought alongside us during the Crusades, who'd laughed and teased, who'd had a hand in giving me my very name…he was my brother! How could he have done this?

I moved toward Much, kneeling beside him as my heart squeezed inside my chest and tears filled my eyes.

Everyone in the gang had become family to us, but it was Allen who had been with Robin, Much, and I since the beginning; Allen who was always at our side, Allen who had sworn himself our brother.

My head ached and my throat constricted as my emotions enveloped me. Part of me wanted to chase after Allen and demand to know why he'd done it. Some part of me almost hoped Robin would catch up to him and kill him.

And yet a larger part of me still loved Allen as a brother and knew I would not relish him dying—and at Robin's hand no less. Robin would not recover from killing his brother anymore than he would recover from being betrayed.

And above it all, I could feel the heartache and compassion of my Father in heaven. He loved Allen, He loved all of us; this situation broke His heart, but violence was not the answer He would call me to.

I was devastated and I was angry, but I knew I couldn't let those emotions consume me.

"We have to forgive him, Much." I took a deep breath, trying to steady myself as the tears began to fall. "We who are the true followers of Jesus here have to set His example."

"Can you forgive him so easily?"

I shook my head as I tried to breathe around the lump in my throat. It would certainly be a powerful testimony of the grace of God to my friends who did not share my faith, but in that moment I did not want to forgive Allen.

Little John had almost died.

Friendships within the camp had grown strained.

We hadn't been able to collect as much of the Sheriff's taxes, and so had a harder time distributing money to those who needed it most.

And he was my *friend*. How could he have done such a thing?

"No. I cannot. I am more angry than I could ever say…but we have to, Much. We have to."

I wasn't sure I'd convinced Much anymore than I'd convinced myself.

I went to my hut that night with a heavy heart. Instead of sleeping, I knelt on the floor and prayed. For comfort and relief from the grief and anger, for answers, and for the strength to forgive Allen. I prayed to be overwhelmed with God's own love and grace and forgiveness so that I could extended the same to Allen.

After all, Christ had forgiven and died for me when I was in rebellion against Him. I had to do the same for Allen—and the only way I could was by leaning into the power of my Savior. I could never forgive him on my own.

I pleaded with God and wept for several hours before exhaustion overtook me and I finally slept.

The children were quietly informed of the news the next morning at breakfast. It was a subdued meal, but it was some small relief that we were all eating together willingly once more, and not because Robin had something important to tell us.

Some members of the gang went to Nottingham that day, others sat in the camp and brooded over the truth that had come to light. In the evening, after the children had been put to bed, Robin took Mark and went to visit Marian in Nottingham.

"I'm afraid of what he might do," I said softly, watching Robin walk out of camp with Mark at his side. I was sitting at the fire with Much and Will. "He wants to kill Allen."

"He won't be able to kill Allen easily," Will said. "Not without the Sheriff catching him. From what I could gather in Nottingham today, Allen is living in the castle now. He's protected."

"I still can't believe he did this," Much sighed. "After everything we've been through…"

"It is horrible," I agreed. "And it isn't much comfort that Allen is living in the castle, Will. Robin won't care, he's too angry. What if he gets caught by the Sheriff? What will we do then? We won't be able to rescue him from prison because we don't have our secret ways into the castle anymore."

Will sighed, running a hand through his dark hair in an agitated manner. "Robin's smart. He won't do anything stupid."

"He's too angry to think clearly."

Will shook his head but he said nothing.

When Robin and Mark returned to the camp later that night, they were subdued. They came to the fire ring quietly. Noticing their return, Little John joined our group at the fire.

"Did you see the traitor?" Little John asked.

"No," Robin replied. "We only saw Marian. You'd be proud of her, Dusty." The bitterness in Robin's voice was unmistakable.

"Why?" I asked.

"She told me not to kill Allen." Robin sighed, looking far more defeated than I'd ever seen him before. As much as the blow of Allen being the traitor wounded me, I knew it must hurt Robin more—he'd known him longer, trusted him longer. And he didn't have a powerful God lending him strength to forgive.

"I can't let this pass," Robin said. "I have to kill him."

"Marian told us something else," Mark said. "She said…"

"She said what?" Will asked.

"She said Allen did what he did in order to protect my father."

"To protect Sir Godfrey?" Much asked.

"How was hurting us going to protect Sir Godfrey?" Little John crossed his arms and scowled.

"It doesn't," Robin said. "Allen is pathetic."

"He's misguided," Mark sighed. "That's what Marian said. Misguided. He wanted to protect my father from a plot to kill him in his sleep. I don't know how Allen knew of that plan…but that was apparently the excuse he gave Marian."

"We could have rescued Sir Godfrey," Robin said. "Allen had no reason to betray us."

"I still don't fully understand," I said. "What does that plot have to do with Allen's betrayal?"

405

"Allen made Gisbourne promise to protect my father," Mark said. "In exchange for that promise, he agreed to give Gisbourne information."

"Marian is right, that is misguided." It hardly seemed like a good reason to betray his family; Robin was right, we could have found a way to rescue Sir Godfrey or stop the plot somehow.

Yet if Allen's excuse was true, his actions had been intended to save a life. He hurt us to save Sir Godfrey. I was still angry, but he meant well…misguided was a good word for it.

"Misguided or an idiot or a downright traitor, whatever he is, I'm going to kill him," Robin said.

"Robin—"

"Don't even start, Dusty. I won't hear of it. Not tonight."

I held my tongue then, but later that night when Will and I were the last at the fire, he asked me why I didn't want Robin to kill Allen.

"Two reasons," I said, studying the fire as I tried to gather my thoughts and still my wild emotions on the subject. "Firstly, because Robin and Allen are brothers in all but blood—I realize that makes this betrayal hurt all the more for Robin, but it doesn't alter the fact that they love each other."

"That is far worse than if he'd been a stranger."

"I know. Even so…Robin is angry now, but it would still torment him to kill his brother."

"Perhaps."

"If Little John betrayed you for some reason and you reacted in anger and killed him...you don't think that would hurt you? And second...I serve a God of great forgiveness and compassion, who had mercy on me when I did not deserve it. I am—not unjustly—called to that same kind of compassion and grace."

Will didn't respond, looking off into the darkness of the night for a time. When he made no sign of continuing his line of questioning, I changed the subject.

"I am sorry I suspected Little John. I know that upset you..."

Will spun back toward me, reaching for my hand. "No, don't." His dark eyes pierced straight through my heart. "I shouldn't have been so angry with you—everything was just so... messed up. Given how close you were to Allen, I imagine it was as difficult to imagine him the traitor as it was for me to imagine Little John as such."

"But you were right; I clearly was not."

"You couldn't have known...and I forgive you."

Chapter 33

ABOUT A WEEK after Allen was revealed to be the traitor and thrown out of camp, I was sitting with Beth and showing her how to mix different remedies for various ailments. She'd shown an interest in my work and was an eager pupil—and surprisingly picked it up faster than Much ever did.

Tension in the camp had fled with Allen—relationships were at ease once more. There was a fury and bitterness toward Allen that most shared, though I tried not to join in, but for the most part the camp had begun to feel like it used to.

The children felt the difference in the atmosphere of the camp and grew less timid once more. Their laughter filled the air as they played, chasing each other across the meadow.

I listened to Beth carefully reciting the uses of the root I had handed her as my eyes wandered the camp.

Little John and Will were sitting at the fire ring—though no fire was lit as it was a warm afternoon—chatting amiably. Little John's wound was healing nicely; he was nearly back to his old self.

My eyes moved past the two of them at the fire to the hut behind them. Much was cheerfully baking in his kitchen. His empathetic heart likely felt the betrayal of our brother on a deeper level than the rest of us. He was spending much more time in his kitchen these days than usual.

As my eyes roamed the camp, I caught sight of Robin casually sharpening his sword as he leaned against the wall of his hut. Undoubtedly he was imagining killing Allen with it.

As I handed Beth another dried flower and asked her to recite to me its uses, pounding hoofbeats filled the air. We both looked up to see Marian galloping into camp—this was a shocking occurrence given she was still under house arrest.

Little John and Will rushed toward her, catching her horse's reins as she dismounted and Mark emerged from his hut to see what was going on. Marian strode across the meadow toward Robin, who had hardly looked up when she entered.

"Marian."

"No time to chat, Robin. Allen is out of control. He's bringing Gisbourne here. Now. With soldiers."

"Allen? Bringing soldiers here?" I asked, getting to my feet as my heart sank. Allen was going to get us all killed? So much for only doing what he did to protect Sir Godfrey. This was going too far.

Marian nodded, and Robin sighed. "Get back to Nottingham before you are missed, Marian."

"What will you do? He's bringing soldiers…there's only six of you!"

"We'll do what we're best at," Robin said, standing up and setting aside his sword so he could hold Marian's hand.

"We'll set an ambush," Will said, leading Marian's horse to her.

"Be careful, Robin. And work fast. They're on their way here; I don't know how I beat them here." Marian then reached for her brother. "Be safe, Mark."

"I'm with Robin Hood," Mark grinned.

"That's what worries me." To the rest of the gang she called out "good luck!" as she swung into her saddle and prepared to ride away.

"Pray," I called back. "I've always found it more effective than luck."

Marian didn't respond as she turned her horse around and rode out of the camp.

"Much, stay with the children," Robin said. "The rest of you, get your weapons and follow me. We have a traitor to catch."

The eagerness in Robin's voice did not put me at ease.

I hurried to my hut to collect my weapons, slinging my quiver of arrows over my back and strapping on my sword and daggers before I grabbed my bow and moved to follow Robin.

I noticed Beth still sitting with the supplies I'd left out. "Don't try to make any remedies while I'm gone."

"Yes, Dusty," Beth said softly. "I'll put it away."

"Thank you."

Within minutes we were all ready and Robin led us through the forest. Our path was not directly towards the main road, but diagonally across the distance between the road and our camp so that if Allen had already led Gisbourne and the soldiers off the road we'd see them.

410

I moved to the front of the group to walk beside Robin.

"Please don't kill him. You would regret it later."

"I highly doubt that." Robin glared at me, his eyes burning with fury. "Don't try and preach forgiveness at me, Dusty. I know you're as angry as I am."

"I am angry, but I can't condone you killing Allen."

"I never asked for your blessing."

It wasn't too long before we came across Gisbourne, Allen, and the soldiers. We could hear them tramping through the forest ahead of us, their boots falling heavy on twigs and underbrush.

Robin motioned for us to take cover and form an ambush. I moved toward a nearby tree and swung myself up into it. As Allen and the rest approached, I nocked an arrow to my string and chose a target—one of the soldiers, and not Allen himself.

I didn't wait for Robin's whistle but rather began firing immediately. The soldier fell to the ground, dead.

Chaos ensued as more arrows flew from myself and my friends and the soldiers searched for the source as their comrades fell. Gisbourne and Allen swung their horses around immediately.

I heard Gisbourne yell over the din of shouting soldiers, "I thought you said we weren't close yet!"

Gisbourne and Allen and a few of the soldiers escaped; the rest Robin had us bury as per usual. As I rolled the last of the soldiers into the shallow graves we had dug, Robin came and knelt beside me.

"I could have killed Allen if you hadn't caused a panic firing too early."

"I know."

Robin studied me, and I met his gaze without shame.

"Dusty…"

"You would regret it Robin—you're angry, you're hurt, but you still love him and it would kill you to kill him. I can't let you do it."

"You don't get to make that choice!"

We returned to camp quietly. As soon as we all entered the meadow, Much rushed over. "Well?"

"We killed a few soldiers," Will reported. "But Gisbourne and Allen got away."

"I almost killed him," Robin said. "Nearly had him. I can't wait any longer. I'm going to Nottingham tomorrow to finish him off."

"Robin, please don't," Much said. "Don't kill Allen. Remember everything he means to you; we're family."

I appreciated that Much felt the same way that I did, but I somehow doubted Robin would take the sentiment any better from Much than he did from me.

"We stopped being family the day he betrayed me," Robin snapped. "He's nothing to me. I can't forgive him. I trusted him, I cared for him…and look what he did to us! He's still dangerous. He almost brought Gisbourne right here to our camp! I can't let him live. He'll destroy us all. And it's only a matter of time before he informs Gisbourne and the Sheriff of Marian's involvement! What would I do if Marian was killed because I didn't stop him first?"

Robin went to Nottingham the next day with the intention of killing Allen, but when he returned he reported that he had not done the deed. Marian had stopped him, telling him the same things that Much and I had—but he chose to listen to her.

The weather began to grow cold once more, just as the gang was growing easy with one another again—Robin had only just started to feel confident enough to start sending us out on extended missions to other cities and shires when autumn drifted into winter and travel became difficult.

Due to the cold, we all spent most of our time while in the camp huddled around the fire, keeping close together and close to the flames for warmth. Often Will would sit next to me and sling his arm around my shoulder—it was comforting and yet also disconcerting.

If he wasn't sticking close to me, he would have little Rachel or one of the other children in his lap—and in spite of the weather he continued to teach young William archery.

One cold evening when Robin returned from visiting Nottingham, he was in high spirits. We were all huddled close together near the roaring fire to keep warm, and he came into camp with a light step and a smile on his face, striding over to join us.

"Mark, I have joyous news!" Robin said as he sat himself between Much and Mark.

"What?" Mark asked.

"Your father is doing better; his health is improving."

"That is good news," Much said.

Mark grinned. "I knew persuading Marian to convince Gisbourne to send for a physician was a good idea."

"She wants your father to come here," Robin said. "She can't stand the thought of him staying in the castle any longer."

"He wouldn't come when we had a chance to rescue him," Mark said.

"Marian is determined this time, whether Sir Godfrey likes it or not."

"Can we even get him here?" Mark asked. "We don't have the secret passages this time."

"He's right," Will said. "You sneaking into the castle through the stables is one thing, but the whole gang wandering in through the stables and courtyard and then traversing the halls down to the dungeons…"

"It would be far more difficult than last time," I said, remembering how they'd snuck into the castle to free Allen— likely the very night that he turned traitor.

"Marian will get him out of his cell," Robin said. "I'm not sure how, but she's forming a plan. She'll get him out and we'll collect him."

"It's a shaky plan at best," Little John commented.

"We don't have details, but we have heart," Robin said, a grin lighting his face. "This is how it used to be, you know. No firm plans, just jumping in and doing the work. It makes it more fun."

"This is serious, Robin," Much chided.

"I am taking it seriously. This is Marian's father, we're talking about. All I'm saying is that I have complete confidence in us; we work well in the heat of the moment."

"But without the passageways..." Will leaned forward, resting his elbows on his knees as he studied Robin across the fire.

"We'll be fine," Robin said. "We won't take the whole gang so we attract less suspicion. We just have to sneak in, grab Sir Godfrey who will be out of the dungeons thanks to Marian, and sneak back out."

"What will my father do here at camp?" Mark asked. "He's not the outlaw type. He still considers Marian and I foolish dreamers for thinking we could do anything to stop the Sheriff or Prince John."

"He can stay with the children; he loves children," Robin shrugged. "And that way we can all go on raids and rescues and not be down a member because we need a nursemaid."

"I suppose it will be better to have all hands on deck," Little John said, "considering we are down a man since the traitor left us."

Robin nodded. "Much, for tomorrow you'll stay with the children. Little John, distribute food and money to the villages around Nottingham. We haven't done enough of that recently, with the whole mess with Allen to deal with and you're the most recognizable among us due to your size. Will, Dusty, you are coming with me to fetch Sir Godfrey."

"I'm coming, too," Mark said.

"That's fine, I expected you to do so," Robin said.

I awoke early the next morning, collecting all of my weapons and taking care not to wake young Beth. The grey light of early morning greeted me as I exited the superficial warmth of my hut and crossed the frost covered ground over to the meager fire Much was teasing into existence to make breakfast for us.

Robin and Will soon joined us. We ate quickly and then made our way to Nottingham. We went around the outside of the city, past every gate, to the place where the castle stables opened into the grassy hillside as a pasture. The large barn doors were sprung wide open and we slipped inside amid the stableboys starting their morning chores to feed the horses housed there. A few of them glanced our way, but continued in their work.

Robin didn't seem concerned by them, and I wondered if he knew them all—he'd been sneaking in and out of the stables for a while now in order to visit Marian under house arrest.

The other end of the large barn opened into the castle courtyard itself. There were guards posted to our right, at the gate that led into the city; there were more guards up on the wall that surrounded the courtyard.

"How do you usual manage this?" Will asked.

"I run." Robin grinned and shrugged, checking the guards one last time to be sure none were looking toward the stable and then sprinting across the courtyard and up the stone steps to the front door. He disappeared a moment later, just as the soldiers on the wall turned around to make their way back the way they'd come—if he'd run at that point, he'd have been seen.

"Well that was surprisingly easy," Will commented.

"You first."

"Not a chance. You make a run for it—if you get into trouble I can get you out."

Knowing Robin was waiting inside without the cover of the secret passages, I didn't argue. I took a moment to wait for the guards along the wall to turn around and head back the other way and then I sprinted as quickly as I could across the courtyard, hoping the pounding of my feet on the pavement wouldn't attract attention.

I bounded up the stone steps and to the door—a door I had never entered before because I'd never been inside the castle properly.

I swung open the door and stepped inside. Robin grabbed my arm and pulled me to the side, glancing down the hallway in both directions.

"Still clear. I think we might just manage this after all."

As soon as Will had joined us inside the castle, Robin began to lead us swiftly through the various corridors, ducking behind corners or into empty rooms whenever we heard footsteps or voices approaching.

Robin seemed to know the castle well, and I suppose that made sense if he'd grown up playing here as a child. Luckily for us, the stone floors and the hard boots of the soldiers made it fairly obvious when someone was approaching.

There were a few close calls with some of the nobles in residence inside the castle because they were not nearly as noisy, but we made our way through the castle to the lower levels without trouble.

As we neared another intersection of hallways, a voice rang out and made my blood run cold.

"Halt!"

I instantly froze, waiting.

Robin paused in front of me, turning around to put his finger to his lips to indicate that Will, Mark, and I be quiet. He needn't have bothered; there was no danger of me making a sound.

"How did you get out of your cell?" the voice beyond the hallway's intersection called out.

Suddenly we heard the sound of running feet and then the unmistakable sounds of an armor clad soldier giving chase. Robin took off running and we followed.

As we sprinted up an empty hallway, we could still hear the footfalls of the soldier giving chase. Robin took a sharp right turn into another hallway and Mark, Will and I followed after him.

Again, it was empty, but we could still hear the sounds of running not too far ahead of us.

The sounds of the soldier chasing who I assumed was Sir Godfrey seemed always just ahead of us, though I hadn't seen anyone yet. They led us on a merry chase through the castle, and this time we did see nobles and soldiers, but we were sprinting past and didn't take the time to stop and see if anyone noticed us or if they would follow after us.

Eventually the sound of what I assumed was Sir Godfrey's voice came echoing down the hallway toward us. "Let go of me!"

We had run nearly back to the front door we'd entered in. Robin grabbed an arrow and raised his bow, rushing around the corner and toward the sounds of the struggle.

Mark, Will, and I followed.

As I came around the corner, I saw the soldier and Sir Godfrey struggling together. Sir Godfrey—a frail, withered old man full of grey hair and wrinkles and far too many bones visible beneath his skin—wrenched himself out of the soldier's grasp just as the soldier plunged a dagger into him.

Robin let an arrow fly, and then sprinted forward and put his own sword through the soldier's chest.

The soldier and Sir Godfrey both clattered to the stone floor.

Robin dropped to his knees, his weapons discarded, as Mark, Will, and I ran up. Robin tried to support Sir Godfrey against the wall, his hands on the man's shoulders.

"Robin..."

"Hang in there, sir," Robin said, his eyes turning to me, wide and terrified and full of tears.

I knelt beside them, reaching for my pouch. "Let me see his wound."

Sir Godfrey wheezed, and then coughed, blood spewing down his chin. "You can't...do...anything..."

"Father!" Mark shoved me out of his way and took my place kneeling beside his father. "You are going to be alright."

Will caught my shoulders and helped me maintain the balance I'd lost when Mark had shoved me aside. Sir Godfrey shook his head at Mark.

"No...I...love...you...tell...tell your sister..." Sir Godfrey turned to Robin and I reached around Mark to inspect the man's wound. It was a deep cut, near middle of his chest, though slightly to the left.

"Tell her, Robin...Marian...it is good...to...dream..."

"Don't try to speak," Robin said. "Let Dusty work."

I pressed my herbs into his wound, but his life was fading fast and I didn't think I could manage this one—I'd never yet stopped a fatal wound. Little John had been close, but it hadn't been this bad.

"She..." Sir Godfrey coughed again, more blood trickling down his chin. "She...will set...all...to...rights..."

"I will tell her." Tears clouded Robin's face and Mark dropped his head to his father's shoulder, sobbing. Before I could do anything else, I saw the life drain from Sir Godfrey's eyes, his expression turning vacant and void.

"We have to get him out," Mark choked through his tears.

"Soldiers," Will said abruptly, standing up. He was right; the sounds of soldiers moving through the castle echoed through the stone hallways.

"News of the escape must be spreading," I said softly. "And we made a spectacle chasing after this soldier and Sir Godfrey..."

"We can't leave him," Mark said fiercely.

"Mark, we have no time," Will said. As he spoke, a group of soldiers rounded the corner from whence we had come and noticed us immediately.

"Hey!"

"Halt!"

"Robin!" Will grabbed his arm and pulled him to his feet. "Time to go!"

I grabbed Mark and hauled him to his feet as well, supporting him as we followed Will toward the nearby front door as the soldiers sprinted toward us.

Robin pulled away from Will. "I'm going to Marian! Get out quickly. I'll meet you at Marcus' home!"

Will let him go, and as Robin sprinted down the hallway, we rushed out the door and across the courtyard followed by the soldiers.

They yelled for the gate to be shut, which the soldiers at the gate immediately did. The doors slammed closed with a resounding thud, but Will led us back through the stables instead.

Stablehands and nobles in the large barn jumped out of our way in shock as we rushed through, making horses whinny in surprise. We burst out onto the frozen hillside and ran along the city wall, heading for Sherwood with the soldiers hot on our tails.

I sent a quick fervent prayer heavenward for Robin's safety.

It was a long run to Sherwood, but the soldiers were armor-clad and slow, so we beat them to the trees and once there it was not hard to lose them.

Once we were free of chase, Mark dropped to the ground and put his head in his hands. I leaned against a tree gasping for breath.

"Robin said to meet him at Marcus' house," Will said, pausing a moment to take a long shuddering breath. "We should return to Nottingham so we can be there when he arrives."

"The gates will be on high alert now, will they not?" I asked.

"Probably. You can go back to camp with Mark; I can wait for Robin."

"No, I'll stay with you."

Mark seemed not to care one way or another, seeming to lose all interest in any of his surroundings so rather than drag him back to camp and then make our way to Nottingham, we simply led him along beside us.

The gates were, indeed, on high alert. The soldiers at the city gate were searching every person walking into Nottingham. We fell into line behind merchants and farmers until the men in front of us reached the front of the line. As the soldiers roughly drew them aside and began patting them down for weapons and staring sternly at their faces to discern if they recognized their features, we bolted.

I held tightly to Mark's hand for fear he wouldn't follow us.

"Halt!"

"Where do you think you're going?"

The soldiers shouts followed us into the city, but our sprinting had caused an uproar and the other people in the line decided to follow our example and not wait their turn. As the horde pressed forward around the soldiers, we were able to duck down a side street and make our way to Marcus' home undetected.

When we arrived at Marcus' home, Will filled him in on what had happened and I sat with Mark, trying to console him. Robin was not long in coming to us.

"Gisbourne is going to arrange a funeral for Sir Godfrey." He spoke softly, glancing toward Mark and then away. "Marian wants to stay for the funeral, but then she is coming to the camp."

Robin sighed, pressing his palm to his forehead for a moment, as though he could wipe away the day's sorrow with his hand. "Will, Dusty, stay here. Get Marian after the funeral and bring her to the camp. I'm…I'm going to camp…"

Robin left.

Mark remained in a stupor until the day of the funeral—two days after Sir Godfrey's death. He revived long enough to attend his father's funeral, in secret of course, blending into the crowds. We saw Much in the crowd as well.

A great horde of people attended the funeral that Gisbourne prepared for Sir Godfrey—Marian and Mark's father had been a beloved sheriff of the area prior to being displaced by the current cruel lackey of Prince John, and the people came in droves to show their respect and to grieve.

When it was over, we snatched Marian from under Gisbourne's nose as she moved through the crowd and we brought her and Mark back to camp.

Chapter 34

WITH MARIAN IN THE CAMP, we once more had no access to the Sheriff's schemes. Caravans began to slip into Nottingham before we were aware of them, and more than one innocent soul was executed before we could plan a rescue.

Winter grew ever colder and snow covered the ground most days, so travel beyond Nottingham once again grew difficult. I believe we all felt in many ways that we were failing England and the people.

Without Allen in the camp to feed information to our enemies, the Sheriff couldn't be aware of our movement when we did plan an ambush or rescue, but the difficulty now was in finding out about the Sheriff's plans prior to them happening. We began to spend more time in Nottingham, hanging around the market and watching—sometimes following Gisbourne as he moved around the city on business, hoping he'd speak to someone openly about the next caravan or execution.

Sir Godfrey's death hung over the camp like a dark cloud, and it only grew darker with every missed opportunity to thwart the Sheriff.

Marian and Mark were both more withdrawn than usual, but I could not fault them for that. When my own family had died, I had gone so far as to forget who I was and become someone else entirely. They did not do anything so drastic, but their grief was evident.

One day I sat at the fire with Much, snow drifting lazily down from the dark sky above us. The camp was empty for once, as Marian had taken the children on a walk through the forest to keep them occupied for a time.

I watched the flickering orange flames of the fire, wondering if there was a way I could approach Marian. We were not the closest of friends, but I understood her grief—there were others in our gang who had lost family as well, Robin for one, but none of them had the true consolation or hope to ease their suffering the way that I did.

I had my dried plants spread out on the log bench beside me, my mortar and pestle in hand as I worked quietly, trying to decide what to do about Marian—and Mark for that matter.

Much was closer to Marian, so I did wonder if I should ask him to point Marian to the One True Comfort if I could not.

"Dusty?"

"Mhm?" I continued to work quietly with my plants for a moment, but Much did not continue so I glanced up at him. "What is it?"

"When you went to Nottingham to free Sir Godfrey…I was worried. I prayed for all of you, and I felt…comforted. Assured."

I nodded. "He does provide comfort when we need it most."

"But…it didn't work. I mean, He didn't answer that prayer."

My hands froze for a moment. Such a deep and complicated question; how could I answer him? I took a deep breath and then I set aside my tools and turned to face Much fully.

"He did. He gave you that feeling of comfort and assurance."

"But Sir Godfrey died anyway."

"I know." I sighed, gathering my thoughts. "Sometimes He works miracles. Sometimes terrible things happens."

"But why?" Much pressed.

"Why?" I repeated, looking up into the sky and the falling snow that caught on my lashes. "We live in a fallen world, Much. It was perfect once, long ago, but that changed when man rebelled. Now it is broken. Tragedy happens because of the broken nature of our world. It wasn't how God intended the world to be, yet He loved us enough to give us free will. Sometimes that means people choose to do bad things. It's sin, Much. It isn't our Savior."

"But you say He's all-powerful. He could stop tragedies from occurring, stop evil men from abusing their power…He could stop all of it."

"Could He? Yes. Does He sometimes? Also yes. Why doesn't He always? I imagine there are a great many reasons." I leaned forward, studying Much intently. "If He always dictated our lives, that would make free will a moot point. There's also the fact that He uses our lives—the horrible, the ugly, the beautiful—to grow and teach us, and sometimes to use us as examples and teachers to others facing similar tragedies. I don't always understand His plan or why He does what He does, but I can tell you with absolute certainty that I trust Him regardless."

"Why, though?"

Why indeed? Why did I trust my God when my life had been so full of tragedy and heartache that I was now terrified of getting too close to people or letting them see my deepest self?

I wasn't afraid to be close to Him though. He saw every piece of me and He loved me regardless.

"That still small voice, Much. You've felt Him; there's nothing that compares. Even when tragedies strike, I can trust Him because I know He is a good God. Scriptures teach that He is good, that He is loving. And if I believe that, then I can rest in it when everything else seems to be falling apart. I won't always understand why, but I can trust that *He* knows why, and He's working it all out for the good of those who love and trust Him."

Much nodded, his brow furrowed as he thought on what I had said. I don't know that he was entirely convinced, but I was. Without a shadow of a doubt, I knew I could trust the Savior who had never left my side through all of the darkness in my life.

Several weeks after Sir Godfrey's death, Robin finally caught wind of a caravan coming through Sherwood and we set about planning an ambush. We were rushed because he only learned of it moments before it was set to go through Sherwood and we did not have time to prepare. We simply grabbed our weapons and ran after Robin to the Sherwood road where he hastily gave our orders.

The caravan came in sight just as I hurried off the road to use a nearby tree for cover. My job today was simply to run forward in the chaos and take a cart. Our supplies were running low since we hadn't been collecting as much treasure and it was becoming increasingly difficult to give money to the poor or to buy food and blankets and other necessities for them.

Robin's whistle pierced the air, arrows flew, and soldiers fell to the ground. Despite our haste to get here, the ambush was proceeding according to our regular routine—and without Allen to spoil that for us, it seemed it would work as well as it had before he betrayed us.

Robin and Mark continued to pelt the enemy with arrows as Much and I both ran forward to drive the carts of treasure into the forest.

As I jumped up on an empty cart, grabbing the horse's reins, I saw Little John fighting soldiers in the road with his quarter staff, and Will standing at his back, firing arrows at the other soldiers in the road.

I directed the horse off the road and heard Little John shout my name. I spun towards him in confusion.

It all happened so quickly.

For an instant I saw Will running toward me, away from Little John.

One moment I was watching Will race toward me with a panicked look on his face, in a split second I'd spun around to see what had scared him and saw an arrow streaking through the air toward me. I felt peace steal over me, knowing I would go to be with my Father.

And then I felt the impact of a body slamming into mine and I flew off the cart, hitting the road with a thud, pain shooting up my elbows.

I struggled to my feet as quickly as I could with the wind knocked out of me, stumbling around the cart to where Will was now sprawled on the ground, the arrow that had been meant for me protruding from his chest.

My heart seemed to stop beating altogether as I knelt beside him. "Hold on, Will…"

"Little John!" Robin's shout echoed over the sounds of fighting along the road. "Get Will back to camp! We'll be there soon. Much! I need your help!"

Little John was beside me in a moment, pulling Will out of my arms. He scooped him up and took off running into the woods.

I jumped onto my cart and directed the horse off the road, thoughts of Will dying racing through my mind. I started to pray as I glanced over my shoulder at those still fighting.

Much was in trouble, too many soldiers bearing down on him. I leaped from the cart, rushing back to the fray. Much blocked the blow of one soldier while trying to sidestep the other two swords swinging toward him. I sprinted forward, whipping one of my daggers from my pocket and flicking it into the neck of one of the soldiers. As he fell to the ground, Much shot me a glance.

"You're supposed to be helping Will!"

"I couldn't let you die first."

"Dusty!" Robin's voice shouted over the din of the sword fighting in the road. "Go quickly!"

I didn't need to be told twice. I darted away from Much as he fought back the two remaining soldiers standing against him, racing toward camp as quickly as I could.

What if I didn't make it in time? What if Will died because I stopped to help Much?

My heart was pounding in my ears and my breathing was ragged, and I knew it wasn't just from running.

When I burst into camp, Marian and Little John were leaning over Will. I ran over to them, noticing they were working on staunching the bloodflow. I dropped to my knees beside Little John.

"Boil me some water."

I yanked Will's shirt over his head to get a better look at his wound. I pressed my hands where Little John's had been a moment before, closing my eyes. "Lord…please use my hands to save this wonderful man…but whatever happens, your will be done."

That last part of my prayer felt wrenched out of me—I didn't want to wait for His will, I wanted Him to save mine.

I took a deep breath to steady myself, focusing on my Savior and His healing power. I tried to tell Him He could do what He needed to for His glory, but I couldn't get the words out.

I felt the comfort and peace spreading through me in spite of myself. He knew.

He knew what I was feeling and He shared my sorrow—I knew He loved Will more than I ever could. If it was in His mind to save Will, He would.

Will had been quiet since the moment he was hit with the arrow, and that worried me.

I set to work quickly; the effort that it took to concentrate on his wound and not to cry, to keep my hands steady rather than giving in to my emotions, left me feeling shaky and I could feel a headache coming on. I ignored all of it and focused my attention solely on the deep cut in his chest, applying my mixtures of herbs and praying constantly, trying to lean into the healing that my God possessed and graciously let me use.

As I worked, Will seemed to come back to consciousness and he let out a groan. I finished applying my herbs and started binding his chest in the bandages that Little John brought to me from the storage hut.

His wound was deeper than I would like, but the angle that the arrow had struck him was such that it had not gone straight in

—it hadn't nicked his heart or his lungs. I felt a confident knowing wash over me; he was going to live.

I looked up at Marian and Little John who were both watching me with pale faces and wide eyes. "I think he'll be alright. Time will tell."

"How can you be sure?" Marian asked.

"I've done this many times before," I replied. "I have seen death, unavoidable and insistent. And I have seen it lingering and impatient. I have also seen it shy, and ready to fly away. This time...this wound. I believe it is the latter."

"That wasn't much of an answer."

"Trust me, Marian. And trust the Lord." I knew she didn't share my faith, but I also knew that if she had, she would not have to be so consumed with worry. I could feel His peace wrapping around my heart even as I turned toward Little John.

"He'll need to stay in bed for a few weeks if he's to fully recover. He's going to protest, but it has to be done. He can't be up and about."

Little John nodded, tears in his eyes. "I'll keep a close eye on him."

"We can see to it he stays in bed," Marian agreed.

Little John gently lifted Will and carried him over to his hut, placing him in his bed.

"We'll have to keep a close eye on him," I said, kneeling beside his bed and running my hand gently through his hair. "He's active and he's stubborn. He won't want to follow the order to stay in bed."

"We'll take care of him," Little John promised. He placed a hand on my shoulder, squeezing in comfort. "He'll be fine. Didn't you say so yourself?"

The children circled around Will's hut.

"Can we help?" young William asked.

I turned to the gathered children at the door, who all looked terrified; I tried to give them an encouraging smile. "If he needs water or just needs company in the coming weeks, I'm sure he'd love to have your help. For now, however, he needs his rest."

"Come on, everyone," Little John said, scooping up Peter —the youngest toddler—and leading the rest of the children away from the hut. "Let's clear some space in our storage hut for the chests of gold and jewels the rest of the gang is likely to bring to us when they're through with the raid."

When the rest of the gang finally returned to camp with the treasure, I was still sitting by Will's bedside. I had left the door to his hut open, so I could see when they trudged through camp, putting away the chests of treasure and making plans to take the horses to nearby farms.

Robin came over to the hut and leaned inside. "How is he?"

"He will live, but he will need plenty of rest and he must stay in his bed for some weeks to heal."

Will began to stir and groaned.

As his dark blue eyes flickered open, mine filled with tears.

Will glanced from me to Robin and his brow furrowed. "I am going to die from lack of exercise if you keep me here day and night."

His voice was weak and frail, but the sound of it made my throat tighten further and the tears escaped my eyes. "You will *not* die, but I have no doubt that you will complain profusely."

I stayed at Will's side as the rest of the gang checked in on him and then went about their business, taking the horses and carts out of the camp as Much prepared our supper.

Will drifted off to sleep and I sat at his side, checking his wound occasionally, and running my fingers through his dark hair.

I was certain he would live, but it had been a near thing and my breathing was only just returning to normal after such a dramatic day.

I bent down and softly kissed his forehead.

"I'm alright, Dusty." Will's groggy voice made me freeze for a moment, before I awkwardly pulled away from his face and sat back down.

"Will. I thought you were asleep."

Will shifted slightly, turning his head to look at me more closely. I dropped my gaze to my hands.

"I was, but it was a pleasant way to wake up."

I didn't respond, studying my clasped hands instead as my chest began to ache. He'd nearly died for me. What was I supposed to do with that?

"Why did you do it, Will?"

"Why do you think I did it? I wasn't going to let you die,"

"But *you* could have died."

"I am well aware of that."

I glanced at his face again, getting caught in the intensity of his dark eyes as he studied my face. I reached out hesitantly and ran my fingers through his hair, relishing the simple fact that he was alive and speaking to me. "Thank you."

"I'll die for you any time." He grinned and winked at me and I shook my head.

"Please don't."

When had I fallen so completely in love with this man? It pained me that he did not share my faith, both because I knew the fate of his soul was at stake and I had no desire for the man I loved to burn in hell, but also because the words of the new testament admonishing believers not to be unequally yoked seemed to ring like bells in my head as I brushed my fingers through Will's hair.

I could not help but love him.

Chapter 35

OUR LIVES CONTINUED in a usual pattern after that; we would gather in the mornings to eat a meal prepared by Much—with the occasional help from Beth and Sarah—and then Robin would send us out to distribute food, money, blankets, and anything else people might need. Occasionally we would get wind of a caravan before it approached and we would ambush it and take the treasure to give to the people, but more often than not in those days the Sheriff collected his taxes because we did not have someone within the castle to give us information.

Allen was sometimes seen around town, and whenever he was noticed a sort of bitter anger would take over the camp for a day or two as Little John growled about the best ways to kill traitors and Mark pitched in his own ideas. They never acted out their fantasies because Robin forbade it—after Marian had convinced him not to kill Allen, he made it clear no one else could either.

One cold evening in the middle of my second winter in England, Robin gathered everyone at the fire ring once we'd all returned to camp from our various duties that day.

"Who didn't follow my orders today?" Robin asked, eyeing each of us with a curious look.

"Didn't follow orders?" Will called from his hut, where he was laying in bed with the door open. "We all did our jobs, I assume. Even me, though my job was just to lie here." He rolled his eyes and winked at me. "Marian was here in camp with me and the children all day."

"We were all busy as usual," I said. "What is this about, Robin?"

"There's someone else foiling the Sheriff's plans," Much said. "We heard about a rescue they did today that none of us did."

Much filled us in on what they had heard in Nottingham of the rescue that none of us had taken part in, and we spent the night discussing the possibilities that the people of England were finally taking their lives into their own hands and not simply waiting for us to save them.

"It will make our lives easier if they can stand up for themselves sometimes," Mark commented.

"But it will be dangerous for them," Robin sighed. "I'm more worried now than I was before. I can't control what the Sheriff will do, and we've failed so many people since losing access to the castle, but at least I had some control over the stopping of executions…if they are doing it themselves, I'll have no way to protect them, I won't even know when or if they are doing it…"

"The people are stronger and more capable than you give them credit for, perhaps," Much said.

"Ignore him," Marian said. "He's just a concerned father to the people now…he's starting to sound a lot like…"

Marian turned away, not finishing her sentence. Mark put his arm around her shoulders from one side, and Robin took her hand from the other. I could only assume they were all thinking of Sir Godfrey, the once beloved sheriff of Nottingham.

Marian and Mark's father had been a good leader according to everyone I had spoken to on the subject. I'd never known him personally or seen him rule, but if he had half of Robin's heart for the people I could believe what was said of him.

After that day, we heard more and more instances of the mysterious someone who was a remarkable archer and foiled the Sheriff's plans when we did not. At first Robin still thought the people might be rising up on their own, but then we started to notice the mysterious archer on our own raids and ambushes of caravans.

It became clear that someone was in the woods with us, shooting down the Sheriff's men—they never shot to kill. Always they left the Sheriff's men wounded. Robin began to become distracted during our ambushes, his eyes roaming the trees trying to locate the mysterious archer helping us, but he never did locate them.

Whenever we heard of a foiled execution or other plot of the Sheriff's after that, we assumed it was this mysterious archer who refused to kill their enemies.

Will was soon allowed to get out of his bed. He spent as much time as he could training with his sword and bow to get back whatever skill he may have lost by his lack of exercise and fighting. I tried to watch over him and keep him from going too far and hurting himself, but once he had been let out of bed there was no slowing him down. He refused to listen to any of my concerns.

One day Robin returned from an early morning visit to Nottingham with a spring in his step.

"Why are you so cheerful?" Mark asked.

"I have finally heard of the Sheriff's schemes prior to them happening, which is always a good day," Robin replied. "The Sheriff is going on a trip."

"To where?"

"Abingdon."

"And what is he going to do there?" I asked.

"Collect his taxes personally." Robin grinned and rolled his eyes. "I do not know why, but it appears our dear Sheriff does not trust his men to carry out such a task and successfully bring his treasure back to Nottingham."

"I cannot imagine why he would feel that way," Much said with a laugh.

"How are we going to stop him?" Will asked. "I assume you have a plan."

"We'll follow him to Abingdon," Robin replied. "Once he's collected his taxes and is heading home, we can…pay him a visit."

We departed for Abingdon later that day—it was the first outing Will had been allowed to go on since getting out of bed, and I could tell he was eager to be back in the action. I, however, felt I would be little use to the gang as I would be constantly worrying and watching over Will to be sure he didn't over extend himself.

Robin set up our ambush a few miles outside of Abingdon, and we sat by the road near our hiding places, waiting for the Sheriff and his caravan to return. The sky above was dark with thick snow clouds, and fluffy white flakes were steadily falling to the ground and piling up around us.

Will was sitting near me, lightly holding his sword. He was rolling his wrist around as though reminding himself how to use his weapon properly.

"Will."

He glanced toward me, his dark eyes twinkling.

"Be careful."

"If you're asking me not to die for you, I can't promise that."

"I'm being serious, Will."

"So am I." Will put his sword down and scooted closer to me across the snow-packed road. "But you don't need to look so concerned. I can handle myself; I'm a good fighter."

"You were, but you haven't been in a fight in weeks, and you are still weak."

"I'll be fine."

"You're also stupid and will do something dumb, like jump in front of an arrow."

441

"I'm never going to regret that and I will absolutely do it again."

"That's the problem."

"I love that you care." Will winked and then swiftly bent down to kiss my cheek before I could react or pull away. "I'll be careful, Dusty, I promise."

"I don't believe you."

"I will be, but I'm not going to avoid danger simply to keep that worried look off your face. Our ambushes and rescues and raids work because we are able to rely on each other; I won't be a weak link and cause others harm. If they can trust that I have their back while we fight, you should, too."

Robin, who had been further down the road watching for the caravan, gave the signal that he'd seen it and we all scrambled into our hiding places. I sent a quick prayer for everyone's safety, trying not to focus my prayer specifically on Will, but probably failing.

As the caravan drew close, I held my bow at the ready, counting soldiers and choosing a target. I wondered if Robin would shoot the Sheriff directly and be done with it. Prince John would likely send a new cruel man to take his place, but still I wondered if Robin would do it.

As the caravan creaked past our hiding places, a lone rider came galloping down the road—not from Abingdon, but from the direction of Nottingham.

Robin's whistle didn't come, so I let my bow arm rest as we watched the rider approach the Sheriff.

"I have an urgent message from Sir Guy of Gisbourne!"

"Well?" the Sheriff asked, clearly impatient. "What is it?"

"Sir Guy said to tell you that he caught the Hooded Rescuer, and will hang him tomorrow at dawn. He requires your presence for such a grand event."

The Hooded Rescuer? That meant Marian!

Robin's whistle suddenly pierced the air and I raised my bow, firing at a nearby soldier. More arrows littered the air and more soldiers fell as the Sheriff urged his mount into a gallop and abandoned both his men and his treasure. We dealt with the rest of the soldiers quickly.

"The messenger..." Will grabbed the reins of a horse tied to a cart, and spun toward Robin.

"We have to get back to Nottingham!" Mark said. "We have to hurry."

"I know!" Robin snapped. "Get the treasure, and come on!"

We all jumped on a wagon or cart and began to lead the caravan down the road as quickly as we could go.

Once we neared Nottingham, Robin called out, "Little John, Will, take the treasure to the camp. Much, Dusty, Mark, come with me. We have to rescue Marian!"

We transferred the rest of the carts to Little John and Will. As I helped Will tie my horse's reins to the back of his cart his deep blue eyes bored into mine. "You have to save her, Dusty. We can't lose Marian."

"Robin won't let that happen."

Marian and I had never grown close, but I knew nearly everyone else in the gang adored her. She was Mark's sister. She and Will had a deep friendship, Robin loved her, Much thought of her as a sister. The people of Nottingham loved her.

We couldn't lose her.

"We'll never get there in time," Mark despaired as we made our way toward Nottingham. "The trip from Abingdon was too long...she's going to die..."

"I won't give up that easily." Robin scowled at Mark. "I won't lose her. Not to the Sheriff."

As soon as we had raced into Nottingham—not bothering to sneak in and undoubtedly putting the soldiers at the gate on high alert as we rushed past them—we went straight to the castle. As we hurried through the streets on horseback, people were forced to jump out of our way, crying out in surprise, but we never paused.

As we neared the castle wall we heard shouting. Mark pulled his horse to an abrupt stop before we exited the street perpendicular to the one that ran along the castle wall. "Robin! Look, up there!"

I pulled to a stop beside Mark as Much and Robin did the same. Following Mark's pointing finger to the top of the wall that ran around the castle courtyard, I could see someone up on the battlements in the Hooded Rescuer disguise.

"That's not Marian," Robin commented, his brow furrowing. "Look at how they're moving. That's not Marian's grace."

A moment later the figure jumped down and hit the pavement a few yards from us with a thud and a gasp of air, then they were up and running down the street to the right, away from the castle.

Sir Guy of Gisbourne came running out the gate with a band of soldiers. I shifted my horse carefully toward the side of the road, hoping to stay out of sight. We weren't in the same street as Gisbourne, but one wrong look and we'd be seen.

The soldiers and Gisbourne searched along the wall and the shops outside the castle for a moment before Gisbourne commended, "Search the city! Find him!"

The soldiers dispersed quickly, though one remained at his side.

"What do we do?" Mark hissed, glancing at Robin. We were in plain view, if Gisbourne happened to turn around to look, he'd see us.

Suddenly I saw Allen creeping down the street toward Gisbourne.

Allen had a sack over his shoulder, and he approached Gisbourne. They appeared to have a whispered conversation that I couldn't catch the sounds of.

"What are they saying?" I leaned forward, hoping not to draw their attention to us, but also wanting to know what was happening.

"I'm not sure," Robin whispered.

Gisbourne and his soldier soon returned to the castle courtyard and Allen leaned against the wall, waiting. Robin backed up his horse just a bit, to keep out of sight, while still remaining close enough to the cross street to be able to see the wall and Allen. Much, Mark, and I shifted to be next to him again.

The unmistakable resounding crack of a hand striking a face came echoing out of the courtyard and then the Sheriff's voice. "You have failed me one too many times!"

Allen shoved off the wall with his sack and moved toward the gate into the courtyard. Robin urged his horse into a slow walk and I followed.

As Allen disappeared into the courtyard we inched along the wall to get a view inside the open gate without being seen by the soldiers within.

Gisbourne was leading Allen toward the stables.

"There she is, Robin!" Much hissed, and I followed his gaze to see Marian being led inside the castle.

"I see her," Robin said. "I don't know what to make of all of this…"

"It appears Allen and Gisbourne saved Marian, which is remarkable," I said. I didn't know how or why they'd cooked up such a scheme, but it seemed to me that Allen had impersonated the Hooded Rescuer escaping so that the Sheriff wouldn't know it was Marian at all.

446

"But on more pressing matters, perhaps we shouldn't sit right here under the castle wall where we can be seen."

Robin reluctantly led us to Marcus' house where we stowed the horses we had borrowed from him for the Abingdon adventure, and then we gathered at Marcus' table while his wife Lillian brought us a bite to eat.

"I could almost forgive Allen after this," Mark said, staring into his mug of ale. "He betrayed us for my father's sake, to keep him safe from the Sheriff's plots. And now he's saved my sister...I can't hate him."

Robin was leaning back in his chair, arms crossed, his brows knitted together as he stared at the wall across the room.

Much touched his arm. "Robin?

Robin shifted, his gaze coming into focus. "Mark and I will sneak into the castle to visit Marian. She might be in the dungeons, but given what occurred today, it seems more likely Gisbourne would have put her back in her own room. You and Dusty go back to camp, if you can get out of Nottingham safely."

As it turned out, the city guards were more invested in finding the Hooded Rescuer who they'd been told was running around Nottingham than in keeping an eye out for Robin Hood's gang returning after their hurried entrance into Nottingham, so it was easy enough for Much and I to fall into stride beside a couple of merchants leaving the city and get outside the city walls without being detected.

Once we were back at camp, we filled Little John and Will in one the day's activities.

"I'm glad Marian wasn't hanged," Will said. "Though now that she's alive, I do have a bone to pick with her. She left the children here alone! So bored by being in the camp, she just left them…"

"William is nearly a young man," I said, placing a gentle hand on his arm. His passionate fatherly tone made my heart flutter—I could picture him being overprotective of our own kids someday before I shut down that particular vision and clamped a tight lid on it. "I'm sure she thought he could handle taking care of the others."

"That's no excuse," Will replied.

Much quietly made dinner for everyone while we waited for Mark and Robin to return from their attempt to visit Marian.

"I wonder why he did it?" young William asked as everyone began to dig into Much's meal. "Why would Gisbourne help the good side?"

"He cares for Marian," I replied.

"But to rescue her in such a manner," Much said, "making it seem like someone else entirely was the Hooded Rescuer…I can hardly believe it happened."

"And Allen helping," Will said. "Let's not forget that. It must have hit Robin hard; he has been so set on hating Allen, threatening to kill him every chance he can get. And now Allen saved the life of Marian."

"I thought Allen was bad," Beth commented, her seven-year-old face scrunched up in confusion.

"He's not bad," I said. "He has made regrettable choices."

"What will we do with him?" Will asked.

448

"Why must we do anything?" Little John growled. "He is with the Sheriff. He is nothing to us."

"Little John!" I scolded. "Allen is a brother to us. He always has been. Even brothers make terrible mistakes sometimes, but that doesn't make him nothing to us."

"And how can he be nothing after saving Marian's life?" Much asked.

"He was never my brother," Little John said. "He was a stranger Robin Hood brought home from the Crusades, whom none of us got to know well before he betrayed us. I have no love of him."

"You'll have to get over that," Robin's voice called out from the darkness.

Will leaned forward, peering into the woods as three figures approached the fire. "Robin?"

Robin, Mark, and Allen came into view. Little John leaped to his feet with a growl, the children instinctively cowered closer to Will.

Robin calmly sat on one of the logs, reaching forward to grab a bowl from the stack near Much's feet so he could scoop some of Much's pottage out of the pan near the fire. "Allen is once more a part of the gang. You'll have to try and not hold it against him too much."

Little John cursed softly as he sat back down.

"You're accepting him back just like that?" I asked, reaching around Much to scoop some of the pottage into a bowl and handing it to Allen. I could hardly believe he was in the camp again, let alone here at Robin's behest.

449

Allen's cheeks were bright red as he stared down at the food I had handed him. He wouldn't meet my gaze, or anyone else's.

"After what he did today…" Robin shrugged. "Besides, Marian told me I had no choice."

"Where is Marian?" Will asked.

"She promised Gisbourne she would stay in the castle."

"Why would she do that?"

"Out of gratitude, I suppose," Robin said. "But also for us. We need someone on the inside getting information from the Sheriff. Too many people have died because we didn't know what he was planning."

Little John continued to glare at Allen, and the children kept their distances, eyeing him suspiciously. Allen ate quietly, keeping his gaze on his bowl of food.

As the gang dispersed for the night, Allen rose stiffly and went to his hut. I hesitated only a moment before I hurried after him, knocking lightly as I pushed open the door to his hut— which had housed only young William after Allen's departure. I wondered how the boy would feel about having his roommate back.

"Dusty." Allen looked up at me from where he sat on the small bed in the hut. He looked wary.

I stepped inside and sat beside him.

"Robin accepted you back into camp so easily?" I didn't hate Allen—I wanted to forgive him. But it seemed unlikely to me that Robin would do so.

"He isn't entirely happy about it," Allen said with a sigh. "I don't blame him."

"He said Marian insisted on it?"

"Yeah…I guess she could see how much I hate myself for everything that happened. Being here isn't helping that feeling."

"Allen…"

"If I could do it all differently, believe me, I would."

My heart broke for him as he dropped his head into his hands, his shoulders slumping.

"I don't hate you, Allen."

"Everyone else does."

"Everyone else is struggling to forgive you for betraying us. Little John almost died because of your actions."

"I know…" Allen groaned into his hands.

"Much doesn't hate you, by the way. He and I are both trying to forgive you as our Christ would do as well."

Allen sat up, his eyes searching my face. "You forgive me?"

"I'm trying to." I sighed, closing my eyes for a moment. I was still frustrated with Allen for the things that he had done, but he had done so to save Sir Godfrey, and now he had successfully helped save Marian's life. I could believe that as misguided as he was, everything he did came from a place of love. "You're afraid to lose people."

Allen stiffened. "What?"

"You're like me; you're afraid to lose the people you love. For me, I close off and don't let people too close to myself. For you…you do outlandish things in an attempt to save them."

Allen relaxed, leaning back against the wall with a deep sigh. "You know me too well."

"I don't think I do. I just put those pieces together in this moment." I studied Allen's face, wondering how I hadn't seen it before. During the years in Palestine he'd mentioned the fact that he'd lost everyone—much as I had. It made sense he would react in some way to the idea of potentially losing his second family. It seemed idiotic of him to do the very thing to push that family away, but I could almost see why he might have thought working with Gisbourne to save Sir Godfrey's life was his only course of action.

"You're an idiot, Allen."

"You don't pull any punches, do you?"

"We could have helped you—helped with saving Sir Godfrey. You didn't have to feed information to the Sheriff and Gisbourne."

"I know! I know how terrible I was, that I made the wrong choice. Believe me, Dusty. I know."

"Well…at any rate, I suppose I'm glad you're back."

"Are you?"

"It means you aren't actually on the Sheriff's side, you thought it was your only choice. I am glad to know you aren't actually evil."

"Did you think I was?"

"I didn't know what to think."

"Life here is going to be awkward, isn't it?"

"Probably. Just avoid being alone with Little John. He's likely to strangle you in your sleep."

"Well that isn't at all disturbing."

After speaking with Allen, I intended to retire to my own hut, but once I was outside, I noticed Will sitting alone watching the dying embers of the fire so I moved across the meadow to sit beside him.

We sat in silence for a time, listening to the sounds issuing from Much's kitchen as he cleaned up the dinner dishes and likely prepped for tomorrow's breakfast.

"I am surprised Robin gave in so easily," Will said softly, breaking the stillness between us. "Marian truly does have an impressive influence over him."

"I am glad of it. I was as hurt as everyone else by Allen's betrayal, but forgiveness needed to happen; reconciliation was needed to heal this group. We are a family, and I hated seeing us torn apart."

"It will be odd to have Allen back though."

"I know. Do you think Little John will forgive him?"

"No. He almost died because of Allen."

"I know…but could you talk to him?"

"Don't expect him to welcome Allen with open arms."

"Could he at least be civil?"

"The most likely outcome is that he won't talk to Allen at all, civil or uncivil."

We continued to sit by the dying embers of the fire long after Much had retired for the night. We sat in silence, both likely lost to our own thoughts.

I wasn't entirely sure how I felt about Robin letting Allen back into the gang. I was surprised, and confused. I was also

453

grateful for the attempt at reconciliation, as I had said to Will. And I did so desperately want to forgive Allen. But trusting him would still be difficult. I was such a mess of different emotions, I didn't know what to do with them all.

Eventually, Will broke the silence. "When we thought we weren't going to make it in time to save Marian…when I saw how torn up Robin was about it…"

Will turned toward me, the moonlight shining in his gorgeous blue eyes. "I couldn't help but think that life is far too short. What we do here is dangerous. We win more often than not, but it is still dangerous."

"I know." I glanced toward Will's chest, where his wound was still healing. I'd nearly lost him.

"I don't want you to die before I can tell you that I love you," Will said, grabbing my hand, his eyes boring into mine. "Dusty…I love you."

My breath caught in my throat. I couldn't say anything. I knew it was true, and I knew I loved him, too, but that terrified me. And more than that, I couldn't do anything about it because of our difference of faith.

"Marry me, Dusty."

"Oh, Will…" I dropped my head to his shoulder. "I love you, I won't deny that…but we can't get married."

"Perhaps not now, but at least when all this chaos is over."

"I can't."

"Why?"

"Because…you don't share the same faith that I do."

Will sighed. "Somehow I knew you were going to have an objection of that nature. I could learn, Dusty."

"It's not just something you learn, Will. It's about owning up to the fact that you are a sinner destined for hell, and accepting God's forgiveness. Please, don't try and have my faith just to marry me." I sat up so I could see his eyes. "That's not the right reasoning; it won't save you."

"Whatever you say." Will sighed, letting go of my hand. "I'm going to bed."

"Will."

Without a word or another glance in my direction, he rose and moved across the dark and empty camp to his hut, disappearing within. Tears filled my eyes as my heart squeezed inside my chest. I'd broken his heart, I was sure of it.

Chapter 36

AFTER A PARTICULARLY long day of distributing money and food to the people of England, we were enjoying a lazy evening in the camp. Robin was in Nottingham visiting Marian, and the children had been put to bed, but the rest of us were lounging around the meadow.

My feet ached from all the walking I had done during the day, and there was a distinct pain in my shoulder as well, but it felt good to be useful to the people again.

Mark was sitting with his back to a tree across the meadow, speaking with Allen who was sprawled out on the ground near him. I could not hear what they were saying to each other but it was a relief to see Allen included in any sort of conversation with a member of the gang. Apart from myself and Much, no one spoke to Allen most days—even Robin kept his distance.

Little John, who was currently fencing with an unfortunate tree near the edge of camp, only spoke to Allen if he wanted to hurl insults at him.

"If he keeps going at the tree, he'll accidentally chop it down," Will said from his spot beside me on one of the benches around the fire. We hadn't spoken of our conversation the night Allen returned to camp. The following day Will had been as chipper and flirtatious as always, and since he never brought up the proposal I had denied, neither did I.

I dropped my head to his shoulder as I watched Little John hacking at the tree.

"Well…" Will said after a brief moment of silence. "We survived Allen being in the camp for nearly two weeks now."

"You were right; Little John won't forgive him."

"Don't sound so sad, Dusty. Allen doesn't deserve to be a part of this group as he was, even if he did save Marian. He's already been given far more welcome than he deserves."

"None of us deserve anything good, Will. We are all fallible creatures who make mistakes and bad choices."

"So you always say."

We sat in silence once more; it wasn't uncomfortable or tense, just quiet as I stayed with my head on his shoulder.

Darkness was creeping into the woods around us and it was growing harder to see Little John hacking at his tree at the edge of the clearing. The fire was casting its orange glow on us and the ground around us. It was peaceful.

It was one of those nights that you could almost forget people were starving and the Sheriff was cruel and we were always in danger. It was a night you might wish could last forever.

I slipped my hand into Will's just as Robin came crashing through the trees into the camp. "Will!"

"What's wrong?" Will sat up, instantly on alert. I could feel the muscles in his shoulder tightening beneath my cheek.

"We have to go. Now!"

"What is it?" I asked, straightening as Will reached for his sword.

"The Sheriff is leaving Nottingham," Robin said as he hurried over to the fire and the rest of the gang gathered around.

"Where is he going this time?" Mark asked.

"To Austria!"

"Austria?"

King Richard was still imprisoned there…

Panic tightened my chest. What was the Sheriff scheming now?

"I just spoke to Marian," Robin said as he hastily moved around the camp, throwing provisions from the kitchen and weapons from storage into small piles. "We have to pack. He's going to Austria to kill the king!"

"No!"

Will, Allen, and Mark were on their feet instantly.

"When is he leaving?" Allen asked.

"Tomorrow morning. Hurry up, all of you. We have to get there first, we have to leave tonight."

"What is our plan?" Will asked.

"I don't know yet…" Robin paused in his work to shove a hand through his blonde hair. "All I know is that we have to beat the Sheriff to Austria and rescue King Richard from Durnstein castle."

"Perhaps the Duke will hand him over if we explain the situation," I said. "After all, we have been paying the ransom all this while."

Robin snorted. "I doubt the Duke will do any such thing."

Robin continued his hurried packing, and we all moved forward to help.

After a few minutes of throwing food, clothes, and extra weapons into sacks, Much suddenly asked, "Robin...what are we going to do about the children?"

Will paused, looking back at Much, and then glancing toward the huts where the children slept. "We can't leave them alone."

"We have no choice, Will," Robin said. "We have to go *now*. I don't have time to make arrangements for the children; the king is in danger!"

"I can ride to Nottingham," Allen spoke up. All activity in the camp seemed to pause as we all looked to Allen and Robin.

Robin whirled around, fire flashing in his eyes. The distrust and anger there pained me, and I could see it hurt Allen, too as he took a step backwards. "And what exactly do you plan to do there?"

"Speak to Marcus," Allen took another step away from the group gathered at the storage hut, putting his hands up in a placating manner. "He can look after the children while we're gone."

Robin eyed Allen suspiciously in the darkness. The tension was thick enough to cut with a knife, so I hurried forward to stand beside Allen. "That is a good idea, Allen."

I glanced at Robin, who was still glowering in Allen's direction. His mind was clearly on betrayal. So I turned back to Allen.

"Set up a place where young William can meet Marcus in the woods, not far from here but not in the camp either. No one can know the location of our hideout."

"I'm aware of that; I'd never bring anyone here."

"You did before," Robin snapped, crossing his arms.

"I didn't though," Allen replied firmly. "Maybe you didn't notice as you were too busy hating me, but I did *not* lead Gisbourne here. I told him and the Sheriff I would in order keep my own life, but I was leading him to a different part of the forest when you ambushed us. We weren't coming here."

"Fine." Robin continued to glare at Allen. "Go to Nottingham, speak to Marcus. But if you aren't back soon enough, we'll just leave without you. *You* can watch the children in that case."

Will reminded Robin that their quickest way of traveling was by using Marcus' horses, so Allen was given a second task when he left for Nottingham, that of retrieving the horses.

Little John went with him, and I knew it was because he didn't trust Allen to do the task alone. Life in the camp had been relatively peaceful since Allen returned—there hadn't been any fights breaking out—but it was clear that the tension was still simmering below the surface ready to come out at a moment's notice.

Will woke young William to tell him what was happening so he wouldn't be confused when he and the other children awoke in the morning.

When Allen and Little John returned with their horses, we all loaded our packs swiftly and mounted. Robin urged us into a gallop almost immediately.

Our travel across England was swift—far more so than when we'd come home from the Crusades. We stopped in taverns

460

and abbeys along the way, but Robin had us up at the crack of dawn each day and rode us into the night every evening.

We did catch sight of the Sheriff's party behind us on more than one occasion, and Robin had snuck back to the Sheriff's camp to scope out the possibility of merely ambushing them on English soil—but they were too heavily guarded. He did discover, however, that Marian was with them.

"Why would they bring Marian?" Mark asked when Robin reported what he'd found to the rest of us. The moon and stars were shining brightly overhead, illuminating the worried look on Mark's face.

"They likely didn't choose to bring her," Robin said. "This is Marian we're talking about."

"That's true," Mark said. "She must have found a way to make them bring her along, which means she's up to something. Maybe she has a plan."

"But how will we know what that plan is?" Much asked.

"We won't," Robin said. "We'll just have to keep an eye out for anything. I hope she doesn't do anything reckless."

Knowing Marian, she would undoubtedly do something reckless. She was no different than Robin or Will or anyone else in the gang in that regard. Worse, probably, from what I knew of her.

Once we reached Dover, we found berths on a ship and sailed across the channel. The people of England were more than accommodating to Robin Hood's gang. Our reach didn't always extend far outside of Nottingham, but we did travel farther when we could, and stories of our exploits seem to travel even farther.

461

Once across the channel, we procured horses and rode for Durnstein castle for several weeks until early one morning, we crested a hill and came in sight of a familiar town.

"Do you think Lord Isenbern might be of assistance to us?" Allen called out as we continued our furious gallop across the countryside.

"Doubtful!" Robin shouted back. "He was loyal to the Duke last time; if he'd known we'd escaped imprisonment he probably would have sent us back."

"Who's Lord Isenbern?" Will asked.

"An old friend from our travels," I replied.

It was early in the morning when the castle came into sight. Robin brought us to a halt some miles from Durnstein. We dismounted, letting the horses catch their breath, as Robin created a make-shift plan to get inside.

"We'll just have to go in the way we came out."

"Right past the guard house?" Much asked.

"It's fool-hardly, but I've got no other options."

"What if they've moved the king?" Allen asked. "What if he's not in the same cell, or they blocked up the hole we created? What if—"

"I know it's not a good plan!" Robin shoved a hand through his hair. "But I've got nothing else. We get in there, we hope to find him, and we get out before the Sheriff arrives."

We crept toward the castle in the grey light of dawn, watching the guards on the wall above the courtyard to carefully time our sprints toward the castle wall while their backs were briefly turned.

462

I held my breath as I pressed myself flat against the cold stone of the castle wall, glancing upward. No faces looked back down at me. They hadn't seen me running.

So far so good.

As the rest of the gang made their way to the castle wall, we began to inch our way along the wall until we drew close to the gate and guardhouse there.

I saw two soldiers stationed at the gate. Robin crept forward with Will right behind him.

This plan of Robins—to sneak into the castle and steal the king—was entirely mad.

We had done a lot of outlandish things over the years, including escaping from this very castle. Yet this adventure felt the most foolhardy of all.

As Robin and Will pounced on the two guards we could see, I sprinted to the door of the guardhouse with Mark close behind.

I rushed into the guardhouse. There were three soldiers there, just sitting down to breakfast and caught unawares. One of them paused with a fork halfway to his mouth, a bit of meat pie falling into his lap.

The element of surprise made the fight easy and short.

As we came back out of the guardhouse with bloodied swords, I saw Much shooting down the soldiers who were up on the wall before they could sound an alarm.

From there, we darted across the open space of the courtyard to the front door of the castle.

The castle felt both familiar and foreign. Our escape was etched firmly in my memory, and yet I had only been inside the castle once, and only for the briefest period of time as we ran. Robin, however, seemed to remember where we were and where to go.

The fact that it was so early worked to our advantage, as few nobles were awake and Robin remembered where soldiers were stationed in various parts of the castle. His memory was far better than mine.

As we turned a corner to another passageway deep within the castle, Robin came to an abrupt halt.

The conversation that we had inadvertently interrupted also halted as a group of noblemen turned to study the strange motley crew that had stumbled across their path. We must have looked a sight with our weapons out, sweaty from our fight and our hair undoubtedly messy by now.

"Gentlemen…" one of the nobles, tilted his head to one side as he regarded us. One of the other's laid his hand on his sword hilt.

"Don't kill them," I said sharply, suddenly speaking in Arabic rather than English. These were not enemy soldiers but simple men. I hated that I killed anyone, but I could justify the other deaths to some degree; this would be going too far.

"What is your business here?" the noble who'd spoken before stepped forward, his eyes on Robin.

"We are here to visit a friend," Robin said smoothly, straightening as he spoke. The quick change from Robin Hood to the Earl of Locksley was remarkable.

"If we don't kill them, they will alert the Duke and other soldiers to our presence," Allen whispered behind me, speaking Arabic as I had.

"They are innocents."

"More so than the soldiers we killed?"

Robin was still speaking with the nobles, trying to persuade them we were innocently visiting friends in the castle. They did not look convinced.

"If we don't kill them, word of us being here will spread," Allen said, still whispering in Arabic.

"We can knock them out," Much said, turning his head toward our whispered argument.

Robin stiffened, his eyes suddenly meeting mine as he spoke in my mother tongue. "I agree."

Robin darted forward suddenly, and in an instant had his arm around a man's neck, stopping his breathing so he would pass out.

The other nobles cried out in alarm, some reaching for weapons while others moved to run down the hall. The rest of the gang sprang into action. I darted forward, whipping out my sword to block the blow of one of the armed noblemen, pushing his sword to the side. Then I ducked under his arm and jumped onto his back, wrapping my arms tightly around his neck in the same fashion Razon had once done to me to demonstrate how to put someone to sleep.

I jumped up to see if there were any more nobles to deal with, but my friends had successfully knocked all of them out. The floor was littered with unconscious men.

"Let's go." Robin marched away from the men on the floor, and we all hurried after him.

Robin led us to the small chamber that led us into the tunnels below the castle.

Unfortunately, when Robin opened the door to the small chamber, two soldiers stood there.

Much raised his bow and shot down one in the same moment Robin rushed forward with his sword to fight the other. The struggle was brief, as Will and Allen squeezed into the room to assist Robin and soon the soldiers were dead.

I waited outside the room with Little John, as there was hardly room for us in there, until Robin pushed past the dead soldiers to open the door to the tunnels and our friends filtered out of the small space.

Robin grabbed a torch off a sconce in the wall as he entered the tunnels, and hurried down the passages without pausing. The rest of us followed him.

"I think we're getting close," Robin said.

"How can you tell?" Allen asked. "There's so many branches and passages down here, I'm not convinced we're on the right one."

"I remember the tunnels," Robin said. "I'm not worried about that. I do think we're close. Keep an eye out along the wall for our hole."

"Which likely isn't there anymore," Allen said.

Robin swung around, the torch in his hand flickering and the shadows on the wall recoiling from the light of the flames. "If you don't want to save King Richard, go home. I didn't want to bring you at all."

"I want to be here, Robin. I only meant it might be harder than you let on."

"I don't need your negativity."

"Enough." Will stepped between Allen and Robin. "We have likely attracted attention with all the soldiers we have killed. We don't have time for arguing. Let's keep an eye on the wall for any sign of a hole, whether it is open or plugged up in some fashion. Let's move."

Robin spun on his heel, marching down the hallway while Allen remained still. As I walked past him I quickly squeezed his shoulder. He was trying to do better, but surely he couldn't fault Robin for his distrust.

Robin waved his torch toward the walls as we walked. I stepped closer to the side of the tunnel, laying my hand against the dirt and followed after Robin. After a minute, I could feel a difference in the earth beneath my hand.

"I think I found it!"

The rest of the gang hurried to gather around me. The wall of the tunnel was dirt and rock, seemingly carved directly from the ground and not built, yet there was a large portion of the wall that was discolored and it certainly felt different beneath my fingers.

Much leaned forward, running his hand along the wall beside me. "It's clay."

"That's it," Robin said. "They filled it in, but that's it."

"The other side is our cell," I agreed.

Robin kicked at the clay, but nothing happened. He passed his torch to Much and began to shove his weight against the wall.

Will crossed his arms, watching. "Should we have a plan before we break that down?"

"We're getting the king before the Sheriff does," Robin grunted.

"What if the king is not in that cell?" Will asked. "What if he is, but so are a bunch of soldiers? What if it is only soldiers, lying in wait for us?"

"Now you sound like Allen."

"Allen has a point." Will stepped closer to Robin, laying a hand on his shoulder. "Before we rush in, we need to think this through."

"We've already rushed in."

"Robin."

Robin sighed, straightening and crossing his arms. "Okay. Okay. Get your weapons at the ready. Little John, smash this in and then duck out of the way—you're too large to fit through quickly. Dusty and I will dive in, Will and Much can cover us at the hole. Mark, stay clear for your own safety."

"You don't have to be protective of me," Mark snapped.

"There's not space for everyone around the small hole we created the last time. I doubt when they plugged it up they made it any larger! Just stand aside, please."

Mark grumbled under his breath, but he moved to one side. Allen moved to stand with him as Robin hadn't given him any direction at all.

Much grabbed an arrow from his quiver and held it at the ready as Little John took Robin's place and began to kick at the clay. I stepped up beside Robin, pulling my daggers out and holding them lightly in my hand.

At first, nothing seemed to happen as Little John kicked at the clay, but then it caved inward.

Robin jumped through the hole and I dove in after him. I rolled to my feet, ready for anything, but there were no soldiers in the dimly lit cell. Only Richard.

He looked up at us, staring at the hole in the wall, and then at us again, and then back.

"Robin?!"

"Richard. We've got to get you out."

"You're supposed to be in England dealing with my brother!"

"And so we have been," Robin replied, pulling King Richard to his feet and shoving him out of the hole. "Right now we have to run because we've undoubtedly attracted attention in here, and because the Sheriff of Nottingham has brought his own batch of vile men to kill you here in Austria. So let's *move*."

As I followed them through the hole, Much shot an arrow past my shoulder. I spun around and saw the shadows of soldiers hurrying through the dungeon toward Richard's empty cell.

Robin pushed the king and began running back down the tunnel, and I ran after them.

Little John took up the rear as we ran, brandishing his quarter staff at the few soldiers who were pushing their way out of the hole in the dungeon wall.

Robin led us back to the castle itself. Shouts followed behind and I spun around, whipping my bow off of my back to shoot at any followers as Little John continued to look threatening but was mostly useless at a distance. Will stopped beside me, and we shot down soldier after soldier, continuing to walk backwards to keep up with our group as we killed off the soldiers following us.

As we rushed through the castle with soldiers on our heels, we startled a few nobles going about their own business but we didn't bother to stop and knock them out.

"Robin!" Richard drew him into an embrace as soon as we'd gotten free of the castle.

"We cannot have a reunion here, Your Majesty," Robin said as he pulled away. "We must be on our way."

Robin hurried everyone away from the castle, to our horses in the nearby cropping of trees where we'd left them, and from there we raced along the road. The nearby town of Vienna crossed our path, and Robin slowed our pace a bit, creeping us along the streets so as to draw less attention.

As we crept along the street of the city, I kept my gaze roaming, on the lookout for any more danger. I was surprised at how easily we had managed to save the king and get away from Durnstein, but before I could truly appreciate that fact I heard the decisive twang of a bow.

Richard fell from his horse, an arrow protruding from his shoulder.

I pulled my own mount to a sharp stop, leaping down and darted forward even as Robin called out, "Help him, Dusty!"

470

I reached for my pouch of herbs, running forward. Suddenly the Sheriff, Gisbourne, and a contingent of soldiers swarmed into the street, and chaos broke out. Arrows flew, swords flashed, and I was forced to defend myself before I could reach the king.

I drew my sword, and blocked the first blow from an opponent, gritting my teeth as I prepared for the fight ahead. This felt so different from ambushing the Sheriff's caravans—this was a fight for the king's life, a fight for England.

I shoved a blade to the side, diving and rolling around my opponent to come up behind them and shove my sword in their back. It wasn't pretty, but I was desperate.

In the midst of the fighting I tried to make my way towards Richard. He was still on the ground, unmoving. Someone needed to defend him. His wound needed tending.

I could see Mark running toward him to keep the Sheriff's men away from him.

I dove to the ground to avoid a sword, rolling to my feet and sprinting toward the king. Gisbourne rushed toward him as well and my heart began to race.

A soldier appeared in front of me, but I didn't have time for nonsense. I slammed the pummel of my sword into the soldier's face as he approached me. He stumbled back, howling in pain and I put a swift end to his life before continuing my sprint to the king.

I heard Gisbourne call out Marian's name as I rushed forward and watched as she put herself between Gisbourne and the Sheriff.

Another sword came bearing down on me and I was distracted from whatever was happening around the king as I once more found myself locked in combat, parrying and blocking and slicing at my enemy until I managed to cut his legs and he dropped to his knees.

I put a boot to his chest and my sword to his throat as I heard several voices scream out Marian's name. One of them was Will, and I had never heard more panic in his voice before that day.

I spun toward the sound of his voice, and saw Marian on the ground, a sword sticking out of her.

Gisbourne was slowly backing away from her, his arm bleeding.

"Lord, help her," I gasped. Robin's cry of anguish rent the air and I closed my eyes momentarily, my hands curling into fists.

The Sheriff was calling for Gisbourne, and I opened my eyes in time to see him pull Gisbourne up onto the back of his horse and gallop away. The rest of the soldiers in the street were either dead or scattering, and I finally had a clear path to Richard.

I rushed forward, though my eyes remained on Marian. Mark had pulled her head into his lap and Robin was kneeling beside her, sobbing uncontrollably.

I knelt beside the king, checking his wound. The arrow was in his shoulder, and it wasn't too deep. He'd had the wind knocked out of him, which was why he hadn't gotten to his feet immediately to help with the fight.

He was also incredibly weak and malnourished from his extended time in Durnstein castle.

I yanked the arrow from his shoulder, causing him to cry out briefly.

"Save Marian, lass," Richard said, sitting up and grasping his bleeding shoulder. He wasn't going to die from his shoulder cut, so I nodded. I ran over to Robin and dropped to my knees beside him, surveying Marian's wounds.

"The king!" Marian gasped.

"He's fine," I told her. "The king will be fine."

I pulled back the cloth of her dress around the blade still buried inside her, trying to see how far the wound went. It was deep—it seemed to cut straight through her and come out the back.

Reaching my hand beneath her, I felt the tip of the sword pressing into the ground. The placement of the sword in relation to her heart and lungs, and how deep it was…I couldn't fix this.

Robin was staring at me, clearly waiting for my miracle. I shook my head in answer to his silent question.

Robin gently put his hands on either side of Marian's face, and I closed my eyes to stem the flow of tears coming from my eyes.

"I'm sorry, Marian love. We can't remove the sword."

"Why?" Marian gasped out, her breathing clearly labored.

I opened my eyes, brushing the tears from my cheeks and trying to speak. How could I explain to her that her wounds were so extensive? The blade still in her chest was likely what was keeping her from dying instantly.

"You'll bleed out," I finally choked past the lump in my throat.

Mark leaned over Marian, his tears splashing down on her face. "I'm sorry, I'm so sorry..."

"Mark..." Marian gasped for air, staring up at her brother intensely. "This is not your fault..."

"I should have stopped him, I was right beside you..."

"Don't...blame...yourself..."

Marian's words were growing slower, her face becoming increasingly pale. I reached for my pouch, pulling out the necessary herbs to ease the pain she must be feeling and carefully pressing them around the blade of the sword into her wound, praying for a miracle.

I'd never stopped a fatal wound before, but maybe...just maybe...

The entire gang seemed to have circled around us, and Marian's eyes were darting around, taking in all of us as I sent a desperate prayer heavenward.

I felt Will's hand press into my shoulder, and I turned to him, burying my face in his shoulder as my body shook with the sobs I had been holding in.

I was a failure. The one time it truly mattered, I was incapable of healing Marian.

"Stay with me, Marian," Robin moaned. I turned slightly in Will's arms so I could see him. He was stroking Marian's hair as tears coursed down his cheek. "Stay with me."

"Marry...me...Robin."

"Marian."

"Please..."

"I can't."

Mark moaned in agony and turned his face away.

I stood, trying to give myself some distance from Robin's grief, from Mark's...I couldn't save them from the horror that was happening now. I couldn't...

Will stood, too, keeping his arms wrapped tightly around me, steadying me.

Marian kept her eyes on Robin as her breathing came out in short gasps. "Ro...Robin..."

Robin took a deep breath, grabbing Marian's hand suddenly. "I, Robin of Locksley, take you, my brave, beautiful Marian, to be my wife. To have and to hold, from this day forward, for better or for worse, for richer or for poorer, in sickness and in health. I promise to love you and cherish you... until...until death..."

Marian smiled through her tears, her mouth opening and closing several times as I she tried to speak. "I...I..."

"It's okay, Marian," Robin whispered as Mark sobbed beside him.

I trembled, my legs buckling beneath me. Only Will's strong arms kept me standing upright as he gripped me tightly.

King Richard knelt beside Robin, taking his signet ring from his finger. "She needs a wedding band, Robin."

Robin took the ring and with a shaky breath he placed it on Marian's hand.

"Kiss…" Marian gasped out.

Robin bent down to gently kiss her.

"Robin…" Marian's chest heaved with the effort it took to speak, and my vision clouded with my tears. "Promise…me… you'll keep…fighting…"

"Marian…"

"Please…England…needs…"

"She right," Richard said. "England does need you, Robin. Especially since I am not going back yet. I have unfinished business here. You must continue to care for my people."

Robin shook his head, bringing Marian's hands to his lips.

"Robin…" Marian's voice was a mere whisper now as she struggled to finish her thought. "Promise…me…"

"I promise. For you, my darling Marian."

Marian's eyes suddenly filled with the vacant distant look I knew so well. I reached past Robin to carefully close her eyes.

I turned my face away once more as Mark let out a scream of pure agony. Will sank to the ground and I fell with him, wrapping my arms around his neck and burying myself in his embrace.

Past the pain of my pounding head, my heart constricting, my throat aching, I could feel Will shaking beneath me, the sound of his cries in my ear piercing my heart.

Everything was a blur of confusion and tears for the next day and half as we traveled outside of Vienna and made camp in the countryside. Eventually, however, I had to come back to reality. We needed to return to England and keep fighting the

Sheriff who was likely headed back to Nottingham and up to no good.

The night after Marian's death, after our companions were sleeping, I moved over to where Robin sat at the edge of our circle, sitting beside the still corpse of Marian. She was wrapped in a blanket as a shroud, frozen in time.

"We have to leave Vienna, Robin. We have to go home," I said as I sat beside him.

"I know."

"We should bury Marian."

Robin winced when I said her name. He took a shuddering breath, pushing his hand through his hair as he so often did when stressed. "I am taking her home. She will be buried in England."

"Robin, you know you can't do that."

"I'm not leaving her here!" Robin was angry, and I could understand that, but I was not letting him carry a corpse all the way to England. The stench alone would be unbearable.

"We have to. We don't have a choice."

"She should be buried with her father." Tears slid down Robin's cheek, glistening in the moonlight.

"I am so sorry, my friend...but we can't carry her dead body on our long journey. We cannot, no matter how much you want to.

"Dusty—"

"No. She has to be buried here. And she has to be buried soon."

"I can't let her go…"

Robin broke down into sobs, his shoulders shaking with the force of his grief as he curled into himself and my heart broke anew. I wrapped my arm around his shoulders.

"Robin." I tried to soften my voice and be less harsh. "We need to bury her. We will do it tomorrow."

"I can't."

"I know. I'll help you."

"Dusty…" Robin clenched his fists, pressing his hands over his eyes.

"I know…I know. I cannot claim to have lost the love of my life, but I did lose my family. I understand this pain you feel. And God does, too. He suffered more than we can imagine, He can comfort you far better than I can."

Robin shoved my arm off of his shoulder. "I don't care for his comfort!"

"I know…but He'll be waiting for you. Believe me, He is crying with you, you have to know that."

"Leave me alone."

I wanted to comfort him, but I did not know how. I was only upsetting him further, so I left him in peace that night. The next day I enlisted the help of the rest of the gang to bury Marian, and then we returned to England, leaving the king behind.

Chapter 37

WHEN WE RETURNED to camp, we all retired to our huts to grieve alone. Our journey from Austria had been quiet and uneventful, with hardly a word spoken between us except out of necessity. Yet the morning after our return home I awoke with fresh vigor; I knew we needed to start leaning on each other for support rather than isolating ourselves.

I had tried isolation before, and it had not been healthy. It wasn't until I'd met Robin, Much, and Allen and begun to open up once more that true healing had occurred. We needed to grieve and not stuff our emotions or wallow to the point of suffocation.

Winter had given way to spring on our long journey to and from Austria, but the morning air was still chill when I emerged from my hut with a heavy heart but the determination to see my friends through this horrible time. I had something they did not—apart from Much: a Comforter that would see me through. It was only right that I should share Him with them.

Much was preparing breakfast as usual, with several of the children gathered around him watching or helping. I sat at on one of the benches around the fire as Allen exited his hut and came to sit beside me.

We sat in silence for a time, watching Much fry up eggs, mushrooms, and the like. When Much brought us plates of food, I thanked him quietly.

"You're welcome."

Silence continued to reign in the camp for a long while. The chirruping birds and the scrape of our forks against our plates were the only sounds to break the stillness.

As we finished eating, Allen offered to clean up the breakfast mess.

"You don't have to do that," Much said.

"I know. But you have been working to keep us all fed this whole journey, though I know you haven't been entirely present. You are grieving and you deserve a chance to do so properly. You've known Marian as long as Robin and Mark; this has to be hard on you more than some of the rest of us."

"Thank you."

As Allen began to gather the dirtied plates, Much wandered to the edge of camp and then disappeared into the trees. I wondered where he would go—I hoped he was turning to our Savior for comfort and peace, as He was the only true source of either.

It wasn't long before Will emerged from his hut.

"Are you hungry?" I asked as he sank to the ground in front of the fire, forgoing the benches altogether.

"Not really."

"You should still eat something," Allen said. He scooped some of the fried eggs and vegetables onto a plate and set it on the ground in front of Will.

It struck me then that Allen was taking care of everyone— it was not something I would have expected from him. Much was a natural caregiver, and Robin would do so from a sense of responsibility and honor, but I was surprised to see Allen watching out for the rest of the gang.

The children who were awake eventually moved off to one side of the meadow to talk and play quietly, and silence fell at the fireside as Allen took a seat and Will ate. As soon as he was finished, Allen jumped up to clean his dishes and then returned to the fireside.

After a few more moments of silence between the three of us, Will said, "I can't believe she's gone."

"I know." Allen reached down to pick up a stone off the ground, bouncing it from palm to palm. "It doesn't feel right."

"She was so good," Will whispered. "All kindness and compassion."

"And fire and conviction," Allen added. "She was…"

Will nodded in silent agreement to Allen's unfinished sentence.

"She was a good friend," Allen said at last.

"Yes, she was," Will agreed. "She took care of us—Little John and I—before you all came back from the Crusades. She was our leader, the heart and soul of our little band back then…I just can't…I can't fathom life going on without her. It isn't right."

The hurt and pain in his voice brought tears to my eyes. I could hardly speak around the lump in my throat. "I am so sorry that this happened. Marian was a good woman."

"I wish…" Allen started, and then stopped.

"We can't play the 'what if' game, Allen," Will said. "It will lead us nowhere fast."

"It is too cruel," Allen replied. "This isn't fair. I'm the traitor, why wasn't it me? Marian was all goodness!"

As we sat in our grief, Much wandered back into camp and took a seat beside me, his keen eyes watching the tears roll down my cheeks. "Are you alright?"

His question was gentle and almost brought a smile to my face. I could always count on Much to look out for me—for everyone.

"No one is alright anymore," Will said.

"But I will be," I said. "Grief is no small thing, but I know the Lord is in control of this situation. And He knows the pain that we are feeling. He is my great comfort."

Allen shook his head. "I see no reason to turn to him for comfort. If he is all that you say he is, you could have saved her, if he really cared."

"Oh, Allen! He does care," I leaned forward, trying to wrap my mind around the peace I could feel curling around my heart, wondering how to explain to Allen how I could feel God's love in my life, even more so in the darkest of times. "He loved Marian more than you or I—or even Robin—ever could. Much like the story of Lazarus, I do believe Jesus is weeping now."

Allen sighed and said nothing.

Will reached up and took my hand in his own. "I am glad that you can find comfort at this time. I feel no comfort, from any quarter."

"Will, if you'd only turn to Jesus. He'd comfort you; He's so willing and ready to do so."

Will smiled at me in a condescending sort of way and shook his head.

"We will need to put up a brave front for the children," Will said. "They will have a hard enough time with the grief that has settled over the camp, without seeing so many grown men and women crying all the time."

"That's a tall order," Allen said.

I glanced toward the group of children playing not too far away—several of them, William and Beth among them, were casting furtive glances our direction. This was, indeed, going to be hard on them.

"Has anyone told the children?" I asked.

"I told them," Much replied. "When they returned from Marcus' home last night."

"When did they get back?" Allen asked.

"Well everyone disappeared into their huts when we arrived yesterday," Much shrugged. "I met Marcus last night to bring them back here."

No one else seemed inclined to exit their huts that day. Much continued to cook our meals, and he would take platefuls to those of the gang who were remaining in solitude inside their huts. And so things continued the next day.

After a few days, Will made a decision.

"We have to continue our work. Marian made Robin promise to do so and I think it is fair to say that that promise extends to all of us. Robin isn't likely to do anything about it right now, but the Sheriff is still plotting and people are still suffering."

"What do you propose we do?" Allen asked.

Will, Allen, Much, and I were gathered around the fireside together, seemingly the only members of the gang with any desire to socialize or exit our huts in those days.

"We are going to Nottingham to keep an eye on things. Dusty, you can continue to travel and distribute food and money. I'll get Little John out of isolation, and he and Allen will come with me to Nottingham to see what the Sheriff and Gisbourne are up to these days, to try and hear of executions and caravans before they happen. Much…you can look after the children and also do your best to care for Robin and Mark."

In the days that followed, we tried to find some sort of sanity and to return to our lives as they had been before our fateful trip to Austria. Robin would wander the woods aimlessly most days, and Mark never left his hut for any reason. The rest of us got to work, however, and tried to keep the people of Nottingham and the rest of England safe from further harm.

My reach was not far and I traveled alone, but I did the best that I could while the others watched for the Sheriff's next scheme. During that dark period of our lives, Will became our undisputed leader. He took Robin's place reluctantly, but he led us well while our leader was unable to fulfill his duties.

I knew with certainty that burying my grief over Marian's death as I had with my own family was not the healthy choice to make, and so I reached out to those around me and we shared our pain together, walking towards healing in tandem. And yet at the same time, watching Robin's complete breakdown over Marian's death sent me spiraling into a panic over Will—what if I lost him?

484

I had faced that fear before when he was injured, but now I could see the aftermath of losing a loved one and not simply imagine it. Would I be as broken as Robin? Would it be worth it to love and lose in such a way?

One day Allen and I were sitting at Marcus' home in Nottingham waiting for Will to arrive so we could share reports of what we'd heard for news that day. Marcus was out on errands and his wife Lillian was at the market, so it was just the two of us sitting at the kitchen table waiting for Will.

Allen was nervously bouncing his legs and he didn't seem to know what to do with his hands.

"Calm down, Allen. We aren't going to get caught here."

"I'm not worried about that. We never get caught..."

"Then why are you so anxious?"

"I'm...I feel out of place."

"Probably because this isn't our home."

"No, not here at this house. I meant in the gang."

"Ah." I rested my elbows on the table, leaning forward. "I understand. I am sorry, Allen. I truly am. But this is, to some extent, your own fault."

"I know. I betrayed you all. I am sorry. You have no idea how sorry I am. It was pointless, and I never meant it to go so far. I do realize now that there were so many better options to try and save Sir Godfrey that did not involve me betraying you. So please, please forgive me."

"You know you are forgiven."

"Am I? Because no one is treating me like I am a part of this gang. You try, and so does Much, but it isn't the same as it was."

"Did you expect it to be the same after everything that happened? You almost got Little John killed. You broke our trust. You hurt us, Allen. That is going to take time to heal. And now everyone is in pain over Marian, which complicates things…"

"I thought you, out of everyone, would be my advocate."

"I'm not saying that I can't forgive you because I do. I do forgive you. But I was hurt, and that is hard to forget no matter how much I desire to forgive you. You just have to give us time."

"I know…but you have no idea what it is like to be an outcast in the gang. I'm part of you, but I'm not."

"You would not know that feeling either if you had made wiser decisions."

"Do you think I don't know that, Dusty? I was an idiot. And I know I'll never be able to make it up to any of you. But I am sorry…so incredibly sorry."

"Forgiveness is one thing, but trust…trust you are going to have to earn."

"I know…"

Chapter 38

WILL SOON HEARD of a caravan passing through Sherwood and eagerly informed Robin, who showed no interest at all.

"We will be running low on money to hand out to the people of England," Will said. He, along with the rest of us—apart from Mark, who never left his hut—was sitting by the fire while Robin sat in front of his hut a short distance from us.

Will pressed on, though Robin hardly looked at him and definitely didn't get up to join as at the fire. "This is how we replenish our supplies. We need to do this ambush."

Robin shrugged.

"When does the caravan pass through Sherwood?" Much asked.

"Two days from now," Will said.

"Then we have time to truly plan an ambush," Allen said.

"I don't care," Robin said calmly from his position by his hut. From the apathetic look on his face, he certainly seemed to mean it.

"Robin." Will stood up and took a step toward him. "The people of England still need us."

Robin didn't respond.

"Okay." Will crossed his arms. "You don't have to help. But we are going to do this; we're confiscating this treasure and continuing to help the people of England survive Prince John's reign and the Sheriff's cruelty."

As Will, Allen, and Little John began discussing a plan for an ambush, Mark came out of his hut and a hush fell over our group. He didn't say a word, but came to sit at the fireside with us.

We greeted him, but were met with no response. His eyes were red and puffy, his shoulders drooping. His eyes held a vacant look. He didn't speak, but he stayed at Will's side as the planning for the ambush began again, and when we left the camp two days later to execute our plan, Mark came with us.

The raid was a success, and we returned to camp with the treasure horde—Will and Little John took the horses to nearby farmers while Allen and I unloaded the treasure and Much prepared a meal for everyone to replenish their strength. Mark went to his hut without a word.

Robin seemed not to care that we'd carried out the ambush or that we'd brought fresh treasure back to the camp. It was disheartening to see him so depressed.

The days began to pass with a sort of routine and rhythm, despite the dark cloud hanging over the camp. Robin was distracted and disinterested in anything, Mark was holed up in his hut most of the time except when there was a caravan of treasure to ambush. Will took charge and gave out assignments in the mornings to myself, Allen, Little John, and Much.

We also heard tale of innocents being rescued though we had no hand in it, and it soon became clear that our mysterious archer was still in business. Even during our ambushes on caravans along the Sherwood road it became clear the mysterious archer was once again helping us, as they always left their soldiers wounded instead of dead.

With Marian dead, Robin out of the picture, and Mark only half there, Will seemed adamant that bringing new members into the gang seemed imperative. To that end, he insisted we try and make contact with the archer, but we never saw them, whoever they were. We'd see their handiwork, but never them.

One day I started sorting through my medicinal supplies, considering taking a trip to Nottingham to look after the sick there. Spring was in the air, but there were lingering colds and coughs from the winter months—and now with all the rain of spring, it seemed more illness would spread.

"What are you doing?" Will asked, entering the storage hut and sitting on the floor beside me.

"I was considering going to help people, but I seem to be low on supplies."

Will didn't respond. I looked up from my herbs and saw he had leaned his head against the wall and closed his eyes.

"Are you alright?"

"No."

"What is the matter?"

"Marian is dead. Robin is useless. Mark is wasting away and there's nothing I can do about it. I'm not qualified to lead these people. I can't do it. I am too insignificant to save England alone."

"You are not alone." I put my herbs away, moving closer to Will and wrapping my arm around his shoulders. "You have all of us. And I believe you are more than qualified to lead our gang. You have been doing it remarkably well so far."

"I just don't feel up to the task. I don't want to let you all down the way that Robin is now."

"You are not letting anyone down. It is okay to take time to grieve; this is not an easy time for any of us."

Will didn't respond. I caught sight of Much outside near the fire and I stood up, kissing Will's cheek before I moved outside to speak to Much.

"Can I ask a favor of you, Much?"

"Of course. What do you need?"

"I am running low on my healing supplies. Can you search Sherwood for the plants I need?"

"Yes, I can do that."

"Thank you." I told him what I would need, hoping his limited training over the years would serve him well. "You should be able to find them easily enough in the woods. If you can't, come back and I can help you."

"I am glad I can be of service to you…but can I ask why you aren't going yourself?"

"Will is especially depressed today. I cannot leave his side."

"Of course. I will be back soon."

"Thank you, my little mouse. I am very grateful for you."

I returned to the supply hut where Will was still sitting on the floor, his eyes closed as he rested his head against the wall. I sat beside him, laying my head on his shoulder. We sat together in that manner for a lengthy period of time, neither of us speaking. I wasn't sure how comforting it was for him, but I wanted to be near him while he was in such a state of depression.

After a time, we moved from the storage hut to the fire where more of the gang had started to gather and discuss the various happenings of our day. Robin was sitting outside his hut sharpening his sword and ignoring the conversation at the fireside as per usual. His dejected attitude sent a sliver of fear cutting through my heart and I glanced at Will sitting beside me. It was for the best that I had denied his marriage proposal, but perhaps I needed to rein in my heart more than I had been.

A fight seemed to break out among the children who had been playing some yards away from the fire so I hurried over to them to bring peace back to their ranks. A few minutes after leaving the group at the fireside, I noticed Much coming into camp—and he wasn't alone.

When Will and the others saw Much entering camp with a stranger—a woman—they all jumped to their feet, apart from Robin who remained sitting on the ground, barely glancing up.

Mark was still locked in his own hut, as usual, but Will, Little John, and Allen moved over toward Much.

"Much!" Will eyed the newcomer beside him. "Who's this?"

Much beamed at Will. "I've found the mysterious archer!"

491

I did not miss the way Robin's head snapped upwards as he finally gave the woman a curious look.

Much had found the mysterious archer, the person who'd been helping the people of England and our gang for months, since before our fateful trip to Austria…

"Are you really the mysterious archer?" Little John asked as Much led the woman and Will back over toward the fire.

"Yes," the woman said.

I stood, leaving the children who were now gawking at the newcomer, and came to sit beside the woman as the gang—apart from Robin who stayed by his hut and Mark who was nowhere to be seen—all settled down on the logs around the fire.

"Are you planning on joining us?" I asked, knowing Will had been intent on that very thing should we ever find her.

"Well…I hadn't planned on…" the woman was hesitant, and glanced toward Robin with a look I couldn't read.

"But you must!" Allen said.

Much nodded. "You have to. All the people fighting for England have to work together."

"It does seem we can do more good when we all work in tandem," Little John agreed.

The woman looked around the group and then she glanced to the side where Robin leaned against his hut, nonchalantly ignoring the conversation.

"I…I'll pray about it," she finally said.

I grinned at her careful pronouncement. It seemed I had an ally in more ways than one. "Now that is a wonderful idea!"

Robin rose slowly to his feet and Will turned to him. "Robin? What do you say to another gang member?"

Robin studied the woman for a minute and then shrugged. "What we really need is a way to get information."

"You need someone on the inside," the woman said.

Marian had been our informant after the secret ways into the castle were discovered—no thanks to Allen—but now she was dead. We'd let too many caravans slip past simply by not knowing about them ahead of time, and far too many innocents were dying that we could have been able to save if we had only known of their executions prior to them happening.

"Yes," Robin said. "We need someone with the Sheriff and…Gisbourne." Robin nearly choked on the latter name, turning from the group for a moment.

"I don't know that I want to be on the Sheriff's good side…" the woman hesitated, "but I'll see what I can do."

Robin nodded briskly, his mouth twitching into an almost smile. "If you're going to stay, you'll need to know who we are. I'm Robin, this is Much, Will, Dusty, Little John…and Allen. Mark is in his hut…he'll come out eventually, I'm sure."

"I'm Lucy. I've…well, to be honest, I've seen all of you in Nottingham before, and recently I've been stalking your ambushes, so I know who you are."

"We've noticed your presence in our raids," Will said.

"You've definitely saved a few of us more than once. The more raids we have, the more soldiers the Sheriff and other lords send with their caravans, the more trouble we have successfully ambushing without falling to harm." Will absentmindedly rubbed his chest where his own wound had once been, and I reached over to take his hand.

"We do appreciate what you've been doing," Little John said. "And it will be good to have eyes and ears in Nottingham again."

"I guess we'll have to build you your own hut as soon as we can," Will said.

"And you should meet the children. Come over here..." I stood, leading Lucy away from the group by the fire ring to introduce her to the children and Robin returned to his mindless stringing of his bow, paying no more attention to what was happening in the camp.

The children gathered around us with bright smiles as I introduced Lucy.

Rachel immediately threw her arms around Lucy's legs, as that was about as high as she could reach. "You're nice, aren't you? I like you."

"I believe you've been accepted," I said.

Lucy grinned at me. "I'm glad."

That night I made room for Lucy in my hut since we hadn't built her one for herself yet. Beth wanted to chat with the newcomer and seemed full of curiosity, but eventually she fell asleep and I was able to bring up the one thing I'd been wondering since Lucy had entered the camp.

Beth slept in the bed, so Lucy and I were sitting on the make-shift pile of blankets that I called my own bed. I leaned against the wall and studied her face in the dim light of the one candle I had lit.

"Given your comment about prayer earlier...do you know Christ personally?"

"Yes, I do."

"I am so glad! I have been in need of a support here in the gang. Much is also a believer, but he is too gentle and quiet to back me up when arguments around faith arise, or when I talk about the Lord. It is encouraging to know I will not be alone."

"You know you are never alone, not when you have the Lord constantly by your side."

I felt a rush of affection for Lucy in that moment. It was a simple statement, but one even Much had rarely said to me. He was young and new in his faith and full of questions. To have someone as deeply rooted in the truth of Christ as myself for a friend...

I grinned at Lucy. "That is very true. Yet sometimes I do long for a like-minded companion to talk to."

"I am perfectly willing to talk to you whenever you like."

"Where are you from?"

"London," Lucy replied, laying down on the pile of blankets I used as a mattress. Lucy stared up at the wooden ceiling of the hut in the relative darkness.

"What brought you so far from there?"

"I've been traveling all over England since my father…" Lucy hesitated, closing her eyes for a moment. "My parents died, and afterwards I felt no need to stay in London. So I traveled, helping people where I could. I rarely stayed in one place for more than a few days until I came to Nottingham. I had heard reports of Robin Hood and his gang, and I was intrigued…and I stayed."

"I am sorry you lost your parents. I lost my own many years ago, and I also ran from the grief."

Lucy nodded. "At any rate, I thought I could help here, so I didn't move on…what about you, Dusty? You aren't from England, are you?"

"No, I hail from the city of Darum in Palestine."

"What brought you to England?"

"Robin. I met him during the Crusades. My family was dead, but Robin, Allen, and Much became my second family, and for them I came to England."

"I am sorry for your loss."

"I am equally sorry for yours. Losing loved ones is never easy." I briefly thought about sharing my deep fear of that very thing and how I questioned loving Will because of it, but I had only just met Lucy and had already shared more than I normally would have with a stranger. Something about her drew me to her —I felt a kinship with her, as a woman, as a Christ-follower, and as an orphan who'd run away from pain and grief. But even so, I held my tongue.

Will took Lucy to Nottingham the very next day to introduce her to Marcus and his wife to make a plan for Lucy to live with them for a while to try and catch the notice of the Sheriff as a visiting noble woman. When they returned to the camp Will gathered the gang together—with the exception of Mark who was brooding in his hut. For once, Robin did join the rest of us gathered at the fire.

"The next step will be spreading the word that you're here," Will said to Lucy. "We want everyone, especially the Sheriff, to know."

"We have to find a way for him to take notice of you," I said.

"I know I'll have to earn his trust so I can get into the castle and start feeding you information," Lucy said.

"I don't think it will be a hard task," Will said. "He'll be desirous to have you stay in the castle once he knows you are a nobleman's daughter. He is rather fond of his reputation. He won't risk snubbing a member of court."

"That's the hope anyway," Lucy agreed.

"It might be best if you didn't let on to the Sheriff that your father is dead," Robin said. "Especially the part where he was killed by Prince John."

"I won't lie, Robin."

"If the Sheriff knows your father was loyal to King Richard and killed because of it then he won't trust you. He'll probably kill you."

"We'll simply omit any information about your parents at all," Will said. "You don't have to lie. As long as he doesn't ask about details, it doesn't matter."

Lucy moved in with Marcus and Lillian soon after that. She spent several days visiting various tailors and embroiderers and jewelers in Nottingham, using both money from our storage and the credit of her reputation as a noblewoman so she could look and act the part and get the Sheriff's attention. Will was right; Lucy hadn't lived with Marcus and Lillian long before the Sheriff heard of her and invited her to stay in the castle.

Some time later, Lucy visited the camp one evening while Robin and I were the only two present—him because he'd done nothing useful all day, and me because I had kept an eye on the children while Will sent everyone else out on various duties for the day. Lucy dismounted and hurried over to the fireside where Robin and I were sitting to tell us she'd heard of a caravan of treasure coming through Sherwood.

"We'll plan an ambush." I said.

"Will we?" Robin asked. He leaned forward heavily, his shoulders curling in as he placed his head in his hands and sat in utter dejection.

I scooted over to sit beside him. "The people will need the money, Robin."

"You'll have to be careful," Lucy said. "Sir Guy is coming to guard the caravan specifically against an ambush."

Robin's head snapped up, his eyes flashing with fire. "We'll definitely plan an ambush!"

"Vengeance is the Lord's," I said softly, watching as his anger transformed his usual dejected manner.

"Hatred won't do you any good," Lucy said after a moment of silence. "It would make you no better than your enemies."

Robin turned his fiery glare toward Lucy. "Don't tell me what to do!"

"I only meant—"

"I don't care. I don't know you, and you know *nothing* about me."

Lucy was quiet for a moment and then she said, "Be careful, both of you. I'll pray for the safety of your endeavor."

She left camp soon after that.

Robin sighed as Lucy disappeared at the edge of camp. "She's just like you, Dusty." There was a mixture of amusement and displeasure in his voice.

498

It was not long before the rest of the gang began to return to camp after their busy days, and Robin and I relayed Lucy's news. The planning for an ambush began immediately.

As we dispersed for the night, Will fell into step beside me as I moved toward my hut.

"It is good to see Robin with us again," he said softly.

"He is only interested in killing Gisbourne."

"I know, but it feels right to have him leading us. This is how the gang is meant to function, with Robin at the helm."

"I personally find you to be a much better leader these days, leading from your compassion and not your hatred."

Our raid was successful in the sense that we confiscated all of the treasure, but Sir Guy of Gisbourne evaded Robin's wrath. At the time it seemed insignificant, but later I began to believe that the Lord was protecting him for His own purposes.

Chapter 39

ONE EVENING some weeks later, Lucy rode into camp just as Much was preparing supper and Will was practicing archery with young William. Lucy dismounted—she often rode horses from the Sheriff's stable when she came to visit us—and moved toward Will and young William immediately.

"Mercy, child, that is not a good way to hold your bow. Let me help you." Lucy gently took young William's hands in hers and started adjusting his position.

"Hey!" Will crossed his arms as he watched her, though a smile was playing about his mouth and I knew he wasn't truly upset. "That's my pupil."

Lucy raised an eyebrow in his direction. "No wonder he's holding his bow so ill."

"I'm rather good with a bow, thank you very much."

Lucy laughed. "Until you can beat the great Robin Hood himself, I won't be impressed."

"No one can beat Robin," Much called from the fireside where he was cooking. Little John, and I were sitting on the benches around the fire, watching the exchange.

"Exactly." Lucy said, laughing again.

Will laughed too, and I tried not to let the sound send flutters through my heart.

"Alright, fine," Will said. "You can assist me in teaching William."

"I would have helped with or without your blessing."

"I know…that's why I gave consent. Saving face and all that."

In the days that followed, Lucy and Will would teach young William together whenever Lucy visited the camp. Young William's skills with the bow did, indeed, improve.

Will and Lucy's friendship blossomed as well. They were very alike in manner, both of them kind, generous people with wisdom and an enthusiasm for life, as well as sharing a similar sense of humor.

One day late in spring, when the flowers were in full bloom in the forest, and all the trees had put forth their fresh green buds, Will accompanied me on one of my trips through the forest to look for fresh plants, roots, and herbs for medicinal purposes.

We walked in comfortable silence for a time, and then I asked, "What do you think of Lucy?"

"What am I supposed to think of her?" Will asked, laughing. "I like her. I think she has been good for all of us; she's brought a spark back to our group and set our dying fire aflame once more. Even Robin is once more trying to save England. She came into our lives precisely when we needed her."

"The Lord does know what He is doing."

"You certainly believe so. The only person Lucy hasn't revived is Mark…"

"What are we going to do about him? He still hasn't spoken to anyone since Marian died. I'm worried about him."

Mark continued to keep to himself while in the camp, and only participated in raids and rescues before isolating himself again. I was not aware of him having held a single conversation with anyone since Marian's death. He wasn't grieving in a healthy manner, that much was certain.

"Just continue to pray for him, Dusty," Will said. I shot him a glance, surprised he would point me back to Christ.

"I am. Believe me, I am. Are you?"

"I don't have that sort of relationship with your God."

"But you could, Will. He's ready for you."

"So you always say." Will didn't say anything further and I didn't press him. I couldn't force him to accept Jesus as his Savior. Part of me wished that I could, but it wasn't meant to work that way.

"I'm worried for Lucy," Will said suddenly.

"Why?"

"We've talked a few times about Gisbourne...she seems very concerned and interested in him."

"I believe she is trying to show him Christ's love."

"Yes, well, I am fearing for *her* love right now. I don't want her to fall in love with that man."

"They hardly know each other, and I can't imagine anyone sane falling in love with a murderer. From what I've heard from Lucy, Gisbourne is distraught over Marian's death."

502

"He should be upset. He murdered her."

"I know," I sighed.

After a few moments of silence, Will said softly, "I miss her."

"So do I."

"She was a good friend to me."

"I am sorry." I slipped my hand in his. He squeezed my fingers and tried to smile.

"Thank you."

"I did not know her as well as you did, perhaps, but I do miss her."

"I know. We all loved her," Will said. "I can hardly blame Mark for not wanting to talk to people. The grief is so great that I don't want to talk to people half the time. I can't imagine what he must feel, as she was his own sister."

"I am afraid he blames himself for her death."

"I would, too, were I in his place."

"I wish there was something we could do to help him."

Will glanced at me and gave me a wry smile. "Keep praying?"

"Well, yes. But do *you* believe so much in my prayers?"

"I know that you believe God hears and answers you, and I know that you are rarely wrong on most matters. So…yes, I suppose I do believe in your prayers."

It was a small step toward faith, but I would take it for what it was.

A few days later, Lucy came to the camp while Much and I were alone at the fireside while the children were scattered around the meadow playing.

"Where's Robin?" Lucy asked as she dismounted and hurried over toward us.

"Everyone is busy," I replied. "Little John and Will are on a trip to the west, distributing our wealth beyond the sphere of Nottingham. Robin heard there was a particularly blood-thirsty sheriff a few shires over and went to investigate, and see if there was anything to be done about it. Mark tagged along, I believe."

"What's wrong?" Much asked.

"The Sheriff, as always," Lucy replied. She told about the Sheriff's desire to kill a man in Nottingham for little more reason than that he was annoyed with him. After relaying her news, she changed the subject, suggesting we pray for Gisbourne.

"Pray for Gisbourne?" I asked.

"God loves him too, Dusty."

I stared into Lucy's earnest eyes for a moment, suddenly ashamed that I hadn't been praying for Gisbourne at all. The radical forgiveness that I received from Christ also applied to Gisbourne, whether I liked him or not. I sighed. "I suppose He does."

"He's horrible," young William piped up. "And so angry all the time."

Lucy nodded. "Precisely why he needs prayer."

Lucy didn't extend the conversation, instead suggesting she could practice archery with those of the children who had been learning, and William and Beth eagerly agreed. So Lucy moved to one side of the open meadow to help them shoot, while the smaller children stayed closer to Much and I.

504

Little John and Will eventually returned to the camp, and Lucy filled them in on what the Sheriff was planning.

Later, once Lucy had returned to Nottingham and Much and I were alone by the fire once more, he surprised me by asking, "Are you going to do what she asked?"

"What?"

"Pray for Gisbourne."

I looked up at the blue sky for a moment, wrestling with my emotions. He'd killed Marian, which filled me with anger and sadness. And in general he had always been a rather cruel man, which did not fill my heart with any pleasant feelings. But Lucy was right—God did love him, and he clearly needed his Savior.

I marveled that Lucy could so easily forgive him, but perhaps it had something to do with the fact that she had not known Marian personally and so could look past his offenses easier.

I met Much's gaze. "She's right; God does love him, too. So yes, I believe I will."

"Have you forgiven him?"

"No."

"Neither have I."

"I am trying," I admitted.

"So am I."

"Well it seems we are in the same predicament then. Perhaps we should take the time to pray together about all the aspects of this disastrous situation."

A few days later, I found myself in Nottingham Square with Will, watching a small crowd gather for the execution that Lucy had informed us of. The rest of the gang—including Mark, who was willing to fight, if nothing else—were stationed around

505

the Square. Will and I had the responsibility of getting the victim to safety while Little John caused chaos among the soldiers in the Square and the rest of the gang used their archery skills to shoot down the Sheriff's men.

The Sheriff strode up onto the wooden platform that had been erected in the center of the market place, two soldiers following him with a bound man between them.

"My people!" the Sheriff called out, spreading his arms wide open as the crowd quieted. "Welcome! This man here—" he pointed to the prisoner, "withheld his money from me—er, the king. Dear King Richard. We must punish him for disobeying the law of the land and not paying his taxes in full! With the king away, harsh action must be taken to keep the people in order!"

The Sheriff smiled out at the crowd in a most sickening way. "Enjoy!"

A shoe sailed through the air toward the Sheriff and he ducked out of the way, before motioning for soldiers to go through the crowd to find the culprit. In that moment of chaos, arrows began to fly from those of the gang stationed in buildings around the Square and soldiers dropped to the ground, dead.

"That's our cue," Will said, leading the way into the throng of people gathered around the platform where the Sheriff and the bound man still stood.

Arrows continued to fly past as we ducked and dodged around the residents of Nottingham and the soldiers in their midst.

When we made it to the platform, Will leaped up and unsheathed his sword, engaging the two soldiers there while I ran up to untie the prisoner. The Sheriff backed away from Will as both soldiers fell to the ground, dead.

A moment later, I had the prisoner untied and I jumped with him off the platform and into the chaotic crowd. Will followed.

"This way," I told the man, throwing a cloak over his back and pulling the hood over his eyes. I led the way through the mass of people while Will distracted the few soldiers who rushed toward us.

I sent a quick prayer heavenward for the safety of Will as I led the man we'd rescued through the streets of Nottingham in a winding way and eventually took him to Marcus' home once I was sure we were not being followed.

Marcus was at the door to greet us, pulling the man inside quickly. "I'm Marcus. You are going to be staying with me for a few days."

"Thank you," the man said, pulling down the hood I'd put over his head. "Thank you so much. I'm Henry, by the way."

"One of two things is going to happen next," I said. "The Sheriff will either get tired of looking for you in the next few weeks and move on to his next victim, in which case you could likely go home. Or he will put a warrant and reward out for your arrest, and make up his mind to kill you if you are ever found. If that is the case, Marcus will make it possible for you to leave Nottingham. We have contacts from here to Scotland if you need to take refuge far from the city. If King Richard ever returns, you will likely be free to come home then."

"For now though," Marcus added. "You'll just live here with me and my wife. The Sheriff has never yet caught one of the prisoners that we have harbored. You will be safe here."

"Thank you," Henry said. "I can never thank you all enough. And lass," he latched onto my arm. "Thank Robin Hood for me."

"I will." I did feel thanking Will would be more appropriate since Robin had little to do with planning any of the rescues or raids these days, but I didn't say as much. "I must go now. God bless and keep you."

"Thank you, thank you." Henry let go of me and I bid Marcus farewell before sneaking out of Nottingham and back to the camp. I overtook Allen on the way there.

"Have you seen anyone else yet?" I asked.

"No, but they may be at camp already."

"I hope so."

When we arrived, everyone did seem to be there, gathered around the fireside. I counted heads quickly, feeling relief wash over me as I caught sight of Will.

"I delivered Henry into Marcus' care," I said as Allen and I joined the group around the fire—everyone, including Lucy, was there. "He said to thank all of you, and especially Robin."

Robin nodded.

I understood perfectly well why he wasn't the carefree man I'd known for so long, but I missed his old self—the smiles and laughter, the arrogance and confidence. All of it. I longed for Robin to heal and be more himself once more.

Spring slowly gave way to summer as Lucy brought news of more hangings to stop and caravans to ambush. The dark cloud hanging over the gang slowly lifted—Mark did not come out of his shell, but Robin started to revive. Anger still seemed to be his main motivation for living, but at least he wasn't disinterested in life anymore.

508

Not many days later, we were hurrying through the forest and then across the hills toward Nottingham. The Sheriff was intent on hanging another innocent victim. Robin, surprisingly, had taken charge of the planning and now as we hurried toward the city, Robin split us into pairs, sending Will and I in first.

We fell into step beside a group of farmers entering the city gates, and slipped past the guards without issue. Once we pushed through the streets and came to Nottingham Square, I was surprised to see how full the market was.

"They don't approve, surely," I commented as Will and I pressed through the crowds to the bakery where we were meant to meet up with the others.

"I doubt it."

Over the heads of the gathered people pressing around us, I could see the gallows that had been constructed for the execution. It wasn't long before the rest of the gang began to trickle into the Square, coming to the bakery where Will and I had gone inside and were now watching from the window.

"That's almost everyone," Little John commented.

"No sign of Robin yet," Will said.

When Robin and Allen slipped into the bakery, Robin immediately started issuing orders again.

"Will, Much, Allen, and I will take up positions in buildings on every side of the Square and use our archery skills to cut down soldiers and keep the prisoner alive when he or she is brought out. Little John, you're on snatch and run duty. Marcus is already ready with horses for the escape, Allen and I stopped there on our way here. We all know this Square and have done this sort of thing a hundred times. You can find the best position; you don't need me to hold your hand. Dusty, keep an eye on the crowd. If the soldiers start harming innocents, I expect you to find and heal them. Mark, you can either work with Little John or be an archer. Any preference."

Mark lifted his bow but said nothing.

Robin nodded. "Very well. You'll be with me. Let's go."

Everyone dispersed, moving back out into the Square and pushing through it to find their places. Robin, Will, Much, and Allen would find places inside different buildings we had used before—many of the inhabitants of Nottingham willingly gave us their aid for such times as these—while I crept through the crowd closer to the gallows so I could keep an eye on the people who would be nearest the soldiers and most likely to get hurt.

Soon the crowd grew more restless as a group of soldiers dragged a woman toward the gallows. People around me were starting to cry, and shout out against the Sheriff and his injustice. Even with the unrest, the people parted and provided a path for the soldiers to drag the woman forward.

Suddenly one soldier fell with an arrow in his chest. Robin's signal.

In another instant, arrows were flying from all sides of the Square as the rest of the gang followed their orders. Soldiers went running to find the source of the arrows, and I caught sight of Little John pushing aside soldiers and residents of Nottingham alike as he barreled through the crowd to grab the woman and carry her out of the Square.

A cheer went up from the crowd, and they began to form a human wall behind him so that the soldiers attempting to follow him could not get through. The soldiers did not hesitate to draw their swords and start hacking down the people, and I rushed forward, keeping out of the way of the soldiers as I moved from one injured person to the next, using my trusty pouch of herbs to mix healing concoctions as I prayed over the wounded and stitched up their injuries.

The chaos in the Square died down as the soldiers took off down the side streets to find Little John and the escaped woman, and I knew the rest of the gang would be hurrying back to camp.

I stayed in the Square, moving from one injured person to another. The friends and family of those who had been struck down gathered around as well, taking those I had healed back to their homes and weeping over those who had died.

Chapter 40

NOT MANY DAYS LATER, Lucy came riding into camp one evening and dismounted before her horse had even come to a stop.

"Lucy!" I moved to greet her. "Any news from Nottingham?"

"Who is the Sheriff hanging now?" Allen asked from where he lounged against one of the log benches by the fire pit.

"The Sheriff isn't hanging anyone." She spoke softly, glancing toward where Robin sat by his hut.

"Is there anything of interest happening in Nottingham?" Will asked from his place on one of the benches by the fire as Lucy and I approached.

"Well…" Again, Lucy shot a glance toward Robin, this time glancing toward Mark who sat by the fire across from Allen as well. "Sir Guy confronted me today, about helping the outlaws. He suspects I am an informant."

"Oh no!" A sharp stab of fear sliced my heart—if Gisbourne knew she was helping us, would he harm her as he had killed Marian? Or would he help her, the way he'd helped Marian save the children that now lived in the camp with us?

"What happened?" Will asked, leaning forward with interest.

"Nothing happened," Lucy said. "I told him he was right."

"You did what?!" Robin snapped, jumping up to move closer to the conversation.

"It's alright," Lucy said, throwing up her hands in a placating manner. "He didn't tell the Sheriff. He didn't do anything at all."

"You've blown your cover! Now who is going to be our informant?"

"I am," Lucy said firmly, giving Robin a sharp look. "Nothing has changed. Guy won't betray me."

"Guy?" Robin's eyebrows shot to his hairline as his voice turned ice cold. "Since when are you so familiar?"

Lucy crossed her arms. "For your information, Sir Guy of Gisbourne and I have been sort of friends for nearly two months."

Robin rolled his eyes. "Oh, splendid. Now our informant hasn't only blown her cover she's also fraternizing with the enemy."

"I live with them, Robin! How can I not?"

"She has a point," Will said.

"I need to get back to Nottingham," Lucy said, standing up. "I only came to let you know what had happened. I am quite thrilled that Guy…Sir Guy…Gisbourne, that is, didn't turn me in."

"Go on then," Robin said. "Run back to Nottingham."

He was sarcastic and angry, that much was clear, but as Lucy walked to the edge of the meadow and mounted her horse, Robin followed her, catching her reins and speaking softly to her.

When he returned to the fireside, he immediately had orders to give. "Will, you are keeping an eye on Nottingham tonight. We'll take turns watching out for any news of Lucy being arrested until we're entirely sure this has blown over."

In the days that followed, we all took turns spending the night in Nottingham and waiting for news of Lucy—good or bad. But she wandered the streets of Nottingham as she always had, passing out food from the castle and visiting the sick in the city. It seemed that Sir Guy of Gisbourne was keeping her secret after all.

I didn't know what to make of that. Was it his seemingly good side creeping forward once more, as it had whenever he'd helped Marian with various things, like saving the children? Perhaps it was mere happenstance, a whim. But if it was the former, did that mean that Gisbourne was falling in love with Lucy the way he had with Marian?

It had always been his love for Marian that drove him to be good in the past—although he'd killed her in the end, so how deep could that love have run?

Summer stretched on, the days growing warmer once more. It never grew quite as hot as my homeland, but summer was my favorite time of year.

A week later, Lucy visited the camp late one evening and joined the circle at the fire ring with an announcement. "I'm going to test Guy, I think," she said as she seated herself between Robin and Much.

"Don't," Will said. "Please, don't do anything foolish. He's unpredictable and dangerous."

"I'm not afraid of Guy. I trust him."

Robin snorted. "You are foolish if you trust Gisbourne."

Lucy shrugged her shoulders. "Then I'm foolish. Regardless, I'm going to ask him to let the children go."

"What?" Much glanced from Lucy to the children playing across the meadow.

"I'm going to ask him to speak to the Sheriff to see if we can get the children pardoned so they can go home to their families."

"That will never work," Robin said.

"Besides, what would camp life be like without them?" Will said. "I'd miss them."

"They belong with their parents, Will," Lucy said. "They need to go home."

She was right of course; they did deserve to be with their families, but they hadn't been separated from them from a lack of any desire to keep them together. They'd been separated so that they wouldn't be killed.

"Gisbourne won't help you," Robin said, crossing his arms.

"He might," Allen piped up from across the fire. "I think he is capable of great kindness."

"Says the man who betrayed my trust," Robin said. "I should have expected you to defend my enemy."

Allen's face flushed and he lowered his head as Robin continued, "Great kindness from the man who murdered my wife? What nonsense."

Lucy sighed. "I need to go. I'm causing more rifts in this camp than anything else I think."

"It's hardly your fault, Lucy," Will said quietly as Lucy rose from the circle and left.

515

"Do you think it will work?" Little John asked no one in particular as Lucy disappeared from into the treeline.

"Of course it won't," Robin replied, sighing as he shoved his hand through his hair.

"But these are the children that Sir Guy saved in the first place," Allen said. "Why wouldn't he save them again?"

"He is evil," Robin said. "I think Marian's death has made that perfectly clear."

Mark hastily stood and left the circle to go to his hut. Robin watched him go and sighed heavily.

I leaned forward, watching Robin's face. "From what Lucy has said, Gisbourne is changing for the better."

"Marian always brought goodness out of him, too," Robin replied, his eyes flashing. "And that led nowhere. Lucy is going to get herself killed!"

It was clear to me that Robin's anger with Lucy had less to do with her desire to use Gisbourne as a tool to free the children, and more to do with his fear of losing another person he cared about. I could understand that fear completely—it was a large part of why I still pulled away from Will.

A few days later, Lucy came to the camp with the news that the Sheriff was pardoning the children after all. She delivered the news and then enlisted my help to gather the children and pack up their meager belongings collected over the time they'd lived in the camp with us.

"How in the world did you convince the Sheriff to leave them be?" Will asked.

"I didn't," Lucy said. "Sir Guy did."

Robin threw a stick into the fire, glaring at Lucy.

"There is good in him," Allen said. "I saw it brought out by Marian."

"And that good she brought out is, I suppose, the reason he killed her!" Robin stood and stomped away from the circle around the fire, leaving a pained silence behind him.

Eventually, Little John spoke, "She was something else."

There were murmurs of agreement around the fire as our thoughts turned to Marian.

"I don't blame Robin," Will said, glancing toward me and sending flutters through my heart as he so often did. "I'd hate anyone who killed my love."

"But hatred will eat you up inside," Much said.

"There's also the Scriptures to take into consideration," Lucy said quietly, "They tell us to love, to forgive. To do good to those who spitefully use us."

I nodded mutely. It wasn't easy to love or forgive Sir Guy of Gisbourne, but by the grace of God Lucy could do it and I was trying my hardest.

"Will Robin ever be happy?" Allen asked.

"Give him time," I said. "The grief is still too near."

"I hate to see him unhappy," Much said. "But Marian…I don't think any of us will move past our grief in a short time."

Will nodded. "True. But it would be nice to have our playful Robin back, rather than this brooding fellow who has taken his place."

"At least he speaks," Allen said.

I sighed, looking over toward Mark's hut. "I do not know what we are going to do with Mark."

"Pray for him, Dusty," Lucy said. "That's what we can do for Mark."

"Something practical might be useful too," Little John rolled his eyes.

There were a few tearful farewells once the children were ready to leave. Little Rachel threw herself at Will crying that she would miss him.

"I will miss you, too," Will said as he scooped her up into his arms. "I will miss all of you, but it will be good for you to be home with your parents."

"I do miss my parents," young William said. "But I want to stay and help! I could be a part of the gang."

"You are far too young for that," Will said.

Before too long Lucy, Will, and I were walking the children back to Nottingham and to their families.

Will suggested the gang take turns keeping guard near the homes of the children's families for a few weeks to be certain the Sheriff would leave them alone, and so we did just that. Yet in the days and weeks that followed, the Sheriff never so much as looked at their homes and it was clear that he no longer cared to punish them for their fathers' crimes from a year before.

One day late in the summer, I went for a walk to once more replenish my medicinal supplies from the plants I could find in the forest—I used many during rescues in the city when I healed the people the soldiers would injure, and both Lucy and I used my store of supplies when visiting the sick in Nottingham and the surrounding villages.

Will chose to walk with me, as he so often did, and son enough we fell into conversation.

"I find it truly remarkable that Lucy was able to not only convince Gisbourne to help the children, but also convince the Sheriff to pardon them," Will commented.

"The level of her influence is impressive," I agreed.

"Do you think Gisbourne is capable of changing—truly changing—or is this more of what we saw with Marian?"

"I don't know. He has done terrible things, not the least of which was murdering Marian."

I caught sight of a plant I could use and knelt, pulling out a small knife and digging the roots free before putting the plant in the satchel I'd slung over my shoulder to carry what I collected.

"My God is a God of forgiveness, and He may yet have His own plans for Sir Guy."

Will's deep blue eyes were searching my face as I stood back up, eagerly taking in all I was saying. I hoped he would truly take it to heart.

"So in the end, yes. I do believe it is possible for Sir Guy of Gisbourne to truly change his ways by the grace of Christ. It will take the Lord's help, but with Lucy being a constant witness to him I am almost convinced that one day soon I might be able to call him my brother in Christ, as strange as that sounds given all he has done."

Will was quiet for a moment as we continued our walk, and then he said, "I love listening to you talk about your faith."

"Do you?"

"You're so passionate, and you believe so strongly in what you say. It is delightful to listen to you, even if I do not understand or agree with you."

"Will—"

"No. Don't. I'm not ready to hear you tell me that I can have that same faith. I just…I'm not ready for that. I can appreciate that it means the world to you, and I can see that it helps you through dark times. And if it will make Gisbourne a better man, so be it. But I am not so easily ready to forgive him for killing Marian, or to accept him as an ally. If that is what your God requires of me, I am not so sure I can follow him."

I wondered if there was more to Will's reluctance than simply accepting that God forgave Gisbourne. Perhaps he didn't want to consider that he had done wrong in his own life and didn't want to amit to his own faults.

It was simple and easy to paint the world in black and white. Sir Guy of Gisbourne was black, a murderer, the darkest of all. Will felt he was a good man, and so saw himself in the white category without acknowledging or addressing the sin that he did carry in his own heart.

But if he wasn't ready to be told differently, I could hardly force him to face the truth.

Chapter 41

A WEEK OR SO LATER, Lucy came to the camp to report that the Sheriff was going to hang a man in the village of Abingdon. She seemed far too cheerful as she relayed her news. Robin, Will, and Little John immediately began planning to rescue the man set to be executed while Lucy drew Allen and I aside.

"Something truly wonderful has happened," she said as she led us a short distance across the meadow. It seemed we were about to find out what exactly had her in such a good mood.

"What is it?" Allen asked.

"Guy told me," Lucy said, her eyes sparkling. "I didn't know about the hanging, but Guy came and told me directly. He knows I'm an informant for Robin Hood's gang, and he told me anyway, knowing what I would do with the information. He's helping us."

"Did he truly do that?" Allen asked.

Lucy nodded, grinning.

"That is crazy!" Allen said. "Good though. I knew he had it in him."

"I can scarcely believe it," I said. "But Allen is right, it is good. Now we have two people on the inside acting as informants. And with Gisbourne being the Sheriff's right hand, we should never miss an execution."

"I'm afraid Robin won't like it," Lucy said, glancing back toward the group gathered around the fire pit. "That's why I didn't tell him. And it would only upset Mark as well."

"I won't tell them," Allen said.

"I will probably tell Will," I said.

Lucy nodded. "I don't want to keep secrets, I just don't want to upset anyone. My friendship with Guy tends to lead to arguments and frustration here in the camp."

She wasn't wrong, though I couldn't blame my friends for hating the man who had murdered Marian.

One morning when Lucy visited the camp, she and Will fell into a discussion of archery—the way young William had improved under her direction despite almost a year of training with Will seemed to pique his interest. They moved off to one side of the meadow to shoot at the trees as Lucy showed Will what she did differently than he.

As I sat listening to their conversation and watching the teasing laughter pass between them, I wondered what could be so terrible about opening up to Will completely. I wanted the ease of his friendship that Lucy had, and I wanted more than that. I could have had more than that—he wanted to marry me.

Or he had.

Watching his eyes dance at something Lucy said sent a sliver of ice through my heart. Will was slowly coming closer to faith in Christ, I was sure of that. But would it be too late for me even if he did come to accept the Savior?

As the days passed, Robin seemed to become increasingly more himself, while Mark curled further into his shell of darkness. I couldn't blame him; he'd lost his sister and he felt responsible for it. I had yet to speak Habibah's name aloud, so I had no room to judge how he grieved his pain.

One day I sat by the empty fire pit—not lit, as it was still summer and the air was warm—with my medicinal supplies spread out before me, mixing my concoctions and replenishing my pouch, my mind lost in thoughts of my family, my grief, and Mark's as well.

Through the grace of God and with the help of Much and Robin I had slowly let go of my pain, and then Will had stepped into my life and helped me open my deepest self even further—though I still held back from him.

I glanced toward Much's kitchen. The door was open, and I could see him working in there. Cooking seemed to be his outlet when he needed something comforting to occupy his mind. Looking down at the herbs scattered around me, I realized my healing work was mine.

It was strange, because on the surface I felt at ease with my family and would be open with them, but if the conversation moved to anything too deep within me, such as my lost family or my fear of love, I would close off instantly. Perhaps I was not nearly as healthy as I wanted to believe.

Much wiped his hand on a towel and came outside to sit across from me. "What is that serious look on your face?"

"I was considering Mark, and his seeming inability to heal from Marian's death."

"It's only been five months."

"I know…I was also thinking about myself. How I hid from my own grief for years, until meeting you. When we went to Darum with the army…that was the first time I truly let myself remember, and grieve…"

Much nodded. "I do recall that. I think we all deal with our grief in different ways, and that's allowed. Mark isn't okay, but he doesn't have to be."

I started packing up my herbs, placing them in the pouches and bottles that housed them in the storage hut when I wasn't using them. Much watched quietly, his eyes so full of empathy and wisdom. He always seemed to see right through everyone.

"It isn't a bad thing if you're still not okay, either," Much said softly when I met his gaze. "Grief isn't something that simply goes away over time."

I sighed, quickly finishing packing my things before I turned back to him. "I know."

Much scooted across the benches to come sit beside me. "Marian's death was horrible for all of us because, well, we loved her. But I could see how it might also bring up old hurts, too."

I nodded. "I'm not thinking about my own family that much—I mean, I do some. But that's not what has me so confused lately."

"Then what is it?"

I looked up into Much's eyes, seeing the care and concern there and relishing the fact that I had a brother I could talk to. I should have talked to him sooner—he always put me at ease. I leaned over, laying my head on his shoulder.

"I'm afraid I love Will."

Much chuckled, his shoulder shaking beneath my cheek. "That was rather obvious."

"But I can't..."

"You can't what?"

"He knows more about me than anyone—even you or Robin. I don't understand it, but I open up to him in ways I never have before..."

"Is that such a bad thing?"

"It's terrifying!" I sat up, shaking my head. "Much..."

Much watched me quietly, not saying a word, not pressing for whatever was upsetting me. Just waiting, patient and gentle. I sighed, relaxing a bit.

"I have been healing from the pain of losing my family, that much is true. Yet somewhere underneath it all, I think I've held onto the fear that if I love again, I'll lose again."

"You let yourself care for Robin, Allen, and I."

"I know, but...I kept walls up. I didn't share everything with you, not my deepest, darkest self. Not my most vulnerable pieces."

Much nodded, reaching over to take my hand and squeeze it gently.

"I want to open up fully, and I started to with Will—but then I think I panicked..."

"So what are you going to do?" Much's eyes bored into mine, intense but still gentle. "Give in to the fear, or trust that God has a plan and will look after you even if you share your most vulnerable self with someone."

"When did you get so wise?"

Much shook his head, a blush forming on his cheeks. "I'm not the wise one; you are. I'm just reminding of you of things you would say to someone else."

"I don't want to choose fear..."

"Then don't."

He was right; he nearly always was. I wasn't sure I was ready to do what he suggested though. In the days that followed, I prayed constantly over my fear of losing Will—and the rest of the gang, my family—and I prayed for Will's salvation, hoping I wasn't praying such a prayer for selfish reasons.

One day when I returned home from a day of distributing food and money to the needy, Much set about cooking us up a delightful supper. As we gathered around the fire, Will and Allen arrived with news.

"There's a caravan going through Sherwood tomorrow," Will said.

"And Lucy wasn't the one to give us that information," Allen added.

Robin frowned, accepting a plate of Much's meat pie and tilting his head toward Allen. "Where did you get the information?"

"From Sir Guy," Allen said. "I met him in Nottingham Square."

"Why?" I asked. "Why didn't he simply tell Lucy and have her inform us as he did before?"

"Perhaps he is simply trying to get close to the gang," Little John said. "Get our guards down so he can kill us, too."

"Lucy knew of the caravan," Will said. "She is the one who came to us and sent Allen to Sir Guy."

"Why?" Robin's frown deepened.

"Because she made a promise to the Sheriff that she wouldn't tell anyone about it," Allen said.

"She did what?" Much asked. I silently echoed his incredulous tone—it seemed a strange promise to make.

"She promised the Sheriff she wouldn't tell us," Will said. "So she had us meet with Sir Guy to hear it from him instead."

"That is ridiculous!" Robin said.

"I agree," Will said. "But it's done now, so it hardly matters where we came by the information. We know there's a caravan of unfairly collected taxes coming through Sherwood, so let's plan where we'll ambush it."

Robin and Will discussed the best places along the road to set up an ambush until Lucy came riding into camp later that evening. She came straight to our group at the fire pit, sitting herself beside me. Robin glared at her for a moment before chucking a stick into the fire.

"We didn't have to go to him," Robin said. "You could have told us."

Lucy stiffened beside me. "Not after I promised I wouldn't."

"You're playing games with us, Lucy."

"I am not. But seriously, Robin, the Sheriff might decide to get rid of me at any moment—he's certainly suspicious—and then you never would get information from inside the castle."

"I still say you could have delivered it. We don't need Gisbourne!" Robin's voice was rising, his eyes blazing with anger and fear and pain. "He's entirely untrustworthy. He. Murdered. My. Wife."

"And he's as tormented by it as you are! More, probably, considering…"

Robin stood and more than one person around the fire flinched. He didn't do anything to Lucy however, he simply stormed off.

"You didn't expect that to go any differently I hope," Mark said, his voice full of venom as he too glared at Lucy. "You can't trust Gisbourne."

"I know you all think that, and I perfectly understand why —"

"Then why are you so insistent?"

"Sir Guy has helped us in the past," I said, trying to ease the mounting tension as Mark and Little John glared at Lucy and Robin muttered curses from across the meadow. "He's made mistakes; massive, unforgivable mistakes one might argue. Yet somehow, he still helps us."

"Even so," Little John said, "in this scenario, Lucy could have simply told us herself, using Gisbourne was superfluous. And more than that, if this is a test, a trap, she should have been much more careful and perhaps not told us at all."

"Well next time I'll just keep my information to myself," Lucy huffed.

"If you are going to do something as stupid as tell us you can't talk to us about whatever you find out, you might as well," Mark snapped.

"Well unlike some people, I keep my promises."

It was rare for Lucy to raise her voice or lash out at anyone, and I sat in stunned silence as Robin stormed back toward our circle and Lucy continued railing at Mark. "You're asking me to break my word like it's no big deal. But it is a big deal to me."

Robin joined the argument as soon as he was back at the fire. "A promise that was forced out of you—"

"It wasn't forced."

"What?"

"It wasn't forced. I didn't have to promise. I only did because I knew you could still get the information without me telling you."

"Lucy—"

"You still got the information you needed, so why does it matter?"

Robin threw up his hands in disgust and stomped away again, and Mark soon withdrew to his hut as a silence settled over the gang.

"That...went about as expected," Will sighed.

"Guy did give me the news without hesitation," Allen said. "Lucy's right. He is helping us."

"I almost believe it myself," I said. "He hasn't given any indication he'd turn on Lucy."

"*Yet*," Little John growled. "There is, however, the glaring truth that he murdered Marian."

The argument over the merits—or lack thereof—of Gisbourne, and the potential danger Lucy was in, continued for some time. Lucy left the camp in a sour mood, and most of those who remained in the camp were equally frustrated.

Chapter 42

SUMMER WAS FLARING toward a close the next time Lucy came riding into camp, her eyes wild with worry.

"The Sheriff knows!" she yelled as she dismounted, running over to where the rest of us were lounging around the empty fire pit.

"The Sheriff knows what?" Will asked.

"That I informed you of the hanging. He is convinced Sir Guy would never betray him, so he's accusing me."

"Oh no." I sat up straighter, looking at the panic on Lucy's face and feeling a weight press down on my chest.

"You've blown your cover *again*?" Robin asked.

Lucy shook her head. "Not exactly. It was this morning that the Sheriff accused me, and as of yet he has done nothing about it."

"You can't go back to Nottingham," Allen said. "He'll likely have you executed."

"Sir Guy will see to it that I am rescued if the Sheriff tries anything, and I'll come to live in the camp with the rest of you. That is if, indeed, the Sheriff decides to harm me at all. I thought he would throw me into prison immediately, but he hasn't."

"I would stay here, if I were you," Little John said.

"I have considered it, but I cannot. I must return to Nottingham. I am greatly needed there. You won't have an informant without me, and—" Lucy bit her lip, refraining from saying whatever it was she had almost said.

"And?" Robin raised an eyebrow.

"And I am simply needed, that's all."

No one wanted Lucy to leave after giving us such news, but she was insistent that she was needed in Nottingham and it was worth the risk.

She was correct in that we wouldn't have an informant and we'd need one—although Gisbourne had been helping us, and perhaps he would continue to do so. But more than anything, I think it was Gisbourne himself that Lucy felt needed her in Nottingham. She didn't often talk about it, but when she did it was clear that they had formed an unlikely friendship and that her heart bled for the pain he was in. She desperately wanted him to know the forgiveness and love of Christ.

She was a far better person than I was.

Until Lucy had put it in my mind, I had never considered praying for Gisbourne's salvation. For his downfall, maybe. But not his salvation.

In the days that followed Lucy's unfortunate news, we spent more time in Nottingham, worriedly waiting for any indication of the Sheriff arresting Lucy, but none came. Lucy continued to visit the camp when she could, and moved around the city helping the poor and needy the same as always.

It seemed that either the Sheriff wasn't going to do anything—or he was biding his time. It was also possible that Lucy was correct in assuming Gisbourne would see to her safety.

One day I was sitting at the edge of the market in Nottingham Square, leaning against one of the shops at the edge of the open space, Will seated beside me. We'd been watching for any suspicious behavior from the Sheriff's soldiers, and waiting for news of Lucy.

She was in the market place herself, across the way from us, speaking to a frail old woman.

"I can't believe the Sheriff hasn't done anything to her," Will said as we watched her.

"Lucy thinks he may have forgotten the incident, though I find that hard to believe."

"The Sheriff's whole mind is bent on finding us—the outlaws—and destroying us. He would not have forgotten anything connected with us, especially someone living under his roof who had admitted to being one of us."

"Yet what other explanation could there be? He has let her off the hook, seemingly, without any punishment. He's either forgotten, as Lucy thinks, or…what? He's too fond of her to hurt her? That doesn't seem likely."

"I can't fathom it." Will shrugged. "But I don't want her staying in the castle—it's dangerous." His voice was filled with emotion, his deep blue eyes roiling with passion.

"You're afraid she'll end up like Marian."

"Yes. I am." Will turned toward me, the pain written across his face evident. "I don't want to lose anyone else."

I could understand that fear, far more than Will probably knew.

"I am worried about her in more ways than one," Will commented, turning to look across the crowd toward Lucy again.

"What else has you concerned?"

"I told you some time ago that I was afraid she'd fall in love with Gisbourne…well, I think she's done just that."

"Really? Because I thought she was simply being kind. She's a good friend to everyone she meets, and I imagine that's no different inside the castle."

"I hope you're right. I don't want him to hurt her."

"You aren't worried about her hurting him?"

"Why would I worry about that?" Will asked, turning toward me with raised eyebrows.

"I have been praying for him, and you'd be surprised what that does to your perception of a person." I shrugged. "When you invest in their lives in such a powerful, spiritual way you cannot help but feel some sort of connection—affection even—for them. I am worried that he will fall in love with *her* and get his heart broken again the same as with Marian."

"I hope it isn't the same as with Marian, Dusty, because he responded to that broken heart in a rather violent way." Will's blue eyes darkened, his brow knitting together as anger became the dominant emotion on his face.

"I know…but I don't think he'd do that again. I am almost convinced that Lucy's witness is going to bring Gisbourne into a true relationship with the Lord."

"Such as what you have?"

"Yes."

"Do you really believe that to be possible?"

"I do, as strange as that sounds."

Will shook his head. "It would take a miracle."

"I believe in a God of miracles, Will."

He didn't say anything else, and I let it go. Somehow we always found ourselves treading this conversation, but he never pursued it. Therein lay the reason I had chosen not to agree to marry him, and therein lay my valid excuse to let my fear of opening up rule me. The two should not have been so intertwined in my heart and mind, but they were. As long as he was not a believer, it didn't matter that I was too scared to let him in—I couldn't marry him anyway.

I could almost hear Much in my mind, demanding to know if I was going to let fear or trust in God rule me, but I ignored it. In this moment, I didn't want to face the choice.

About a week later, I returned from a long day healing the sick in the villages around Nottingham to find only Much in the camp. He was carefully cutting up thick slices of cheese and freshly baked bread, laying them out on plates for the rest of us when we arrived.

I took a seat on one of our benches, propping my feet up on the stones of the fire pit. It was a warm night, and no fire was lit.

"How was your day?" I asked as he brought me over a plate of bread and cheese.

"Nothing of interest to report," Much replied "Yours?"

"It was a calm day." We hadn't had to stop any executions or had any violent ambushes recently; it seemed apart from the tension surrounding Lucy, our lives were falling into a reprieve from the chaos.

At that moment Lucy came bursting into camp.

"Lucy?" I sat up, forgoing my relaxed state. "Are you okay?"

Lucy seated herself across from Much and myself, her hands shaking slightly. "The Sheriff almost killed me."

"What happened?" I asked, leaning forward. Apart from her shaking hands and wild eyes, she seemed unharmed.

"He was upset that you knew about the caravan and he was sure I must have told you so he tried to kill me."

"But he didn't," Much said. "I mean…you're alive."

"Yes. Guy saved me. I don't know how he got there so quickly, but he was there and he and the Sheriff had a moment of altercation and then…"

"Guy and the Sheriff fought?"

Lucy shook her head. "Not exactly. After Guy blocked the Sheriff's initial blow that was meant for me, they glared at each other and argued for a bit…and then the Sheriff left me alone."

"You aren't safe going back," I said. "The Sheriff is sure to punish you this time."

"I don't think so. Guy convinced him in the moment that I wasn't the one who told you, which is the truth. I wasn't."

"You are walking a rather delicate line with the Sheriff."

"It is the path I must take if I want to be an informant for all of you—and therefore help stop some of the cruelty in Nottingham, and help the people—while also maintaining my integrity as an honest woman."

"Do be careful, Lucy," I said. I clasped my hands together to keep them from growing as shaky as Lucy's had been when she arrived. Her position in the castle was growing ever more precarious, and the fear of losing her the way we'd lost Marian was mounting.

She trusted Gisbourne to keep her safe so completely. Didn't she know what he'd done to Marian? I wanted to forgive him and offer him the grace that Christ would, that Lucy clearly did, but in that moment all I could think was that her life was in danger and putting herself into Gisbourne's protection was the worst thing she could do.

"Are you sure you'll be safe in Nottingham?" I asked. "You would be more than welcome here.

We do need an informant, but your safety would matter more; Robin would understand."

"No, thank you, Dusty." Lucy shook her head, straightening her shoulders and speaking with conviction. "Guy needs me. Keep praying; he's close, I think. So close to making the most important decision of his life."

"We'll keep praying," Much said.

"Just be safe, Lucy," I told her.

She left the camp soon afterward, and I began to pray—for Lucy's safety with the Sheriff, for Gisbourne to fully embrace Christ and His forgiveness and therefore become a true ally to Lucy, one I could trust with my friend's safety. I prayed for my own fear and worry to be removed, and instantly felt the peace and comfort of my Savior wrap around me.

When the rest of the gang returned from their duties that day, Much and I informed them of what had happened with Lucy. Robin and Will were upset and insisted Lucy should have stayed at the camp as her life was worth more to them than having an informant in the castle.

"I don't know how she manages to stay alive," Robin said, shaking his head and shoving his hand through his hair. "She's only blown her cover half a dozen times at this point. What will it take for the Sheriff to get tired of her?"

"Well he did try to kill her today," Mark said. "He sounds pretty tired of her."

"We need to pull her out of there," Will said. "Gisbourne might not be around the next time the Sheriff tries to kill her."

"She won't come," I said.

"She is an expert with both a sword and bow," Allen commented. "She can protect herself if it comes to that."

"I hope so," Robin said. "But I would feel much better if she wasn't trusting her life to our temperamental Sheriff and the man who murdered Marian."

Only a few days later, Lucy visited the camp one night with a guest—a frail looking old monk.

Robin stood as soon as she entered the meadow. "Lucy, who is this?"

"Friar Tuck," Lucy said, leading the old man over to where we'd all gathered at the fire as per usual. "He's a very dear friend of mine. He was as a father to me when I was growing up in London."

Robin sat back down as Lucy and Friar Tuck joined the group.

"What brought you to Nottinghamshire?" Will asked.

"Lucy did," Friar Tuck replied. "I have been anxious to see her since she left home so many years ago."

"I told him he could live in the camp, if that's okay, Robin," Lucy said. "I think he'd be safer here."

Robin studied her for a moment. "You don't trust Gisbourne then?"

"I—"

"That's fine. Friar Tuck, you are more than welcome here."

Robin seemed pleased with the idea that Lucy wanted her friend in the camp with us rather than in the castle with Gisbourne. He commented on it more than once over the next several days as the men of the gang gathered materials and built a hut for Friar Tuck to use.

I watched with interest as Will began to spend any spare moment with Friar Tuck, asking questions and drinking in his wisdom. I felt an equal amount of joy at the prospect of him coming to know Christ through the monk's gentle wisdom as I did fear at the thought that I'd have to face my reservations eventually if the excuse of his unbelief stopped being valid.

If he came to believe as I did, then what excuse could I have for giving into my fear?

Nottingham was soon bursting with merchants and tourists as the time of the Nottingham Fair drew close once more. A year ago we'd found out Allen was betraying us, but now he was back at our side fighting to free the people from the cruelty of the Sheriff and others like him.

When the day of the Fair arrived, Robin suggested we keep an eye on things in town, and so he along with Will, Much, and myself made our way to the city.

The Sheriff's men patrolled the streets in groups, and we carefully stayed out of their way. Most of the people ignored the groups of soldiers and continued about their business, but when

Gisbourne walked through the crowds, the conversations around him would fall silent and people would send furtive glances his way. For his part, Gisbourne looked as tormented as he ever did, scowling at everyone in his path.

"I don't see whatever good in him that Lucy does," Will commented.

"I don't think it's about whether or not he is good," I replied as Will, Much, and I walked through the jostling crowd in Nottingham Square, moving through the extra merchant booths set up for the Fair and pushing past street performers to find a place to stand along the edge of the Square and watch for anything suspicious. "Lucy chooses to forgive his past, and hope in his future whether or not he deserves such."

"I do think at the very least he is conflicted," Much said. "He does vile things, like murdering Marian. He does decent things, like letting the children go, and not turning Lucy in, and such. He wavers back and forth…"

"You're right," Will said. "It might be less of a good or bad question and more that he simply lacks the conviction to stick with one or the other. I don't have the same problem…when I know what I believe and what I want, nothing will sway me."

Will slipped his arm around my waist and winked at me and I tried not to give in to the desire to pull away from him.

He loved me, that I knew with certainty. And I loved him. But could I accept that?

Could I let him in to see every part of me without being overwhelmed by the fear that the closer I got to him the more I would be destroyed if I ever lost him?

The Fair itself was an interesting and entertaining experience. There were singers and dancers and jugglers and other performers to entertain the crowds. There were merchants selling all kinds of goods. Much gravitated toward booths selling various foods that he could savor. I merely watched it all, taking it all in. Someday, if we ever won this war against the Sheriff, I'd come to the Fair openly and not as an outlaw and be able to truly enjoy it.

As summer melted in the coolness of fall and the trees burst forth in bright shades of gold and red, Will and I found ourselves in the village of Leicester. We'd spent the day distributing food and money to the people there; our baskets were empty, and the villagers were once more well-stocked. As we moved down the street toward the edge of the village to head back toward Nottingham, Will glanced at me and then away.

"Do you have something to say?" I said, holding back a laugh at his nervous nature.

"I've been thinking…"

"About what?"

"About you and me."

I didn't respond. What was I supposed to say?

"Dusty, I want to marry you. I want to spend the rest of my life on earth with you, however long or short that life may be.

I want to raise a family with you, spend my whole life making you smile."

"Will…"

Will smiled at me and I found myself transfixed by his perfect blue eyes. "Don't worry. I know you want to say no so that you aren't 'unequally yoked' as you called it before. Friar Tuck explained that to me in greater detail."

"If you already know what my answer is—"

"Dusty." Will stopped walking, setting his empty basket down and pulling mine out of my hands as well. He set it in the dirt, turning back to me with confidence. Before I knew what he was doing, he slipped his arms around my waist and kissed me right there in the middle of that dusty street.

"Will Scarlett!" I pulled back from him, though a large part of me didn't want to.

"You aren't hearing me," Will grinned. "I realized that this whole thing—your faith—isn't just for you and Lucy and people like you who seem to have an extra zeal for God. It's more personal than that. I have my own sin that is deserving of death, and Christ died to save me from that—He died for Will Scarlett. I do accept that. And having done so, how can I not live my life for Him and Him only? I understand your passion now, Dusty. I share it."

"Will!" I didn't know what to say, but I could feel tears forming as my vision clouded.

Will pulled me into his embrace. "I knew that would please you, but I didn't know how to tell you when it happened... I've wanted to marry you for so long, but I didn't want you to think I was accepting your faith only so that I could marry you, or that I was faking the whole thing to have you, or something of that nature."

I pulled back enough that I could look up into his face, though I stayed comfortably in his arms. "When did you accept Christ then?"

"I've been having a lot of conversations with Lucy and Friar Tuck over the last few weeks, coming to terms with everything you all believe and trying to decide how I felt about it...and then I encountered Him myself—the overwhelming love and grace of my Father who took my punishment on Himself so that I could live. He's everything you ever said He was, Dusty. I *know* Him."

Tears were filling Will's eyes and I reached up to brush them from his cheek as they fell. "Oh, Will..."

"I wanted to tell you immediately, but I knew as soon as I did, I'd want to ask you to marry me, too. And I didn't want you to misconstrue my intentions..."

"I wish you had told me, so I could have celebrated with you."

"I do have to ask one more time," Will said, a smile forming on his lips again. "Will you marry me?"

Could I?

He was a Christian, apparently. I could see the truth of that in his eyes. He wasn't lying to me. So that particular excuse was invalid.

The more pressing issue now was whether or not I could let go of my fear and open up to Will fully. I smiled up into his blue eyes, my breath caught in my throat.

I loved him. And I loved my God, who so graciously brought this man into my life.

"Of course I will!"

When we returned to the camp, Little John was the only one there. Will hurried over to him with a bright smile and a spring in his step. "I'm getting married, old friend."

"It's about time," Little John replied, laughing. He seemed entirely unsurprised by Will's pronouncement. I could only assume being Will's best friend, he must be aware of Will's affections. "Will you get married soon, or wait until all of this chaos is over?"

"There's no telling when the war with the Sheriff might end, or when King Richard might choose to come home after dealing with whatever he wanted to deal with in Austria," Will said. "I would prefer to marry Dusty sooner than later."

I nodded, feeling almost giddy with joy. It wasn't something I was used to feeling. "It might do the gang good, too, to have something pleasant to occupy their thoughts. Everything's been rather depressing since the trip to Austria—understandably, of course. I wouldn't have expected it to be any other way, I just…"

"It will be good to have something to brighten our days," Will said. "I'm sure Friar Tuck will be happy to perform the ceremony, and then…you'll finally be my wife."

He bent and kissed my cheek and I let the joy of the moment wash over me—how had I ever thought forgoing this emotion was the better option? I couldn't imagine letting fear rule me again.

As the rest of the gang began to trickle into the camp, we eagerly informed them of our news. Robin and Lucy were the last to arrive, walking into camp together. I ran over to Lucy to tell her myself.

"We're getting married."

"We are?" Robin asked, a grin spreading across his face.

"Not you, Robin!" Lucy laughed as I playfully swatted his arm.

"Who?" Robin asked.

"Dusty and Will of course," Lucy laughed. "Where have you been, Robin, that you didn't see this coming?"

"When are you getting married?" Robin asked. "And who said I haven't noticed?"

"We haven't set a day," I said. "But Friar Tuck will marry us. And you have to be here, Lucy."

"Of course. Just tell me when and I'll come."

"Didn't he ask you before and you refused?" Robin asked.

"No." I shook my head, trying to find the words to explain why I hadn't agreed to marry him the first time. "Yes."

Robin raised an eyebrow. "No…yes?"

"He asked you to marry him and you refused?" Lucy asked.

"Yes, he did ask. No, I did not refuse him exactly…I've always loved Will. He asked before Marian…" I paused. Robin's eyes darkened a shade and I hesitated to continue. "But I couldn't marry someone who didn't believe the same as me."

"That's absurd," Robin said.

"No it isn't, Robin."

Robin quirked an eyebrow at me and then glanced at Lucy and shrugged. "I will never understand the two of you. I am glad, however, that there will be a wedding to brighten our days. We need something cheerful to liven things up. Life has been…" Robin sighed. "Dark. It's been so dark since Austria."

"Will and I thought so, too," I said. "That's why we won't wait until after all this," I waved my hand in a vague manner, "to be over. We all need something good to hold onto these days."

Two weeks later, we were saying our vows under the brilliantly colored autumn trees near the stream that ran past the camp. Lucy had taken me to a tailor in town—insistent on purchasing material for a wedding dress to be made for me and though I felt she did too much for me, slipping on the beautiful silk and lace gown that morning had me feeling like a princess for the first time since my father had died.

When Lucy led me across the meadow and through the trees to the stream where everyone waited, I could feel my hands shaking and hear my heart pounding in my head. But as Will came into view, I felt myself steady.

His dark blue eyes caught mine, shining with tears, as a bright smile graced his face. I walked confidently toward him, knowing I was walking to my home. I was unafraid, and ready to love Will with everything that he deserved—to open up to him, to share my deepest self with him. I knew without a doubt that he would accept and love me, too.

Will took my hands as Friar Tuck led us through the ceremony and our vows. I had asked Will to use my name—not Dusty, not the Saracen, but Andaleeb, the name my father had given me; Nightingale.

Will had gone even further than that. He spoke all of his vows in Arabic. Hearing the sound of my mother tongue on his lips made me smile, and when he said my name, Andaleeb, I couldn't stop my tears from flowing.

As soon as it was over, Robin slung his arm around my shoulders.

"I hope you both will be very happy, of course, but do try and hold off on any children until after this chaos is over."

"Robin!" I tried to scold him, but I knew I was blushing and I let myself laugh.

Will shoved Robin's arm off of me and slipped his own around my waist. "You should know that I expect a house full of children some day."

"I'd expect nothing less, given the way you doted on the children who lived here at camp," I replied.

I was happier than I thought I deserved to be and forever grateful to my God for bringing me not only to Will but to the rest of my family here in England.

Epilogue

MARI-LU WATCHED WITH HORROR as Aunt Lucy closed the leather-bound book, focusing on the present and the empty clearing in front of her once more.

"That's not the end!" Mari-Lu gasped.

"Well, it was the end of Dusty's journey," Aunt Lucy laughed.

"But what about Gisbourne proposing to you? What about Robin Hood getting caught?"

"What about Gisbourne coming to know Jesus?" Edmund asked. "What about the village that was almost burned down?"

"What about the Ida," Mari-Lu continued, "we didn't even meet her!"

Aunt Lucy laughed again. "You already know how the rest of our adventure in Sherwood took place, but it was not entirely relevant to the story that Dusty wanted to tell. She told Will her side of things, and she stopped at their wedding at first, likely because that is when she felt her journey to let go of her fear of loss had ended."

"You said she stopped the story there at first?" Edmund asked, eagerly leaning forward.

"Well…" Aunt Lucy's eyes began to sparkle. "Dusty did have a few final thoughts that she told Will and he added to the end of their little memoir…"

Aunt Lucy turned the final page of the book and Mari-Lu and Edmund eagerly leaned forward to read the words that Aunt Lucy spoke…

It was a freezing cold night the night I gave birth to our firstborn. When Will was allowed in to see me and was handed his son, he wept.

The Lord had greatly blessed me, and I was overcome with love for my God, for my son, and for my husband. I only wished my own mother and father could have met their grandchild, and that Habibah and Daniyah could have seen him and lived to be his aunts. Yet even so, I am more blessed than I can say.

Our son is older now, and we have a sweet daughter—Daniyah—who brightens our lives. Our lives have not been without hardship since the days of our first Sherwood adventure, but even with the trials and struggles, I have been more blessed than I deserve. I am precisely where I am meant to be…

Acknowledgments

As always I have many people to thank for their help in making this book a reality and that includes both those who took part in fashioning *The Song of the Nightingale* into a real book and those who helped on the original *Dusty*.

Rebekah for being my encouragement and my critic (and pointing out the similar breath units in my sentences...the kind of thing only you would comment on). The original words I wrote for you in the previous version of this book still apply: it was hard to write this book without you right beside me, but I do appreciate when you are able to read for me.

Elizabeth Hutchinson for your editing work on the original and the new version of this book. You are the absolute best and I am always grateful for you.

The amazing women in Quill and Cup—my writing community. You are undoubtedly how I was able to rewrite (and publish) this entire series in a single year. You keep me accountable, you encourage me when I'm having a hard month. I love you all and there are too many of you to name, but...you know who you are.

Susannah Schmidt and Sarah Loewen for your encouragement and critiques on the original version of this book.

Kristin Milligan for stretching and challenging me when I first set about to write Dusty's story. You pushed me to work harder than I thought I could and I know my writing is better for it.

My parents will always get a thank you for their never-ending support.

And of course, an even bigger thank you to my God. For giving me stories to write and helping me to do just that. You inspire my passion, and bring a true joy to my work. I could not do this without you!

www.ingramcontent.com/pod-product-compliance
Lightning Source LLC
Chambersburg PA
CBHW072008020726
47501CB00006B/1737